Their Woman in Lerwick

The story of one woman's lust for power in an independent Scotland

John McDougall

Author's note:

This is a work of fiction. The characters are entirely a product of the writer's imagination. The Scottish parliament, Shetland Isles Council and the Anderson High School are real, but they have been given complete transfusions of personnel. If any resemblance remains to any person living or dead, this is entirely accidental and the writer apologises for it.

Acknowledgement

The author would like to thank Police Scotland for their unstinting help.

Cover photograph: Patricia Enciso

Chapter 1

Friday, 4th December

The principal was a tall man with silver hair and a confident manner. He beamed at us, casting a quick glance at Pamela's cleavage.

'Ladies, to what do I owe the pleasure?'

He should have known. How could he have failed to notice that critics of the Party were falling silent? He thought he was different? He couldn't imagine that anyone would try to stop a man as important as *him* from speaking his mind?

He was arrogant and stupid. On top of that, he was a sleaze bag and a hypocrite. I felt no pity for him.

Pamela had a brown A4 envelope with her. I'd been responsible for the contents of many such envelopes over the past two years, and usually the crisp colour photographs therein had shown me in a starring role. This time, however, was different. This time, Pamela – patronising Pamela I called her – had decided that I was 'past my best' (while she, pushing forty, was no doubt still in her prime). So she'd decreed that I should move from being the bait to a new role as trainer. I'd recruited Louise, a blonde, peachy-complexioned student who was also an ardent Party member, and together we'd established several things: the principal attended many staff-student events; he had a penchant for blondes; his grace-and-favour flat, to which these young ladies were sometimes invited, had a hard-bitten, hard-up cleaner who was looking for more regular employment; she'd be happy to accept the guarantee of a job with a Party sympathiser in return for letting in, before she left, a technician who would install suitable cameras in the principal's bedroom. (Actually, Pamela's technical boys already had a perfectly good camera that could be concealed in a necklace or a brooch, but Pamela decided – and Pamela was never wrong – that the principal was such a nuisance to the Party and Louise was so inexperienced that nothing should be left to chance.)

Strictly speaking, the man had done nothing illegal, because Louise could be considered a consenting adult. But she was one of his students. Besides, the film from which the stills were taken contained some images that were totally grotesque – so grotesque that it was hard to see how he would not offer *anything* rather than let them be publicised. I waited to see how far Pamela would go in threatening to humiliate him.

I have jumped into this scene because our visit took place on the morning of the day on which Pamela told me I was going to Lerwick; so the events are forever implanted in my mind. I realise, however, that I should go back a little and fill in some of the background for you. I assume you know how the Scottish National Party finally persuaded the electorate that the revenue from Shetland's newly discovered oil fields made an independent Scotland financially viable. But did you realise that the change of leadership which took place within the National Party shortly after independence amounted to a putsch, when certain elements decided that the 'figureheads' who had won the referendum were far too moderate? ('Moderate' in the sense that they accepted the idea of multiparty democracy.) These 'elements' have never been properly characterised – about the only label that commentators have agreed on is 'populist' – but it's probable that most of them were

opportunists, flocking to the banner of the National Party only when independence was assured. Then, when they saw power within their grasp, they weren't going to let namby-pamby 'reasonable' politicians meekly give it away to rainbow alliances. (Can you blame them? Who would want to be almost a somebody and then go back to being a nobody?)

This putsch, let me say, wasn't properly covered by the media, because for a long time the implications were unclear. I myself didn't see through the fog until one day, in the school where I'd landed, I heard a colleague refer not to the National Party but simply 'the Party'. *Of course*, I thought, *of course*.

So that was the moment when the trajectory of my life intersected with the course of Scottish history – when I realised that if I wanted to escape from the treadmill of teaching I had to ingratiate myself with the Party. I asked my colleague to introduce me to some party members, and I quickly recognised that silencing critics and neutering political opponents was the name of the game. I had one friend who was a private detective and another who – much like Pamela's techie boys – was good with cameras; with their help I began some serious neutering. In less than a year, I had made a reputation for myself and my acceptance into the Scottish Intelligence Services was a foregone conclusion. I had to suffer patronising Pamela, but the leap from the tedium of the classroom to the buzz of manipulating grown men was exhilarating. Even my mother benefited: she was able to reduce her dosage of citalopram because she enjoyed so much boasting to her friends and neighbours about how her daughter, the girl from Pilton, had outshone all those pretentious private-school types to win a job 'in government'.

But to our tale. After a very few pleasantries, Pamela tapped the brown envelope against a rather fleshy knee, and said, 'Principal, it has come to our notice that you and some members of your staff have been making slanderous statements about the government.'

The principal's demeanour changed at once. He tilted his head back so that he literally looked down his nose at Pamela. 'Slander? I don't think so. Legitimate expressions of free speech? Certainly.'

'Really?' Pamela could not be out-patronised. 'You have made accusations of cronyism in business. Accusations of intimidation. Accusations of promotion in public bodies only for supporters of the government. You have evidence for all this?'

'I could certainly gather it.' He shook his head like someone who found such nonsense beneath him. 'I'll tell you what. Why doesn't the government sue me?'

Pamela snapped like a crocodile. 'Because you're not worth it.' She pulled a photograph from the envelope. We were both sitting on a couch facing the principal's desk and I was concentrating on the man's eyes; so I didn't see which photograph it was. But it could have been the one with the dog collar. 'Look at this,' she said, 'and tell me if any sane person would think you were.'

One glance and the arrogance drained from his face. He did his best to recover, but his voice shook. 'This is ridiculous. This is a totally illegal invasion of privacy.'

'Oh?'

'Heads will roll for this.'

'Yes, yours first.'

'You don't scare me. Everyone knows that photographs can be easily faked.'

'You just said that this was an invasion of privacy.'

He side-stepped Pamela's thrust, blustering. 'An invasion that will get you nowhere, for the reason I've just stated. You can't prove this is genuine.'

Pamela was smiling with pleasure that wasn't faked any more than the photograph. 'You think not?' she said. 'Date and time stamp on the photographs. GPS stamps also available. Likewise witness statement from the young lady. But how about this? We'll release a few copies to certain websites and then *you* can sue *us*.

'Copies?' That came out in an anguished croak.

Pamela spread her hands in mock sympathy. 'Digital technology makes copying so easy.'

There was one copy Pamela didn't know about. Ever since I'd started working for SIS officially, I'd kept meticulous records of every case I handled. I noted who gave me the orders – it was nearly always Pamela and on two nerve-jangling occasions I'd even worn a wire so that she could never deny it. I also noted the time, the place, the victim, and the victim's sins. When the job was over, I made sure I had my own copy of the film and, judging a thumb drive too easy to steal, I stored everything on my cloud account. I couldn't have said quite why I did all this; I had the vague notion that at some time in the future I might need the insurance.

The principal stared at her. 'Blackmail? You'd stoop to blackmail?'

'We'll defend the public interest.'

He was looking at Pamela, but he wasn't seeing her. 'What do you want?'

'What do you think we want?'

'You want me to stop criticising the government.'

Pamela laughed. 'If only it were that easy. I'm going to give you two choices. Listen carefully. I can release this film. You will be forced to resign; you will be denied your pension; your wife will divorce you and your children will never speak to you again. Even better, you will be a laughing stock for all time. Or...'

He'd been hanging his head with each punch. Now he raised it, because he knew he had to pay attention to whatever came next.

'Or you will do whatever we tell you to do.'

'How can I agree to that?'

'How can you not?'

He hid his face in his hands and muttered, 'Oh God, oh God.'

'God won't help you. Do you agree or not?'

He took his hands away, sat up then slumped, and I thought he was going to cry.

'Well?' Pamela said.

He whispered, 'I agree.'

'Say it. Say you will do whatever we tell you to.'

'I will do whatever you tell me to do.'

'Good. But I have to test you. Take off your clothes.'

'*What?*'

'You heard.'

His face went scarlet. 'That's impossible. My secretary could come in at any minute.'

'She won't do that. She knows she might interrupt a threesome.'

He didn't move. Pamela made to stand up. 'Well,' she said, her tone implying that the interview was over.

6

The man was pathetic. He got to his feet and took off his jacket, tie, shirt – everything except his underpants.

Pamela put a husky note in her voice. 'Your pants too.'

'Oh God.' He pulled off his pants and stood naked, his hands covering his crown jewels.

Pamela gestured to me. 'Carol.'

Though I knew what was coming, I said, 'What?'

'The camera.'

I took it slowly out of my bag. She'd phoned me at breakfast to tell me to bring it. Now I wished I could say I had forgotten it.

'No,' the principal begged.

'Hands on hips.' She waited until he did what he was told. 'Take a couple of shots, Carol.'

I clicked twice. I know I said that I had no pity for this victim. That's true, but nonetheless I felt distaste, even disgust, with Pamela. Let me try to explain. As long as I could stand outside myself at critical moments – you'll get my meaning – I enjoyed my job. I enjoyed it because I enjoyed playing a game, acting a role; I'll admit that I also enjoyed the power, and to some extent the feeling that I was exacting a due vengeance. But I had no interest in taking the next step into out-and-out sadism.

'You may sit down.'

He crossed his legs in a ludicrous attempt to preserve his modesty. I made a mental note to congratulate Louise on being able to fake unbridled lust with this man.

Pamela said, 'Initially, as you have guessed, we want you to stop your criticism of the government. Within a month, we want the first signs of a tentative admission that you have been wrong on this issue or that. We'll let

you choose the issues, except that one of them must be the government's very sensible policy of concentrating some subjects in a few institutions and abandoning altogether others that can show absolutely no contribution to the public good – the kind of subject that you have been defending from an arty-farty, élitist point of view.'

'But I've been so clear,' he wailed. 'People will know that I've been got at.'

Pamela didn't care. 'No bad thing, if it discourages other troublemakers. But anyway, after a while people will forget what rubbish you used to spout. People do forget. So in a year you will be an ardent supporter of every government policy. Now your staff…'

'My staff?'

'Your staff. You'll start with MacAlister in the sociology department. He has a bee in his bonnet about newspapers abandoning their "traditional" function of examining official policies. All he's doing is sowing discontent. You will shut him down within a month.'

'But how can I shut him down? He'll say academic freedom is the last…'

'Bollocks. Who cares what he says and who cares how you shut him down? Find an irregular expenses claim. Find an unauthorised leave of absence. Find a misuse of resources. Get plenty of witnesses. Start a whispering campaign. Then sack him. Let the penny drop in the sociology department and elsewhere that this is a warning. After that, you will be on the watch for, and you will deal swiftly with, any other agitators.'

'I'll lose all respect.'

'Respect?' Pamela laughed again and picked up the photograph that still lay on the desk. It *was* the one with the dog collar. 'I'll let you finesse a little,

find nuances here and there. But there will be no variations from the timetable. Understood?'

'Oh God.' He held his head again. 'Understood.'

'Now get dressed, you sorry excuse for manhood.'

It was a Friday. Pamela chose a country pub for lunch, saying I 'could' drive her home afterwards.

She sent me to the bar for drinks – gin and tonic for her and ginger beer for me – and when I brought them back, I thought I'd try an innocent-sounding question.

'Any plans for the weekend?'

'Not really.' She took a swallow of her gin. 'Hugh's home.'

Her answer surprised me, because it so nearly gave her away. The rumours that went round SIS were consistent: at any given time, Pamela had at least one paramour from those who stalked the corridors of power, but she also had a liking for young men, fifteen to twenty years her junior; the mature chaps from Holyrood squired her during the working week, whereas the boys were summoned at short notice, especially on a Friday night, when her husband – bald, overweight and ageing – was away on one of his business trips.

'And you?' she said.

'Nothing much. I don't have a significant other at the moment.'

Pamela could have taken out patents on her patronising glances. This one said, *You poor dear. What is it like when you just don't have it?* Then she examined the menu. 'I think I'll have chicken fricassee. Have you decided?'

'Sea bass.'

'How plebeian. Go and order, will you?'

Halfway through her second gin and tonic, she said, 'I had coffee with Arnold yesterday.'

'Oh?'

Arnold was the minister responsible for SIS. With his white hair and deceptively casual manner, he could have been your favourite uncle. In fact, he was a ruthless operator, the person to whom the new leaders turned if a critic was too vociferous or a Party member stepped out of line. He was also shrewd: he'd have no illusions about how Pamela – whose official title was the *Deputy* Director of the Scottish Intelligence Services – went about her business, but he'd make sure that, for him, everything was deniable.

'He's a worrier, you know.'

'Yes.' Arnold wasn't a *worrier*; he was a *thinker*. Pamela just liked to run people down.

'So first of all he gives me a row for being too stridently anti-Russian.'

'*Too* stridently anti-Russian? Is that possible?' I was sucking up to her, of course.

'Quite.'

I should point out that the Russians, together with the Chinese and some Arab states, were helping – a little – to bring down the fiscal deficit. While the Arabs leased shooting estates and the Chinese invested in infrastructure projects, the Russians were paying exorbitant rents on 'storage and repair' facilities at sites like Prestwick Airport, the Western Isles rocket range, and the Machrihanish base near Campbeltown. The money wasn't in the same league as the revenue from Shetland's oil, but it wasn't to be sneezed at. However, there was a faction within the Party, to which Pamela belonged, who were adamant that the Russians' motive was to make Scotland

dependent on them in the long run so that Holyrood could be bent to the will of the Kremlin. (Why the Chinese and the Arabs weren't accused with equal ferocity I could never work out.)

'And then,' said Pamela, 'he brought up Shetland.'

'Shetland?'

'There are some nutters who call themselves the Free Shetland movement. It's hard to take them seriously – who would want to cut themselves off in a tiny state in the North Atlantic? – but Arnold's such an old woman. "What if… what if… what if?" – that's his refrain.'

What if the government lost all that lovely oil revenue? I could see Arnold's train of thought, however unlikely the scenario. If that did come to pass, the generous welfare benefits that kept the Party in power would have to be sacrificed. What would be the alternative? Go plunging deeper and deeper into debt until your creditors demanded savage austerity? It was a measure of Pamela's divorce from reality that she should criticise acceptance of Russian money *and also* refuse to share Arnold's prudence about Shetland.

Pamela went on: 'There's a super-nutter – his name's Eric Sorenson – who appears to have taken the movement by the scruff of the neck. He's a powerful orator, so they say; the way he can fire up an audience, you'd think he was Hitler reincarnated. I doubt if it's going to last – the Shetlanders will soon get back to their favourite pastimes of arguing amongst themselves and drinking each other under the table – but Arnold wants us to take this Sorenson down; he's confident that if this cement is removed, so to speak, the whole edifice will collapse. There's talk of an indicative referendum; it would be good to do the demolition job before the council even discuss this.'

'I see.' Well, I didn't quite see. Not yet.

11

'The problem is that Sorenson seems squeaky clean. The IT boys tell me they can get absolutely nothing on him They've tried trolling him, but that hasn't put the slightest dent in his popularity. So Arnold, who's been reading too many spy stories, wants to go back to old-fashioned methods. He wants someone to settle into Lerwick as a sleeper, sniff out or engineer a way to bring Sorenson down, and do it.'

'A sleeper?' Now I was beginning to see: that sleeper would be me. 'Under what cover?'

'Schoolteacher. Suits you perfectly. There's a high school in Lerwick that's short of English staff. They've just readvertised two posts. You'll have to fib that you left your last appointment to care for your ailing mother, who is now better, but otherwise I don't see a problem. This, by the way, will be in the same department as Sorenson's wife, a perfect place to start.'

'A schoolteacher?' I kept my voice neutral, but the full horror was clear. I'd be back in a classroom. And Pamela wasn't talking about a week or two in Shetland; she was talking about *months*.

I couldn't object. You didn't argue with Pamela.

'You'll find the application form online,' she said. 'Closing date is Monday; so fill it in this weekend. Give you something to do.'

I hated Pamela. I hated the way she held my life in the palm of her hand and wasn't going to let me forget it. If I could see a way to get rid of her, I'd jump at it.

Chapter 2

Saturday, 6ᵗʰ February

Settling into Lerwick took a little while. I swear that for the first three weeks I never saw the sun and the temperature never rose above two degrees Celsius. I bought an expensive parka, a sturdy pair of gloves and a dozen hand-warmers. Even so, I found myself rushing from house to car and from car to school to avoid frostbite.

I enjoyed one piece of luck. The girl who secured the other job in the English Department – a redhead called Sharon who told me she'd had a 'rough' time with an abusive husband – was a Shetlander returning to her old school; she was able to put me in touch with a potential landlady, one Betty Dawson. Betty had a pleasant flat on the upper storey of her grey but solid villa in the New Town, and she wasn't asking an exorbitant rent. When I agreed to take the flat, she said with a straight face that the only demand she'd make as a landlady was that I should submit all my boyfriends for inspection. I replied that I didn't have even one boyfriend, to which her comment, delivered with a face not quite so straight, was: 'Not yet, my dear, but I'm sure the men of Lerwick will be pleased to meet you.'

To begin with, though, I had no more energy for socialising than I had for scoping out my target; I found it so hard to get back into the teaching groove. If you've never been there, I don't suppose you can imagine it. There's the preparation, which becomes ever more fine-grained as you come to know the needs of each pupil. There's the marking, which weighs you down like a sack

of coal. There's the administration – the registers, the referrals, the recording of targets set and targets met, the logging of homework, the letters to parents, the report cards… And there's the teaching itself, the performance in front of every class. In those first few weeks, I would curse Pamela as I drove home. 'Sympathy' wasn't in her vocabulary; she would expect me to make progress no matter how tired I felt.

Gradually, very gradually, I did make progress. Eric Sorenson's wife taught in the room next to mine. Her name was Joy, and she was, shall we say, interesting. She was slim, not unlike me in build; she had a sweet choirboy face without a trace of makeup; her hair was short; she usually wore trousers and a mannish shirt. Need I say more? There was also a hint of mischief in her green-blue eyes, a glance or a smile at me now and then, that told me I could have stumbled on an open door into the Sorenson household. I began to return her smiles.

Then she invited me to her house. We were walking along the corridor to our respective classrooms, one Friday lunchtime, when she said, 'Doing anything tomorrow night?'

'No.' I'd dropped into Sharon's flat on the last couple of Saturdays, but I knew she was going to Yell this weekend, taking her son Robert to see his grandparents.

'Like to come for dinner?'

'Well, thank you. That would be nice.'

'It'll be just Eric and me, my crotchety old dad, who'll lust after you, and Colin Carruthers, Eric's economics adviser.'

'Economics advisor?' Eric was a councillor; so there was room for confusion here. 'Does that mean he advises Eric as a councillor or as the leader of Free Shetland?'

'The latter, although he also works for the council. Like Eric, he has to wear two hats and not get them mixed up.'

'Otherwise?'

'Otherwise Colonel Blimp will jump on him.'

I'd gathered in the staffroom that Colonel Blimp was the nickname for the council leader. In real life he was Douglas Stewart, but he defined himself, so people said, by the bushy moustache, the upright bearing and the clipped manner of an ex-army officer. *British* army, that is: he'd been as vehemently opposed to Scotland breaking away from the UK as he was now to Shetland leaving Scotland.

'And is Colin a Shetlander?'

'Born and bred, apart from a stint at university. He's split up from his wife, but I think he's still too morose to make a pass at you.'

'So I'll be quite safe?'

'Oh I wouldn't go that far.'

There I was, then, on the first Saturday in February, closing the door of my flat and hurrying down the crazy paving across Betty's front garden. I was hurrying because a cold sleet was falling and I couldn't wear my gloves. Why not, do I hear you ask? Because Pamela, when she grudgingly agreed to fund a car, had decided that this vehicle must fit my supposed poverty; in other words, it must be old and decrepit. It was a Honda Civic, *so* old that you didn't open the door with an infrared beam. Oh no. You had to fumble with real keys, and I couldn't do that with my gloves on.

My fingers were numb as I slid into the driver's seat, turned the key in the ignition and switched on the heater. Here was the car's second flaw: the heater took a full ten minutes to clear the windscreen. I'd forgotten my hand-

warmers, but I made do with pulling up the hood of my parka and putting on my gloves. I could have used the time to do some tidying, because the glove compartment, the well of the gear stick and the inside of both front doors had been used as wastepaper baskets for far too long. But thinking was top priority.

This would be my first chance to meet Eric face to face, to find his flaws or to worm my way into his confidence so that I could find them later. I had to discredit him in some very dramatic fashion, but I wasn't sure that the usual methods would work. Just before I left, Pamela had said to me in her office, wiggling her high-heeled shoe on the tip of her toe as if she were seducing one of her Holyrood contacts, 'I doubt if you'll manage a honeytrap.' From the little I'd heard about Eric, I feared she could be right.

But you never knew. Another scenario flitted through my imagination. Suppose... just suppose Joy's father and Colin could be shooed out of the door in good time... how far might a free flow of wine dissolve inhibitions? I had one of those trusty micro cameras, hidden in plain sight at the centre of a shiny pendant. Could it be positioned to catch the leader of the Free Shetland movement and his wife engaged in the despicable seduction of a young schoolteacher who was too drunk to resist? Might that work?

No. That was the stuff of phantasies.

Still...

The mist had cleared from the windscreen. I put the car into gear.

Lerwick is little more than an overgrown village. From my flat to North Road took two minutes; from North Road to the edge of town took another four or five. When I turned up the hill away from the sea, there was nothing

16

in the way of suburbs; twenty yards past the last car dealership, my headlights caught a sodden Shetland sheep staring out from a clump of windswept grass.

The location that Eric and Joy had chosen for their ranch-style house was sheltered from the worst of the Atlantic blasts by a low hill, though that same feature deprived them of what would have been a spectacular view of the ocean. A potholed track lead down to a sweep of gravel where four vehicles were parked. One was Joy's little Toyota. A Nissan pick-up I thought must belong to Joy's father – I'd been told that he owned a croft. A newish Vauxhall I deduced was Colin's. The fourth car was a BMW; as far as I could see, it was old but well-maintained, and that was interesting, because Joy had once declared in my hearing that Eric had only two ambitions in life: one, to lead Shetland to independence and, two, to buy a new BMW with every gadget known to man. A weakness there?

Bright light shone from a big kitchen window. Clutching my bottle of Sauvignon, I ran through the sleet to the nearest door. It opened into a little porch, which opened in turn into the kitchen. A man shaped like a barrel was framed in the doorway.

'Saw you from the window,' he said, in a flat, even unwelcoming voice. Sorry I can't shake hands. I'm dripping in Omega-3.'

'You're Eric?'

'Yes.'

I'd envisaged a tall, commanding, Viking-like figure with a physique that would allow him to throw you over his shoulder before he carried you off to rape you. I'd been well off the mark: Eric was short; he might be called sturdy, but the only thing truly Viking-like about him was his reddish-brown beard.

'And you're the chef?'

'Yes. I like good food, well cooked. I once thought other people did too.''Really? You were disappointed?'

'Long story.'

I thrust the bottle of wine at him. He took it without looking at the label. 'Thank you.' He shouted over his shoulder, 'Joy!'

Joy appeared, in a white cotton shirt with brown buttons. Under the thin material, her breasts didn't need, and didn't have, any support. A green necklace of some semi-precious stone glinted round her neck. She caught me by the hand and pulled me in, kissing my cheek. Her scent was delicate – lily-of-the-valley – and I felt a mild tingle.

She said, 'You found your way?'

'No problem. Not too many wrong turns you can take in Shetland.'

'Not too confident about that. It depends if you're talking metaphorically. Come on through. We'll leave Eric to the intricacies of salmon mousse.' She waved me into a hall. 'Let me take your coat.'

I shuffled off my parka. Underneath, I wore a Fair Isle cardigan over a slightly tight, slightly scooped white teeshirt.

Joy said, 'Think you'll be a bit warm in your Fair Isle knitwear. Eric likes to keep the place like a greenhouse, even though it costs us a fortune.'

I took the cardigan off, conscious that my bra made my nipples poke out like periwinkles. Joy smiled in their direction.

'Nice top. Like your pendant too.'

'Thank you. And that's a nice shirt.'

Another smile. 'As I told you, if there's one person who'll notice your top, it's my dad.'

Not to mention you.

18

'Hold on,' she said.

She draped my parka and cardigan over some pegs outside the kitchen door, while I cast a glance round the rest of the hall. On the walls, which were immaculately painted in white, hung several paintings of boats and sunsets. I said, 'You have a lovely house.'

'Lovely mortgage too, I can tell you – which is a sore point.'

'A sore point?'

'Yes.' She grimaced. 'I should fill you in before Eric and my father start bickering. Eric quit the merchant navy to join his parents in developing a hotel chain on the mainland. He imagined he could be a good chef – well, he is. But he went over the top: he had the idea of transforming the hotels into go-to places for fine dining in the north of Scotland. Trouble was, the custom wasn't there. So, about five years ago, he changed tack, came back here and married me. We built this house with a huge mortgage, relying on the big windfall we thought we'd get when his parents sold up. But they haven't sold up, because they can't. Who wants to buy failing hotels in the middle of nowhere?'

'And how does your father come into it?'

'Ah. He's minted – made a fortune trading jade and amber and whatnot from Burma to China – and he thinks the only reason Eric married me was because he had his eye on my inheritance. I mean,' – she rolled her eyes – 'why *would* anyone marry me? So my dad refuses to give us a penny. And Eric calls him a mean old git.'

'Oh dear.'

'Yes,' Joy said. 'Oh dear. If the two of them start sniping at each other, just ignore them. Anyway, come and say hello.'

19

She took a few steps along the hall, opened a door on the right, and ushered me ahead of her. An alcove held a table that was set for five. In the main part of the room, the sitting area, two men occupied the ends of a long sofa, to one side of an electric fire. They stood up.

Joy's father had the same boyish face as his daughter, its contours largely unscarred by age. The slightest of gleams came to his eye when he saw me.

'Carol, this is my dad – Sven – and Colin.'

I shook hands and mumbled, 'Nice to meet you.' Even though I might have been jumping to conclusions, I felt I had the measure of Sven. Colin, however, took longer to assess. He was slight and of medium height; he had mousy brown hair, parted at the side; his nose was straight, his features clean-cut but unremarkable; and he wore a blue and purple checked shirt that belonged in the nineteen-fifties. Then I realised that what really caught my attention was the way he looked at me. He had recently separated from his wife; he was free to play the field, starting with me; yet his expression, was glum, hang-dog, melancholy. He might be echoing my 'nice to meet you', but he wasn't saying, '*Well,* nice to meet *you.*'

Joy said to her father, 'You two have put the world to rights?'

Sven had the unhesitating air of a man who was sure he could do just that if he was given the chance. 'The world's too full of idiots, blinkered and myopic.'

'Absolutely full?'

'Present company excepted.'

Joy paused, then changed direction. 'Oh well. We'll be back to catch your repartee in a second. I'm just going to give Carol a quick tour of the mansion.'

Sven grunted, 'Better get on with it before the bank forecloses.'

20

In the hall, Joy's laugh tinkled like a cow bell. 'Didn't I tell you he was a grump?'

She led the way and threw open a door on the left. 'Master bedroom, scene of wild nights of passion – not.' She barely gave me time to take in the king-sized bed before she hustled me on to the next door. 'Guest room. Rather Spartan.' It was. 'But you're welcome to stay the night if you've had a glass too many.' She took me round a corner and pointed to her right. 'Shower room and toilet. Now come and see the only interesting space in the house.'

This was a big untidy studio at the very end of the hallway. Two wide windows were curtained in a deep red. An easel stood next to a desk that was cluttered with paints, brushes, jam jars and multiple sketchpads. Cardboard boxes on the floor contained rolls of paper that might have been drawings. A chaise longue looked like something borrowed from an artist's garret. Floor-to-ceiling bookcases along one wall were overflowing with books and folders and models of ships. At the back, a computer system – desktop, printer, router – was plugged into the wall. I drifted towards the books, which were covered with a layer of dust.

'Most of those are Eric's,' Joy said. 'Check out his Graham Greene library.'

Indeed, one shelf held everything from *Brighton Rock* to *The Heart of the Matter*. I said, 'What does he like about Graham Greene?'

'Good question. I think he identifies with all those ageing, unfulfilled men.'

'But he won't be unfulfilled if he becomes president of the Republic of Shetland.'

'You've hit the nail on the head.'

So Eric's motivation centred on his ego? Though it wasn't a fair comparison, I thought at once of a failed artist who'd surfaced in Weimar Germany with a fierce determination to make it as a demagogue.

Joy had stayed at her desk; she didn't really want to talk about Eric and his books.

I said, 'What kind of things do you draw?'

'Well, anything. I enjoy playing with light and its effects. But what I like best is life drawing.'

'That's what the couch is for?'

'Yes, although I haven't used it yet. Every summer, I go down to Edinburgh, to what used to be the College of Art, and I do one or other of their life drawing classes. In Shetland – well, you might be surprised how broad-minded people are, but even so I can't say to everyone I meet, "How d'you fancy being a life model?"'

I came back in from the bookcase, sat on the couch and spread my arms along the top, pushing out my lips in a parody of a kiss. One of the first rules of intelligence work is that you have to keep all doors open.

'What you need is someone who is both uninhibited and discreet.'

'Exactly.'

Joy hesitated. I knew why. She was wondering if she should seize the moment and make a date for our first session. Then she picked out a roll of paper from one of the boxes on the floor. 'Tell me what you make of my masterpiece.' She began to clear a space on her desk.

I came over as she placed a jam jar on each corner of the paper. The drawing showed a young woman, naked, sprawled on a sofa. I studied the shading – I thought it was done by charcoal – and realised that, however Joy had managed it, she had caught perfectly, with the half-closed eyes, the

lolling of the breasts, the casual splaying of the thighs, the spirit of abandonment. This girl wasn't merely proud of her body; she loved it.

'Wow.'

Joy was pleased. 'That was more or less the tutor's comment. He said I had an inside track to eroticism.'

'Was he hitting on you?'

'I don't think so. He wasn't stupid.'

I examined the full mouth, half open with the hint of ecstasy fulfilled. 'Doubt if I'd have the patience to be a model.'

'Multiple glasses of wine are an essential lubricant.'

Right.

In the living room, Colin was on his own. I sat on the sofa with him.

'I hear you're a Shetlander,' I said.

'Yes.'

'And an economist?'

'Yes.' He flicked a glance at me with each answer, then flicked it away again. I couldn't work out why. He didn't like what he saw? He didn't know how to chat a girl up?

I surveyed the model ships that sat on top of a display cabinet. Someone – Eric? – was obsessed with ocean-going yachts.

Colin said, 'You're a teacher? You teach with Joy?'

'I do, yes.'

'You like it?'

'I'm sure I will, but it's hard to begin with.'

'Ah. You will like it. Shetland's a great place, you know.' He almost looked at me; this must be him at the peak of enthusiasm. 'Everyone's your neighbour.'

Except unfaithful wives. But wait. Joy hadn't said that his wife was unfaithful; maybe the poor soul had just pined for some eye contact.

This, by the way, wasn't the first time I had heard a claim such as Colin's. If you lived up here in the land of perpetual cloud, you had to find some explanation for your own choice, to prove to yourself that you weren't barmy.

But I played along. 'Not like the big city.'

Joy's father reappeared, holding a bottle of wine. 'You drink Chilean red?' he said to me.

'What are we eating?'

'Fish.'

'I'd probably prefer white.'

'Suit yourself. Colin?'

Colin shook his head. 'No, thanks. I'll have a glass with my dinner, but I have to drive home.'

'Don't want to get stopped by Billy, eh?'

'He's in CID. He doesn't catch drunk drivers. But I don't want to get stopped, period.'

'Who's Billy?' I asked Colin.

'My brother.'

Sven poured himself a glass, left his bottle on the table and came to sit on an armchair. He waved his glass at me. 'You deny the benefits of resveratrol?'

'That's the stuff in red wine?'

24

'Found in the skin of red grapes. Proved in countless studies to contribute to a healthy heart.'

He looked a healthy specimen, I had to admit: a mane of silvery hair, sharp eyes, a wiry frame. But I've always found it intensely irritating when people try to give you lectures on food and drink.

A hatch between the kitchen and the dining area rumbled open. Joy placed a tureen of pink mousse on a mat. 'Sorry,' she said. 'I should have offered you an aperitif. Never mind. Sit up and we'll eat.'

Eric's opening sentence to me was: 'Where do you stand on independence?'

Joy, who'd poured wine and encouraged us all to dive into the mousse, was aghast. 'Eric, give Carol a chance to breathe. My God.'

Eric's eyes were like little brown marbles, set in pouchy skin that appeared to limit their movement. He turned his whole head to speak to Joy. 'You know I hate small talk. Why avoid the big issues?'

Joy backed off; I had the impression that she'd learned to manage her husband's temper.

I said, 'I'm not sure. I'm not a Shetlander, after all.'

'But you've studied our website.' That wasn't a question. 'What do you think of our proposal for a sovereign wealth fund, for example, as opposed to the Scottish government's lavish expenditure on welfare?'

Sven interrupted. 'The old Gordon Brown trick. You remember Gordon Brown?' He didn't give me the chance to answer. 'Chancellor for ten years and what did he do with the oil money that rolled in all that time? Invest it for future generations? Oh God, no. He used it to dish out benefits and keep

the economy boiling. More or less what our so-called National Party is doing as we speak.'

I knew all this, although in Edinburgh now most people didn't speak so frankly.

Eric snapped, 'Let her answer the question.'

I didn't have a name?

'Well,' I said, 'wouldn't an independent Shetland have a welfare system?'

'Of course, but you have to have a balance between helping those who are in real need, on the one hand, and investment, on the other. We can't *squander* the huge sums that are coming to us.'

'Huge sums? You're sure of that?'

He scowled. 'Work it out. It's simple arithmetic. Eight billion divided by twenty thousand gives you a very different answer from eight billion divided by five million.'

'Yes.'

'That's the projected oil revenue divided by the population of Shetland as opposed to...'

'Yes. I get it. But what if you have another virus pandemic and the price of oil slumps again?'

He peered at me. How dare I question him? 'It's hardly rocket science. You store your oil until the price recovers.'

There was more discussion about the figure of eight billion, Colin throwing in some cautionary tales about the complexity of the parameters involved, and yours truly taking the opportunity to extricate herself from the conversation. Joy, I noticed, said hardly anything. She finished her mousse, topped up her glass, Eric's and mine, finishing my bottle of Sauvignon, and started to clear away the plates.

A phone trilled across the room. Eric rose without a word to answer it. I was able to tune into his conversation because Colin was quietly explaining to Sven likely trends in the market for oil. 'Paul,' I heard Eric say, and there was an edge to his voice, 'I am not going to have time to read a book before Wednesday. We have agreed to reconsider the strategy, I know, but in the meantime there is nothing else to say.'

Joy began to push through the hatch tureens of potatoes and broccoli, and behind them individual helpings of some kind of fish. When she saw that I was still eating, she said, 'Colin, could you...?'

'Sure.' Colin cut short his exposition to help. Sven, sitting across from me, was much closer to the hatch. His bottle of Isla Negra was half empty, but he wasn't drunk, certainly not so drunk that he couldn't carry plates. I wondered why Joy hadn't asked him.

Eric was still on the phone. 'Yes,' I heard. 'Unst on Monday, Yell on Tuesday. Back to Lerwick on Wednesday for the council session and then our own meeting in the evening. No, Paul, it's better, as we agreed, if you leave the public meetings to Colin and Billy. You have your own forte.'

Joy came through from the kitchen with a second bottle of wine. 'Hey, Mr Spreadsheet Man,' she sang to Colin, murdering Bob Dylan, 'can I pour a glass for thee?'

'No thanks.' Colin grinned. I didn't know he *could* grin.

'Mr Spreadsheet Man?' I said.

'Oh yes,' Joy said. 'Twice a day or more, we get an email from Colin with a spreadsheet attached. Scratch our hard disc and you'll find a thousand spreadsheets.'

'Why so many?' I asked Colin.

He squirmed, the very picture of diffidence. 'It's all the… the variables involved in predicting the fiscal position of an independent Shetland. Not just the oil. And each of these variables shifts continually. So I have to keep sending Eric updates and then updates to the updates. Also, I must confess, sometimes I hit the Send button before I've finalised the presentation.'

A feeble light glimmered in my brain. 'The council don't mind you clogging up their servers?'

'Oh no, no. We can't use our council emails. We have to use personal accounts.'

The glimmer turned into a full light-bulb moment. It wasn't *Eric* I should set a honey-trap for. If I could get into *Colin*'s bed, I could probably get into his computer, and from there, with a little help, I could get into Eric's and wreak all sorts of mischief.

That help was available, for I had my secret weapon.

Chapter 3

Yes, my secret weapon. Let me tell you about her before I return to the dinner party from hell.

On my first Sunday morning in Lerwick, I went to Tesco. The store was very quiet. I was pushing my trolley up the fruit and vegetables aisle when I saw an employee with straggly blonde hair kneeling to restock the broccoli and at the same time cocking her head to listen to the radio programme coming from a speaker on the wall above her. My shoes made not a sound, and she must have thought that no one was near her, because as I came closer I heard her say, softly but distinctly, 'Fuck them, fucking hypocrites.'

It took me a second to realise that she was reacting to what was being said on the radio. A man was warbling on about the pleasures of living on Shetland and declaring that Shetlanders were all one big happy family. (Yes, *that* theme again.) This woman, clearly, had strong views on the subject.

'I agree with you,' I said.

She jumped, whirled, and said, 'Who the fuck are you?'

I had to be conciliatory. 'Not a Shetlander.'

She was wary, a mere step away from being angry. After all, I'd crept up behind her. But I had an intuition that she could be useful. So, when she said nothing, I offered another olive branch. 'How d'you stand it in this God-forsaken town?'

A look around – there wasn't another person within twenty yards – and then she hissed, 'Because I fucking can't go home.'

I dropped my eyes, to imply that she'd hit a nerve. 'Me neither.'

Some of her caution disappeared. 'Why the fuck not?'

'Because I've an ex-partner who might fucking kill me.' What's a lie here or there?

'Jesus Christ.'

We stood looking at each other. 'I'm Carol,' I said.

'Helen.'

I had to push a little. 'When d'you get off work? Want to go for a drink and a moan?'

She made a sound that was halfway between a snort and a bitter laugh. 'You're not a dyke?'

'No.' I had no trouble sounding indignant.

She snorted again and made a face that said, *Who gives a fuck?*

'All right. Half five at the Norseman. You can buy.'

Her surname was Flett, and the reason for her hatred of the Shetlanders came pouring out after a few drinks. She'd come from Orkney about fifteen years earlier, escaping from the wrath of a string of women whose husbands she'd sampled. (This part of her story she related with some satisfaction.) She'd quickly drifted into prostitution, and one of her earliest clients was a 'genius' – her word – at computer hacking. He was also a heroin addict and dealer – heroin was, and perhaps still is, pretty much the drug of choice in Shetland. Soon she was living with him and smoking heroin herself. Through long, drug-fuelled nights, she learned 'a huge amount' about hacking. Then, one morning, her boyfriend, who was called Frankie, took an overdose; the ambulance was slow to come and by the time Frankie reached hospital he was dead. She'd cursed the Lerwick health service ever since.

But that wasn't all, because she too was addicted. In a burst of lucidity, she'd seen the spiralling degradation ahead of her and gone to a GP for help. He, so she said, had been unbelievably condescending: she should 'stabilise her chaotic lifestyle by switching from heroin bought on the street to methadone prescribed by a doctor'. If she'd been from a respectable Lerwick family, with a pushy mother and a well-connected father, she was sure she'd have been given at once a road map to a comprehensive recovery. As it was, she'd struggled on, feeling abandoned by the whole of Shetland, until she'd chanced upon a Christian couple from Bressay who'd been so desperate to rescue their own son that they'd built a padded room in which any addict could go cold turkey. It had been 'murder', but she'd come through, and her benefactors had even intervened to find her a job. It was a rich irony, as she put it, that they were incomers from Kent.

The next Sunday – I had decided that Sunday morning was a good time to go to Tesco – Helen was on the only checkout where you could talk to a human being. She suggested that after her shift we should take a fish supper out to her house and she would show me her 'toys'.

These turned out to be pieces of hacking software left by the departed Frankie. As Helen laboured to explain the intricacies of vulnerability scanning, Excel exploits, piveting, payloads, rootkits, backdoor access, etc, etc, etc, I might have caught the gist here and there, but the details were overwhelming. If you're thinking that this knowledge should have been part of the armoury of any SIS officer, you'd be right – but you don't know Pamela. She had a policy of divide and rule, which meant that if any of us in the field needed help with 'computing issues' (i.e. hacking), we were supposed to call in the services of the IT department. Her purpose was, first,

to watch our movements and, second, to ensure that no one could carry out an operation single-handed and so claim all the credit for its success.

You'll see where this is going: it occurred to me, as I tried to follow Helen's convoluted exposition, that if hacking were an essential step in bringing down Eric, I could circumvent Pamela (though I'd need to think up a good excuse for such boldness) and present Arnold with a fait accompli that would bring the glory where it belonged.

So there I was, enjoying my light-bulb moment at Joy's dinner table. But the way ahead wasn't totally illuminated. I had to persuade Colin to give me a lift home on the grounds that I'd had too much to drink, and then I had to work my charms on the road to Lerwick. Neither should be difficult. However, I also had to keep Joy sweet; I couldn't overtly give her the push, as it were.

When Eric came back from his phone call, he saw, as I had already, that Sven's bottle of Isla Negra was well on the way to empty. 'Hey,' he said. 'You shouldn't be drinking like that in your condition.'

Sven went red with anger. 'What do you mean, in my condition?'

'You know what I mean. It was *you* who asked *us* to do your shopping for you because you didn't want to drive in to Lerwick and trundle your trolley round Tesco on a Saturday.'

'That's a big deal? You take week about. Every second Saturday's too much to ask?'

'Not the point, and you know it. I'm talking about not adding alcohol to a problem you've already recognised.'

'You're saying that because I have the slightest tremor in my hand now and then I can't have a glass of wine?'

32

'You've had a lot more than one glass.'

The old man glared. 'You'd be happy if some quack banned me from driving altogether and maybe from blowing my nose and breathing?'

'I don't want you banned from anything.' Eric was stiff-lipped, prim and preaching rather than compassionate. 'But it would be sensible to have yourself checked.'

Sven topped up his glass. 'From what I gather, the treatment for Parkinson's is worse than the disease. Cheers.' He had a long, defiant pull at his wine. 'Anyway, what's the problem? You have a spare room. I can crash there.'

Joy looked at me. 'But Carol…'

I cut in, with the tone of a peacemaker. 'Don't worry. I'm sure Colin can give me a lift home.'

'Of course, of course,' Colin said. Was he *keen*?

'But your car,' Joy said to me. 'It'll be here.'

'I'll think of something.' If I remembered right, Sharon had said she was coming back from Yell on Sunday morning when her parents went to church. She'd drive me out.

A lull in the hostilities between Eric and Sven allowed us to finish our meal – and the second bottle of Sauvignon. I helped Joy clear away the debris while Eric poured himself a whisky and Sven had yet another glass of Isla Negra. Colin ferried plates through until Joy asked him if he'd mind trying to keep the peace between her husband and her father. I started to load the dishwasher.

Joy bent and stroked my arm. 'So you're dumping me?'

I blew her a kiss. 'Hardly.'

We were both leaning over the machine. She brought her face closer to mine. 'You sure?'

'I'm sure.' I didn't pull away. If anything, I moved closer. I knew I was giving her an invitation.

She took it. Her lips were soft. I tell you, her kiss was sweet.

'I want you,' she said, and kissed me again, her lips caressing mine.

It's nice to be wanted. But I said, 'Don't think you can have me tonight.'

'Soon?' Another kiss, the essence of gentleness.

'Soon.'

We pulled back, Eric came in wanting water for his whisky, and the spell was broken. When we returned to the living room, Eric and Colin were discussing data that Colin hoped to supply before Eric's tour of Unst and Yell, while Sven was half listening, half sleeping.

But the conversation was desultory. After twenty minutes or so, I muttered that I had a mountain of marking to do before the weekend was out.

When I stood up, Colin followed my example, but only after he'd looked round like a man who'd now decided he needed an escape route.

In the car, Colin said, 'How big is your mountain?'

'Actually, I don't have one, not this weekend.'

'Oh.'

I waited for him to come back at me with some flirtatious follow-up, but he didn't. So I said, 'I thought it would be nice to drive back with you.'

'Oh.'

The car crunched across the gravel to the track and bounced up to the main road. I realised I had no time to lose.

The heart of the matter: 'Joy told me you and your wife had split up.'

'Yes.' A guarded tone. A stare straight ahead at the swirling sleet.

'What happened? Did you just get fed up with her?'

'It wasn't like that at all.'

I could imagine. But this conversation had to be carefully managed, because otherwise I could set him off down memory lanes that turned into wretched cul-de-sacs – and that could take all my precious minutes.

So, the moment for flattery: 'Really? But, Colin, you're a good-looking chap. You won't…'

'You think?' A look that harboured suspicion. He thought he was being patronised.

'Yes.' *Don't over-elaborate.*

Next tactic: empathy.

I fed him more or less the same lie I'd given Helen: 'I've just come out of an unsatisfactory relationship myself.'

'Well, one thing's for sure: *you* won't be without a partner for long.'

That was said with vehemence, even bitterness. Colin was sorry for himself.

I had to turn this round. 'What do you mean? I've got a placard round my neck – *Come and get me*?'

'No, no.' He was flustered now. 'I didn't mean that at all. I meant… you're *hot*.' That burst out of him like a pop of escaping gas, but it wasn't said entirely as a compliment, because some of that bitter tone remained. He meant, I think, *Why can't you be honest? You're out of my league.*

'I am?'

I had more work to do. I slid down in the seat and curled towards him, as if the only thing I wanted in the world was to snuggle up beside him. 'Colin,' I breathed.

'What?' That was much less aggressive, much less bitter. It was amazing what signals the curl of a body could send.

I wrote a hesitation into the script. Then I said, in a rush that even to me sounded spontaneous, 'Can I give you a hug?'

He yelped. 'Not while I'm driving.'

I inched my head towards his shoulder. 'Promises, promises.'

His glance now was totally different. It spoke of hope – not outright anticipation, just a rebalancing of probabilities. It was enough, I thought; despite unfavourable conditions, the fish was hooked.

We didn't say any more until we came down the hill to the lights of Lerwick. I hadn't hit the bull's eye yet, because I didn't just want a peck on the cheek when he dropped me off. I wanted to see where he lived, to pick his life apart and scan for openings.

We were almost at the roundabout at the Toll Clock Centre when he said, 'Where's your flat?'

'In the land of twitching curtains.'

'Oh.'

That 'oh' would drive me nuts. But the breakthrough came: 'Do you want... to come to my place?'

'Well, I would.'

'If what?'

'If you didn't think I was... forward.'

Colin lived on Harbour Street, on the top floor of a solid, attractive block of flats. When I pressed my nose against his living room window, I could see the darkness of Bressay Sound and some of the lights of Bressay itself.

He'd taken my parka – the room was pleasantly warm. 'Sorry the place is a mess,' he said.

He was right on that one. Tendrils of lint and fragments of material spotted the wooden floor. Big bundles of books had been taken from the bookcases, causing the volumes that remained to tip over. The sole armchair, facing a space that should have housed a television, was piled high with empty coathangers. The mantelpiece – a traditional structure that had been retained even though the fireplace itself was boarded up – was littered with opened envelopes, scraps of paper and up-ended photographs.

'Would you mind,' Colin said, 'if I checked my emails? We have meetings on Monday, Tuesday and Wednesday and it would be really useful if I could update my economic models for Eric. To do that, I need some data that one of my contacts in the oil research business should have forwarded to me. If he hasn't, I'll have to remind him that it's urgent.'

How romantic, I thought. But I said, 'Go ahead. Of course.'

A computer system stood on a long pine table opposite the window. Colin switched it on and sat on an upright chair. I flipped over one of the photographs on the mantelpiece and saw a dark-haired woman with a full, even plump face. Her plunging neckline was meant to be provocative, though it hardly rivalled Pamela's décolletage, and she wore a necklace, earrings, and makeup that could have been supplied by Dulux.

'Is this your wife?'

'Yes.'

'What's her name?'

'Margaret Ann.'

There was a second upright chair, a few feet from the other one. I moved over, still holding the photograph, pulled out the chair so that it angled,

37

slightly, towards Colin's, sat down and picked up a book that lay on the table – something about the oil market. He had just logged on to his computer, because the operating system was almost ready.

He loaded up his browser and went to AOL – I didn't know that people still used AOL. From the way his fingers hovered over the keyboard, I could tell that he touch-typed. That was good.

For those of you who don't touch-type, a brief primer. Your left hand sits above the keys 'a', 's', 'd', 'f' and your right above 'j', 'k', 'l', ';'. To reach other keys, you stretch your fingers up or across or you curl them down to hit the bottom line. Once you've touch-typed a few hundred documents, these movements become automatic. So, when you're watching someone else, you have two chances to detect the keys he hits: you can see the keys themselves or you can detect the finger movements. When it's a password that's being typed in, the user is often quite slow and deliberate, because it's such a pain to make a mistake and have to start all over again, and this nearly always gives you a good chance to catch at least a few of the letters.

I had to observe Colin closely, but without being obvious. My solution was to pretend to read the back cover of the book on oil and to make comments, so that I had a pretext for looking towards him.

'This looks complex,' I said.

His fingers were poised to input his username. 'It's like anything else. It's not too bad when you get into it.'

'Mm.'

The fingers started. He was certainly not at the speedy end of the spectrum, but still I missed the first letter. For the second and third, though, he moved the third finger of his right hand up and then back down. So: 'o' and 'l'. This had to be his first name. I missed the fourth letter but I caught

the 'n', then a full stop. I missed the next letter but he hadn't used the Shift key for upper case. I missed another, but I caught 'rr' and 'u' and that was all I needed. His username was 'colin.carruthers'. Not a surprise.

As he hit the Return key to take him to the page for his password, I said, 'Colin, I suspect that you are really, truly brainy.'

'Huh.'

His password. Second finger on the right down to the bottom line, I thought. So: 'm'. Had he used the left Shift key? I wasn't sure. Third letter: 'r'. Fourth: 'g'. Sixth: 'r'. Eighth: 't'. His wife's name. Right pinkie away up to the very top. So: '-' or '_'. I missed the next letter but I thought he used the right Shift key. Then an 'n' twice, then possibly an 'e'. So: 'Anne', not 'Ann'. His password was 'Margaret_Anne' or 'Margaret-Anne'. Perhaps the whole lot was lower case, but I didn't think so. Anyway, I had enough for Helen. She'd get into his emails, after one or two tries at the most, observe what kind of material he sent to Eric and devise some malware that would destroy Eric's reputation. I had every faith in her.

'Ah,' Colin said. 'It's here.'

'You pass it straight on to Eric?'

'No, I incorporate it into my model.'

'That must take time.' I stood up, ready to go home, since I had everything I needed. 'Maybe I should leave you to it.'

'Oh. No, no, no. Sorry. I just had to check it was here. I mean, I really…'

You mean you really do want to screw me? Tough. You blew it.

He closed his email, quit AOL and his browser, shut everything down. Looking at his keyboard, he said, 'You know, Margaret Anne and I are getting a divorce.'

39

He was telling me that he was free? That we could have a real 'relationship'?

'I didn't know.'

He directed his gaze towards the photograph, which I'd left on the table, then looked back again to his keyboard. 'I'm going to scrub all traces of her. Tomorrow.'

Oh no. It was an odds-on bet that one of those traces was his email password. After I'd gone to all this trouble.

So I had to screw him after all, and hang around long enough to catch his new password? *Damn.*

But if that was what I had to do, I would do it.

'Good,' I said.

'Well...'

I couldn't be bothered waiting for him to finish his sentence. The *Mata Hari Manual*, which I'm going to write as a companion volume to *Spying for Dummies*, will suggest that in a situation like this there is nothing better than good old-fashioned teasing. With that in mind, I toyed with my cardigan, slipped it off, rolled my bum a little, and posed with one hand on a hip.

He didn't quite lick his lips, but he did gulp. 'I'll just...' He started forward, stopped and started again like a jerky robot. 'I'll just put the heater on in...' He went through a doorway in the corner.

I felt about as randy as a comatose slug. But come *on*. Colin wasn't bereft of intelligence, and he couldn't be *altogether* lacking in experience. Surely he'd earn at least a beta plus?

Chapter 4

Saturday, 6th – Sunday, 7th

I won't keep you in suspense. The best I could give him was a beta double minus.

The condom issue was a bad start. I always kept one in my pocket – I carry a backpack sometimes, but I have a horror of handbags – along with a sachet of lubricating jelly. I applied the jelly in the bathroom, but I didn't produce the condom in case this hinted at promiscuity and frightened Colin off.

So we're sitting on his bed in our underwear and I say, 'Colin, I'm not on the pill or anything.'

He froze.

What in hell had I done wrong?

I said tentatively, 'But you can use a condom, can't you?'

Suddenly, he snarled, 'Oh yes. Naturally.'

'What do you mean?'

'Why would a married man, whose wife was on the pill, have a condom? Tell me that.'

'I don't know.' Okay, maybe he didn't have a condom, but why on earth was he so upset?

'Because she insisted, that's why, for the best part of a year. Oh she *said* it was a different pill and she didn't trust it, but that was a lie, a stupid lie. I *knew* it was a lie. It wasn't getting pregnant she was scared of.'

'I don't understand.' Actually, maybe I did. But I couldn't trample all over his pride. 'She didn't think you had caught… she didn't think you had been playing around?'

'Huh.' He twisted his mouth. '*She*'d been playing around. *She*'d caught an STD. *She* didn't want to admit it, until I forced it out of her the day she left.'

I thought Margaret Anne had been pretty reasonable, making sure she didn't infect her husband.

'Colin, that's awful.'

After that, I had an uphill struggle. I managed to get him into bed, although we kept the remnants of our clothes on. I held him close, I smoothed his hair, I stroked his cheek. Most of all, I whispered reassurances: he shouldn't throw out a whole barrel because one apple was rotten; Margaret Ann had been wrong for him, but his life lay ahead; he was young, he was handsome, he was fit, he was intelligent; lots of women would want him; well, I could think of one.

'Really?' he said.

'Really.'

I got up and took my bra and pants off. Climbing back into bed, I slipped my hand down under his boxers. Where there should have been a maypole, there wasn't much more than a lifeless log.

Eventually, the maypole rose. Now Colin did produce a condom, but he was clumsy, rushed, tense. And he forgot all about me.

'Sorry,' he said. 'Sorry. I was too quick.'

The business of massaging a man's ego – you might know this – is a never-ending task. 'Colin,' I said, 'don't be silly. It was nice. I'm a bit tired. And it was only a rehearsal.'

I kissed him on the cheek and shoulder and cuddled into him. The wind rose, blowing hail against the window, and in moments he was asleep. I lay and tried to remember the last time I'd given a man a straight alpha.

I was slow to wake. Colin had showered, brewed coffee, and set the table for breakfast before I came into the living room.

He was dumping the photographs from his mantelpiece into a plastic bag. 'Should have done this weeks ago,' he said. 'I was kidding myself. You've helped me face up to reality.'

'But, Colin, you don't need to *face up to* reality.' I wagged a finger at him. 'You can *enjoy* it.

'Yeah?'

His coffee was good. I enjoyed my breakfast and asked just enough questions about his economic models to keep him talking. It was clear he wanted to get to work on these, because, when he asked if I needed a lift back to Joy's to fetch my car and I said I'd ask Sharon, he didn't object too much.

'Sharon?' he said. 'I think I've met her. She teaches English?'

'Yes. She and I are the newbies.'

'A quiet sort of girl? She's had some sort of trauma?'

'Why d'you say that?'

'Her eyes. She must have had a problem sleeping. Over a long period.'

'She had an abusive husband, but she stayed with him because she wanted her son to have a father.'

'Oh my God.' To him, I supposed, Sharon's story was more proof that marriage was a bad idea.

He poured me another cup of coffee and made more toast. When he sat down, he fiddled with his black cherry jam before he said, trying to sound casual, 'How do you spell your name?'

'My name? C-A-R-O-L.'

'No "e"?'

'No "e".'

'Do you have a middle name?'

'Lynn. L-Y-N-N.'

'Carol Lynn.' He said it dreamily. 'I like it.'

I observed that his computer had not been switched on.

He said, 'Can I call you through the week?'

Well, if a man's going to use his new girlfriend's name as his email password, it's only sensible to check that she wasn't a one-night stand.

'I'll be crushed if you don't.'

I waited until I was outside before I phoned Sharon, just in case she wasn't available and Colin insisted after all on driving me out to Joy's.

Sharon and Robert were almost back at Lerwick. 'Of course I'll take you,' she said. 'Get you at the Toll Clock Centre?'

'That would be great. Thanks very much.'

'Don't be silly. You're my bff.'

'And you're mine.'

It had been very easy to slip into the role of Sharon's friend. She'd adopted me on my first day in the school, when Peter, the head of the English department, hadn't been available to greet me. He'd left a note that he'd see me after the morning interval and I should start my second-year class on *Ring*

of Bright Water, which was 'in the cupboard'. One of the secretaries took me along the corridor and we were lingering outside the cupboard when Sharon appeared. She seemed to take to me at once, showing me my classroom, giving me a quick summary of departmental priorities, and then taking me back to hunt for the books.

'*Ring of Bright Water*?' she muttered. 'God knows where it is.'

The cupboard was neat, but it held boxes upon boxes of books, some of them on shelves so high that you had to stand on a chair to see what was there. Sharon was methodical – she'd encountered this problem before – and finally found the thirty well-thumbed copies at the end of the second-top shelf.

'Hope you're into otters.'

'Um… Not really.

'I can give you Maxwell's autobiography,' she said. 'It puts everything into perspective. Shows you quite clearly how he grew up into the kind of guy who could fall in love with an otter.'

And we'd gone on from there. In the few weeks since I'd arrived, we'd shared insights on other members of staff, not least Peter and Joy, dissected Gavin Maxwell's psyche, watched a scary movie on one of those Saturday nights, and confided in each other that we were not in favour of an independent Shetland. An observer would have said that we were inseparable.

I met them at the Toll Clock roundabout – Sunday morning in Lerwick is so quiet that you can stop almost anywhere without causing a traffic jam. After an unsuccessful attempt to banter with Robert, who was in the back

seat, engrossed in a game on his handheld computer, I said to Sharon, 'How was your visit?'

She made a face. 'Not fantastic. I couldn't sleep.'

Even from the side, I could see that her eyes were more pouched than usual. Those dark bags, and the mental scars they hinted at, would be with her for the rest of her life. I'd have liked to take her away, find a good plastic surgeon, give her two months' holiday without Robert, and engage the services of an effective counsellor.

But I couldn't. I said, 'Something specific?'

'Well, a certain person' – she jerked her head towards the back seat – 'was girning for Scotland. And my dad was so *stiff*. He's stiff at the best of times, but he was all worked up about a meeting of the community council, of which he's a stalwart, this coming week. They've to make a recommendation to a special session of the SIC, which is going to discuss whether to hold an indicative referendum – something that dad is vehemently opposed to.'

The SIC was Shetland Isles Council. But a special session? I remembered Eric's phone call, and said, 'I heard the SIC is meeting on Wednesday. Is this the special session?'

'No. There's no date for that. They're going to discuss the date on Wednesday.'

'So they're going to discuss when to hold their discussion?'

'You've got it.'

I said, 'That's local government for you. Will the SIC ever actually *do* anything.'

'The problem is that they might.'

Joy's Toyota was parked on their gravel sweep, but no one was in. Having established that, I came back to Sharon's car.

'Let me take you and Robert for lunch at the Skipidock.'

Her face lit up, then at once she frowned. 'Ah. It's closed on Sunday.'

'Damn. Know anywhere else?'

'Not really. At least no place suitable for Robert.'

Now there was an anxious look in her eyes, and I could guess why. She didn't want to go back to her flat to endure the rest of the day alone with Robert. She was about to invite *me* for lunch. But this was another thing I couldn't do, because, while it would be easy to get up and leave the Skipidock, it would be a different matter abandoning her in her poky little living room. I could get trapped, especially if I did manage to establish rapport with Robert. And I *had* to go to Tesco, because I *had* to activate Helen.

'Let's make it a date,' I said, 'for next Saturday. Robert can eat chips to his heart's content, and you and I can talk.'

The sunshine came back to her face. 'I'll look forward to it all week.'

I realised that that was probably true.

I was in Tesco by half past three. This Sunday, Helen was restocking the cauliflower and cabbage while the radio played some screeching fiddle music. She saw me at once, and the glazed look that comes from utter tedium dissipated.

'Hi,' she said.

'Hi. What's new?'

'Not much.'

'Natasha busy?'

Natasha, who was an immigrant from central Europe, shared Helen's house. Though Helen herself claimed to have left prostitution behind at the same time as heroin, Natasha still dabbled in both.

Helen placed her last cabbage on the display. 'Not particularly. She's on a downer. Some guy was rough with her. Now she's started looking in the mirror, examining her wrinkles. Big mistake, looking in the mirror.'

Given that Helen's face was pockmarked and makeup-free, and her hair was invariably tied with a rubber band, it was easy to believe that she didn't spend too much time gazing at her reflection.

I'd taken a trolley and started to fill it with groceries, because I didn't want Helen to get the impression that I'd come into Tesco just to see her. My approach had to be low-key.

'Hey,' I said, 'want to have some fun with Free Shetland?'

'Fun?'

'I came across a guy who emails Eric Sorenson regularly. You know Sorenson?'

'I know him. Pompous little shit.'

'So this guy has an AOL account. I know his username and I think I know his password.'

'How the fuck did you manage that?'

'Well,' – I laughed – 'pillow talk.'

'You fucked him?'

'Well...'

'Bloody hell. I wanna know all about it.'

I raised my eyebrows. *Really?*

In fact, she was more eager to play with her 'toys' than to hear about my sex life. 'He emails Sorenson regularly? Any attachments?'

'Excel sheets.'

'Right.' She was pensive. 'Not as easy to put bugs into Excel as it used to be. Still, I could lurk in his account, find the version of Excel, probably unearth an exploit. Then I could work something out.'

'You could get into Sorenson's computer?'

'You dumb fuck, I could *take over* Sorenson's computer.'

'Interesting.'

'Wanna buy me a drink when I come off my shift?'

'Sure. Now give me one of your cauliflower.'

The Norseman was one of the few old-fashioned pubs left in Lerwick. I liked it because it had good food, although the menu was limited, and multiple nooks and crannies, marked off by green banquettes, where you could have a quiet, civilised conversation.

Helen knocked back her first vodka with alarming speed. 'God, I needed that. A day at Tesco and you turn into a zombie.'

I didn't rush to offer her another one.

'My round, I suppose,' she said.

'I'm not ready,' I pointed out. I'd had about three sips of my cider. 'But you go ahead.'

She did. This time, she drank much more slowly. 'So,' she said. 'Who's this guy who gives away his password after a good fuck? I assume it was a good fuck.'

I wasn't going to answer the second question. 'His name is Colin Carruthers. He's got an AOL account and his username is colin dot carruthers, all lower case.'

'And his password?'

'I'm almost certain it's Carol underscore Lynn. That's C-A-R-O-L underscore L-Y-N-N. I think the 'C' and the 'L' are upper case and the rest is lower case. It might be Carol hyphen Lynn, but that seems less likely.'

'Carol Lynn? Is that you?'

I shrugged modestly.

'Bloody hell. How long have you known this guy?'

'A night.'

'Fuck me. You think he's going to change his password on the basis of one night?'

'I'm fairly sure. If it doesn't work, it doesn't work.'

'What if it does? Do you know anything about Sorenson's computer skills?'

'His wife implied that he was sloppy. At least, he doesn't keep his hard disc tidy.'

'Sounds good.' She chewed the inside of her lip. 'He probably logs on as administrator. You'd be amazed at the number of idiots who do. That'll make my life easier.'

'So what'll you do, exactly?'

'Exactly? I tried to explain this to you before. I'll need to find an exploit. Then I'll choose a payload. I'll kill Sorenson's antivirus, migrate my shell to something other than Excel – probably svchost – and upload a toolkit including a rootkit and a backdoor.'

I shouldn't have asked.

'Could this be traceable to you?'

'No. You can hide whatever you want with a rootkit and when I've finished I'll clear the event log.'

'So after that the sky's the limit?'

'Sure is. But let me get set up first. Then we'll plan our campaign.'

This was perfect. 'Let's have something to eat,' I said. 'I'm going to have steak pie.'

'Make mine fish and chips.'

She was assuming that I would pay. I went up to the bar and, as the barman was busy, rested my elbow, then my back against the counter.

There was a man behind our seats, in another banquette nest, reading *The Shetland Times* and at the same time listening to an iPod, or something like it, on Bluetooth headphones. His body was lithe and well muscled under a blue seaman's jersey, and his face was somewhere between handsome and roguish. Black hair hung over his ears and his cheek showed the beginnings of a very dark stubble. For some reason, he didn't seem to me to be a Shetlander.

I ordered our food and was taking two glasses of water back to the table – in the hope that I might reduce Helen's alcohol intake – when the mystery man looked up and smiled at me. I have to say that something stirred inside me.

When Helen had scoffed her meal, she went to the toilet. A voice with a rich, deep timbre came from nowhere. 'May I sit down for a moment?'

It was him. From up close, he was even more handsome than I'd thought. Strong nose, strong jaw, dark hair and eyebrows, that dark stubble, and most of all dark, laughing eyes. There was a burr in his consonants that suggested he wasn't a native speaker of English.

'A moment?' I said.

He took that as a yes and slid into the seat that Helen had vacated. I was imagining what his body would be like if he removed his jersey. There was

51

an easy power about his movements, just as there was an easy confidence in his gaze. 'Can I buy you a drink?' he said.

I tried to place the accent, but couldn't. He could be from Eastern Europe, the Balkans, or some corner of Scandinavia . Yes, he could be a modern Viking.

'And who are you?'

'I'm Gregor.' He shook my hand. 'There. We are formally introduced.'

He hadn't, I noticed, asked *my* name. 'Where are you from?' I said.

'You can't tell?' His voice went even deeper. 'I'm from Mother Russia.'

'Russia? What are you doing in Shetland?'

'Aha.' He seemed to take great delight in my questions. 'I'm a mad scientist – evil, of course. I'm scheming to bring my country world domination – in halibut.'

'*Halibut?*'

'Halibut. You know the problem with halibut?'

'They're expensive?'

'Well, yes they are, but the first problem is sex.'

'Isn't it always?'

He cast me a glance of amusement. 'You must come up and see my hatchery some time.'

'And where's that?'

'Unst.'

'*Unst?*' That was as far north as you could go; I'd always assumed you needed an icebreaker to get there. 'You have to commute to Lerwick for a drink?'

He said, 'We have an apartment, provided by a grateful government.'

Helen returned, took a look at Gregor, and said to me, 'Uh huh?'

'This is Gregor. Gregor, this is Helen.'

He shook hands again. Helen, who wasn't used to such civility, stared at him.

She said, 'Guess I'll be on my way.'

'Don't be silly. Have another drink.'

Her glare was withering – God knew what signals I was giving off. 'Maybe not.'

'You'll keep me up to date on that matter we were discussing?'

'You got it.'

Helen had hardly left us when I fired off another question. I didn't plan anything, you understand; I wasn't playing games; I was genuinely curious.

'What did you mean by saying the first problem with halibut is sex?'

He frowned, admitting an error. 'I should have said sex determination. You see, halibut that end up as female grow much bigger, with the same nutrition, as those that end up male. So they are much more valuable.'

What do you mean "end up"?'

'The crucial question. We humans are used to the idea that our sex is genetically determined. With certain species, that is not true. Take crocodiles. The sex of a crocodile depends on the temperature of the egg at certain stages of development; sex determination in this case depends on epigenetic factors – you know, factors that increase, decrease or turn off completely the expression of different genes. Likewise with halibut: the eventual phenotype – whether the fish appears to be male or female, in this case – also depends on epigenetics. So it is my job to experiment with the optimum arrangement of these factors.'

'My goodness.' This wasn't the usual kind of man you met in a pub, the kind who hopes to impress you with his scintillating repartee.

53

'And why Unst?' I said.

'Because the temperature of the sea there is about right, and it's also roughly where the temperature of the water off Russia will be in six or seven years' time.'

'I see. And what about humans? Can you change *their* phenotype?'

He was serious; I liked that. 'Sort of. You can't interfere with the embryo to change its sex, but it's possible that epigenetic factors do affect the full expression of sexuality.'

'Doesn't this kind of study diminish your sense of the magic of sex?'

'Not at all.' His eyes were very steady; he gave me the impression that he wasn't going to steer this conversation; he was going to let it run wherever it ran. 'Rather, it shows me – I know this is a cliché – the wonder of the universe.'

'Don't tell me you're religious.'

He smiled at that. 'No, although I have been known to sing religious songs. And I have some sympathy with the view that if your belief in God helps you to live a more contented life, then it doesn't matter if your belief is well founded.'

'I'm uncomfortable with that.'

'Why?'

There was magic *here*, in having this discussion in the Norseman, with a man I had just met. I'd forgotten all about Pamela and the Scottish Intelligence Services and Helen and the future of Free Shetland.

But I wasn't entirely sure what I wanted to say. 'I'll need to think about it.'

A pause. Another steady gaze. He said, 'That drink?'

I didn't want to linger in the Norseman. 'My car's round the corner. I could get arrested for driving over the limit.'

'Just leave it. This is a very law-abiding place.'

'It is.'

'You could come back to my apartment and try my slivovitz. It's the very best slivovitz there is.'

This was ridiculous; I couldn't be *that* easy.

But *bugger* it. Why faff about? Why play hard to catch? Why not simply admit that, like any girl, I needed a treat now and then?

'As long as it's safe slivovitz.'

Chapter 5

Sunday, 7th – Monday 8th

Gregor's apartment was in a nondescript building not far from North Road, on the edge of one of those undefined Lerwick spaces where taxis are parked and optimists have set up workshops and small businesses in overgrown sheds. We entered by a plain white door, though it had an electronic lock, and climbed a timber stairwell.

The living room was in marked contrast to the exterior. The floor was of laminated wood, two of the walls were painted in muted magnolia, the others in a warm brown. Framed photographs and paintings showed Shetland scenes: waves crashing on cliffs, sea birds wheeling above their nests, empty beaches, the Northern Lights, sunset over shining voes. Across the room, beside a window that overlooked the workshops, a sturdy table was big enough for two. Next to a couch of a deep russet stood a smaller table on which a chess match was in progress. There was no television, but there was a huge monitor for a tiny computer, and two big speakers. No log fire and no hearth rug, I noticed. Oh well.

I sank onto the couch. Gregor went into the kitchen and returned with two glasses of slivovitz. He sat beside me and clinked my glass.

'Your health.'

'And yours.'

I sipped the spirit. It was freezing cold, but my taste buds detected the plums.

I said, 'Who are you playing chess against?'

'A friend in Moscow.'

'Why do Russians love chess so much?' Don't imagine, by the way, that I was avoiding the moment of truth; rather, I was postponing it so that I could savour the anticipation.

A tease lurked in the play of his eyebrows. 'You could say it's the long, cold winters. Or you could say we've all got devious minds.'

'How devious is yours?'

'Very.' He sniffed his Slivovitz. 'Although, if I wanted to be kind to myself, I might prefer the word "flexible". How about you? I have a feeling that your mind is flexible too.'

'I like to think it is.'

'So,' he said, 'any advance on our discussion? On why you are uncomfortable with a belief in God bringing you contentment?'

Unless I was badly mistaken, he was playing the same game as me.

In fact, my subconscious must have been working on the question, because an answer jumped out of me. 'Because it means that your life is based on self-deception. You're not fully human if you don't stare into the abyss of reality and share your feelings honestly with others.'

'The abyss of reality? You mean the meaninglessness of life?'

'That's right.'

Both of us stared at the place where the log fire should have been. Both of us knocked back the slivovitz.

Gregor said, 'I sometimes think that the question of meaninglessness exists on two levels. When we're on our deathbed and we look back at the sweep of history and our puny achievements, that'll be one kind of meaninglessness. But more important – more meaningful, if you'll pardon

the expression – is the question of what we do at any moment. What desires do we have *now* that are genuine, untouched by conditioning? What do we want to do *now*?'

He suddenly grinned like a boy; I think he'd realised that his words had, so to speak, a double meaning. I laughed, we both laughed, the glasses went down beside the chessmen, and we were kissing furiously. I was so *wet*.

He carried me through to the bedroom, somehow pulled back the downie, and deposited me on the vast white sheet. Gently, he began to undress me.

'Condom?' I said.

'Of course.'

When I was naked, he took off his own clothes – and, boy, was he ready.

He took his time – the very opposite of Colin – and I felt he could hear the music of my body. He could tell when I wanted an allegro, an andante, a largo. He knew what instruments to choose – his lips, his tongue, his nose, his hand – and how to make them work together. He could turn up the intensity at will, turn it down so that my pulses had time to recover, then turn it up, up, up. I just let myself go. Let's talk about meaning. When at last his hard masculinity fused with my wet, wet eagerness, when nothing mattered because I was lost in animal desire, *that* was meaning.

I lay in contentment, my head on his shoulder. 'Carol,' he said, 'I have a confession to make.'

'Mm?' I didn't want to come awake. Then I did, abruptly. 'Hey, how do you know my name?'

'Aha.' He was unabashed. 'That's part of my confession.'

I sat up. 'Let's hear it, then.'

58

'Well' – he was choosing his words – 'it's like this. Even in these supposedly liberal times, when a Russian goes abroad, he may be given other duties by the government. He isn't *asked* to carry out these duties; he is *told*. The intelligence services of Mother Russia know who *you* are – don't ask me how – and they knew that you were coming to Shetland. So they *told* me to make contact with you.'

'You *arranged* this?' I pulled away from him. 'This was planned?'

'But it didn't work out as planned.'

'What do you mean?'

He turned towards me. 'I mean… I guess I fell for you on the spot.'

'You fell for me?'

'Yes.'

I should have got up, got dressed and walked out. He'd deceived me in the Norseman, a big deception.

But how often do you meet a man to whom you give an alpha double plus?

'And what,' I said, trying to be aloof, 'do your intelligence services want from me?'

'They say you have a boss called Pamela something-or-other, and she, for some reason, doesn't like Russians.'

'You could say that.'

'Do you know why she persists in looking gift horses from Russia in the mouth?'

'Your intelligence people told you to ask me that after you'd fucked me?'

'Carol, they only told me to try to find the answer to the mystery. They're perplexed. Scotland has facilities that Russia could use; Russia has money that Scotland could use. Why not put the two things together? Why is this Pamela person so obstinate?'

I let my wariness slip a little; I do believe I already had it in my mind to forgive him. 'Pamela adopts a position. She assumes that any opinion she has must be right. Then, even if the evidence against her appears to mount, the evidence has to be wrong.'

He nodded. 'The Soviet Union used to have a lot of individuals like that.'

'Where is this going, Gregor?'

Where was *I* going? Did I trust him or not?

Now he sighed. What did the sigh mean? That he really didn't care about the machinations of his government? 'I'm told that our government thinks it would be to everyone's advantage if Pamela were replaced.'

'Replaced?' I dared to hope. A relationship with Gregor might bring advantages. 'How would that be managed?'

'I don't know, but apparently she's promiscuous. You're aware of that?'

'Word gets round.'

'Normally, the FSB – or, to be more precise, the SVR – would be able to use that to get plenty of kompromat. But, so I hear, Pamela is very, very careful – last-minute change of plans, last-minute change of rooms, that sort of thing.'

'Hold on. You want *me* to help you get the kompromat?'

He sighed again. 'It's nothing to me. I just want to get back to my halibut, although… well, I'd like to keep seeing you. But, yes, that's what the SVR has in mind.'

'Treason? They want me to commit treason?'

'If treason means betraying your country's interests, no. They want you to work *for* your country's interests.'

I didn't comment. Did I give a damn about Scotland's interests?

Gregor said, 'If Pamela lost her job, would you be interested in it?'

Would I indeed? If I wore Pamela's crown, I would move in exalted circles; I would meet interesting people; Gregor might only be the first.

'Possibly.'

'You would have a good chance?'

'Perhaps.' My brain was humming with the probabilities. I had a good record, and I was sure that Arnold was sweet on me.

He rolled onto his back. 'Could my government help you at all? They could provide funds, but I doubt if that would be relevant.'

'What about information – on the rival candidates and the members of the selection panel?'

'That should be possible. And they'd certainly be happy to begin a new era of cooperation once you got the job.'

Cooperation would be two-way. I would be a sort of double agent. The very idea sent a thrill through me. When I walked down a street and saw ordinary people in mindless pursuit of pointless goals, I could hold my knowledge like a hot-water bottle.

'We have to think about this,' I said.

'Certainly.'

I got out of bed and started to get dressed. 'Where are you going?' he said, and I thought I heard disappointment in his voice. So… maybe he really had fallen for me… maybe he was telling me the whole truth. That would be nice.

'I need to be a little discreet. If I'm seen returning to my flat at the crack of dawn, tongues will wag.'

And some tongue would eventually wag to Colin. I didn't need that, because it was impossible to say if Colin had outlived his usefulness.

'You're right,' he said. 'But I'll see you again?'

'If you're a good boy.'

I put his phone number into my Contacts, gave him a quick peck on the cheek and left. He was definitely disappointed.

I fell asleep thinking of Gregor, I dreamed about Gregor, I woke up thinking of Gregor. When Joy said to me in the English corridor before classes started, 'Well?' I for a second imagined it was Gregor she was talking about.

Then I remembered Colin. 'Well, what?' I said.

'How was it? Cough.'

'He's a very nice guy.'

'And?'

'He just needs to relax a little.'

'He's bound to be a little tense. He's like a golf player who needs to ease back into his swing.'

'That's not a bad analogy.'

'In the meantime,' – she fluttered her eyelashes – 'as soon as you want to swing…'

I pretended to be amused, wanting to deflect attention from the possibility that we might make a tryst right now. I had my hands full enough with Gregor and Colin.

'Can one ever get too much golf?'

First period of the day. My Fifth Year were sitting a prelim exam across in the Clickimin Centre and I had to invigilate. If anything was ever designed to bring down your mood, it must be invigilation. There's the boredom, which I'll leave you to imagine; the frustration – as you watch your pupils struggling with questions that should be easy; and the joyless anticipation –

as you calculate how many days your share of these scripts will wipe off your life. I was glad to get back to my classroom to welcome my Second Year.

They brought my good mood back. Some people will claim that this is what teaching is *really* like, when young people whose minds are filled with insatiable curiosity lift your soul. I tell you, that doesn't hold true very often, but sometimes it does, through some random shuffling of genes and some chance interaction of personal chemistry.

'Hey, miss, got our essays marked?'

'Hey, miss, saw you in Tesco's yesterday.'

'Hey, miss, what're we doing today?'

It helped that they'd got off to a flying start, because *Ring of Bright Water* had been an unexpected success. A lively debate had developed between those who took pleasure in the unquestioning devotion of their own pets, especially dogs, and those who suspected from the first few pages that there was something 'odd' about Gavin Maxwell. I'd set them a concluding essay with the title 'Heavy Petting', and invited them to consider any aspect they liked of the relationship between humans and their pets. I handed out their papers now, let them consider my comments, and then took a few back in so that I could read out choice excerpts. With some good-humoured discussion between each read, the period passed quickly. Everyone, I thought, enjoyed it.

As the class dismissed, I spoke to a boy called Jason Young who I knew lived on Unst. I asked him if he was aware of anyone on the island who was experimenting with halibut.

'Sure do, miss.' He had an appealing, fresh-faced, tousled-hair look and an open, engaging manner. 'The Russians. Everybody knows about them. They come into the town every so often for supplies, and sometimes for a

drink at the hotel. My dad says they're generous; if they order a round of beers, they don't bother about the change.'

'The town? Baltasound? Haroldswick?'

'Baltasound, where I went to school. I'd be there still, but my social worker thought I should come to Lerwick after primary school.'

'Because you're so brainy?'

'Because my dad and mum are always fighting.' He said this with a nonchalant air, but that could have been a pose. 'My mum keeps going down to Glasgow to see her boyfriend and my dad keeps drinking at the hotel or at his pal's.'

'I see.' You could never guess at the experiences that lay behind a young face. I should know. 'So, anyway, you've been to the Russians' place?'

'You can't get in. They have a big sign up, *No entry, for reasons of biosecurity.* Their boss, Gregor, explained it to me, but I didn't really understand it.'

'How did you meet him?'

'They have a flat in Lerwick. He gave me a lift in once when I'd missed the school bus.'

'But you tried to get into the site on Unst?'

'And I won't try again. I'd taken two steps past the sign when this nasty guy – I'd never seen him before – comes up with two big thugs and starts hurling abuse at me. Asks me if I'm stupid, if I can't read, and stuff like that. I just ran for it.'

'But you could show me the way?'

'Yeah. Why would you want to go there?'

'I'm curious.'

Curious to know how much of the truth Gregor was telling me.

64

For lunch, I'd brought a sandwich to eat at my desk because I wanted to do as much preparation as possible before Peter handed out the exam scripts. I was scribbling a lesson plan when I realised I didn't have a single spare jotter left in the room. Not good. With the wrong class at the wrong time, it's amazing what an irritant such a trivial thing can be. I went along to Peter's cupboard to pick up a new packet.

The cupboard was a big one, and Peter had arranged a little interview space – three chairs and a table – under the window. On one of the chairs a long rake of a man sat alone; I could have sworn he leered at me as I came in.

'Hello,' I said. 'Where's Peter?'

The man gestured towards the door that led into Peter's classroom. 'On the phone.'

Now I could hear Peter speaking. He had a booming, resonant voice that the pupils called, with mock reverence, the Voice of God.

'Who're you?' the man said.

'I'm Carol Rutherford.'

He shook my hand without getting up. His face was mottled round the cheeks and nose, and he had a wolfish, unpleasant twist to his lips. 'You're new,' he said. 'I'm Paul McIntyre. You know Free Shetland?'

'Of course.'

'I'm the Communications Director.' He definitely had capital letters there.

Paul? Eric had been talking to someone called Paul. 'So what does your role involve?' I said. 'You mastermind their online campaigning?'

He snorted. 'Oh yes. I would, if Eric Sorenson and his lily-livered liberals would let me. I could have the referendum sewn up in a few easy moves. I trained with the best, you know.'

'Oh? Where?'

'St Petersburg.'

These Russians had a finger in every pie. 'That's impressive,' I said.

'Yeah. The Russians know everything that's worth knowing about... achieving your ends through the Internet.'

Achieving your ends? He meant, *manipulating people.*

I said, 'So how would you start – sewing up the referendum?'

'*Start?*' He made my choice of word sound like an insult. 'I'd do some mining on Facebook, I'd set up a few bots and websites and accounts to promote the news that's favourable to us, I'd buy a few hundred "likes" and "shares" and "followers", and I'd troll like fury those who try to troll *us.*'

'All this is legal?'

He snarled, 'Show me the statute in Scots law that says it isn't.'

He'd caught me there. I said, 'But Eric doesn't agree with that approach?'

Another snort; he had quite a repertoire. 'Eric Sorenson and his cohorts think that the shining light of reason and the white doves of peace will win the day.'

I scratched my head. 'But you're not in here to campaign?'

'Don't be stupid. I'm in here to see *him.*' He jerked a finger, clearly in anger, towards Peter's room.

'What's up?'

He should have told me it was none of my business, but his indignation was in full flow. 'I've been telling him, ever since my daughter came to this school, that she has dyslexia and ADHD. But has he done anything about it?'

'But it's not up to him. That would be a matter for pupil support.'

'But they ask him for his opinion – don't they? – as her class teacher. And he says there's not enough evidence. And people listen to him because he's been here since the Boer War.'

That was rubbish. People listened to Peter because he gave honest, considered, balanced responses.

I thought I might redirect the conversation. 'It must be a nuisance to you having to come in here on a Monday lunchtime.'

He looked at me suspiciously. 'When you have three foster children, you have a lot of responsibilities, and you have to carry them.'

In other words, he didn't have a job. The state paid him to foster these children and here he was hoping to attach to one child a few labels like 'dyslexic' or 'ADHD sufferer' so that it would be easier to claim some allowance that he could pocket.

Peter had come off the phone. I muttered that I'd have to go, stood up, helped myself to a packet of jotters from the stack in one corner of the cupboard, and beat my retreat. I was sure that McIntyre would waste the rest of Peter's lunch hour, and not think twice about it.

Peter didn't manage to parcel out the exam scripts. Oddly, I was disappointed. I know I said I wasn't looking forward to the marking, but now I was left with nothing to do in the evening. There's nothing worse than twiddling your thumbs.

Oh yes there is. You can browse the Internet.

I browsed the Free Shetland website, on the grounds that I might find some useful information on the forthcoming meetings.

The two that were being held on Unst and Yell were 'local consultations to clarify the arguments for Shetland's independence'. That wasn't quite what Sharon had said, but it wasn't surprising that Free Shetland should have their own perspective. As for the one on Wednesday evening, this was 'an opportunity for paid-up members of Free Shetland to reassess strategy in view of the impending decision of the SIC'. I assumed that the 'impending decision' referred to the vote on whether or not to hold the indicative referendum.

I also noticed that there was yet another meeting – 'a forum for all Shetlanders' – to be held the next Wednesday, the 17th, in the atrium of the high school. Eric was moving up through the gears.

I should have stopped there, but the Internet is addictive. I went to the council website and flicked back through the minutes of previous sessions. It was in November that Eric had first proposed a non-binding ballot, and some of his words were quoted: 'If a majority of the Shetland electorate declares that they are in favour of independence, pressure can then be put on the Scottish government, in the name of democracy and justice, to hold a vote that *will* provide the legal basis for Shetland becoming a new, autonomous state...' This didn't tell me anything new, it shouldn't have affected my spirits. But it did, because it spelled out to me how carefully planned Eric's blitzkrieg had been. The only weapon I might have was Helen's malware. If that turned out to be a dud, Eric's tanks would roll all over me – and Pamela would throw the remnants to the dogs.

Chapter 6

Tuesday 9th – Wednesday 10th

I was in a hurry. I needed to get into Eric's computer sooner rather than later.

But I couldn't phone or text Helen. If I tried to pressure her at all, she would smell a rat.

During the day on Tuesday, and all through the evening, I kept hoping that my phone would beep. It never did. About eight o'clock, I took twenty minutes off from my marking to sign up online with Free Shetland, reasoning that if Helen lost interest or was unsuccessful, I could at least go to the meeting on Wednesday and see if there was another spanner I could throw in the works.

On Wednesday, I checked my phone at the morning interval, lunchtime and the end of every class. Nothing from Helen, though I seemed to remember that Wednesday was her day off. At long last, as I was packing up, I heard the beep I'd been waiting for.

But it was Colin. *Back in Lerwick. You going to the f s meeting tonight?*

It hadn't occurred to him that I might never have joined the Free Shetland happy family.

I typed back: *Sure.*

Will come by your flat about 7.15? I had told him where I lived as we sat at breakfast.

See you then.

I went out to the car park and was about to start up the Honda when my phone beeped again. This time it *was* Helen.

Everything in place. Want to come round after school? She had no idea of the time.

I typed: *Will come now. Fish supper?*

And some wine. Been working at this all day.

I guessed I was paying. But I didn't care. I detoured to the Coop, then the Hungry Haddock.

Helen and Natasha had a downstairs flat in what people call 'social housing', so far out on the north edge of Lerwick that it could hardly have been less convenient for Tesco. Their garden was a wasteland, their windows unwashed, and their front door in sore need of palliative surgery. Inside, the hall was cluttered with plastic bags and cardboard boxes that had no apparent function, and the living room was strewn with teeshirts, underwear (clean, thank God), pairs of jeans, shoes, towels, magazines, packets of Pringles and the wrappings of chocolate bars. Only Helen's computer corner, it seemed, was ever tidied.

Natasha sprawled on the couch. She was a striking girl, slim, with a long nose that would have given her an elfin look if it weren't for the first signs of wear and tear round her eyes. She had endless legs, which she flaunted by wearing the shortest of skirts. As I sat next to her feet, she had her knees raised, displaying her white panties. I could see how easy it would be for her to catch men's interest.

'How are you?' I said.

'Fine.' She was fiddling with her smartphone.

She'd been 'on a downer' on Sunday and now she was 'fine'? That was Natasha for you.

Helen, who'd gone into the kitchen to fetch two glasses – Natasha wasn't eating with us – came back and said, 'Natasha, you're fine *now*. You've known this latest guy how long? Two days? Wait till *he* turns rough.'

Natasha was one of those people who'd be scrolling down her phone as the world came to an end. She barely stopped long enough to say, 'He won't. He's good to me. You'll see. He should be arriving any minute.'

Her phone trilled. She jabbed at it with a purple-nailed finger. I heard a male voice grunting something and she said, I thought, 'zdravstvuyte.'

I said to Helen, 'She speaks Russian?'

'Two words.' Helen threw up her hands. 'But you'd think she was going to honeymoon in Moscow.'

The conversation was very short. It ended with Natasha saying in a sultry voice, 'Okay.' She stuck out her tongue at Helen. 'See. He's just round the corner.'

'What's his name?' I said.

'Ivan.' She giggled. 'Ivan the Terrible.'

A car stopped outside, a door banged, footsteps clumped on the garden path. Natasha jumped up and ran into the hall. I heard her say 'zdravstvuyte' again, before a long pause. Then she came through, dragging her client by the arm.

'Ivan, this is Helen – you know – and Carol.'

'Zdravstvuyte.' Ivan was as shy as a suitor being introduced to a girl's parents. He was bulky, and somehow untidy, his beard and his hair in need of a trim.

'Hi,' I said.

There was an awkward moment before Natasha pulled him away. 'See you two later.'

Helen and I ate. I had half a glass of wine and she had half the bottle. Finally, I said, 'Everything set up to play havoc with Sorenson?'

She brightened. 'Yup. I've got full access and I've done some programming. When Sorenson sends an email with an attachment, a few lines of code will be added.'

'An attachment to the attachment?'

'If you like. This code will sit on the computer of the guy who receives it until *he* sends an attachment. Then it will forward itself. Each time it forwards itself, it will delete the My Documents folder of the computer it's leaving.'

'So this will go on all along a chain?'

'Yeah. The other thing the code will do, after the attachment has been received, is display a short URL, and a message inviting the user to view Eric Sorenson's naughty pictures. Not everyone will be stupid enough to click this, but those that do will be taken to Sorenson's treasure trove of child pornography.'

I spoke before I thought. 'Christ, we can't do that.'

'Why the hell not?'

'We'll put him in jail.'

'So? I've got news for you: I've done it.'

I was getting soft. Spying was a rough game, and people got hurt.

'You've covered your traces?' I said.

'You think I'm stupid? I told you, you can hide whatever you want with a rootkit. On the other hand, when Sorenson emails somebody with an

address at shetland.gov.uk, their intrusion detection programs will be on to it like bloodhounds. He'll get the blame, not to mention the police on his track.'

'You are a fiend.'

Helen accepted the compliment. She finished her supper, drank more wine and began to tell me her worries about Natasha. Really, I just wanted to get away, wanted to go back to my flat and have a shower.

'This Ivan,' she said, 'she hardly knows him.'

'He's definitely Russian?'

'Yeah. Works on a fish farm on Unst.'

Did he? That couldn't be a coincidence. I decided not to mention Gregor. Helen hadn't asked what happened after she left the Norseman.

She was venomous about Natasha's clients. Apparently, safe and gentle sex wasn't high on the list of their priorities, and Natasha didn't always stand up for herself. Helen's chief concern was that any more nastiness could increase the chances of Natasha sliding back into the embrace of heroin.

Natasha herself reappeared, flushed, after about an hour. 'Hey,' she said, 'Ivan says he could take me out to his fish farm. What d'you think?'

Helen was never going to make the diplomatic service. She screeched at once, 'Are you nuts? How many men are out there?'

Natasha flipped from excitement to hurt in a second. 'I don't know.'

'And when d'you think they last had sex? How many hookers do you think there are on Unst?'

I thought Natasha was going to cry. 'What are you talking about?'

'If you go out to some fish farm and his mates want a shot at you, d'you expect him to protect you?'

'You're *horrible*.'

She was about to turn and scurry away when I said, in my most compassionate voice, 'Natasha, you've got to be sensible. Get to know Ivan better, see him a few more times, let him take you out, talk to him, don't rush. If he likes you – and I get the impression that he does – he won't abandon you.'

Her expression hovered just short of misery. She'd thought her life was taking off and Helen had brought her back to earth.

'I guess you're right.'

'So go out for dinner tonight. Send him through here while you make yourself irresistible. That won't take you long.'

'Dinner?' She pursed her lips. Going out for dinner wasn't usually on her agenda. 'Yeah. Why not?'

I made my escape shortly after that. I went home, had my shower, and put on some clean clothes before Colin arrived. All the time, I was trying to assess what Helen had told me about her hacking. What had impressed me was that she just took it for granted that her coding would work.

The meeting was being held in Lerwick town hall, about five minutes' walk from my flat. Colin and I set out in a light drizzle and I sensed that he wanted to hold my hand. I slipped my arm through his – how far should a girl go on a second date?

I asked how he and Eric had fared on Unst and Yell.

'Fine.'

I hate that answer (though I'd taken it from Natasha) and I told him so. It's what people say when they can't be bothered finding adequate words.

'Sorry,' he said. 'I don't know how I can describe the process. Eric was at his best, shall we say. I've never heard anyone so brilliant at holding an

74

audience. He's go some sort of sixth sense about what buttons to press, when to pause and have them begging for more, when to crack a joke, when to give them a bit of information, and when – especially – to build up emotion.'

So Pamela was right: Eric was an accomplished orator. I felt a sneaking admiration for him.

We were outside the hall. A sturdy man about Colin's height emerged from a group who were waiting for one of their number to finish a cigarette. 'Hi,' he said to Colin, and cast an appraising look at me.

'Hi,' Colin said. 'This is Carol. Carol, this is Billy, my brother.'

We shook hands. It was my turn to size up Billy. He was older than Colin, and quite different. Where Colin was slight, even skinny, Billy had a comfortable layer of flesh; it gave him an air of contentment that Colin hadn't found.

'Just a few questions, madam.' He affected a deep, authoritarian voice. 'You do not have to say anything, but anything you do say may be taken down and used in evidence against you. What first attracted you to my little brother?'

He was joking. Wasn't he?

I joked back: 'I heard that he had a brother who was really hot.'

'I'm sorry, madam. His brother is happily married with two cute little boys. Now…'

'Hey.' Colin cut in, perhaps because he was uncomfortable with the conversation. 'We'd better get in and get a seat.'

Lerwick Town Hall, built in the 1880s during a boom in herring fishery, is a source of great pride to Shetlanders. The stained-glass windows that grace its main hall – the council chamber can also be booked for meetings,

75

but it's smaller – are world-renowned. They had quite recently been renovated, and I couldn't help noticing that the scenes and people from Shetland's history were in sharp, bright colours. We found seats which would have been under the eye of Hakon Hakonson the Old – if he hadn't been squinting off to his left.

The room was full – too full. The body heat from more than two hundred Shetlanders, many of them heavy, bearded men in heavy pullovers, was combining with the warm air rising from the radiators to make the atmosphere oppressive. I pulled off my anorak and jersey.

At seven-thirty exactly, Eric came in and strode to the lectern holding only a small sheaf of notes. A white-haired woman took a seat to his left, and Paul McIntyre was to his right.

Colin was right: Eric commanded his audience well. He looked people in the eye, and he rejected the microphone in favour of projecting his voice along with his message to the very back row. He had an air of being in complete control.

'My friends,' he said. 'I thank you all for coming. You are the vanguard. It is you who will go across the islands, in the days before the council holds its extraordinary session, listening to hopes, reservations, arguments, persuading voters to persuade their councillors that it is time to take the great leap forward. Now, let me say first what most of you will know already: SIC agreed this afternoon that the date for their decision on whether or not to hold an indicative referendum will be… Monday, 1st March.'

Monday, 1st March? That was less than three weeks.

No one else in the audience seemed to be surprised by the date, and in any case Eric pressed on. 'Paul has asked that we reconsider tonight what we

might call our digital strategy, but first I want to re-summarise and re-emphasise the manner of persuasion that we have agreed on.

'The first question that will spring to people's lips will be about the economy. Will they be better off or worse? Let's be clear that they will not want bland, patronising answers. They will want details. So I am about to email to each of you an updated discussion, with clear conclusions, on each of the pillars of Shetland's wealth: the fish and aquaculture, the lambs and other agricultural products, the tourism, and – of course – the oil. I urge you to get the main headings, get the summary of summaries, but also get the fine points that will convince every fisherman, every guesthouse owner and every farmer. But use the details sparingly. *Listen* to the other person. It is as important to listen, and to be seen listening, as it is to bombard the other with statistics.'

He was 'about to email'? Surely attachments would be flying across Shetland within twenty-four hours?

'That brings us,' Eric said, 'to the question of what we will do when the other person is not ready to be persuaded. I know you have been practising these scenarios in your role-playing exercises, but I would like to restate what we agreed. What we will *not* do is jump in at once with our arguments. What we *will* do is sympathise. We will attempt to tease out the real reason for the other's opposition. Is he afraid of the unknown? Is he concerned about his financial future? Is he worried about being cut off from family and friends on mainland Scotland? We will, in short, try to get inside his head, try to show him that we are on his side. Only then will we draw out from the rich array of our policies the one that will show him his welfare really lies with us.

'And what about direct abuse from implacable opponents? We agreed this too, you will remember. What we will *not* do is meet abuse with abuse, because then we will not only lose for certain the vote of these opponents; we are also likely to lose the votes of those who witness the nastiness. We have to convince the electorate, ultimately, that our policies are sensible *and* *also* that we are decent, reasonable people – as we are.

'Now we voted before that exactly the same principle must apply to online abuse – to trolling, as they call it. However, Paul considers that the trolling against us has reached new, vicious heights, and he has asked that we re-think our whole approach to social media. I thought it better to bring this to you, to discuss it and to vote again, rather than have the disagreement festering within our ranks. So, Paul, over to you.'

This hadn't been quite the heady rhetoric that I was expecting, but I would concede that Eric had made a competent speech. His purpose, after all, was to instil discipline into his own troops rather than inspire the electorate. It remained to be seen how the troops would respond.

McIntyre – I couldn't think of him as 'Paul' – came to the lectern. His facial muscles were working as he tried to assemble a serious expression, but a snarl wasn't far away. I could smell the aggression.

He started with a swipe at Eric. 'This has to be said. God bless Eric, but he is a pacifist. He agrees with me that we should put up defences, but he doesn't want to launch attacks in turn. There is a time for pacifism, but this isn't it.'

Away to my left, I could see a group of colleagues from the school. In the middle of them was a man called Matthew. He taught Maths, and that seemed to me to typify his straight-line thinking. He very often sat in the staffroom, with the same group that now surrounded him, and was scathing about

anyone who questioned the 'sums', as he put it, of Free Shetland's economic case. Now he was nodding vigorously, as were some of his companions, even before McIntyre got into his stride.

McIntyre bounced from one cliché to another. The best method of defence was attack; fire had to be fought with fire; show weakness to an enemy and you were finished; now was the time and now the hour to hit the trolls of the Scottish government in the solar plexus; why land a few jabs when you could go for the knockout? It was very clear that there was nothing that McIntyre would like more than to give rein to his bitterness on Facebook and Twitter.

But then he changed course. All at once, he was giving us a lecture on how every electoral upset since the days of Rodrigo Duterte had been made possible by a 'comprehensive digital strategy', especially one that concentrated on 'micro-targeting' of 'persuadables' through the techniques of Facebook advertising. Not that he used the word 'advertising'; he talked of 'spreading the news'. I knew immediately that this news would be slanted, exaggerated or even totally false; also, it would be spread by the bots, the anonymous accounts and the bought 'likes' that he'd boasted of to me.

McIntyre rambled on about the uses of artificial intelligence, claiming it could identify, among other things, 'suitable influencers' and 'suitable tweaks to headlines for a person's newsfeed'. I had read about such techniques being exploited during Brexit, Donald Trump's campaigning and the second Scottish referendum, and as far as I could gather – at least as far as tweaking headlines was concerned – it wasn't much more than repeated A/B testing of different versions of propaganda, embedded in an algorithm which did the tweaking as a result of each test; in other words, there wasn't much 'intelligence' about it.

When McIntyre had finished, Eric stood up. 'There we have it,' he said. 'Paul is a fierce advocate of a digital strategy; I am an implacable opponent, at least of trolling and partial news. Before we vote, however, I would like to call on Alison to make her case. As you know, she has strong opinions on what kind of society we would want to establish in Shetland, and the uses and abuses of the Internet are very much part of her vision. Alison.'

Alison was the lady with the white-hair. I remembered that I'd seen the name Alison Dalrymple on the website. If this was the same person, she was Eric's official deputy.

And 'lady' was the right word, because she had a quiet, assured manner and a quiet, assured patrician voice. But what she said, I thought, was at first a load of twaddle.

In her view, Shetland had an opportunity that might come only once in history: to recreate something of the 'exhilarating democracy' and the 'cultural magic' of the city states of ancient Greece. In high culture, there would be no limit. Shetlanders had long enjoyed their own music, literature, expertise in the arts and sciences, mastery of diverse crafts. Now they could concentrate on becoming the Athens of the north Atlantic, bringing in visitors from across the globe to share their vision of what it meant to be human. They would form a small state, but a beautiful one.

Maybe, I thought.

'Now democracy,' said Alison. 'We Shetlanders will have – if not direct democracy where every person can speak in the assembly – at least a system of government in which the primary means of communication will be talking face to face. We will use modern technology, of course, but we will not hide behind a digital mask. Consider the kind of 'communication', so called, that takes place on the Internet. There you have no idea if any recommendation

comes from a human or an algorithm; you have no idea if any video you watch is a deepfake; you have no idea if what appears on your screen as 'news' is accurate; you have 'friends' you never see and enemies who hurl at you abuse that they wouldn't dare utter in your presence. If we base our electioneering on this farrago of deceit and cowardice, we will not be Shetlanders. Our opponents in the Scottish government may try to use such tricks against us, but we must have confidence in the good sense, in the reason and reasonableness, and the openness of ourselves and our neighbours. If we do not have such confidence, then we have nothing.'

Alison received sustained applause, though I had my doubts. Certainly – I wonder if you'll find this strange – a part of me wanted to believe that impassioned rhetoric could still win elections and referenda, but I didn't really think you could ignore the tricks and traps of the Internet.

Eric stood up as she sat down. 'Thank you, Alison,' he said. 'Now I'm well aware that a vote on this may not be a simple matter. What I'm going to suggest is a five-point veto. If we don't get agreement on that, then we'll pick apart the points one by one. So I'm suggesting: no fake news, no fake accounts, no bots, no bought advertising, and no trolling. Let's try a simple show of hands. If you are in favour of that five-point veto, please raise your hand.'

Once again, I had to admire Eric; he wasn't ducking the issue. If the vote went against him, would he quit?

Hands went up, but hesitantly, and at first I thought there wouldn't be a majority. Then two or three groups seemed to come to a consensus and enough hands went up, I was sure, to carry the vote.

'Those against such a veto?'

A fair sprinkling of hands, including those of Matthew and his group, but definitely a minority.

Eric didn't allow himself a note of satisfaction. He waited for the buzz of comment to die down, then he said, 'We are a democratic party, as this vote has shown. But we are also a disciplined party. Once a vote is taken, we stick together. We will go ahead with a unity of purpose and a unity of procedure, and the electorate will recognise it.'

The meeting was almost over. Eric went briefly into lyrical mode, encouraging his listeners to 'weave threads from Alison's inspirational material into the fabric of their persuasion', and to remind the fiddlers and the singers, the knitters and the quilters, the poets and the writers that the flowers they tended would bloom in the 'nurturing atmosphere of independence'. (I would have said that he was running a bit wild with his metaphors, but you can't please all of the people all of the time.) After that, there was some discussion about what medium the voters should use to put pressure on their councillors – every medium, but especially heart to heart talking, was the answer – and finally a small, earnest group engaged in a certain amount of hand-wringing about how independent an independent Shetland could be; in particular, would they, should they, could they seek to join the EU?

Eric cut the agonising short. It could certainly be argued, he said, that there was no point in cutting loose from Edinburgh only to become subservient to Brussels, but the time for that argument was *after* independence, when a whole range of potential alliances, both political and economic, would be up for debate. In the meantime, such a discussion would merely distract them from their main purpose.

The audience seemed to accept this, but what I found intriguing was a little interaction between Billy and Colin. When Eric used the phrase 'subservient to Brussels', Billy glanced at his brother and raised his eyebrows in some sort of question. I couldn't guess what the question was.

Anyway, I thought as we filed out and down the stairs, none of this mattered. One thing I had learned tonight was that there existed in the Free Shetland ranks no charismatic, unifying figure who might step into Eric's shoes. When Eric was disgraced, the movement would fall apart in internal squabbling, just as Pamela had predicted.

All I had to do was wait a couple of days.

Chapter 7

Thursday, 11th

When I woke up on Thursday morning, I was annoyed to find that my mood had flipped again. I was on edge. I *hated* waiting.

Something else had annoyed me: a conversation I'd had with Billy and Colin as we stood outside the town hall. Billy suggested a drink. I declined, rather quickly, my real reason being an acute attack of paranoia: I was worried that this sharp-witted detective might pepper me with questions that would raise in Colin's mind doubts about my sincerity. The only excuse I could think of, on the spur of the moment, was pressure of work.

Colin was all sympathy. 'Schoolteachers have a hard life.'

I said, 'Ah, but I come alive at weekends.'

Bad mistake. Colin said at once, 'How about Friday night? Drink? Something to eat?'

And bed? Oh no.

But Detective Sergeant William Carruthers was witnessing this. So I said, 'Sure.'

And – would you believe? – I had a third source of malaise. My damn period. It came early, catching me off guard, meaning that I was up at four and just managed to make it to the bathroom before the first flood. Sleep

eluded me until about six, with the result that I was tired and irritable and the period pains that sometimes annoyed me were quite intense.

At school, I went on autopilot. When the morning interval came, I trailed up to the staffroom to see if there was any talk about Eric.

There wasn't, except that Matthew and his cohort were grumbling about his 'timidity'.

On my way back to the English corridor, Joy fell in beside me. 'What's happening this weekend?' she said.

'I'm not sure.'

'Want to come out on Sunday afternoon? Eric's got yet another meeting, this time on Fetlar.'

'I'd like to.' This wasn't entirely true. I was still obsessed with Gregor; I was wishing I hadn't played such a determined game of hard to catch. 'But I might have a problem with the curse.'

'The curse? Ah. Well, give me a ring. I'm not doing much.'

Lunchtime arrived, and the staffroom still wasn't agog with gossip. I didn't linger, but went back to my room to keep on top of my preparation so that I'd have the evening clear for the exam scripts.

Sharon came in. 'Got a minute?'

'Of course. How are you?'

In she came, closing the door. 'A bit tired. Woke up at five.

'Your mind's buzzing?'

'Yes. Too many things to do. And I've just given myself one thing more.'

'You haven't?' If I couldn't arrange a two-month holiday for her, I should at least bring her to see that she mustn't feel responsible for everything.

'I have. I was talking to Brian and he was saying how the pupils should get the chance to debate the issues round Shetland's independence, and before I knew what I was doing, I'd volunteered to help – in fact, to arrange it – and to coach one team while he coached the other.'

Brian was the music teacher, a jovial fellow with a wry sense of humour and a passion for his subject. He was reputed, however, to be well short of the mark when it came to administration, which would explain why he'd manoeuvred Sharon into doing the donkey-work.

'He can't organise it?'

'He says he's busy with a concert coming up. Anyway, I agreed. He says I should get permission from George the Second, because it's a delicate matter. What d'you think?'

George the Second, the headteacher, was so called to distinguish him from George the First, a local worthy who ran almost every charity that existed in Lerwick.

I didn't want to tell her that I thought she was mad. 'I certainly think you need permission.'

'So George said he could see me today, at five o'clock.'

'And you've got Robert…'

'Could you – I'm so sorry to ask – could you pick him up from the child minder and just plug him into one of his games?'

'Not a problem. I'll take some marking with me and get on with it.'

'Thank you. What would I do without you?'

I didn't like the idea of a debate. I'd been assuming that Free Shetland would soon be consigned to the dustbin of history. Now, if the school pupils voted for independence, the whole subject might be kept alive, with or without Eric.

When I picked up Robert, the child minder tried to engage me in conversation.

'He's got big problems. He's totally withdrawn.'

'You know I'm not his mother.'

'But you're her friend. You've got to get her to take him to a psychiatrist.'

God, I thought, that would terrify the boy. He needed... what the hell did he need?

Robert said nothing on the way home. He said nothing when I took his coat. He said nothing as we both sat on the couch and stared at the electric fire. I cudgelled my brain trying to think what *I* could say.

The boy felt abandoned by his father; I sensed that. In fact, I knew something of how he felt, because – I haven't mentioned this before, but let me tell you now – I'd been abandoned by *my* father when I was sixteen. I'd come home from school and found my mother crying her eyes out. She'd told me through her sobs that she'd learned my father had had two families for years – it was easy when you drove long-distance lorries. I remembered wondering to myself whether there could ever be a greater betrayal.

But how did that help Robert? He wanted everyone to make up for the betrayal, though no one could, and Sharon, in trying, was building a harmful pattern in his little mind. Now he wanted me to run after him the way she did. He wanted me to make him an offering – a drink, a conversational opening, a bar of chocolate, some entertainment – so that he could girn and refuse it. Then I'd have reinforced the pattern. You didn't need to be a psychiatrist to see that.

I sat, and made up my mind that I would not speak first.

He said at last, 'Can I have a drink?'

'A drink?' I gave him my full attention, but didn't leap to my feet.

'A drink,' he repeated. I could see he was perplexed; he didn't know whether bawling would work with me.

'Sure.' I smiled at him, but still didn't stand up. After a while, I said, 'What do you like to drink?'

'Orange squash.'

'Right.' Again, I took my time about speaking. 'You'll need to show me how to make it.'

'Okay.' It was he who leapt to his feet.

The transformation was astonishing. In the kitchen his instructions were eager: so much squash and so much water. I had little doubt that offering me the benefit of his expertise was bringing him as much pleasure as the drink would.

He said, when we were back on the settee, 'What can I do?'

'Do?'

He giggled; I think he had recognised my verbal ping-pong. 'Will you read me a story?'

'What about?'

He produced a book, something about a boy and girl going to the seaside. I didn't like it much, because the sandcastles, bucket and spades, swimming costumes and sun hats were far removed from any experience he might have on a beach in Shetland. Still, I read it, and he seemed to listen, until I realised that his breathing had slowed. He was sound asleep.

Sharon laughed when she came in. 'Hey, what magic wand do you have?'

'I guess I'm just very boring. How did you get on with George the Second?'

She sat beside her son, careful not to wake him. 'He agreed, on certain conditions.'

'What are they?'

'That Brian and I remain strictly neutral. We can coach the teams on rhetorical techniques and manner of delivery, but we mustn't put words into their mouths.'

'Fair enough.'

'Would you believe that between lunchtime and end of school the senior pupils had already agreed their teams? Two girls with me, arguing against independence, and two boys with Brian, arguing for. The girls are certainly keen – they came to see me while I was waiting for George – but I'm not sure that they've got many coherent ideas yet.'

I saw an opportunity here. I'd been looking at the downside, but what if the pupils voted *against* independence? That could be the final nail in Free Shetland's coffin? I should feed the girls arguments, filtering these through Sharon. She was so impulsive that she'd talk and talk and pass the ideas on without realising that she was doing what George had told her not to, and without even remembering, probably, that I was the source.

'Still,' I said, 'you could throw questions at them. That wouldn't be putting words in their mouths. The university issue, for instance.'

'What university issue?'

'Well, at the moment our school-leavers can go to any university in Scotland, and I'm sure a lot of them are dying for the day when they can go to Aberdeen or Glasgow or Edinburgh and let their hair down. If Shetland were independent, what would they do?'

Sharon put her head back against the settee. 'Hadn't thought of that.'

'Then, if the girls are any good, they could have a lot of fun with the soon-to-be-established University of Lerwick. You know, students from across the world flocking to do postgraduate studies in fiddle music and whisky drinking.'

She chortled. 'I like it.'

Robert stirred. I decided that for the moment I wouldn't make any comment about his psychological development. The very last thing I wanted was to make Sharon anxious.

So I stood up. 'I'd better go.'

'Stay for tea.' She was pleading.

'Sharon, I can't. I have that damn marking to get on with.'

That marking. I did get on with it immediately after my meal. There were only six scripts left when my phone rang.

Pamela. On WhatsApp.

Let's be clear: Pamela wasn't going to give me ideas above my station by handing me some expensive, triple-encrypted Motorola handset. Not when I could use WhatsApp's end-to-end encryption for free. So what if our metadata might still be tracked? She was arrogant enough to believe that no one would ever make anything of it.

I had to answer. 'Hello?'

'What the hell do you think you're doing?'

And good evening to you too.

'What d'you mean?'

'Ever heard of phoning in reports?'

'I've nothing much to report?'

'Why the hell not? Honeytraps not working? No other bullets in your rifle?'

I couldn't risk *not* telling her something of what I'd done. She'd sack me on the spot if she found out by other means. So I gave her what I thought was a careful summary: I'd found a weak link – Colin; I'd discovered his password; I was 'in the process' of taking over Eric's computer.

Pamela pounced. '*In the process?* What does that mean? You passed this to our IT boys without consulting me?'

I'd thought about this. So I said, 'I decided that if our IT department installed the malware and it was traced back to them, you would be in an impossible position.'

'*What?*' There was indignation in that screech, but there was caution too. One thing Pamela did worry about was covering her back. 'You don't think our computer people are expert at laying false trails?'

I had to build on her doubt. 'There's a very active, very skilled hacker community up here. If they mounted an investigation, I wasn't confident that you'd escape their eagle eye.'

'Really?' She was trying to be patronising, again, but this time not quite succeeding. 'So what have you done? You don't have the expertise to install malware yourself.'

'I've recruited one of the hackers, who has a grudge against the Shetland Isles Council. I haven't blown my cover – I've posed as just someone else with a grudge. As far as she knows, we're going to create mayhem for the sake of it.'

'What kind of mayhem?'

'Wipe files when Sorenson sends someone an attachment, and provide a link to his favourite child pornography site. I can't see how he's going to survive that.'

'Mm.' She paused, because she was impressed despite herself, but then she shot back. 'But this all depends on a rogue hacker, who could be flaky.'

'She's not flaky at all.'

'You think? If this goes wrong, I'm going to hang you out to dry.'

That wasn't an idle threat, I knew it. At the same time, if everything went well, she'd do the usual, that's to say she'd try to steal the credit.

She said, 'I'm coming up tomorrow, to assess things for myself.'

'Oh.' *Oh shit.*

'Arrange a meeting with this hacker.'

There was no point in trying to dissuade her. She *might* want to check up on me, but it was more likely that this was the Pamela weekend itch. She was the cougar who gave cougars a bad name.

All the same... 'What's our legend? Why do you want to meet her? How did she come up in our conversation? Who are you, after all? How did *we* meet?'

'Yes, yes. We're friends from university. Now I'm working for the government – no need to hide that – and I'm looking for a hacker to whom I could outsource especially delicate operations.' She paused, thinking. 'Actually, that's not such a bad idea. Anyway, I mentioned this to you, because I'd heard hacking is a boom industry in Shetland, and, lo and behold, you had met this – what's her name?'

'Helen.'

'Okay, Helen. You thought she might fit the bill.'

'But how did we meet at university? I mean, we're not quite of the same vintage.'

'You think?' She was about to take umbrage, then thought better of it. 'Okay, I was doing my Ph.D. while you were doing your first degree. We were in the same department.'

'What was your Ph.D. on?'

'Bugger it. Is she going to care? Is she well read?'

'Not particularly, but she's not stupid.' Pamela was breaking every rule in *Spying for Dummies*. She didn't think the rules applied to her.

'Oh God knows. You're the one who read English Literature. Think of something and fill me in when I come up, before I meet her. I'll be at the Ross Hotel. Be there at six o'clock.'

Yes, ma'am.

'Sure.'

The Ross Hotel? Upmarket and discreet, the perfect place for a tryst. Did Pamela have something arranged or was she going to go hunting in Lerwick? When she ended the call, excitement ran through me. Did I have the courage to accept Gregor's offer?

Damn right I did, if it meant there was a prospect of getting rid of Pamela.

I texted him: *Hi. Where are you?*

The reply was immediate: *In Lerwick. Want to come round?*

On my way.

Gregor opened the door at street level, and pulled me in. Then he did something I'd never expected: he wrapped his arms round me and crushed me in a hug.

You know the song? *That dizzy, dancing way you feel, when every fairy tale comes real...* Let me admit it: for a second or two, that summed up my swirling emotions.

But the next line wasn't going to fit. I, Carol Rutherford, did not – would never – fall in love.

Mind you, I could fall in lust. I nestled against his chest, revelling in its strength and its warmth.

He took me upstairs, offered me a glass of wine. I noticed that the chess match was almost finished: one player had his king and queen left, the other his king and a rook.

We sat on his couch, thigh to thigh. 'I thought you'd never call,' he said.

I liked that; it seemed a straightforward statement that he wanted me.

'I was going to call anyway, but I've got news for you.'

'News?'

'Pamela's coming up tomorrow. She's staying at the Ross Hotel. Well, she told me to meet her at the Ross Hotel.'

'You want to launch Operation Kompromat?'

'I do.'

'Right.' He touched my arm. 'It shall be launched.'

'What'll you do?'

'All *I*'ll do is make a call. She might not be *staying* at the Ross Hotel, of course, and she might work the room-changing trick, but we can leave the details to the experts. If they miss her, they miss her. In the meantime,' – he put his hand on my knee and squeezed – 'you and I should concentrate on enjoying ourselves.'

I turned and kissed his cheek. Then I said, 'Gregor, I'm sorry. I've got my period.'

He swapped his wineglass from right to left and put his arm round me. 'My dear, we can wait. We have all the time in the world.'

'We do?'

'Of course we do. Tell me about other things. By the way, the men who pull my strings told me *why* you are in Lerwick – although that wouldn't have been hard to guess. Is there any help you would like in that respect? Is everything going well?'

I laid my head on his shoulder. One thing that was going well was this fire that we had kindled. Right now, the coals were giving out a steady, comforting heat, but in due course the flames would roar higher again, licking over both of us. I murmured, 'Your government would help there? They don't want Shetland becoming independent?'

He nuzzled my hair. 'I should imagine they couldn't care less, but what they do care about is Pamela, and her replacement. Anything they can do to establish a good relationship with that replacement, whoever she might be' – he rubbed his nose into my scalp – 'they would do it.'

'I might not need them,' I said, 'but then again I might.'

Chapter 8

Friday, 12th

I thought Eric was *never* going to send an attachment. Friday morning crawled past without incident. Lunchtime came and went. I was beginning to look forward to my one free period of the day, the very last period of the week, a lull in which I could finish off my six scripts.

Then, as my Third Year streamed out, Peter appeared at the door. He waited until we were alone.

'Sorry. I'm going to have to give you a please-take.'

'Oh no.'

'Joy's gone home. She's very upset.'

'What's wrong?' I said, but my pulses raced.

'Mm.' Peter wasn't one to gossip. 'It's Eric. He's… in trouble.'

'He's ill?'

'No. Oh, you're going to find out soon enough. It seems he's been sending people links to pornography.'

'For goodness' sake. Eric?'

'Apparently so, though it might be a malicious prank.'

'Who would do something like that?'

'Your guess is as good as mine.'

I accepted the please-take – not that you ever had any choice in the matter. Fortunately, Joy's class had plenty to occupy them; they were busy on a

group assignment, each group preparing a talk on some aspect of the tourist industry. I didn't have to do much except sit at the desk and scowl at those who were becoming too exuberant. On the other hand, I couldn't concentrate on my marking; those six scripts still weighed on me.

Sharon came along when the pupils had gone. 'What's this about Eric?' she said. 'Something about pornography?'

'Sending people links to porn sites, Peter told me. I don't believe it.'

'I'm not sure. I had an argument with Joy this morning. I don't know how we got into it, but I was saying how disgusting it was men looking at porn and she got quite worked up, told me how holier-than-thou I was. I wonder if… well, I wonder if she maybe caught Eric…'

'And the rumours aren't nonsense at all?'

'Yes.'

Poor Eric. He was hung, drawn and quartered, and this was before the phrase '*child* pornography' hit the rumour mill.

I was asking myself what I should do. Should I go out and see Joy, to console her, or should I merely phone? I had a busy evening ahead: I was meeting Pamela at six, and she and I were meeting Helen in the Norseman at half past – I had already texted Helen to the effect that 'a woman I knew from university' was in Lerwick and would like to meet 'an experienced hacker'. Also, I was supposed to see Colin at some point. All in all, I'd like to go back to the flat and do not very much for an hour or two.

But a friend's gotta do what a friend's gotta do. I told Sharon I was going to Joy's, reminded her of our lunch date at the Skipidock, and went out to the car. Groups of teachers were talking in the car park. No prizes for guessing what was on everyone's lips.

97

There were six cars on the Sorensons' gravel: Joy's, Eric's, Colin's and three others. A council of war was in progress.

No one answered my knock on the back door. I stepped into the kitchen and heard voices from the living room.

The door to the hall was wide open, and the one from the hall to the living room couldn't have been fully shut. I stopped and eavesdropped.

McIntyre was speaking; I recognised the snarl. 'Eric, what I'm proposing is nothing to do with fake news. Okay, we don't know *how* the Scottish government did this, but we know *that* they did it. So we get our supporters to flood social media; every possible tweet and retweet, every possible "share", every possible post on their Facebook walls. Let me emphasise – we are only getting people to believe the truth, that the Scottish government has tried to blacken your good name, because they want to sink our campaign for independence.'

Someone – it was a soft female voice that sounded familiar – mentioned the police. McIntyre let loose again.

'The police analysts will take *months* to examine Eric's computer. Whether *they*'ll find the infection or not, I don't know, but I've got *my* copy of the disc. I'll make another copy and send it on to my friends in St Petersburg…'

A deep baritone I'd never heard before said, 'That won't cut any ice in court, Paul. If you find the infection, the police will say that you could have altered the original data.'

'Steven.' McIntyre was cutting. 'If the police are any good, they can detect tampering. But look, we can't hang about. We need the social media campaign *now*. We should lay our plans this evening. I'll get going, take my

copy of the disc away before the police get here and confiscate it, then I'll come back and we can work out our every last move.'

I retreated on tiptoe to the back door and came clumping through. 'Anyone there?' I called. McIntyre emerged as I approached the living room.

'It's you,' he said. Like every word he uttered, it sounded like a criticism.

'It's me.'

'Whose side are you on?'

'What are you talking about?'

He did his best leer. 'I saw you at the meeting on Wednesday and yet I hear you're best friends with that bitch – Sharon MacIntosh? – who's poisoning the school kids against independence.'

'Don't call Sharon a bitch.' I glared at him. 'And don't be ridiculous. Sharon's not poisoning anyone. In any case, don't you think it's possible to be friends with someone even if you don't agree with them. You haven't heard of tolerance?'

Joy appeared. She had a weary look. 'Stop your squabbling.' I thought this was addressed to McIntyre. 'We'll see you later, Paul.' She shooed him away and said to me, 'Paul's all worked up. Aren't we all?'

'That's why I came out. I was worried about you.'

She kissed me on the cheek. 'You're very kind. Yes, I'm upset, though I've calmed down a little. Come in.'

Everyone was sitting round the dining table: Eric and Colin, Alison Dalrymple and a middle-aged man wearing a bow tie and a hearing aid. This was Steven, whom Joy introduced as 'our lawyer', though whether that meant he was the family solicitor or legal advisor to Free Shetland I had no way of knowing. Each person in the room wore an air of gloom like a black cloak.

99

Eric's face was taut, and his arms were folded across his stomach. He barely acknowledged me before he said, 'So, Steven, notwithstanding Paul's heroics on the social media battlefield, should I step down, temporarily, until I clear my name?'

'Your call, Eric.' Steven spoke loudly; perhaps he was making sure that he could hear himself. 'But Paul's right, that the police could take a very long time to examine your computer. And all the while a cloud will be hanging over both you and Free Shetland.'

Alison said, 'But to step down might be seen as an admission of guilt.'

'Not at all,' Steven said. I didn't take to him; I didn't like the bow tie and I didn't like the over-confident manner. 'It would be a statement that Eric cares more about Shetland's independence than about himself. That's a powerful thing to say.'

Alison addressed Eric: 'Eric, at least take your time. Don't rush into anything.'

Steven was generous. 'Oh yes. Take a few days.'

They all stopped talking. Eric stared into space like a man who was already convicted. 'Bloody mud,' he said. 'People like to make it stick.'

Joy said brightly, 'Anyone like a cup of tea?'

Everyone except me muttered yes, although their tone suggested that they would have preferred hemlock. I said to Joy, 'I'll give you a hand.'

In the kitchen, I filled the kettle. 'Listen,' I said, 'I just came to see if there was anything I could do.'

She was putting mugs on a tray. 'Thank you, but I don't think there is. You don't want to linger for the wake?'

I patted her elbow, deciding that I'd made a mistake in coming at all. 'Joy, it'll blow over. Crises always do.'

'Maybe.'

I walked into the hall and put my head round the living room door. 'I'm not staying. Hope things go all right.'

Colin looked across. 'I'm sorry. I won't make it tonight.'

'Don't worry about it. Text me sometime.'

Joy walked me out to the car. 'We'd better forget about Sunday.'

I was happy to forget about Sunday; I had too much on my mind. I said, 'Phone me if you want to talk or anything.'

She stroked the sleeve of my parka. 'D'you know the worst thing about this?'

'No.'

'Eric seems so… so *beaten* that I wonder if there's truth in it. I wonder if he's really been *caught*.'

First Sharon, I thought, now Joy. With friends like that, who needed enemies?

On my way back to Lerwick, I passed a police car going in the opposite direction. Was I sorry for Eric? Not really.

As I parked outside my flat, Betty, my landlady, was conversing on the pavement with a neighbour. This was Kirstie; I'd seen her around with her two children. The older one, a boy, was forever kicking a football up and down their drive, while her daughter, a timid little thing of eight or nine, was always, as now, hanging onto her mother's coat-tails.

I stepped over to say hello. As I approached, Kirstie was saying, 'He just stood at the shallow end, looking.'

Betty glanced at me. 'You seem very serious. What's up?'

'I've just been out at the Sorensons' place – you know, Eric and Joy's.'

Kirstie had a thin, beaked nose and made a sort of pecking motion as she said to me, 'Are you a friend of theirs?'

I didn't need to concoct a story. 'I'm friendly with Joy; we work in the same department. But I don't know Eric very well.'

'He used to go to the swimming pool, you know. And one day he just stopped.' She delivered the last sentence like a prosecutor who considered that no more need be said.

Perversely, I wanted to jump to Eric's defence. 'Maybe he gave up on trying to keep fit.'

'Yes, Kirstie,' Betty said, 'we mustn't hang a man before he's convicted.'

'Huh.'

At six precisely, I walked into the lobby of the Ross Hotel. Pamela was in one of the hotel's deepest armchairs, talking to a conservatively dressed middle-aged couple, and her cleavage, which would have raised eyebrows in Edinburgh, never mind Lerwick, had the husband transfixed.

She stood up, *not* introducing me and *not* offering me a drink. 'Must go,' she said to the couple. '*So* nice to meet you.'

Her coat was over the back of her chair. She bent forward as, apparently, she struggled to put it on. The man goggled recklessly.

Outside, she said, 'Bloody hell, it's cold.'

'Afraid so. I told my hacker that we'd meet at six-thirty. Do you want to walk or what?'

'Bloody hell.' She should complain – at least it wasn't sleeting. 'We'd better walk. Then no one can listen in.'

The wind, which must be cutting through her smart city coat, was behind us as I set off at pace up the Esplanade.

'Jesus Christ. Slow down. We're not in training for the bloody Olympics.'

Yes, ma'am. No, ma'am. Three bags full, ma'am.

She said, when she'd caught her breath, 'Right. Don't faff around. My taxi driver told me that Sorenson's in trouble. Is he finished?'

'I would say so. I think he'll be helping the police with their enquiries as we speak. On the other hand, it's hard to be absolutely sure of anything.'

'You're not sure? So what's Plan B? What else have you got on him?'

Not much. 'He's in financial trouble – too big a mortgage; his wife's a lesbian; he collects models of sailing ships; and he likes Graham Greene.'

'Bloody hell. Everybody has a Graham Greene phase, even me; we can't make a lot of capital with his reading habits. And a lesbian wife – that doesn't cut any ice these days. But money – that could be different. What's your plan?'

'I don't have a plan yet. I don't think we'll need it.'

'You'd better be right. And this hacker – she's covered her traces? She's reliable?'

'I'm sure of it.'

'We'll see. And what was my Ph.D. on?'

She'd caught me off guard, a typical Pamela move. I'd forgotten all about her damn Ph.D. So I had to ad lib. 'Take a leaf out of Sorenson's book. Go Greene.'

'What? Oh very funny. Be precise.'

'Ok. You investigated the way his books hold up a mirror to his life, the way his protagonists are often middle-aged men running after young women and not seeing how pathetic they are.'

103

'Give me some examples.'

'The one set in West Africa – *The Heart of the Matter* – and *The Quiet American*.'

'The one in Vietnam? Yes, I did read that. Right, that'll do.'

She was being careless. If she blew my cover with Helen, I'd have to pack up and go home.

Helen was early, which had enabled her to commandeer a corner banquette in the Norseman. She had washed her hair and was wearing a blue blouse that I had never seen before. She looked almost presentable.

Pamela shook hands as if she was afraid that she might catch some infection. Helen must have smelled the condescension because she went on the attack as soon as Pamela took off her coat. 'Fuck me. You like to let it all hang out.'

Pamela, who expected deference from everyone, reddened but recovered. 'My dear, if you've got it, you may as well flaunt it.'

Helen came back with an even harder jab: 'Are you flaunting it or giving it away?'

Pamela flinched. I should have let the fight develop and sat back to enjoy it, but for some reason, some ingrained notion of social decorum, I said, 'Drinks?'

Helen growled, 'Double vodka with lime.' She already had an empty glass in front of her.

Pamela pursed her lips. 'I'll have a G and T.'

I scurried round to the bar, collected the drinks, including another G and T for myself, put them on a tab, and scurried back. It seemed that Helen had decided to tone down the aggression, though there was still an edge to her

voice. I heard her say, 'So you met at university? How come you're longer in the tooth than she is?'

'I'm not *that* much older,' Pamela said, 'but all right: I was doing my Ph.D. while Carol was on her first degree.'

'You did a Ph.D.? On what?'

I suspected that Helen was hoping for some esoteric subject it would be easy to make fun of.

'Graham Greene,' Pamela said, 'and the way his male characters reflect his own attitude to women.'

Pamela, don't mess this up.

'Yeah?' Helen was sceptical. 'I read one of his books – *The Human Factor* – and the guy in it – what was his name? – had a black wife. Are you telling me this means Greene had a thing for black women?'

Pamela flicked a glance at me. There were two questions there, and I would bet that she didn't know the answer to the first one. I was sorely tempted to let her stew in her own juice, but that would be cutting off my nose to spite my face.

'You're talking about Castle,' I said as I handed them their drinks, 'and the first reason his wife is black is because the story demands it. But if you dig a little deeper, you'll hear Greene say, "Look how open-minded my characters are, just like me." And then, if you dig deeper still, you might hear another voice, one that he wouldn't admit to, saying, "It's not important what colour a girl's skin is; what's important is whether or not she'll let me fuck her."'

Helen sniggered. Pamela didn't even have the grace to look grateful. Her glance flickered again, this time over our shoulders towards the bar. I could hear some new male voices; she'd be sizing up their owners.

'Well, anyway,' Helen said; she'd lost interest in Pamela's imaginary doctoral thesis. 'What do you do now?'

Pamela tugged her attention back to us. 'I'm a civil servant.'

'But what do you *do*?' Helen let no one get away with vagueness.

'I provide information to ministers, about security matters. Let's say, about possible sources of disorder and dissent.'

Helen took a slug of her vodka. 'I see.'

Pamela coughed, which was odd, because it indicated a degree of hesitation. 'Carol told you? In my position, I would find it useful to have someone outside official circles who could undertake certain tasks discreetly for me.'

I was waiting for Helen to say, 'Fuck off.' But she was almost civil. 'She told me you're looking for a tame hacker. How would this hacker get paid?'

'That's simple: by bank transfer from a company with an innocuous name. But... before I offered you the job, I would need some reassurances. First of all,

are you in favour of Shetland being independent?'

'Are you kidding me?' Helen nearly choked on her vodka.

Her unmissable spontaneity lightened the mood. 'Quite,' Pamela said. 'The second thing is that I'd need to set you some kind of test. I'm thinking I could bring a project up with me next weekend – or, if I don't come back up, I could communicate it to you...'

'This project would be paid?'

'Of course.' Now Pamela was gracious.

Helen said, 'I'll have to think about it.'

'Naturally.' Dear Pamela looked over our shoulders again. 'Excuse me for a minute.'

She went in the direction of the bar, but I didn't follow her progress immediately. Helen grunted at me, 'She's a pain in the arse.'

'Helen, she works for the Scottish government. What do you expect?'

She grunted again. I said, 'And you want to work for *her*?'

'Doubt it, but I could use the money.'

I sipped my G&T, Helen finished off her vodka. Then, simultaneously, we turned to see what was going on at the bar. Pamela was in the middle of a group of young men and was already making eyes at a big, tall fellow who wore a jersey saying 'Lerwick Port Authority'. From the body language, you could easily jump to the conclusion that they were going to fall into bed.

But whose bed? His or hers? My future could depend on that.

Very shortly, she came over. 'Change of plan,' she announced. 'Roddy's going to take me down to Captain Flint's.'

Neither of us said a word.

She smirked. 'Sorry, but what's a girl to do? I'll catch you later.'

We didn't watch her go. I went to the toilet and texted Gregor an update. When I returned, Helen said, 'Did she pay the bill?'

'Shit.'

'Don't worry. I'll get it out of her.'

'How will you do that?'

'Trust me.'

Chapter 9

Saturday, 13ᵗʰ

After we left the Norseman, I went home and waited for a message from Gregor. Midnight passed. One o'clock passed. Nothing. I resigned myself to the only possible conclusion: Pamela and Roddy hadn't gone back to the Ross Hotel – and we didn't have our kompromat.

I was restless all night. When I hauled myself out of bed, my mood was downbeat. I should have been happy that in all probability I had holed Eric's man-o'-war below the waterline, but – you know what it's like – you've no sooner achieved one goal that you'd set your heart on than you're obsessed with another. For me, the next goal – Pamela's job – was the big one.

A text from Gregor was on my phone: *No go. We'll try again. Have to go to Unst. Back mid week.* The only good thing about this message was that he'd checked in like a regular boyfriend.

Sharon and Robert arrived at half past twelve and we walked up to the Skipidock, Sharon and I taking one little hand each and every so often lifting Robert off his feet to give him a swing. He whooped, enjoying the attention.

Between swings, Sharon asked about Eric – she'd heard nothing more – and I gave her a one-sentence summary: he might step down from Free Shetland but then again he might not. She said, 'Do you think that either way it's a mortal blow to the independence movement?'

'Hard to say.'

'My girls came to see me yesterday.' She was referring to her debating team. 'They expect the debate to go ahead because, as they put it, the fundamental issues remain the same. And then they said, "What *are* the fundamental issues?" So I, like the neutral mentor I am, turned the question back to them.'

'And they said?'

She paused to give Robert a double swing. 'Greed, they thought, was first. Sorenson's playing on people's greed. But they couldn't quite decide what word to use for the second issue – "patriotism", they suggested, or something like it. I thought maybe "identity", but if you consider Shetland is a country, "patriotism" is as good a word as any. So they said, "What exactly *is* patriotism? How does it arise?"'

'What is it? I trotted out the old maxim: '*Patriotism is the last refuge of a scoundrel.*'

'Who said that?'

'Can't remember.'

'Is it adequate?'

'Good question. I'd need to think about it.'

We'd reached North Road and the maze that they call the Toll Clock Centre. The Skipidock – which is easier to reach by circumnavigation of the whole building than by plotting a course through its inner channels – was busy. Shetlanders like the place because it serves filling, usually wholesome food at reasonable prices, and also because the staff, who might be Thai, are invariably friendly. We occupied the last empty table, across from an old lady who was dipping her spoon carefully into a bowl of broth.

Sharon and I had lamb hotpot, while Robert worked his way through a large helping of macaroni and chips. Our conversation was inconsequential – thoughts of Eric and Colin and Pamela and Gregor came crowding in on me, and I was irritated, unreasonably, that I couldn't talk honestly about any of them. When we'd finished and I'd fetched two coffees, I produced a modest present I'd brought for Robert: a jigsaw of no more than thirty pieces, showing a boy of about his age with a lamb in his arms. The old lady, who I thought might be in her late seventies, sat within touching distance of Robert and was now nursing a cup of tea. She looked over and said, 'Ooh, a jigsaw. I love jigsaws.'

I had a sudden humanitarian impulse. This old soul was probably as lonely as hell. We could make her day. You might find it hard, dear reader, to see me as a good Samaritan, but every villain has her moment. 'Come on, Robert,' I said, picking up the jigsaw and taking hold of his hand, 'Let's see if this lady can help us.' I had him across to the other table before he could object.

I tipped out the pieces of the puzzle and pushed them back so that there was ample space. Then I propped up the cover picture, which was a photograph showing the pieces clearly marked off. 'What's your name?' I said to the old dear.

'Mary.'

'Mary, this is Robert. I'm sure he'll be a good pupil.'

She was quick on the uptake. Picking up one of the edge pieces, she said to Robert, 'Do you know what this straight edge means?'

Robert was too overcome by shyness to utter a word.

'Well,' said Mary, ' it means that it goes somewhere on the top or the bottom or this side or that.' She held the piece against the top left-hand corner of the photograph. 'Does it match that one?'

Robert looked at her blankly.

'Are these two pieces the same?'

He didn't answer.

'Okay.' She moved along the top. 'What about this one? Do *these* pieces match?'

He shook his head.

'You're right.' I could see that Mary was hiding her delight at getting a response. 'Let's keep going.'

None of the pieces on the top was a match. 'Mm,' Mary said. 'What'll we do now?'

Robert jabbed a finger. 'The bottom.'

'Right.'

On the bottom edge they were soon successful. 'What now?' Mary said.

Robert picked up another edge piece. All this time, he and I had been standing. I pulled his chair across – the lunchtime crush was thinning – and lifted him onto it. 'You're good at this,' I said to Mary.

'I've had lots of practice. I had three grandchildren.'

'What do you mean, you *had*?'

She made an odd grimace. 'They moved to Aberdeen. I don't see much of them now.'

'That's a shame.'

Robert had identified the position for his new piece. He looked at me, then Mary.

'Well done,' she said. She screwed up her face, pretending to cry. 'But you don't need *me*.'

'Yes I do.'

They had a game going. I watched them for a minute or two before I sat down again with Sharon. 'You're marvellous,' she murmured.

She was exaggerating. Still, reader, you know why I've described this little episode? I'm showing you that I'm not a monster, because I fear that you may incline to that conclusion as my story unfolds.

Sharon and I began to talk about boyfriends. Colin had sent me a text, apologising for the day before and asking if I would like to meet around seven for something to eat. I'd hesitated, wondering if I could dump him *now*, but then I'd accepted, partly because I hoped he could update me on how Eric had fared with the police. When I told Sharon that I had a 'sort of date', she became quite animated.

'Who is it?'

'Colin Carruthers,' I said, adding that I wasn't entirely confident how well it would go.

'Grab him with both hands,' she advised. 'He's decent.'

I didn't argue, merely turned the conversation to the question of how *she* could re-enter the dating scene. She put up various objections: she was tired; she was wary of men; she had commitments.

I took it that 'commitments' referred to Robert. So I said, 'You need a regular, reliable baby-sitter. Then you can hit the town with gay abandon.'

Robert and Mary had finished their jigsaw. Mary, who must have had sharp hearing, leaned across and said, 'If you need a baby-sitter, I'd be

delighted to help. I have a whole stack of jigsaws in my house that Robert and I could work through.

Sharon was pleased. Mary was pleased that she was pleased. You've got it: I was pleased that both of them were pleased. Don't you think it's beyond doubt that someone who brings such sweetness and light should be in the running for sainthood?

I was back in my flat shortly after three. I had a nap – the hotpot had left me sleepy – then did some cleaning since the living room in particular had acquired a clinging overcoat of dust. I had finished that chore when Colin texted: could we meet at Captain Flint's?

I replied: *No problem.*

Captain Flint's is older and darker than the Norseman, with enough creaking timber to make you think it really has been rebuilt from a Spanish galleon. Here too there are banquettes, though they're not arranged in such a way that you can have a private conversation. Billy and Colin – I hadn't expected to see Billy – were sitting in a nest opposite the bar.

It was obvious that something was wrong, because Colin had his head in his hands and Billy was talking to him as if trying to persuade him not to jump off Victoria Pier? I slipped in beside them. 'What's the matter?' I said.

Colin's head came up, but it was Billy who answered. 'He's feeling guilty, though he's got nothing in the world to feel guilty about.'

I was astonished. 'Colin, what have you done?'

He made a glum face. 'I've crossed my own red lines.'

'But how?'

Billy drained his glass. 'He's talking rubbish, but he won't listen to me.' He stood up. 'I've got to go, or Janine will feed my dinner to the dog.'

Colin said, 'Tell the boys I'll be over for a kickabout tomorrow afternoon. We'll be finished by then.'

'Sure.' Billy addressed me: 'You could come too.'

He wanted to welcome me into the bosom of the family?

'No, thanks all the same. I have a ton of work to do.'

'Have you?' He looked at me – sharply, I thought. 'Well, look after my little brother. He's a sensitive soul.'

As soon as he'd gone, I put my hand on Colin's arm. 'Tell me what's happened? I can't believe you've done anything wrong.'

He shook his head. 'I swore I'd never have anything to do with deceiving people. But Eric was so down, when he came back from the police station…'

I shouldn't have interrupted, but I was dying of curiosity. 'What happened there?'

'Not a lot. They'd taken his computer when they came out to the house and they weren't going to charge him with anything until their specialists examined it. But even the process of being questioned left him in despair. He was on the very edge of quitting. Then Paul was insistent that we could repair the damage and Eric wavered and I wavered… and the decision was made…'

'What decision?'

'On the face of it, just to set up two supposed news sites that will defend Eric. Paul and I have been working on them since last night. Two pillars of disinformation…'

He tailed off as a big group of men at the next table suddenly erupted in raucous laughter. Captain Flint's is a bit like that: it cultivates a wacky atmosphere and its clientele often want to give the impression that they are

having an absolutely hilarious time. These chaps began to hurl wisecracks at each other, making our conversation impossible, and I said, 'Come on. Let's get out of here.'

In the street, he staggered and I grabbed his shoulder. 'What's wrong? You're not drunk?'

'Wish I was. I'm just exhausted. I've been glued to a computer screen all day. Then I had one beer on an empty stomach.'

I pointed across the road to a little restaurant called the Phu Siam. 'Let's get a carry-out and go back to your place. Once we've eaten I'm going to tuck you up in bed.'

He acquiesced rather than agreed. In the Phu Siam, a girl who was definitely Thai wore an anorak and a woollen hat. She took our order smartly enough, though her English was rather broken. 'Please sit,' she said.

We sat. She brought our food. We walked up Commercial Street in a cold rain. I realised as soon as we reached his flat that he'd been making an effort to move on from Margaret Anne. The photographs of her were all gone. A new Dyson cleaner had been used to suck up the pieces of lint from the living room floor. The bookshelves were tidy; the entire mantelpiece had been swept clean, and a calendar of Shetland views covered one of the bare patches on the wall. Only the seating options were the same, and the blank space where the television had been.

Colin had a new microwave. We heated the food and carried everything through to the table in the living room. I let him eat his dinner before I put him under any pressure.

'Can I see your websites? I still can't believe they're as bad as you say. And I'm curious to know how you're driving traffic towards them.'

He pinched his nose. 'We only have one finished so far. And I only helped create it. Driving the traffic is Paul's business.' He woke up his computer. 'The first one is called *The Shetland Examiner*.'

A website loaded up, its headline screaming 'HOLYROOD ACCUSED'. There was a main piece credited to 'Our staff reporter', a few small photographs of lambs and fish catches, and links to articles about tourist attractions and Shetland's economic future.

Colin said, 'It was my job to put together the peripheral material – all the good news about Shetland. I've done this for the other site too. Paul just has to finish the op-ed.'

I said, 'He's your staff reporter?'

'Yes. He's going to put his name to it on the other site. He didn't think he could do that twice.'

I scanned the main article. The gist of it was much as you would have expected – that the Scottish Intelligence Services had used their 'extensive cyber resources' to hack into Eric's computer and attempt to discredit him – but this was expressed as a fact rather than an allegation, at least until you came to an inconspicuous sentence which said, 'Such was the unanimous verdict of a panel of recognised experts who reviewed all the evidence.' It was the kind of vague blandness that a careless reader might not even notice.

'I take it that this panel of experts doesn't exist?'

He shook his head. 'The whole thing sets out to mislead, to suggest that there is certainty where there is none.'

'You're *not* certain that Eric is innocent?'

'There's been talk.' He hesitated. 'Where does Eric get his sexual satisfaction from? In view of...'

'Joy's sexuality?'

'Yes.'

I thought, *Irony of ironies. Has Helen taken a random stab and hit an artery?*

But Colin had an over-developed conscience. I said, 'You're feeling guilty because you *may have* deceived people? I've read a lot more blatant lies in supposedly reputable newspapers.'

Another grim shake of the head. 'Lies are only the first thing. You asked me about driving traffic to the sites. If your name is Paul McIntyre, you don't just set up a news site; you also set up a corresponding Facebook page and then you employ a dozen tricks, the kind of tricks that Free Shetland voted to outlaw.'

'Bots and fake accounts? That kind of stuff?'

'I don't exactly know.' He was ashamed, like a boy scout caught cheating in one of his badges. 'We were in Paul's computing room. I was tired, after staring at the screen for so long. I sat on his couch and dozed off. When I opened my eyes, I caught a glimpse – only a glimpse, I admit – of one of the Facebook pages where you can buy advertising, using all those micro-targeting techniques. There was a figure in dollars – I think it was three hundred and something. That would be the cost – the funds Paul would be transferring to Facebook.'

'Who would be paying for this?'

'That's the question. Not Free Shetland, after they explicitly rejected the idea. And not Paul, I would say, because he's famous for being as mean as sin.'

'Who, then?'

He screwed up his face. 'It could be anyone, anyone who wants to break away from mainland Scotland. Some of the fishermen, for example, who're

already making a fortune, would like it if Shetland's fish were *not* shared with the rest of Scotland.'

He opened Facebook and clicked a few times. 'See. I *knew* it. '

'What?'

'Look. This is the page corresponding to the news site. Five hundred "likes" in a day. And dozens of comments. He's bought these likes, I'd bet on it. You can buy pretty much anything if you're unscrupulous enough.' He groaned. 'I can't believe I'm involved in this.'

I was trying to assess the damage. True, it wasn't good news for me if someone was supplying dark money to back Shetland's drive for independence, but this kind of targeting, which involved the drip-drip of propaganda, needed time to be effective. And McIntyre didn't have time; to save Eric's skin, he needed something much more dramatic; he needed a bombshell.

Colin's phone rang. He snatched it up from the table.

'Eric?' he said, and to me, 'Excuse me.'

I moved away, hearing the rasp of Eric's voice but unable to make out what he said. Colin's face, however, told me he was listening to bad news. He didn't say a word for quite a while, then he blew out a breath. 'Eric, give it time. Radio Free Shetland's conducting another of their telephone polls on Tuesday. Suppose the numbers were okay or even good… yes, I know that's not going to affect the money situation, but something might turn up. Oh God, Eric, we forgot next Wednesday. Nobody else can bring everyone together… No…no…definitely not. Okay, Eric, okay.'

He put the phone down and stared at his hands. I went over and sat down, waiting. At last he said, 'Eric's in a pit. He wants to step down now. I told him he can't. We have the meeting for all of Shetland on Wednesday. No

one can inspire people the way he can. Alison can't; she's too... too gentle. And Paul can't either; he'd alienate everybody.'

So Free Shetland was finished?

Still, I was perplexed. 'Has something happened? I thought Eric agreed that you and Paul could work to retrieve his situation.'

'Yeah.' Colin hung his head and stuffed his hands in his pockets. 'Fate kicks you when you're down. You know about Joy and Eric's financial situation?'

'The big mortgage? Yes, Joy told me.'

'Eric had a letter from the bank this morning. Unless he can come up with a solution within the next four weeks, they're going to foreclose on his mortgage. Apart from the... *mess* with the pornography nonsense, he feels he has to step down from Free Shetland so that he can get a job. If he had a wage coming in to add to his meagre allowance from the council and to Joy's salary as a teacher, he thinks the bank would grant him a stay of execution.'

'There's no other solution?' I struggled to hide my satisfaction.

'There's Sven and his bulging bank account. But Sven makes Shylock look like an easy touch.'

Chapter 10

Monday, 15th

An eerie calm hung over me on Sunday and most of Monday. I heard a lot of mutterings about Eric, in Tesco and again in the staffroom and school corridors. A few people, quoting the 'evidence' on Facebook, were convinced that he was the victim of a plot. Considerably more were, like Kirstie, ready to hang him high. And in the middle a fair number either muttered that there was 'no smoke without fire' or were mainly incensed that his 'carelessness' had allowed malware to erase important files on their computers. On balance, it was clear that the pendulum of sympathy had swung hard against him.

Joy was subdued. I walked out to the car park with her after school and asked how Eric was coping. She said he hadn't yet made up his mind to quit, but he was very close to it.

Then, at six o'clock, everything exploded. My suspicions fell on McIntyre at once, because it was the kind of bomb I'd said to myself he needed. Okay, it wasn't a literal bomb, but it felt like it.

I'd put on the Scottish news quite by chance, because I was waiting for my oven to heat up. When I saw what the 'lead story' was, I forgot all about my dinner.

The cameras were live at a press conference in an Edinburgh hotel. A speaker was coming up to a lectern draped with a banner that said 'Popov Systems'. He was smooth, young, black-haired, smart-suited.

The assembled journalists settled down. Mr Smoothie arranged a small bundle of notes and switched on a projector that was linked to a laptop. 'Let me start,' he said, 'at the beginning.' He had the faintest trace of an accent that I couldn't place. 'On Saturday, Popov Systems was contacted by a customer in Shetland who uploaded the contents of an entire hard disc. He was sure that malware was hidden somewhere on this, and he was right, though it took our experts a long time to uncover it.

'The malware was embedded in the code that controlled the sending of email attachments. Here is the essential section.'

He put up a screenful of hexadecimal code that contained just enough internal comment lines to convey the general idea of its purpose. He pointed out what he said were the significant sections before clicking on to another slide. 'Here,' he said, 'is what the lines say, in effect.'

IF this code has already been forwarded

THEN delete the My Documents folder

AND send the text, *Click here to see Eric Sorenson's naughty pictures*

END IF

I, of course, in common with probably ninety-nine percent of viewers, had no idea if that was what the hexadecimal gobbledegook really meant, and in any case the code could have come from anywhere. All this, if I believed Helen's talk of rootkits hiding everything, was pure bluff; it could be that McIntyre had reported to Popov what the malware was doing and Popov had simply reverse-engineered the algorithm.

The speaker continued – he was Russian, I'd decided. 'The conclusion is unavoidable, that the hacker's primary purpose was to embarrass and discredit Mr Sorenson. But the story by no means ends there.

'The question is, who sent this? He or she used TOR, which is supposed to guarantee anonymity because each relay node shows only the node that came before and the one that comes after. Now TOR isn't quite foolproof, but to find the sequence of relays can be tedious and sometimes impossible. Suffice to say that at Popov we have one analyst who was able to cut the Gordian knot. He has a good knowledge of the political situation in Scotland and he asked himself who could have or would have sent this malware. He came to an educated deduction – not a guess, let me emphasise. He suspected an organisation – let me call it for the moment Organisation X. By a piece of good fortune, he knew the IP address of Organisation X. *How* could he know that, do you ask? Well, the Scottish government and other Scottish bodies have an extensive range of static IP addresses, many of which they bought from the UK government when Scotland became independent. But you may *not* be aware that most of these addresses have long been known to the authorities and others in Russia. There's your answer. In any case, our analyst was able to use all the tools of the ethical hacker to breach the computers of Organisation X and, much to his surprise, he found – unencrypted and residing in a folder helpfully marked "Payloads" – the exact same code that I showed you a moment ago. He had successfully short-circuited the entire process of tracing the data through TOR.'

Now I knew for sure he was talking nonsense, doing no more than producing a long-winded smokescreen, but I didn't know *why* Popov would do this.

'Laymen,' he went on, 'imagine that an IP address will provide only an approximate physical location of the relevant computer, but there are ways in which this can be refined. The IP address in question belonged to a particular building in the New Town of Edinburgh.

'You want to know who occupies this building – of course you do.' Mr Smoothie fancied himself as a teller of tales, a builder of suspense. I wondered if I was the only person to have guessed the answer. 'But I have to tell you first that, when we at Popov recognised the political implications of what we had discovered, we went to the Russian government and said, "What should we do with this?" Their reply was unequivocal; I will quote it: "The Russian government has no interest in interfering in the politics of Scotland. This is a matter for the local authorities, in particular Police Scotland." So we took that advice, and we passed all our evidence to Police Scotland.'

He paused, drank from a glass of water, shook his head, donned a mask of sadness, and said, 'So, Organisation X? I can inform you with complete certainty that the building in the New Town is occupied by the Scottish Intelligence Services.'

This brought gasps and exclamations from his audience. As soon as the session was thrown open, many of the questions were pointedly aggressive, along the lines that the Russians might *claim* they didn't want to interfere in Scottish politics, but wasn't that precisely what they were doing? Mr Smoothie's replies were all variations on a theme: Popov Systems wanted only that the truth be known; they were not in the business of covering up anything.

Reporters were clamouring to speak. One, stuttering in indignation, declared that Popov had acquired their information by illegal means and this would never be admissible in a court of law. Smoothie was saying, in effect,

that the niceties of Scots law weren't Popov's problem – when my phone rang.

Pamela. I cursed, though I'd expected the call from the moment I heard the phrase 'Edinburgh New Town'. She would be furious. She would lash out, she would blame me.

I didn't answer; I needed time. I waited until the ringing stopped and then put the sound on Mute. I had a second phone, one with a Pay As You Go SIM, which I kept for personal calls. I used this now to call Helen.

She barely let me say hello. 'Did you see that fucking rubbish on the news? Fucking *fucking* rubbish.'

'I saw it, yes. What d'you make of it?'

'Well, *we* know it's rubbish, because the Scottish Intelligence Services had nothing to do with it, and I didn't even use TOR.'

'Are you saying other people might not recognise it as rubbish? They might think it's plausible?'

I knew the answer already. Once Paul McIntyre got going – this time with the impetus from Popov propelling him – once he put a few more indignant articles on websites, a few hundred more 'shares' on Facebook and a few thousand more tweets on Twitter, the allegation that the Scottish Intelligence Services, and therefore the Scottish government, had stooped to the dirtiest of tricks would solidify into a 'fact' that was set in concrete.

'Oh it's *plausible*,' Helen said, 'just plausible, if you believe the Scottish Intelligence Service is full of sloppy buggers who don't protect their systems. And I'm sure Popov will produce a trail that looks authentic. By the way, how the hell d'you suppose Popov got wind of it in the first place?'

'I can tell you that. Paul McIntyre, who calls himself communications director for Free Shetland, uploaded Eric Sorenson's entire hard disc to them.'

'Did he? Why Popov?'

'Don't know. McIntyre claims to have trained in Russia. Maybe he had friends there. But I don't get it: would he have the clout to persuade Popov to make a false allegation?'

'How would we know? Of course, it's an allegation they are never going to be able to prove. On the other hand, no one's going to be able to *dis*prove it.'

'What would you guess Popov are trying to do?'

'God knows. I looked them up. They're a fairly new outfit, scrambling to get some market share in the security business. It could be that they wanted the publicity, on the grounds that all publicity is good publicity.'

'And what will happen now?'

'Nothing, for a long time. The police will sit on the stuff Popov has given them. And then sit on it some more. Anyway, who the fuck cares?'

I saw that my other phone was ringing again. Apart from me, Pamela cared.

'I'd better go,' I said. 'See you at the weekend, when our dear friend from the Norseman comes back up.'

'Aah. We'll screw her.'

I answered Pamela's summons. She didn't bother with hello either.

'Where the hell have you been?'

'Sorry. I was in the shower.'

'Why?'

Why? What was that supposed to mean? It meant that she didn't believe me.

'I was sweaty after a day at school.'

'Really? You saw the news?'

'Yes. A load of nonsense.' Oops. How did I see it if I was in the shower? Pamela didn't notice. 'Neither the great Scottish public nor our revered representatives at Holyrood know it's nonsense. Some idiots are calling for my head.'

'That's ridiculous. Surely all you have to do is point out to Arnold that Popov's allegations are unprovable.'

'Do you think I'm stupid?' She was shouting so loud that I had to hold the phone away from my ear. 'Of course I've done that. Let me tell you, I think you've messed up. This hacker of yours – she's sold the story to the Russians.'

'How could she? She didn't know that SIS had anything to do with it.'

'She didn't need to. She sold a story she thought was false. Gives her some money, gives Popov a chance at publicity. Everybody's happy, except you, me and Arnold. When I come up at the weekend, I'll grill her.'

'Pamela, you can't grill her. You're not supposed to know about this exploit of hers. Besides, I know how Popov got involved.' I told her about McIntyre.

She wouldn't let go. 'You don't know the relationship between her and McIntyre. I'll get the truth out of her.'

Christ. Pamela was going to have a second shot at blowing my cover wide open.

I said, 'Arnold's taking your side?'

'For the moment. Do you know what he said? "I'll give you the benefit of the doubt." The *doubt*? What doubt? He's a bastard.'

'He's a politician.'

'I could wring his pansy neck.'

Arnold wasn't a pansy. Anyway, Pamela should be grateful she hadn't been sacked – yet.

She wasn't finished. 'And Sorenson? He'll be off the hook. Probably profit from a sympathy vote. You'll need to think of something else. Have a Plan B ready for me for the weekend. Same as last time. Six o'clock in the Ross. And a rendezvous with your hacker.'

When she'd ended the call, I had a lot to consider. On the plus side, Gregor and I would have another chance to get some kompromat; I should alert him as soon as possible. On the negative side, very definitely, was the requirement for a Plan B – and Pamela's likely reaction if she didn't get one.

I needed help; I needed someone to bounce ideas off. Who else but Gregor?

I texted him: *Need to talk. Urgent.*

There was no immediate response. I didn't know where on Unst his halibut hatchery was, or whether he had a phone signal. In the meantime, there was nothing I could do except make my dinner.

I wasn't hungry.

I'd eaten and tidied my dishes when my phone rang. I swept it up, but it was Colin.

He was in some noisy place. I could hear the laughter and the clinking of bottles and glasses. 'Hi,' he said, sounding too cheerful to be sober, 'would you like to come for a drink? We're celebrating.'

'Celebrating what?'

'You haven't seen the news? Eric's exonerated.'

'Of course. Where are you?'

'Oh. The Norseman.'

'Great.' I felt anything but great, but perhaps a drink would cheer me up, or at least take my mind off Pamela. 'I'll be up in ten minutes.'

In the Norseman, the scene was a full-blown party, a gathering of true believers relieved that their messiah had not been taken from them. They were crammed in the area round the bar, reluctant to sit down, I supposed, in case they missed some of the repartee. As I entered, the massed ranks moved a little, and I caught a glimpse of McIntyre propped against the counter with several bottles of beer in front of him. A group who I thought were well-wishers were crowding round and behind him.

Colin and Billy, each holding a bottle of beer, were at the back of this group. Colin saw me, gave his beer to Billy, and came over.

Billy was watching; I had to put on a good show, choosing a smile from my palette – 'warm', 'happy', with a splash of 'caring' – and encircling Colin with a hug. He kissed my cheek, his breath smelling of beer.

'A party?' I said. 'Are people buying Paul drinks?'

'Yes.' His expression changed from pleasure to doubt, then back again to a sort of forced pleasure. 'He persuaded Popov to hold the press conference. His friends in Russia must be pretty influential. But come and have a drink.'

He took me across to Billy, asked me what I'd like, then left the two of us while he pushed his way to the bar.

Something about Billy annoyed me. It might have been the way he did not see the need to make conversation.

128

I said – and it came out more barbed than I had intended – 'I thought that you policemen were always busy with overtime.'

His eyebrows went up. What the hell were they saying? *You want our hostility out in the open? And you're hostile because you know that I know you're only toying with my brother?*

'Ah,' he said, 'not quite, but we're always on duty after a fashion.' He took a pull from his bottle of Shetland Lager. 'You came from Edinburgh?'

'Yes.'

'What school did you teach at there?'

Maybe it was a polite enquiry; maybe he wanted to make up for being so taciturn. Or maybe he was snooping. At any rate, I couldn't answer the question without giving him a lead that he might use to investigate me. I trotted out the story that I had 'done supply' before I stopped to look after my mother.

'She's better now?'

'Yes. Fortunately. I couldn't have afforded to stay unemployed for long.' I wanted to steer the conversation away from my previous teaching experience. 'And you? Did you work somewhere else before you came back to Shetland?'

'Edinburgh.'

No. My paranoia bloomed. He would have contacts, and *they*'d have contacts. He could have a net of enquiry across the city within a week. He could even capture a photograph of me from one of Lerwick's cctv cameras and send that down with the message that this search was urgent... Billy could ruin me.

Colin returned, not before time, with a bottle of cider for me. He took his own bottle from Billy and I saw Billy's eyes flickering between the two of us. So I clinked bottles with Colin before I asked him if he'd spoken to Eric.

'I did, just before I came out. He thinks his luck has turned. There might even be light at the end of his financial tunnel.'

'Oh?'

'Steven has said that he should be able to sue the Scottish government for defamation, *and* there's a potential buyer for one of his family's hotels.'

Either or both of these rainbows could turn out to have no pot of gold at the end, but that wasn't much help to me now, not if the glimmer of hope persuaded Eric that he didn't need to stand down.

'Good news all round. So Eric will be back on song for the big event on Wednesday?'

'He will. Thank God.'

I suffered the party for almost an hour. There were a lot of jokes, many of them coarse, about Police Scotland and their 'extensive experience' of pornographic websites. Billy dealt with these, I had to admit, with easy banter and the atmosphere didn't descend into nastiness. It was a different story, however, when McIntyre lurched through his band of admirers on the way to the toilet.

He saw me and sneered. 'Your pal gonna tell her debaters about those criminals at Holyrood? Eh?'

'Who's her pal?' somebody asked, and I felt a lot of eyes upon me.

I tried to stare McIntyre down, but his face was flushed and it was clear he was drunk. Billy stepped in, literally, edging between McIntyre and me. 'Come on, Paul. It's nothing to do with her.'

McIntyre couldn't confront me without pushing past Billy's considerable bulk. He spluttered and cursed, then backed down, allowing one of his friends to jolly him along to the toilet.

'Thank you,' I said to Billy.

'Think nothing of it.'

But I was uncomfortable, and said so. 'I think I'll just go home,' I added.

Colin had just bought himself and Billy more lager. When he offered to walk back with me, I told him, perhaps more sharply than I needed to, that I could look after myself.

On my way home, my mood was pitch black. I had no Plan B and no idea where it might come from. I had my suspicions about Billy's and *his* suspicions. And I worried that the identity of 'my pal' would be known to all those drunk, aggressive men before the night was out. If they mounted some kind of hate campaign against Sharon, I would boil over with anger.

I'd left my phone in the flat, and a message awaited me, from Gregor. *Back on Wednesday. Dinner at eight? My place?*

I had to go to the meeting in the school, because I wanted to catch the mood of the general population, and that meeting didn't start until seven. So I replied, *8.30? Even 8.45?*

He replied in turn: *Of course. A pleasure postponed is a pleasure enhanced.*

Can't wait.

I shouldn't have sent that. But I needed him. I needed just to be with him even more than I needed a Plan B.

Chapter 11

Tuesday, 16th – Wednesday, 17th

Throughout Tuesday, my nerves twanged like overstretched guitar strings. I told myself over and over that I should wait for Gregor's input, but my mind ran – no, sprinted – round the question of how to find a Plan B. The faster the sprint, of course, the greater the tension and the slimmer the chance of hitting upon a solution. I should have known that what I had to do was stop, relax, have a glass of wine or two, and wait for ideas to pop up from my freewheeling neuronal circuits.

When I tuned into Radio Free Shetland at seven o'clock, I was on my second glass and those circuits were still not cooperating.

The presenter, who was chirpy and blessed with clear diction, reminded her listeners of the two basic rules of their telephone poll. No one was allowed to reply to the telephone call with 'I don't know'; anyone so tempted had to imagine that he would be shot if he didn't cast an unambiguous vote. And, secondly, anyone who had changed his mind since the last time – the same one thousand people were questioned each month – had to give a reason. That was it. The results last month, she reminded us, were 508 for independence, and 492 against; it could hardly be closer.

Drum rolls. Clashing of cymbals. Radio Free Shetland was having a bit of fun. A male voice, imitating – or mocking – a BBC presenter of the fifties, read out the results. For independence, 515; against, 485; number who had

changed from 'for' to 'against', 3; number who had changed from 'against' to 'for', 10. My stomach churned.

When people changed their minds, their reasons were recorded verbatim. These recordings were played back now. Of the three who had changed to 'against', none explicitly said Eric was a pervert, but they all used phrases like 'losing confidence in Free Shetland's leadership'. Of the ten who switched in the other direction, two claimed that they had been persuaded by the economic arguments, while the rest were very clear that they had been 'disgusted' – or words to that effect – by 'the actions of the Scottish government'.

The presenter introduced Alison Dalrymple and another woman, who were going to discuss the results on behalf of the opposing camps. I couldn't listen to them, because I was too worried about Pamela. She was going to come up on Friday and deliver an ultimatum: offer a plausible Plan B or resign. After a minute or two, I closed down the computer and stared at the wall.

On Wednesday, the whole school was buzzing – you'd have thought independence had already been declared. I had to fix a mask that said I shared in the general excitement. I had to ask Joy cheerily if Eric had his mojo back – he did. And I had to respond with great good humour to endless questions from my classes.

'Hey, miss, will we have our own passports?'

'Miss, d'you think I could join the Shetland navy?'

'Hey, miss, will we get to put in a team to the world cup?'

Their exuberance was a bombardment demolishing the remnants of my morale.

Sharon, having arranged that Mary would break her babysitting duck, was going to the big meeting. So was Colin. Both of them had offered me a lift, Colin by text. I'd declined both, saying that as I was coming in to the school anyway, I was going to arrive half an hour or so early, to 'catch up with a few things in my room'. The truth was, of course, that I didn't want anything or anybody to slow me down in my escape to Gregor's.

At a quarter past six, I parked at the Clickimin Centre – so that my getaway would be even faster. In my classroom, I pottered around for twenty to twenty-five minutes, tidying, marking a few jotters, looking at preparation that I should do but couldn't. About a quarter to seven, I went along to the atrium.

The atrium. The architects' pride and joy. A futuristic, spaceship-like, dazzlingly white space that could be used for anything from assemblies to dances to banquets. Its seating capacity was about a thousand, and once it was full not another soul would be admitted, because Shetland Isles Council were sticklers for health and safety. I thought I had left it too late, because I couldn't see a seat. But there was one, at the back beside the wooden stairway. I caught sight of Joy and Sven, and Sharon sitting with her girls and chatting to a man the back of whose head looked familiar. It was Colin, I realised. *Well.*

A microphone had been set up for the debaters. At a minute past seven, Peter, who was chairing the proceedings, no doubt because of his reputation for fairness, led out Eric and a bearded, bespectacled, bejumpered fellow who – I knew because I'd seen his photograph in the newspaper beside his

frequent, nay incessant, comments on Shetland's culture – considered himself to be some sort of sage, mystic, poet, social commentator and Socratic philosopher all rolled into one.

His name was Harry Watt, and he'd been chosen by the Remainers to be their spokesman. When invited by Peter to speak first, he said, after a few remarks about the privilege of being born and bred in Shetland, 'Now, I want to remind you, before I say anything else, of the beauties of Shetland. Bear with me, for this is totally relevant.'

Was I the only one who groaned?

I suppose he thought his description was the ultimate in lyricism. Let me give you a taste. 'Ah,' he said, in his umpteenth paragraph, 'the sound of the sea skelping the skerries, the call of a thousand baagies who call a ness their home, the slicht glide and breathtaking dive of a whaal, the bleating of peerie snow-white lambs in spring, the magic of simmer dim or da Mirrie Dancers…'

He wasn't just singing Shetland's praises, you'll gather. He was saying, *Amn't I at home with the dialect?*

But so what? When Harry was satisfied that his gifts as a wordsmith had been sufficiently brought to our attention, he went on: 'Every day in Shetland, as you drive along an empty road and the mist blows away to reveal the majestic sweep of a voe, you are reminded of the grandeur and mystery of the universe, and in particular of this corner of the universe in which we have the good fortune to live. Now here's the thing. Do you want to spend your time contemplating this grandeur, moving in and out of a state of peaceful transcendence, or do you want to find your day filled with the administrative minutiae involved in governing a state? Make no mistake: the politicians in Holyrood are not our masters, they are our slaves, freeing us

from mundane responsibilities, giving us, in effect, freedom to move to matters of a higher plane. When we are not awe-struck by our natural surroundings, we can attend to our music, our arts and crafts, our drama, our simple but hugely profound communion with each other.'

Harry was full of hot air, and his audience would see right through him. Da Mirrie Dancers were all very well, they'd be saying, but they didn't put Cornflakes on the table or buy the kids shoes.

Then he changed direction; perhaps he'd merely been softening us up.

'But let's put aside, if we can,' he said, 'all thoughts of the meaning of life, the universe and everything. Let's focus on gritty economic details. When you read carefully the website of Free Shetland, what do you find? Vagueness, generalities, many a statement of probability and nary a statement of fact. What will the level of income tax be? Well, we're not sure. And VAT? And council tax? And who's going to pay for what you might call the fripperies of government – the embassies, the passport office, the mint, the central bank and the civil service? Then there are pensions. Many of you will have, or will be looking forward to, pensions from a public agency. Can Free Shetland confirm that they would have either the financial resources or the administrative capability to continue these payments? Can they really?'

It was Project Fear all over again. Harry was doing his best – and his best was quite good – to make people worry about money.

'Now,' he said, 'fossil fuels. In an age when the world knows that it must move decisively from producing more and more carbon, on what is Shetland going to base its economy? Advances in electric vehicles, and in the production of non-carbon energy, are being made almost every week, are *accelerating* almost every week, and yet Shetland is going to put all its

money on the turn of one card: the demand for oil. My friends, this is madness.'

Harry had hit an important target. I realised that he was annoying me, and I was astonished. Whose side was I on?

He gave us a lot of information on renewable energy, the targets of the Scottish government and the opportunities presented for Scottish manufacturing. He went into endless detail on electric cars, on joint ventures between this company and that, and on 'game-changing' batteries. In fact, he probably gave us more than we needed, and, as the audience began to shuffle, he seemed to recognise that he might be losing them.

In his peroration, he went back to a broader brush. Remove an external enemy, he claimed, and history showed that a population fell to fighting amongst themselves. The Scottish government wasn't an enemy, but it could be cast as such; it could certainly be cast as a scapegoat. Shetlanders 'had been known' – he said this with a knowing smile – to squabble. If they had no one else to blame, these squabbles over resources could become poisonous indeed. Then no one would even notice da Mirrie Dancers, and everyone would be the poorer for it.

This conclusion didn't exactly stroke the collective psyche, and the round of applause that Harry received was muted. Still, he must have crystallised a lot of doubts – and he'd managed it without breathing a single snide word about Eric.

Eric himself stood up, adjusting the microphone and whistling into it to produce an eerie sound. Then he said slowly, 'Aye, aabody in Shetland feels the same ettersome wind, and hears it howlin' in the cowlin'.'

He grinned and cocked an eyebrow. I looked round and saw faces relaxing in amusement. Eric had pitched his response just right. *I too can speak the dialect, but I won't go on and on about it.*

Eric did indeed have his mojo back. He gave us a concise apology for the malware that had spread from his computer and caused huge inconvenience throughout the islands. However, he said, the real culprits, the real criminals, were those who had engaged in hacking in order to sabotage the democratic rights of the Shetland people, for in a democracy the first thing people were entitled to was the truth.

He didn't labour the point, which was a good move, because it implied that the matter wasn't really worth discussing. 'This brings me at once,' he said, 'to the heart of the matter, to the meat of Harry's presentation: the economic case. Harry is right that our website speaks of probabilities, not certainties, but the truth is this: *any* economic forecast is a matter of probabilities; to claim anything else would be deceit. How *do* we, after all, estimate the revenue and expenditure of an independent Shetland? It is established – I'm surprised Harry didn't say this but I will – that the expenditure per Shetlander, for services like education, health, transport, the post, is greater than for the rest of Scotland, simply because of the far-flung geography of our islands. On the other hand, it is also established that the revenue per person is higher, because we have much lower unemployment, so that income tax and corporation tax, to take two examples, bring in proportionately more. On our website, we have set out a range of estimates – yes, based on a range of probabilities – but overall our best guess is that the fiscal effect of Shetland's independence would be broadly neutral. That is, before we consider oil.

'Yes, oil. You will know that new seismic survey techniques and new methods of analysing subsea geological structures have already discovered huge new fields in what will be Shetland's exclusive economic zone, and you will know it is likely that they will discover still more. You will also know that techniques of subsea recovery now make production much more cost effective. You will be aware that the contribution from Shetland's oil to the Scottish budget is already almost six billion dollars per year, and it is likely to rise to eight. Harry is right, of course, that the world is hoping to move away from fossil fuels, but that hope is very far from being realised. If Shetland had, say, ten years – a conservative estimate – of this kind of income – and that's before we consider a Norwegian style of financing – we could build a sovereign wealth fund that would transform these islands for the foreseeable future.'

He outlined uses to which this fund could be put: investment in healthcare, infrastructure, 'the knowledge economy', agriculture and aquaculture, the upgrading of tourist facilities, the encouragement of a 'vibrant' culture… He didn't go into detail on any of these, and I had the impression that he merely wanted to convey the impression that utopia was round the corner, rather than risk anyone nit-picking about how the treasure might actually be distributed.

Then Eric acknowledged that he was about to deviate from his main theme. He gave us a tour d'horizon of constitutional, defence and financial arrangements: full independence, no 'British Overseas Territory nonsense'; no immediate application to join the EU, although that would be open to discussion; likewise with NATO; a Shetland pound, to be launched at parity with the British pound, thereafter to be freely floated; interest rates to be set by the Bank of Shetland; slim-line government; no embassies across the

world – arrangements would be made with friendly countries... The tour lasted about five minutes, before he paused and poured a glass of water. His cri de coeur was about to come.

'Now,' he said, 'money. And the kind of society we want. The two go hand in hand. Let's ask: at present, what does the Scottish government *do* with our six billion a year? Let's be blunt: they use it to reduce their fiscal deficit to somewhere near manageable proportions.

'What causes this fiscal deficit? It is caused, in large measure, by the dependency culture of mainland Scotland, by the overblown public sector, which guarantees so many people a comfortable job, and by the over-generous welfare system, which guarantees to so many people that they don't need a job at all.

'Make no mistake. Dependency is an insidious poison. And it is self-reinforcing. Take PIP. You know PIP? Personal Independence Plan, a scheme to make life bearable for those who are severely disabled? On paper, a good, humane idea, and I am certainly not suggesting that this benefit should be taken from those who need it. Yet I am going to focus on PIP because it illustrates *perfectly* the difference between the culture of Shetland and the culture of mainland Scotland. Did you know that, once you have been awarded PIP, this results in considerable additions to other benefits? It is, in other words, a huge financial boon to be declared disabled. There are genuine claimants, of course – I have already conceded that – but there is also an enormous grey area in which some people *might* be considered disabled or might not. Small wonder, then, that there are endless sources of advice, in the towns, villages and housing estates of Scotland, on what boxes to tick on the form, what answers to supply, what methods to use in order to circumvent your doctors. Crucially, it is helpful if you *consider* yourself disabled,

because the correct answers become automatic. Then, certainly, the vicious circle has begun. You live the life of the truly disabled, you can't get yourself out of bed, you can't go for a run or even a walk, you can't control your eating and you can't, most important of all, work.

'Is this good for you? Of course it's not. But once you're in this mindset, do you want your PIP to be cut or cancelled? If the National Party wants to lose your vote, what's the easiest way to achieve it? So how does the National Party, which assuredly does *not* want to lose your vote, get the money to keep it – to pay for your destructive pattern?

'Well, as I have said, they get a lot of it from us. *We* are helping to destroy – this language is not too strong – the lives of thousands of people on mainland Scotland.

'I put it to you that this is the very opposite of the vision that Shetland should offer the world. We have a way of life that is incomparably healthier. We get up at dawn, or before it, no matter how ettersome the wind, we go out to dig our potatoes, to tend to our lobster traps or our lambs, to sail the seas for fish. In doing these things we interact with other Shetlanders and we understand their point of view even if we don't agree with it. When our work is over, we enjoy our families and our community activities. In short, we centre our lives on the old wisdom that work is good for you. Work not only brings material prosperity, it rescues you from vice and in particular from the vice of utter self-centredness. Work makes us fully human.

'The conclusion must be that we are not quite a different species – homo shetlandensis – and not quite a different race. But by our way of life and culture, by our view of ourselves and the universe – indeed, by all those things that Harry listed – we might as well be. Still, Harry's conclusion is nonsense. Do we think that we can keep all that we value and yet be

141

subservient to Holyrood? How ridiculous. How self-contradictory. Rather, we should listen to Alison Dalrymple, because she's right: just as poets and playwrights and philosophers sprang from the peculiar circumstances of classical Athens to bring to the world insights and compass points of everlasting importance, so we *could* be a beacon of light for humanity, as bright as the torches of Up Helly Aa in a January night.'

Eric sat down. I thought he might have been rash to confront the question of benefits, but most of the audience stood clapping and cheering. On the basis of this evidence, Free Shetland were rolling on a tide to victory.

Peter asked for questions, and there were some. Would Shetland issue its own government bonds? Probably not, because it wouldn't have any need to borrow, except possibly in the very short term. Would Shetland have its own passports? Absolutely. Would Shetland be able to defend itself if it wasn't a member of NATO? Well, defence, especially of fish stocks, was an important issue, but there were rules and international courts which were hugely preferable to military confrontations. Would Shetland retain links with the British monarchy? Eric conceded that this would have to be a subject for debate, but in his opinion the answer was an emphatic no – because subservience to a monarch was an anachronism that should have been recognised as such many centuries ago.

That seemed a fitting place at which to call a halt. Peter said that as the time was twenty to nine and the lease of the hall ran out on the hour, he would now put the issue to a simple show of hands. Did the meeting recommend to the council that they should go ahead with an indicative referendum, on the basis of the proposals heard tonight and those laid out on the website of Free Shetland? Yes?

The majority wasn't in doubt, though the hands were not an uninterrupted forest. 'Carried,' Peter said, and then I lost sight of him as people in front of me stood up again to applaud.

I bumped into Joy on the way out. 'A drink?' she said.'

I shook my head. 'Sorry. I'm not feeling well at all.'

'The curse, still?'

'I'm not sure.'

She was full of concern, but didn't hold me back. 'Early to bed,' she called after me.

A gale was brewing up, sweeping rain in from the west. I waited for my windscreen to de-mist. So Free Shetland was stronger than ever? *Gregor*, I thought, *where art thou?*

Chapter 12

Wednesday, 17th – Thursday, 18th

I knew where Gregor was, in a topological sense. But I couldn't park outside his door, because Lerwick's gossip squad would have started a public enquiry within hours. So I left the Honda outside my flat and set out to walk. The only problem was: which route to take? I didn't want to be seen, in particular by Colin. He might come back from the school by North Road and Commercial Road, but he might cut down King Harald or St Olaf Street and go down Harbour Street from the west. I almost ran up King Harald Street.

I had nearly reached the relative safety of King Haakon Street – these Norwegians sure left their mark on Lerwick – when I saw headlights coming down from the direction of Commercial Road. I jumped into a driveway and cowered behind a bush.

The movement of the lights slowed, the car came level with the drive, I saw the outline of Colin's face, the car slowed still more, I saw him peering out, not quite in my direction. He'd caught a movement? He was going to stop the car and come to look? He was going to catch me hiding behind a bush?

But the car didn't stop. It swung left into Harbour Street, and I breathed out.

Still, I was annoyed. How on earth had I got myself into a situation where I was playing hide and seek in the streets of Lerwick?

Gregor was waiting for me; he calmed me down, took me upstairs, poured me a glass of some special wine. A heavenly aroma reached my nostrils.

'What's that lovely smell?'

He took my parka away. 'Some fish,' he said.

The table was set for two, complete with a bottle of white wine in an ice bucket. The time was almost nine-thirty, and I was already thinking that maybe I wouldn't make it to school in the morning.

He produced two whole sea bream, poached in a wine sauce with mushrooms, herbs and a sprinkling of vegetables. He must have been reading the *Guardian* weekend supplement. I enjoyed a few mouthfuls and half a glass of wine before I spoke.

'You heard about Eric Sorenson?'

Gregor was freshly shaven and looked well slept. It seemed that nothing would ruffle him. 'I heard he was accused of accessing child pornography and then Popov Systems held a news conference to exonerate him.'

'Yes. And tonight a poll showed a swing of support towards him.'

'That's what's urgent?'

'Yes. Also, Pamela's coming up again on Friday.'

Now he showed mild surprise. 'She likes her diversions. The Ross Hotel again?'

'So she says, but with Pamela and her paramours you can never be sure of anything.'

'Yes. As far as that's concerned, it'll be just like the last time. My colleagues will do their best to catch her. If they can, well and good. If they can't, it's too bad. But our friend Eric? He's a different issue.'

'You said your government might help me.'

'Absolutely. You have a plan?'

145

'There's the problem. I don't have a plan, and I don't have a clue how to find one.'

He poured more wine. 'I don't like to see you worrying. Eric will have weaknesses. There will be something we can use. Do you have to go to work tomorrow? We should examine our target in depth, you and I.'

'I'm already thinking of calling in sick.'

'That would be nice.'

We gazed into each other's eyes like a pair of lovestruck teenagers. The wine was working on me, dissolving my anxiety. *Take no thought for the morrow.*

We ate and drank. Gregor refused to accept that we would *not* come up with a plan, that we would *not* sabotage Free Shetland, and that I would *not* be in the running for Pamela's job. Then he enquired about my possible rivals. I listed them, describing their strengths and weaknesses, their experience, their political allies.

The sea bream had been picked clean when the subject was exhausted. 'So,' Gregor said, 'if it couldn't be you, who would your choice be?'

I didn't take long to think. Pamela didn't encourage her subordinates to socialise, or even interact very much, but I was friendly with one girl, Susan Ferguson, who was very methodical, very calm and, so it seemed to me, had antennae like a mosquito's. She and I had agreed once, after a couple of drinks, that we were in favour of 'sensible cooperation' with the Russians.

I passed this on to Gregor.

'Anyway,' he said, 'it will be you.'

We finished the wine. Gregor said, 'I'll take two minutes to clear the dishes and five to set up the attempt to get kompromat on Pamela. Why don't you…'

'Warm up the bed? My pleasure.'

The bed was indeed cool. I hugged myself and waited for Gregor. When he slipped in naked beside me, I cuddled against him. The rain battered against the window as my hand slid down from his chest.

This time was very different. Gregor was incredibly tender. He knew, by some heightened power of intuition, when I wanted to be stroked or kissed or merely held. *I* knew that he was erect, but I also knew that if he sensed I wasn't ready, he would never press the issue; he would find a way to make me feel good about just lying there with him while the rain poured down and the wind howled.

My desire took a long time to build. But when it peaked, the urgency was overwhelming.

I didn't want to fade into oblivion; the moment was too precious. My mind bounced to Sharon. 'D'you know that saying,' I murmured, '*patriotism is the last refuge of a scoundrel*?'

'Mm. Samuel Johnson?'

'Was it? D'you think it's adequate, as a description of patriotism?'

He woke up a little. 'I don't think we can take it at face value. Johnson, as far as I remember, was a lifelong Tory. What he meant, I believe, was that the *profession* of patriotism is the last refuge of a scoundrel who can't find any other way to buttress his arguments.'

I was rather ashamed that Gregor knew more about English literature than I did.

'Suppose,' I said, 'we did take it at face value. *Then* would it be adequate?'

'Mm. Too vague.'

I pressed him. 'How would you adapt it? What could be wrong with patriotism?'

'Patriotism is…' – I thought he was too drowsy to concentrate – '…the last refuge of… someone who is looking for meaning. No, the second last refuge.'

'The last one being… religion?'

'Exactly.'

'And the two often go together?'

'Mm.'

I had to let him sleep. I should sleep myself. But I lay for a while, pondering. What kind of meaning was a patriot looking for? When he found it, was it satisfying?

I woke to the sound of rushing water. When I put out a hand, Gregor wasn't there. I'd heard the shower.

The time was twenty past eight. For staff at the school, the rule was that if you were ill you were supposed to phone in by half past, so that one of the deputy headteachers would have time to issue please-takes to your unfortunate colleagues.

I stretched, running through my timetable in my head. First period, I had my second-year class. Who in the department had a free period? Sharon. She was the only one, I was sure. And 'free period' was a serious misnomer if

your name was Sharon MacIntosh. I should dress, rush back to my flat, brush my teeth and speed round to the school. I would just have time.

But the bed was comfortable. I was in that wonderful state where you're still drowsy and content. And I'd been looking forward to a leisurely breakfast with Gregor.

Damn. Sharon would forgive me. And I'd make it up to her. I got up and found my phone. What could I claim was wrong with me? Migraine? Flu? Back ache? Food poisoning? What could no one disprove?

'Migraine?' said the office assistant, in the tone of one who could smell a malingerer at a hundred yards. I recognised her voice: she fancied herself as a dragon.

'Yes.'

'Will you be in this afternoon?'

'No.'

'Tomorrow?'

'I should think so.' *Well, I have to go out drinking in the evening with patronising Pamela and harridan Helen. Any more questions?*

'I'll tell them.'

'Thank you.'

I was standing naked as Gregor emerged from the bathroom. 'Good morning,' he said. Though he wasn't erect, I thought I could interpret his grin.

But the phone call had spoiled my mood. He picked up on that immediately and said, 'Are you all right?'

I explained my feelings of guilt. He frowned. 'You're too conscientious. Have a shower and wash your discontent away. I'll put the coffee on.'

His coffee was good, his muesli was tasty and, though the wind had dropped, the rain bouncing off the roofs of the vans parked outside made me glad I was in a warm apartment.

He saw me looking out the window. 'It's a good day,' he said, 'to stay indoors and plot.'

In a way, I didn't want to plot, but we had to. 'Shall I give you a list of Eric's weaknesses, apart from being a numbskull with computers?'

'Please do.'

I gave him a slightly different list from the one I'd given Pamela. 'He likes whisky; Joy – his wife – is a lesbian; and he may be short of money.'

'Doesn't the National Government have trolls who can use that sort of thing to rubbish his reputation?'

'They do, and the trolls have tried, but so far they've had little success.'

'What about the money? Why might he be short?'

I explained, as best I could, about the debts from Eric's hotel business, the mortgage on the house, the BMW fixation, and the possible recovery in his finances. Gregor said, 'But this recovery might not materialise. Even if it did, it might not meet all his needs. Would he be open to bribery?'

'To sell Shetland's independence down the river? Definitely not.'

'What about Joy's family? Any money there?'

'Her mother's dead, but she says her father, whose name is Sven, is wealthy. Only thing is, he's a mean old bastard. He refuses to help them out.'

'But she'll inherit eventually?'

'Eventually.'

'This Sven's fit and healthy? How old?'

'Early sixties. He has the beginnings of Parkinson's. He refuses to ask for a diagnosis, because he might have to stop driving, but you can see his hand shake, and I don't think there's any doubt about it.'

'Really?' Gregor was grimacing. 'Parkinson's is horrible. It killed one of my aunts. I watched her as *she* watched death approach with every tremble of her hand. Then she got side effects from the medication: couldn't swallow, couldn't move her bowels, couldn't sleep, got hallucinations. We wouldn't let a dog die like that. It makes you wonder, does it not, about those who preach that human life is sacrosanct.'

'You don't think it is?'

'Well, in the first place, the same preachers turn a blind eye when the lives that are lost are far away, belonging to those who have a different skin colour or a different religion. And, in the second place, 'sacrosanct' is the wrong word, because that means something's protected by divine edict – which is rubbish. You have to replace 'sacrosanct' with 'valuable', and as soon as you do that you hit the question, can one human life be more *valuable* than another?'

'And can it?'

'What do *you* think? Take Sven with his Parkinson's. How much life will he have left? Five years? Ten years? We don't know. But we do know that his life will become more and more a living hell. Is that worth more or less than the life of a child whose every smile brings joy? Or the life of someone like you, who could bring quarrelling countries together for everyone's benefit?'

'I could do that?'

'Of course you could, if you replaced Pamela.'

'But, Gregor, how is this relevant to Eric?'

'Let me think. More toast? More coffee?'

'Yes, please. Both.'

While he was in the kitchen, my thoughts played around what we'd just been saying. What a shame it would be if I did *not* replace Pamela.

Gregor brought the toast and coffee, and also a jar of Scottish heather honey. 'Try this,' he said. 'It's as sweet as life itself.'

I buttered my toast and spread on the honey. It stuck to my teeth, too sweet for my taste.

Gregor liked it; he sniffed the perfume.

'Suppose,' he said, 'just suppose that Eric put Sven out of his misery and managed to conceal it, managed to frame someone else, and then paid off his debts with the money his wife inherited, would we blame him? Would we not applaud him for having the courage to find a good solution to everyone's problems?'

'*We* might, but most people wouldn't.'

'Because their minds are tied up by this notion of sacrosanctity?'

'Suppose you're right. So what?'

'Well, now suppose we made it *appear* that Eric had done this, except that his attempt to frame someone else failed. That would get rid of Eric, that would finish off Free Shetland. So it would solve your problem as well as Sven's. So would we not deserve equal applause for finding these two solutions?'

'Gregor, are you suggesting we murder Sven and frame Eric?'

'I'm suggesting we might – might – release Sven from his misery.'

I could think of nothing to say.

'Carol, this is no time for false modesty.' Gregor was very earnest. 'You and I are not like other people. What did we say about ourselves? That we

are willing to look into the abyss of reality and acknowledge that there is no ultimate meaning? Is this true? *Can* we survey the universe of possibilities? *Are* we free spirits?'

I stared at him. 'I don't want to go to jail.'

He stroked my knuckles. 'Neither do I. But we wouldn't take any risks.'

I swerved into the realm of practicality. 'But how,' I said, 'could we possibly do it? Kill Sven without being caught *and* frame Eric?'

'I don't know – yet. But tell me, does Sven do his own shopping?'

'Not really. Joy and Eric take turns to collect the bulk of his groceries from Tesco on a Saturday.'

'Do they? Anything he gets every week?'

'A bottle of Chilean red wine. Isla Negra.'

'Why Isla Negra?'

'I told you, he's as mean as sin.'

'Mm. It will be a screwtop.'

'So?'

He laughed, a self-deprecating laugh. 'If this were a puzzle, I could supply you with a piece. Before I left Moscow, I had dinner with a friend who told me that the scientists in the intelligence services have taken a toxin called batrachotoxin and manipulated the chemistry so that it is tasteless, colourless and odourless – the odour was a major problem – but still amazingly fast.'

'Fast?'

'It kills a man in about a minute. What's a minute of pain compared to five years of hell?'

'We'd put it in Sven's wine bottle?'

'We'd have to get an identical bottle, prepare it, and swap the bottles somehow.'

153

'How?'

'That's a detail. Listen, I'm sorry, but I'll have to go to the toilet. Don't finish that jar.'

I buttered another slice of toast, but I skipped the honey. In the school, first period would be grinding to a close.

The view out of the window hadn't changed; the rain still washed the dark heart of Lerwick. I felt trapped, because tomorrow night Pamela would demand a plan. I didn't want to be trapped.

The coffee was strong. I could feel it kicking at my brain. The pieces of Gregor's puzzle weren't all there, but that was the thing about a puzzle: you had to get the shape, work out what was missing.

When he returned, I said, 'Gregor, we could, in theory, kill Sven, putting poison in his wine, or whatever. But how exactly *could* we frame Eric? And how could we lay a false trail to suggest he tried to frame someone else? Who would the someone else be? And how would we make that false trail discoverable but not too discoverable? It's impossibly complicated.'

This time, Gregor's laugh seemed ridiculous. How could this list of difficulties put him in a good mood?

'You don't play chess?' he said. 'But you know that we Russians do. We love to think out moves and counter-moves and counter-counter-moves. So here we have a different game on our board. Let's have fun with it.'

'And how would we start?' There was no harm in this, as long as I saw it as a theoretical exercise.

'Well.' He clasped his hands in his lap. 'We can't tie down the details until we have done a full reconnaissance. You will have to insinuate yourself into the life of Eric and Joy. You'll have to observe the patterns of their

behaviour, so that we can decide how to switch the bottles of wine in the first place…'

'How could we reseal the bottle after we'd put the toxin in?'

'You add a touch of glue. Then there's a little resistance when the top is opened, as everyone expects.'

'You've done this before?'

'Don't be silly. I'm hypothesising. Next, for framing Eric, we might need to plant evidence in his house, for example. So we'll to know where and when and how to do that. You'll have to worm your way into their house, so that your presence there is unremarkable. Can you do that?'

I noticed our verb tenses; I was using 'would' and he was using 'will'.

'Can you?' he repeated.

I thought of Joy's ambition to draw me nude. 'I think so,' I said.

'Good. It will help if, as part of your reconnaissance, you also insinuate yourself into Sven's life, or at least his mind. Don't become a regular caller at his house and *never* phone him. If you did, you'd be on the list of suspects at once. But find a way whereby you might be able to manipulate him, if necessary. Might that be possible?'

Now I thought of the gleam in Sven's eye when I was introduced to him.

'I could try.'

'Excellent.'

'But I still don't have the *faintest* clue about the false trail.'

'No?' Gregor swept a hand over his jaw. 'I think the false trail might itself be part of the evidence against Eric. If he *seems* to have lain a false trail, the police will ask, why would he do that if he's not guilty? Give me time to play with an idea. Eric will have a smartphone, and so will Sven. Everyone does

155

these days. Joy will have both numbers on *her* phone. And you have Joy's number?'

'Yes.'

'Can you give me it?'

I found the number and read it off to him. He wrote it on a notepad on which he'd scribbled a series of chess moves.

'I can give this to my friends in Moscow. They can access it, get the numbers for Eric and Sven, and access *their* phones. In fact, they can take them over, do anything with them that their owners can. What is a smartphone, after all, if not a computer on a network? So they can send messages that will appear to come from Sven or Eric, delete them, make phone calls, access emails, take photographs. We can use this, I'm sure, although I don't yet know how.'

I could dimly imagine possibilities. Pamela's technology boys might have offered something similar, but I couldn't approach them. With the possible exception of Pamela herself, no one around Holyrood should have any inkling of this.

I was thinking about *doing* it?

Chapter 13

Friday, 19th

'Feeling better?' The dragon in the office handed me the little form on which you had to tell all your lies about why you had been absent. She was a solid matron, a big cheese in the Women's Institute, and I could see that she thought I was a wimp. Why should I care? I was here today and I'd be gone tomorrow.

But I did care.

'Yes, thank you.' I wasn't going to give her a list of imaginary residual symptoms. She'd see at once that I was protesting too much.

I filled in the form on the spot and hurried out, almost bumping into Sharon.

'Hi,' she said. 'Feeling better?'

Same words. Very different sentiment. But I couldn't tell even Sharon the truth. She was looking bright – too bright, perhaps.

'Yes, thank you. Did you get a please-take for me?'

'I did, but don't worry about it.'

'I'm sorry. You must be so busy.'

'Well, my debating girls are keen. But it keeps me going.'

She needed something to keep her going?

She said, 'Will you have a minute after school?'

'For you? How can you doubt it?'

I lost count during the day of the number of times I was asked about my health. A few of the enquirers might have been concerned, but most, I felt, were either ritualistically polite or else, like the dragon, downright sceptical. *Feeling stressed, were you? Aren't we all?*

Joy was probably sceptical, but at least she wasn't snide about it. 'Migraine?' she said when I met her at morning interval. 'Nasty.'

She came into my room after the last class had gone. 'None the worse for a day in the classroom?'

'No. In fact, it's good to get back into a routine.'

'You've been doing too much? Too much sex?'

She didn't – she couldn't – know about Gregor. So she really thought Colin was insatiable?

'Not exactly.'

'You need a quiet weekend, reclining on a couch.'

Ah.

'Oh?'

'Eric's off on another electioneering tour from Saturday. Fetlar first – the visit he should have made last weekend – then Foula.'

'He's on full throttle?'

'Well.' She hesitated. 'I'm not sure for how long, because the offer for the hotel in Sutherland hasn't materialised yet. Some question mark over the survey. That could put a damper on his spirits. But a girl has to live while she can. Why don't you come out on Saturday afternoon?'

Gregor and I had agreed that we would go ahead *as if* we were going to implement our plot. He would order the batrachotoxin – he made it sound like something you could buy on Amazon – and I would start the reconnaissance. So this invitation was the one I needed.

'You still want to draw me?'

The twitch of her lips was at least mischievous, more probably lascivious. It was certainly a yes. 'Say two o'clock? Then you'll be able to get back into Lerwick for more sex in the evening, if required.'

'Of course.'

I had almost forgotten about Sharon, but she appeared as soon as Joy had gone.

She was frowning. 'I've just passed Joy and she's still not talking to me.'

'Because of your spat about Eric watching or not watching porn?'

A twitch had developed below Sharon's left eye. 'Don't know.'

She sat down, and her conversation jumped, as it often did. 'I'd have texted you yesterday, but I heard you had a migraine and I thought you might be sleeping. Are you sure you're all right?'

'I'm sure. And you? How's Robert?'

She beamed. 'I'd go so far as to say he's a changed boy. He and Mary got on really well.'

'Good.'

She said, 'What are you doing this weekend?'

I told her – a little – about Pamela, and then about going out to Joy's on Saturday. We had a midterm holiday on Monday, but I didn't comment on that, because I hoped I might have the day in Gregor's arms.

She made a face. 'Oh well, we can hit the town another time. I wanted to ask you about something. The girls are still saying to me, what exactly *is* patriotism? How does it operate on a psychological level? Why are people patriotic? They feel – quite rightly, I think – that it's *the* central issue.'

I'd meant to consider this, because I wanted to provide all the help I could. 'Somebody put it to me that patriotism is the last refuge, not of a scoundrel but of someone looking for meaning.'

'I don't get it.'

I wasn't sure that I did either. 'Well, maybe it's when you're not sure who you are or what the purpose of your life is, then you drift towards a group or a belief that seems to give you an identity.'

'So patriotism is a fig leaf for insecurity?'

'Yes.'

'Isn't that pathetic?'

'Of course it is.'

'I wonder if the girls can put that over.'

'Stress the positive. Stress how wonderful it is to accept your insecurity and so open your mind to everything and everybody in the world.'

'Debbie might be able to do it. She's the star of my team.'

I left Sharon pondering strategies, and went back to my flat meaning to call Colin. We hadn't been in contact since Monday, when I'd left the Norseman to walk myself home. I wondered whether he'd just been busy or whether he'd sniffed the air and deduced that I wasn't keen. If the latter, this might be the perfect moment to give him the old story, *You're a really nice person, but....*

I picked up the phone and put it back down again. The temptation to end the relationship was strong. It would be so pleasant to walk to Gregor's openly, with no need to jump behind bushes. Hadn't Colin served his purpose?

Yet I was wary of Billy, because I felt *he* was wary of *me*. If I hurt his little brother, he might step up enquiries in Edinburgh.

So, when Colin answered his phone – he was still at work – I told him about 'my old friend from university' who was 'coming up for the weekend', but then I suggested that I go round to his flat later.

He said, 'Are you sure?'

Here we were. Any hesitation, any coolness of tone, anything other than full-throated certainty would convey a message he couldn't miss.

'Of course I'm sure. It might be around ten o'clock.'

'That'll be fine.'

I had already phoned Helen and suggested we meet at the Norseman at seven. I called again, just to be sure, and she said she was looking forward to a blowout at Pamela's expense. I asked what her extortion plans were, but she wouldn't tell me.

Pamela was waiting in the Ross Hotel, sipping a G&T. More significant, she was chatting to a tall man with long black hair who could have been an ambassador for the Chippendales. Her dress was almost modest, with only a genteel décolletage, but she had some kind of bra that pushed her breasts up and out. For someone her age, she was adept at catching the eye.

Mr Chippendale, however, was neither ogling her nor flirting with her. As I approached, from behind Pamela, I caught a phrase about 'the structure of the industry'. I took this to mean the oil industry, and I assumed that Pamela was interested in this fellow on at least two levels. Yes, sex and money.

Again, she didn't introduce me. Indeed, after saying hello, she virtually ignored me, taking her time about finishing her drink and standing up. 'Where are you having dinner?' she said to Mr Chippendale.

He stood up too, the gallant gentleman. 'The Shetland Hotel.' I couldn't place his accent.

'I may see you later.'

'It would be my pleasure.'

Out in the wind, I said, 'Who's he?'

'Mind your own damn business.'

'I see.'

She scowled at me. 'Sometimes, Carol, I don't like your manner.'

'Sorry.'

She stomped along for a few yards. 'Right. Plan B?'

'Hold on. Are we ready for Helen?'

'What d'you mean?' Pamela was ready to bite my nose off. 'I'm going to grill her about how Popov got that story. See if she slips up.'

You couldn't argue with Pamela. I pleaded, 'Just don't give me away.'

'Christ.' Her fury was boiling over. 'Will you stop implying I'm stupid? Now tell me about Plan B.'

I was reluctant, because Plan B could be a phantasy – and if it wasn't, Pamela could use it against me at some later date. But I couldn't stall her, not in her present mood.

'Sorenson's stuck for cash. His bank is about to foreclose on his mortgage. His father-in-law is rich but has terminal Parkinson's.'

She got it at once. 'Christ. You're going to kill the father-in-law and frame Sorenson.'

'That's it.' I'd *decided*?

'How?' Pamela didn't give a thought to the morality.

I couldn't give her all the details, because I didn't have them. What could I do but bluff?

'I'll tell you if you want, but I'm not sure: if I tell you too much, won't you be an accessory?'

'Shit.' She thought about that, as her curiosity fought with her desire to cover her back. 'I suppose you're right. But give me a clue.'

'Suffice to say there will be poison in a bottle of wine Eric buys for his father-in-law.'

'What poison?'

'Not quite sure yet.' I certainly wasn't going to tell her about Gregor and his batrachotoxin.

'Mm. You said that Sorenson was a Graham Greene fan. There's a bit in *The Human Factor* – I actually re-read it this week – where Castle's colleague gets poisoned by aflatoxin. If you used that, it might provide a small piece of circumstantial evidence, the suggestion being that Sorenson got the idea from Greene.'

'Good point.' I didn't think it was a good point at all; 'evidence' like that would hardly swing a case.

In true Pamela style, she wanted to pursue her own brilliant idea. 'How could you source it?' she said.

'Aflatoxin? I'd need to look into it. Might be difficult.'

'*I* could source it, but I don't want to leave a trail.'

'Leave a *trail*?' I feigned surprise, to imply that an expert in spycraft would find that a trivial problem.

She said nothing for quite a while – she'd be wondering how she could organise a cut-out that was fail safe – and then said, 'Yes. Yes. Okay. My supplier – let me call him that – is very efficient. If he has it in stock, so to speak, he'll get it to you by the beginning of next week. Your landlady wouldn't open any parcels?'

'Absolutely not.'

I was pretty sure that I wouldn't be using aflatoxin. Pamela might find out eventually that I hadn't, but by that time, I hoped, she would be out of a job and bereft of power.

We walked for fifty yards. 'You can get away with this?' she said. 'If you get caught, you're on your own.'

'Understood.' *Thank you for your support in this matter.*

Helen was in the Norseman, at the same corner banquette. This time, she hadn't washed her hair and was wearing a tatty old tee-shirt. This time, they didn't shake hands.

When Pamela took off her coat, Helen fired her first missile. 'New bra?'

I sighed. Helen, I suspected, was ready for an all-out war; she'd considered the idea of working for Pamela and rejected it, because some things weren't worth any money.

Pamela snapped, 'You pass a lot of remarks.' Then she controlled herself and said to me, 'Carol, why don't you get us some drinks?'

We'd all taken a seat. Helen, sitting opposite Pamela, had fixed her with a very steady gaze. 'Wait a minute,' she said. 'You owe Carol forty quid for last week. You fucked off before you'd paid your share. Plus, we need another forty as an advance for this week.'

164

Pamela's face went through a series of rapid transformations. First, there was fury – *How can anyone be so insubordinate?* Then, realisation – *If I don't pay up, this meeting is over.* Then, a blank – the acknowledgement that she had no answer to naked aggression. And, lastly, the pretence that this was all a good joke.

'Hah, you drive a hard bargain.'

'Too right.' Helen waited.

Pamela turned to me. 'Did you know this ambush was coming?' She was trying to keep her voice light, but she'd skin me alive if she thought the answer was yes.

I shook my head. 'Helen's a law unto herself.'

She raised an eyebrow. 'I can imagine. What's eighty pounds among friends?'

'Nothing,' Helen said, 'as long as you pay up.'

Pamela reached into her bag, pulled out four twenties from a purse and handed them to me. 'I'll have a G&T,' she said, her smile as sincere as a crocodile's.

I went up to the bar, ordered two G&Ts and a double vodka. I returned to the table just as Pamela said, 'D'you know a man called Paul McIntyre? I believe he's another Shetland hacker.'

'McIntyre?' Helen was still truculent. 'He's a Free Shetlander fanatic. So I don't know him and I don't want to know him.'

'Right.' At least this was what Pamela wanted to hear. 'So you don't know if he gave that story to Popov Systems? You heard their press conference?'

'I heard it.' Helen snatched her vodka and took a gulp. 'I think it's quite likely that he did.'

Pamela pressed on. 'I can see how the allegation about the Scottish Intelligence Services would be in Free Shetland's interests, but I can't see why Popov Systems would go along with it. How would they profit?'

'Yeah.' Helen dropped her belligerence momentarily. 'Carol asked me the same question, but I don't know the answer. The best I can come up with is that they wanted the publicity. Still, it's odd.'

Helen's puzzlement was obvious. So much so that Pamela seemed satisfied there was no leak to be discovered here. She said, assuming that peace had broken out, 'What about my job offer?' She reached into her bag – I presumed to produce the details of the test that she wanted to give Helen.

Helen, however, finished her vodka and shrugged. I knew for sure what the shrug meant. She'd decided that a truce would be pointless.

'Let's get this right,' she said. 'You want me to install keyloggers, Trojans and the like on the computers of unsuspecting people who have the nerve to argue with your *Party*' – she spat that out – 'the nerve, in fact, to expect free speech. Then you'd dig some dirt and intimidate them into silence. Yeah?'

Pamela jerked backwards. She was so stupid that she hadn't anticipated this. She stumbled for words. 'That's… a very negative way of putting it.'

'Oh?' Helen stretched and blew out a scornful breath. 'Well, let me put it simply. You can fuck off.'

'Food?' I said like an idiot, picking up one of the menus on the table. 'They do a good steak pie here.'

Dignity was everything to Pamela. She drew herself up like a dowager duchess and said to Helen, 'You have an attitude problem.'

Helen sneered. 'Trying to scare me? Be careful. Want to get doxed?'

166

Pamela would have only the vaguest idea of what doxing was. She pretended to look down at the menu, then said, 'I think I'll go up to the Shetland Hotel.'

'We'll stay here,' Helen said. 'We're not used to wine bars and bistros where everyone's up their own arse.'

I thought that was rather hard on the Shetland Hotel, but I wasn't going to argue. Pamela stood up, put on her coat, gave Helen a glare. '*So* nice to meet you,' she said to Helen.

'Fuck off.'

We needed more drinks after that. I fetched another vodka and another G&T. 'You were brilliant,' I said to Helen, though I feared Pamela would make me pay for the débacle. 'I don't know how I ever became remotely friendly with that prima donna.'

She didn't seem interested in the question. Downing half of her vodka in one gulp, she said, 'Didn't I tell you we'd get back at her?'

'You did.'

We drank, I ordered food, and after a while I went to the toilet to text Gregor, giving him a description of Mr Chippendale and saying that I was sure he was staying at the Ross Hotel. His reply came quickly: *This time.* The two words sent my hopes soaring.

About ten o'clock I walked round to Colin's. He had been sitting by his electric fire, reading a book. He looked tired and thin, swathed in a big thick jersey. The room was still a long way short of inviting. He needed to do something with his boarded-up fireplace, he needed a more cheerful source

of heat, he needed to buff and polish his floor, he needed curtains that weren't threadbare, he needed… I didn't know what he needed.

I sat on the arm of his chair, still in my parka. 'How did the evening go?' he said.

I might as well tell the truth. 'Awful. My friend from Edinburgh fell out with my friend from Lerwick. You could have cut the atmosphere with a knife.'

'Dear oh dear.'

His voice was so flat and dead that I wondered if I could change my mind there and then about dumping him.

He offered me a drink.

'No, thanks. I've had enough.'

Silence. Either I went forward or I went back.

'Colin?'

'Yeah?'

'Could I have a shower? Might warm me up.'

'Sure.' He hoisted himself up. 'I'll get you a towel.'

He fetched the towel and switched the shower on. It was one of those electric things that heated the water instantaneously.

'Colin?'

'Yeah?'

'Why don't we have a shower together?'

A flicker of life came to his eyes. 'Good idea.'

It worked, more or less. He soaped my breasts and got an erection. When we were in bed, I pinned him down and made him kiss my nipples. I'd been thinking that one of the reasons for his beta double minus might lie with me.

168

Maybe the act that was good enough for middle-aged men who were blinded by their own importance wasn't good enough for a diffident soul like Colin. So now I threw myself into my performance and he responded, though not spectacularly. All in all, I felt he deserved a beta.

Postcoital tenderness, however, was another challenge; I didn't trust myself to converse, merely snuggled into his shoulder until his breathing slowed and deepened.

For me, sleep was a long time coming. It was dawning on me that, in my manoeuvring for Pamela's job, I had the time scale wrong. It could take me a month or more to get rid of Eric – always assuming I could manage it at all. But if Gregor did get the kompromat tonight and his masters wanted to exploit it immediately, then Pamela could be sacked – and Arnold could convene a selection committee – next week. I wouldn't be ready; I wanted to arrive in that interview room fresh from destroying Free Shetland.

If Gregor got that film, he had to hold it back for a few weeks.

Chapter 14

Saturday, 20th

At breakfast, when Colin had checked his watch for the third time, I said, 'Got a busy day ahead?'

He grimaced. 'I'm supposed to be going to Fetlar and Foula with Eric.'

Marvellous.

I said, 'I didn't know *you* were going. When should you leave?'

'Soon. I'm really, really sorry.'

'Colin, don't be *silly*. What's your role in the electioneering?'

'Well, Eric likes me to orchestrate the audience.'

'Orchestrate?'

'Yes. I mean, if there are some groups we know are sympathetic to us, I can encourage them discreetly to applaud at the right time, or laugh at Eric's jokes.'

'Eric makes jokes?'

Colin didn't react; he wasn't into jokes much either. 'Yes, he recognises that argument isn't everything. Sometimes, you have to win people's sympathy as a person before you start to win their sympathy for your policies. And then there's Paul.'

'What about Paul?'

'He thinks, since the Popov business, that he's the star of the show. Up till now, Eric's been able to persuade him to stay away from public meetings, because Paul's always liable to lose his cool and so throw away a bundle of

votes. Eric's allowing him to come this time because it's so difficult barring someone who seems to have saved your skin.'

'You have a role in relation to Paul?'

'Yes. It's agreed – by Eric, Paul and me – that I have to stick close to him; if I feel he's getting aggressive, I have to touch his elbow and he'll back off.'

'Will it work?'

'It'll have to.'

'People management?' I said. 'You've got many talents. So when will you be back?'

'Not till Monday. We're staying on Fetlar tonight, flying to Foula on Sunday and spending Sunday night there. But we're hardly back before we're away again. We're going to the west side on Tuesday or Wednesday.'

Even more marvellous. That was my first thought. My second was, *If I'm so glad to see the back of him, how long can I keep pretending?*

I walked to my flat, let half an hour pass so that he'd be clear of the town, then scooted up to North Road.

Gregor had been finishing his breakfast, listening to what sounded like a news bulletin in Russian.

'Late night?' I said.

He clicked off the radio, which had been playing on his computer. 'Till two o'clock. Pamela has stamina.'

'You got film?'

'I did. Give me a minute and we'll watch it together.'

He tidied away his plates. Then we sat on the couch like Derby and Joan.

The first file wasn't a film at all. It was an audio recording, captured, so Gregor said, in the bar of the Ross Hotel. I heard Pamela and a male voice I thought was Mr Chippendale's.

They chatted about Shetland and its awful weather, before Pamela said, 'Your room? Mine's a mess.'

Gregor commented, 'That's her equivalent of switching rooms at the last minute.'

Mr Chippendale agreed that his room would be suitable. Pamela said she'd be there in two minutes.

The recording ended, and I turned to Gregor. 'How did you get this?'

He grinned. 'Ah well, Lieutenant Colonel Mikhail Vasiliev is an experienced operator.'

'A honey trap?' I found that hilarious. 'And you had both rooms wired?'

'No expense spared.'

He started the film, then immediately paused it. 'We had to be prepared,' he said, 'for Pamela arguing that our film was a deepfake. So we've built in various safeguards. One is the capture of her voice. Of course, you can deepfake voices too, so we have taken other precautions. Both the audio and video recordings have GPS and time/date stamps – you'd have guessed that. She'll find it hard to argue these away. Besides, you will see that the video has another telling feature. At least, I think you will.'

He clicked a button, and it wasn't long before we were treated to a full frontal of Pamela lying on the bed and then, when Gregor toggled a switch, one of the young man coming out of the bathroom.

'You had two cameras?' I said.

'Yes. Both high definition. It means that both faces are very clear.'

So they were. I imagined that that would make the production of a deepfake all the more difficult.

'Toggle it back,' I said.

He did, and I peered at the screen. I commented, 'Pamela has quite distinctive aureolae.'

Gregor chuckled. 'Very good. That's the feature I mentioned. There are some gentlemen in Holyrood who will readily recognise them. These good fellows will certainly want to see Pamela dismissed as soon as possible, in case footage emerges of *them* in a similar situation.'

The lieutenant colonel was lightly muscled and well endowed. I had always thought that Pamela might be rather too fleshy for a fit young fellow's taste, but this chap had no difficulty in finding wood. We watched rather too much – I was beginning to feel like a voyeur by the time Gregor clicked off the viewer.

'In due course,' he said, 'a respected journalist – still to be chosen – will be fed the information that Mikhail is a lieutenant colonel in the GRU. Mikhail will be reprimanded, of course, but will acknowledge that he is the man in the film. That should be the final nail in Pamela's coffin.'

'In due course?' I said. 'I wanted to ask you for a delay of about a month.'

'A *month*?'

I explained my reasons. Gregor frowned, then added quickly, 'But of course. Moscow wants you to get the job. It won't be a problem. All the same, we should get ahead with our plan, don't you think? What's to be gained from putting things off?'

I had no answer. In fact, I worried that there would be factions in Moscow who wouldn't want to wait a month.

Gregor said he had to go back to Unst to oversee some step in the feminisation of his halibut. Two 10ml containers of batrachotoxin, securely wrapped in what looked like an Amazon package, would arrive in his absence and be delivered to me.

I told him about Pamela's aflatoxin.

'Mm,' he said. 'Don't throw it away. I was thinking that we shouldn't try to plant batrachotoxin in Eric's house, because that would be too obvious, but if the police discovered *afla*toxin, a prosecutor might argue that this showed Eric had been investigating toxins in general.'

'So I'd have to plant the aflatoxin?'

'Yes.'

I said, 'Why *two* containers of batrachotoxin?'

'Well, suppose we reconnoitre Tesco a few days in advance and we find that they have two kinds of cheap Chilean red – I would say it's unlikely that they will have more than two. We won't know which kind Eric or Joy is going to buy for Sven.'

'So we'll have to have two doctored bottles ready?' *All right, future tense.*

'Yes.'

'How do we find out which bottle to use? And how will we do the swap?'

'I'm not sure about either of these yet. First we need very precise detail on Joy and Eric's routines – do they take strict turns in buying Sven's groceries, for example? – and also Sven's routines, in case, say, he's in the habit of having friends or neighbours round and they could turn up at some critical moment.'

The die was cast, the Rubicon crossed. I said, 'I'm visiting Joy this afternoon. I'll see what I can do.'

I thought it might be worthwhile to check out the location of Sven's croft. I had gathered that it was called da Kame and lay a few miles west of Joy and Eric's house. So, before I set out to launch my career as a nude model, I had a look at Google Maps.

There it was: da Kame, on a long track on which and near which no other habitation was marked.

The track was easy enough to find. A wooden sign pointed left and beside it a big black mailbox was emblazoned in gold with 'Henderson, da Kame'. I pulled in and tried to note everything that might be relevant. There wasn't a single house with a view of the turn-off, and the track dipped quickly down the side of a ridge; after a minute or two, any car on it would not be visible from the main road, although its headlights might. The road itself wasn't busy, even on a Saturday afternoon. After dark, when the business of the week was over and the traffic had dwindled further, I would be very unlucky indeed if my car was recognised.

I did a U-turn and drove back towards Joy's.

She was pleased to see me. 'Come in. You still haven't brought your toothbrush, but you can still stay the night if you want to.'

She took me into the kitchen, where she was making coffee. I had a quick scan round for a bag that might contain Sven's groceries, but there wasn't one.

When she poured the coffee, I said, 'Can I have some milk?' I went to the fridge and glanced round. Here too there was no bag or item that was clearly separate from everything else.

Sven's groceries were already at his croft.

We sat at the kitchen table. 'Any change with Colin?' she said. 'Is he relaxing yet?'

'Ah.' I wondered whether I should lay some groundwork, so that it wouldn't come as a complete surprise when I finally gave Colin the heave. 'Not really.'

'Dear oh dear.' She shook her head. 'Shall we go through and get started?'

'Sure.'

In the studio, she'd pulled her desk out towards the sofa, and cleared it of everything except an A3 piece of drawing paper and some pencils. She had a stool beside it, which she sat on as she drank her coffee. I sat on the sofa and drank mine.

'I thought I'd do two drawings,' she said. 'Both of them with you reclining. One facing me and one facing away.

'I hope you do justice to my bum.'

She finished her coffee and put the cup on the floor. I did likewise.

I didn't feel embarrassed at all. There are things that are a lot more humiliating. When my clothes were a neat bundle beside the sofa, I said, 'So? What's first? Full frontal?'

'Why not? Just lie against the back of the sofa and make yourself as comfortable as possible.'

I did my best, though the material under my skin was a little scratchy. Joy did some ready reckoning with her pencil and her fingers, made some marks on her paper and then said, 'Here we go. I find it best just to let it flow.'

Her pencil swept across the paper. I had to admire her confidence and skill, because she didn't once have recourse to a rubber. At first, I followed the direction of her gaze, so that I knew when she was focusing on my head, my shoulders, my arms or my legs, but then my attention began to wander

and I became quite drowsy. When she gave me official permission, as it were, to close my eyes, I might have dozed off if the couch had been a little more comfortable.

I couldn't have said how long she had been drawing and I had been drowsing – maybe an hour and a half – when all of a sudden she threw down her pencil and said, 'What was that?'

I woke up. 'What was what?'

'I thought I heard a car.'

As the parking circle was on the other side of the house, I thought she must have superhuman hearing. But, sure enough, in another few minutes we heard a door bang.

'Who the hell is that?' She put down her pencil and went off to investigate. Very quickly, she was back. 'It's dad. I'll need to see what he wants. Sorry.'

She didn't close the door behind her. I slipped across, pulled it further open, and listened. The two voices were barely audible – I thought they were coming from the kitchen. Could I learn anything? Some detail that Gregor and I could use? I tiptoed along the hall to the corner where it turned down to the living room and kitchen.

Joy's voice was now clear. She was saying, 'You could hurt yourself.'

I slid into the living room and checked the hatch into the kitchen. It was partially open, forcing me to stay out of the dining alcove. Never mind: I could hear them perfectly.

Joy was agitated. 'But you know your hand shakes. And the sheep's completely slippery with its own blood. You could cut your hand off.'

A grunt. 'Stop fussing. I've been butchering my own sheep for years.'

'And if Charlie Mann saw you, he'd report you in a shot. He's dying to get even.'

Who was Charlie Mann? A neighbour? And what had Sven done to him?

'Huh. Charlie wouldn't dare. Now do you want this lamb or not? It won't all go in my freezer.'

'What am I going to do with you?' Joy was softening. 'All right, thank you.'

A phone – the landline – shrilled beside me, making me jump. *Damn.* I was going to get caught.

But there was another phone in the kitchen. Joy answered it. 'Hello? Jenny? Good to hear from you. How… ? Oh no… Oh no.'

There was a long pause. I should have hurried back to the studio. Then Joy said, 'I'll come down next weekend… of course I will.'

It really was time to go. Sven could come wandering through at any moment.

I went into the hall and was at the corner when I heard a deep rumble. 'Hello, there.'

I turned my head. He was looking at my bum, and I knew what I had to do. *Get him begging.* So I faced him, declaring that I was quite happy he should see me naked.

I said, 'What are you doing here?'

'Bringing Joy some lamb. What are *you* doing?'

'I'm modelling for her.'

'I don't believe you're a lesbian.'

I let my gaze roam over his stubble. 'Sometimes, the Viking of one's choice is not available.'

His eyes shone. There's no fool like an old fool.

'You must come and see my croft sometime.'

178

I raised my brows. I had to express interest, no more. It would be overdoing things if I suggested unbridled lust.

There was something I needed to check. 'I wouldn't like to intrude on your social gatherings,' I said.

'I don't have social gatherings.'

That seemed blunt enough.

'Dad!' Joy had finished her phone call. 'Where are you?'

She came into the hall, saw the tableau, and exclaimed, 'Dad! What are you doing?'

Sven smirked. 'Having a chat.'

'Have you no thought for a girl's modesty?'

I got in quickly, imagining that I might stir Sven's interest even further. 'This girl has no modesty. Don't you have naturists in Shetland?'

'*Well.*' Joy, for once, was stuck for words.

'Did I smell coffee?' Sven said.

'Not for you.' Joy took his arm and started to bundle him back along the hall. 'You're going home. We're busy.'

'Can see that.' He let himself be bundled, though he looked over his shoulder to wink and say, 'Catch you later.'

I heard them arguing all the way to the back door, she telling him to get a girlfriend of his own, he saying that she couldn't expect to keep every attractive woman to herself. I supposed I should be flattered.

In the studio, I examined the model ships. There was one in particular – of a luxury yacht – that must have taken ages to build. I gripped the superstructure in my knuckles and found that it lifted off, revealing quite a spacious interior. I replaced the deck, then turned to the books, picking out

The Human Factor and flicking through the pages to see if I could track down the mention of aflatoxin.

Joy came in and said, 'You made a hit there, but I'm telling you, don't give him an inch or he'll take a mile.

I put the book back. 'He hasn't got a girlfriend?'

'He's a lonely old git. Everybody avoids him. I can't remember the last time even we went out for dinner. His idea of a good Saturday night is slow cooking a leg of his own lamb and then at eight o'clock opening his wine.'

This could be gold dust. 'Eight o'clock? On the dot?'

'His habits are more entrenched than the British army at the Somme.'

I settled on the couch. Joy sat on her stool and picked up her pencil. After a few sighs, she restarted her drawing. My mind was running on what I'd learned. Sven opened his wine at eight? And Charlie Mann? Somebody Sven had made an enemy of? If Eric were going to try to blame someone for Sven's murder, would Charlie Mann be a candidate?

Suppose… suppose Gregor's associates, when they'd taken control of Sven's phone, sent a fake message to Eric that Charlie Mann had visited, and suppose this message could somehow be revealed to the police as a fake… I couldn't fill in all the moves.

How plausible was it that Eric would cast Charlie Mann as a fall guy? What kind of person *was* Charlie? Would it help if I went to his house and had a snoop?

Joy had thrown down her pencil. 'My concentration's blown,' she said. 'I got a call there from a friend of mine who's been diagnosed with breast cancer. I can't help thinking about her.'

'What can you do? Where is she?'

'Edinburgh. I promised to fly down next weekend.'

180

Next weekend? So Eric would do Sven's shopping.

'You're very loyal.'

She was staring at my breasts, and I'd have been willing to bet that she was seeing not mine but her friend's. This was a special friend, I deduced.

'Shall we call it a day?' I said.'

'I'm so sorry. I think I should call her back.'

I dressed slowly, not wanting to appear too eager to escape. We carried the coffee cups through to the kitchen, and she apologised again. I told her, just as I had told Colin, not to be silly.

One of those thick Shetland mists had come down, blotting out what little daylight there was. I headed towards Lerwick just in case Joy was observing me, but after a mile or two I turned and drove back. If Charlie Mann was a neighbour of Sven's, I should be able to find him.

It was difficult in the mist, but I drove slowly, looking out for signposts on the left. I was about half a mile beyond the turn-off to Sven's when I saw another track. A cottage with some outbuildings was visible from the road, a bare light in an uncurtained window only adding to its bleak appearance. I pulled in and my headlights caught a rotting wooden sign. When I clambered out and walked over, I could just about decipher the words *White Knowes*. A mailbox that had fallen off the post – I could see the mark of the clamp – was lying on the ground, where it had been sprayed with mud by passing vehicles. I had to go back to the car and fetch a tissue to wipe off some of the mud before I could read the name. It was Mann.

So what could I deduce about Charlie? His mailbox hinted that he wasn't on top of his life, but was he sour and bitter or merely lazy? Did he have a serious grudge against Sven? I needed more information.

I turned the car again and steered cautiously through the mist to Lerwick.

I was closing the door of my flat behind me when my phone beeped. A message from Helen. *Have a look at these photos. From natasha at the halibut place on unst. Something very odd.*

So Natasha had ignored Helen's warning.

I took off my parka and put the fire on before I examined the images. The first one showed a structure like a quay, curving along the side of a bay; about half way along, extending over the water, was a darker shape. In the second, it was clearer that this shape was a shed or boathouse.

But the third and the fourth photographs were the ones that startled me. They revealed that beside the boathouse, in the sea, lay a black object that I guessed – though nothing offered itself as a yardstick – was about two metres long. It had a formation on its back like a dorsal fin, two more on its sides like pectoral fins, and a tail. From the rear and from a distance, you might have thought that it was a shark.

But it wasn't a shark. It was a vessel of some sort, perhaps a submarine, certainly a drone, because it had no hatch and I was sure it was too small to accommodate even one person. This – I *knew* – had nothing to do with halibut; it had some military purpose.

A cold sensation, somewhere between embarrassment and fear, curled round my stomach. Gregor was no mere halibut farmer. I had closed my eyes to the obvious.

He was an utter bastard.

I had no sooner condemned him than I scrambled to excuse him. Maybe he had been economical with the truth because that was what his masters demanded. You could hardly expect a spy to be utterly candid. Maybe –

wasn't this what mattered? – he at least hadn't been lying when he said he was attracted to me.

I had to check beneath this stone. Making up my mind there and then, I packed a bag, including my binoculars and my night vision goggles. Then I consulted the ferry timetables, because I had to go to Unst.

Chapter 15

Sunday, 21st

To get to Unst from Lerwick is a slow haul, but not a long one. On the first leg, you drive up the Shetland mainland until you reach a place called Toft. I'd decided not to set off until the morning, and my plan was to catch a ferry there at 9.45. It's only twenty-eight miles; so I left at five to nine, thinking I'd have plenty of time.

I hadn't reckoned with the mist, which hadn't cleared at all. It blanketed the road, with the result that no one could see to overtake, and gradually a long convoy built up, crawling along at not much more than thirty-five miles per hour. It was 9.43 on my watch when I rolled onto the terminal and into the open jaws of the blue and white ferry.

The crossing took a mere twenty minutes. On Yell, another convoy, though shorter, formed ahead of me. As green pastures – surprisingly green – slid past on my left, my thoughts jumped to Gregor. Had I been *totally* naïve to trust him?

I ran through the arguments. On the one hand, he did know a lot about halibut, and I couldn't disprove his claim that the intelligence services had recruited him only temporarily. On the other, he managed, with suspicious ease, to order up batrachotoxin, and produce a young stud to tempt Pamela . I had to assume the worst and follow the evidence. That was why I was here.

The convoy slowed when it swung across the barren heather moor that sat at the centre of the island, then it slowed again, dramatically. I wasn't

concerned. The time was 10.25 and, as far as I remembered, there was a ferry at eleven. I would be on Unst at ten past, and in Baltasound, which I had decided would be my first port of call, by the half hour. Since I didn't know where the halibut hatchery was, I needed a guide, and who better than Jason Young, from my second-year class? He had told me that his father drank at the hotel, and there was only one hotel on Unst – the Baltasound, where I had already booked a room. The proprietor would surely be able to direct me.

The mist thinned, the convoy stopped. About a dozen sheep ambled off the road, encouraged by a shaggy collie. A mud-splattered tractor swung off behind them. Now the convoy lumbered into motion and hit a staggering forty miles an hour as we bypassed Mid Yell and turned north.

We looped round the head of a sea loch – a voe – and headed east towards the ferry terminal at Gutcher. The mist blew away completely, revealing a splendid view across the water to another island – I thought it might be Unst. A ferry was in mid-channel, like a toy in a child's bathtub, but it was heading away from the terminal.

Gutcher consisted of a few houses dotted round another of those green swards that break up the brown Shetland heather. To the right of the terminal was a café, in a good state of repair but deserted, and on the left a causeway led between a loch and the sea towards a rather ugly quarry and a big forbidding house that sat below a row of wind turbines. There were four lanes at the pier. Lanes One and Two – 'Booked' and 'Unbooked' – were for Belmont on Unst, and both were empty. I pulled into Lane Two.

Lanes Three and Four were for Hamar Ness on Fetlar. A single vehicle, an old, dirty Vauxhall estate car, sat in Lane Four. When I went to speak to the driver, an old chap with a grey ponytail, he wound down his window.

'Hi,' I said. 'The next ferry is at eleven?'

185

'Aye, for Hamar Ness. Twelve-fifty if you're going to Belmont.'

'Damn. I must have misread the timetable. Any place I can get a cup of coffee? I see the café's shut.'

'You could try the Old Post Office. They might take pity on you.'

'Thank you.'

The Old Post Office, recognisable by the red phone box standing outside, was a neat building, its windows freshly timbered, its stone smoothed with careful rendering. But there was no one in.

Though the sky was now blue, the wind that had blown away the mist had brought the temperature down several degrees. I could go back to the car and run the heater or I could go for a brisk walk.

I chose the latter, heading south. In a couple of minutes I passed some farm buildings and after that there was no sign of life except for the ubiquitous sheep. After about a quarter of an hour, I was coming down a gentle slope towards the mouth of a sizeable burn when I saw, fifty yards ahead of me, stretched on south-facing rocks, what seemed to be two bundles of brown carpet.

At thirty yards I saw that they were otters, turning their faces to the sun like beach babes who wanted to polish their tan. I may have made some slight noise, or perhaps they caught my scent, because they sat up, one twitched a head towards me, then they slid down into the water.

They made me think at once of Gavin Maxwell and his Camusfeàrna. The Outsider – l'Etranger – that's what Maxwell was. Like me. Sometimes, just sometimes, fine words, such as Maxwell's or Gregor's or mine, don't cut it; sometimes, being an outsider makes you shiver.

I was beginning to shiver for real, because that wind was cutting through my parka. When I turned, the icy blast took all feeling from my forehead. I

marched back to the pier, waved to the man in Lane Four, climbed into the Honda, and switched on the heater at full blast.

The ferry for Hamar Ness came sidling in, two vans came off and the dirty Vauxhall drove on in regal solitude. A Landrover pulled in behind me. This was excitement, Gutcher-style.

This crossing was shorter – ten minutes. The drive up through the moors to Baltasound took another ten or so. I was defrosting, just a little, by the time I'd checked into the hotel, ordered a bowl of fish soup, told the landlord I was a teacher in Lerwick and asked about Jason Young.

'Jason? You've come all the way from the deep south to check that he's doing his homework?'

'Not exactly. We have a holiday tomorrow, and I thought I would see the wilder shores of Shetland. So Jason seemed like a promising guide to the wonders of Unst.'

'The wonders of Unst? You into birds?'

'Birds? Not really.'

'Radar masts?'

'Er, no.'

'Viking longhouses?'

'Seen one, seen 'em all.'

'No worries. Jason'll take you round all the night clubs and opium dens.'

'Great.'

He gave me directions, which sounded straightforward. The Youngs lived in a cottage, 'in need of some whitewash', on the road towards the school; a big pile of orange gas cylinders in the front garden should act as a flag. I

finished my soup, which was very good, and set off under a sky where grey clouds from the east were already spilling over the blue.

The Youngs' house was unmissable, but no one answered my knock on the front porch. I pushed the door open, trod carefully through wellington boots, fishing rods and lobster creels, and tried the main door. It opened.

'Hello? Anyone there?'

Apparently not.

I went out to the road and along to the next habitation on the left. This was another cottage, in rather better repair, its whitewash newish, its windows picked out in dark red paint. A buxom middle-aged dame in severe black glasses came to the door.

'Yes?'

I explained that I was looking for the Youngs.

'Who *are* you?'

'I teach in Lerwick. I teach their son, Jason. We've got a holiday and I thought he might show me around a bit of Unst.'

She looked me up and down. I was wearing walking shoes, black jeans and my parka. Surely I didn't look like a child-molester?

'Show you around?'

'Yes.'

'In *February*?'

'Yes.'

She examined my face. I supposed that on Unst you never knew when you might have to pick someone out in a line-up. Taking off her glasses, she scraped a piece of something out of the corner of her eye, then put her glasses back on and examined me some more.

188

'They'll be fishing.'

'Ah.' Finding Jason, which I had thought would be simple, might turn out to a road with many turns. 'The whole family?'

'Mrs Young is not there.'

'I see.'

'Jason will probably be round the harbour somewhere.'

'Right. Thank you.'

When she didn't add anything, I stepped back and repeated, 'Thank you.' When she still didn't speak, I said, 'Bye for now.'

She watched me all the way to my car.

The harbour, less than fifty yards from the hotel, was formed by a big quay shaped like a hook and a smaller hook inside the big one. I parked and walked along the main quay, on which a blue sign declared – in five languages – that the landing of animals from abroad was not allowed. By now, the wind was merciless, and the dome of the sky was shaded in grey almost from one horizon to another. Some containers festooned with nets sat above a forlorn fishing boat and I wondered if Jason might be sheltering among them.

He wasn't, and there was absolutely no one around.

As I retreated towards the car, a grizzled man in yellow oilskins stepped out of a red-roofed bungalow-like building. 'Can I help you?' he said.

'I'm looking for a boy, Jason Young. His neighbour told me that he might be down here fishing.'

'Too cold for that.'

'Yes.'

He waited, I waited.

'Jason in trouble?' he said.

'Not at all. I'm his teacher and I have a day's holiday. I thought he might show me around.'

'Show you around?'

Not again.

I nodded.

'Well,' he said, waving an arm towards the smaller quay, 'he'll be at the marina. The Browns' boat. Go up the pontoon. Second from the end on the right.'

'Thank you.'

'You're welcome. Ah, wait. The entrance to the pontoon may be locked. If it is, come back and get me.' He jerked a thumb towards the bungalow.

There *was* a lock, set in a weatherbeaten blue door, but someone had left it on the snib. I stepped down onto the pontoon, which ran straight up the middle of the little marina, and saw that the boats were nearly all cabin cruisers. The one that was second from the end wasn't the smartest; it was wooden, for one thing, and I reckoned that the algae marring its once-white paint would take a lot of effort to sand down and obliterate.

Three figures, all of them wrapped in hooded parkas, were sitting round a table in the cabin, playing cards. They didn't notice my arrival.

I shouted, 'Hi.'

Three faces turned. I recognised Jason. He put down his cards and came out onto the deck.

'Hey, miss, what you doing here?'

'I thought I'd see the sights of Unst.'

A young man with craggy, handsome features had emerged. He stepped forwards and said, offering his hand, 'Come on board.'

I clambered on and let them lead me into the cabin. The third person was a girl; locks of blonde hair escaped from the neck of her parka and her bright blue eyes smiled at me.

We introduced ourselves. I said I was Carol, though Jason knew me as Miss Rutherford. They were Malcolm and Annette.

'Mr and Mrs Brown,' Jason declared.

They seemed a happy couple. I said, 'Just married?'

Malcolm put a big arm round his wife's shoulder. 'Two years.'

'With number one on the way.' Jason was determined to spill their secrets.

I said to Annette, 'When's the new arrival due?'

She patted her stomach. 'The middle of June.'

'That's handy. Jason will be able to take the baby for a walk in the pram during his holidays.'

Jason spluttered, 'Aye, right.'

Annette said, 'Would you like a cup of tea?'

There was a tiny stove in a corner, and beside it a collection of mugs any one of which, surely, would bring acute bacterial poisoning. But Annette wanted to make me feel welcome, and I hadn't the heart to say no.

We played cards, I drank the bitter, milk-free tea, they poked fun at Jason about being a godfather and the serious duties it would involve. Sleet began to swirl against the windows, turning more and more to snow, blotting out the world except for the four of us.

I had the absurd feeling that I was on holiday. Then that slid into an emotion even more bizarre. On the ferry from Gutcher, I had fallen through a wormhole into another universe. What was the difference in this one? I couldn't say exactly, but it was something in the bright eyes of the other

three, in their quick smiles and their laughter, in the way they accepted me and were willing to cement a friendship within minutes.

But tomorrow I would go back through the wormhole, to that other world of plotting and subterfuge and struggles for power.

We played for half an hour or so, until a phone rang inside Annette's parka. She fished it out, and her laughter died as she answered it. 'Oh,' she said. 'Right.'

'What's up?' Malcolm said.

'It's Mum. She's had one of her turns. We'd better go.'

I gave Jason a lift to his house. He had a bucket with three silver-and-black fish that I hadn't noticed in the cabin. They had been neatly gutted and decapitated. When I pulled up, he gestured at them and said, 'Want some fish and chips?'

It was only half past four. Despite the greyness and the snow, some daylight lingered. My plan, in so far as I had one, was to approach the hatchery under cover of complete darkness.

'Sure.'

Mr Young still wasn't at home. Jason switched on an electric fire in the untidy living room and took his fish through to the kitchen. I followed.

Two big frying pans and a pot of oil with a drainage basket stood on the cooker, which was connected to a gas cylinder like the ones in the front garden. Jason poured a little oil into each pan and turned the cooker on. From an oversized brown bag behind the back door, he pulled out dirt-covered potatoes, transferred them to the sink and began to wash, then peel them.

I said, 'You make chips from scratch?'

'How else d'you do it?'

'Buy them already prepared from the supermarket.'

'No Tesco's on Unst. And no spare cash.'

In any case, he was so deft and quick that in a race against oven-ready chips he would have won. He had the whole process – preparation, cooking, serving – completed in about twenty-five minutes. We carried the plates to the living room, where he removed a *Shetland Times* from the table to reveal two placemats.

We ate greedily – the food was tasty and comforting – before he said, 'What d'you want to see on Unst?'

There was no point in being coy. 'Remember I asked you about the Russians and their halibut hatchery?'

'Yeah.'

'Where is it, exactly?'

'Woodwick beach. It's not far, but they don't allow visitors. Didn't I tell you?'

'You did. But there's talk that odd things are going on there. I thought it might be fun to spy on them.'

'They'll see you a mile away.'

'Not if we go in the dark.'

'You want to go *in the dark? Tonight?*'

I felt guilty – perhaps there would be unpleasantness if the Russians caught us and accused us of trespassing – but Jason didn't take much convincing. I supposed he wanted to show what an intrepid guide he was. He put together a picnic consisting of bread and cheese, chocolate from his mother's 'stash' and a thermos flask of tea. We were about to leave when I asked whether he shouldn't write a note to his father.

'No point,' he said. 'He'll be out till at least midnight.'

I could see why Jason's social workers worried about him.

The snow had stopped, though the road was slushy. He directed me – 'Right… straight on… right…left' – and it wasn't far at all before he told me to stop. Lights shone behind us in the windows of a croft and to our left we could just make out a track, lightly covered with snow, curving up a gentle slope.

'The Russians built this,' Jason said. 'It was all grass before.'

The track was fenced on both sides, making it impossible to lose your sense of direction. We walked slowly but steadily, the wind behind us. According to Jason, the distance was 'a bit more than a mile'.

We didn't talk, but I was glad of his company.

After about a quarter of a mile, we'd reached a watershed. The track bent to the right, running along a flat-bottomed dip between two low, rounded knolls. We plodded on, sheltered now, until we began to lose height.

I stopped. 'I'm not seeing any sign of life.'

'We will, any minute. There's a sort of cliff that overhangs the place where they've built their bunkhouses.'

We went on. I smelled the sea. There was a burn to our left, its gurgling more noticeable as the slope became steeper. All at once, lights shone away to our right, I heard the hum of some machinery, and saw the outline of a big rectangular sign, presumably the one that forbade us to go further.

I pulled Jason back. 'How do they get electricity?'

'They have a wind turbine.'

I took the night vision goggles out of my rucsac and swept the scene. Nothing moved.

Jason glanced at the goggles. 'Where did you get those?'

A glib lie: 'My father used to go out watching owls.'

He didn't question that. 'There's a ruined croft down the hill a bit. I think the track splits in two there.'

'I've seen a photograph. They've built a quay along the south side of the bay. That's what I'd like to look at.'

'Let's go, then.'

The fences ended and the track did split, one branch turning off in the direction of the bunkhouses and the other heading down to the sea. I held a finger to my lips and pointed seawards.

A shape like a giant beehive loomed up. This had to be the hatchery, and I was reassured to think that at least Gregor hadn't been spinning a web of total lies. But I wasn't interested in halibut. We had to get right down to the water.

A pebble beach lay in front of us, the burn skirting its left-hand side. I sensed that the tide was out – the moaning of the sea seemed to be at a distance – and I stepped out rashly.

At once, my foot crunched on a patch of shells. We were well out of the wind now and apart from the sea there was very little noise. Any sound we made would travel far.

I grabbed Jason's arm and pointed at our feet. He understood, and jerked a thumb towards the burn. We had to cross it.

The task might have been simple in daylight. But this was a dark, dark night. We came closer to the bank and tried to gauge the difficulty.

We weren't facing a rushing torrent, but neither could we simply wade across without getting very wet. We went downstream a few yards, being careful what we stood on, then up. The most promising spot was above a

little waterfall, where two or three rocks seemed to form an island in the centre.

I jumped, aware that in a fraction of a second I could break an ankle. I landed, slipped – there was a light splash as my toe dislodged some gravel – then I jumped again before I could think better of it.

Jason was more sure-footed, but even so he cannoned into me and cursed. I put my finger to my lips again.

We waited for a few tense minutes. No sound, not a murmur. The grass here was pebble-free, allowing us, when we did move, to walk with confidence. In moments, we were on the quay and I could see the overhanging structure that resembled a boatshed. It was exactly the same as in Natasha's photographs, except that there was nothing in the water.

I stepped along the concrete as far as I could – a solid door prevented me going into the shed itself – and peered into the blackness under the overhang. No, there was nothing; no glint of metal, no fake shark fins.

A cry from behind made me turn. A big black shape had swept up Jason, who was wriggling like a fish. A second shape was coming for me.

There was no place to go. The palm of a meaty hand hit me on the side of the head, spinning me round. Then two arms that could have crushed me to death plucked me into the air.

Chapter 16

Our captors carried us like weightless bundles of groceries. They strode up the slope and into the nearer bunkhouse, throwing us down on a wooden floor with such force that they were able to truss us like chickens before we could recover our breath.

'Miss, what'll they do with us?'

My guilt was heavy. 'I don't know, Jason, but it's my fault. I'm sorry.'

A scowling man with a full grey beard marched in and thrust his face into mine. I could smell the garlic on his breath.

'Who are you?' he demanded to know.

I tried to preserve some dignity. 'My name is Carol Rutherford and this is kidnapping.'

'Pah. You are spies.

'No.'

One of the thugs had emptied our backpacks. The bearded man, who wore a dark blue sweater, held up my night vision goggles and said, 'Only spies use these.'

'And bird watchers.'

The door was thrown open again and this time it was Gregor who came in. He looked at us in astonishment. 'Carol? Jason? What's going on?'

'You tell me,' I said.

All of a sudden, a furious argument erupted between Gregor and the other man. It was in Russian, of course, and I didn't understand a word, but I formed the impression that Gregor might be saying we were harmless while

the man with the garlic breath was sticking to his accusation that we were spies.

In a lull, Gregor bent down to untie me, and his colleague fired off another salvo. Gregor ignored him and began to untie Jason too. The bearded man's snarl reached a peak – perhaps he was infuriated by his own impotence – and then he stormed out. Gregor spoke to the two man mountains and they too, after some hesitation, disappeared into the night.

I realised we were in a kitchen. I sat on an orange plastic chair at a Formica table. Gregor and Jason sat down too, and I wanted to be first with the questions.

'What did that man say as he left?'

Gregor spread his hands. 'He said it was on my head.'

'What was? Letting us two spies have our freedom?'

'More or less.' His expression grew more serious. 'Carol, what are you doing here?'

If this was an interrogation, I was determined it was going to be two-way.

'Gregor, what is there to spy on? What are *you* doing here?'

He grinned – I'd have said it was totally spontaneous. 'I told you. I'm an epigeneticist with an interest in producing halibut that are phenotypically female. Aaah,' – his horror seemed real – 'you didn't go into the hatchery?'

'No.'

'Thank God for that. The risk of contamination is high.'

'All right, but what's your naval friend doing?'

'What makes you say he's in the navy?'

'Gregor, stop being evasive.' I didn't know why I thought the other man was in the navy; it was a guess, based on no more than that blue sweater.

He laughed. It was the laugh of a little boy who'd been caught in some minor prank. But then he paused. He was calculating.

'Okay, you got it in one.' He laughed again, but this laugh was phony. 'Hey, I'm a terrible host. Are you hungry? Jason?'

Jason, who was remarkably calm, said, 'Could be.'

'I'll get our cook.' He opened a door behind me – I hadn't paid any attention to it – and shouted. A burly man in a sauce-splattered teeshirt appeared.

'This is Joe, best cook this side of Moscow.' He exchanged a few sentences in Russian with Joe and then said to Jason, 'Fish and chips or meat balls? Limited menu, I'm afraid.'

Jason thought. 'Fish and chips. I've had it already, but I'll have it again.'

'Carol?'

'No, thanks.'

'Maybe you and I could take a walk.'

Jason said, 'Something you don't want me to hear?'

Gregor punched him lightly on the shoulder. 'You're a smart boy.'

We walked along the front of one bunkhouse, and then to the end of the other. Gregor opened an unlocked door, switched on a dim light and ushered me in.

It was a spartan room: a single bed with a dark-coloured downie; a folding chair beside a card table; a panel heater on the wall giving out the merest breath of warmth; two piles of clothes neatly stacked in a corner. I could see why Gregor liked to come to Lerwick.

'Bed or chair?' he said.

'Chair.' I sat down and swivelled towards the bed so that I could watch his face. 'So, Gregor, what is the Russian navy up to?'

He puffed out a breath; it might have been theatrical. 'I'm not supposed to broadcast this, but I think you must have a fair idea already. Basically, the navy are freeloading; they knew we had this base, and it suits them to make use of it. For sonar experiments. They say they have to test their sonar in a number of different oceanic environments. I suppose that makes sense.'

'For military purposes?'

'Not necessarily. There are a lot of commercial applications: fishing, for one; and prospecting for oil and other deposits, as the Shetlanders will tell you. Then there are scientific applications: the oceans are as unexplored as Mars.'

'But military needs come first. Otherwise, why would your colleague be so paranoid?'

'My colleague – his name's Yuri – is always paranoid. But fair enough,' – he did that spreading of his hands, a gesture of openness – 'in the minds of many people in Moscow, military purposes *do* come first – although you shouldn't underestimate how commercial and military power often go closely together.'

'So what's Yuri doing with his sonar?'

Gregor shook his head like someone who was deeply frustrated. 'I don't know. The niceties of sonar physics are not my speciality.'

I was thinking about the submarine drone and wondering how to phrase a question about it when he said, frowning, 'What brought you here, though? What convinced you there was more here than halibut?'

I didn't answer. His face cleared and he snapped his fingers. 'Natasha. Right?'

He knew I knew Helen. He must know that Helen and Natasha shared a house. I would give him this one.

I said, 'How come Yuri allowed Natasha to stay?'

He paused, processing my implicit admission, before he damn near giggled. 'You don't know the half of it. Yuri had been away in Moscow for three or four weeks – I forget exactly. When he learned about Natasha, he went absolutely mad. Gave Ivan a tongue-lashing. Gave me one too. I found it all good entertainment, which made him even madder.'

Now this, if it were true, would imply that Gregor wasn't a professional spy, or at least not as professional as Yuri.

Gregor chortled some more, then he said, 'Have you reported this place to Pamela?'

I stared at him, suddenly startled. Was this the information he *really* needed? If I hadn't reported to Pamela, he could throw both Jason and me off a cliff and no one would know about Yuri's sonar.

I said carefully, 'I haven't, but I left an envelope on my kitchen table. *To be opened if I disappear.*'

His face went cold. 'Carol, Carol, that would be easy to check.'

Now I was angry. 'Gregor, Gregor, if you don't trust me, how can I trust you?'

I faced a crunch. If he was going to kill me – well, I could do nothing about that. But if I could walk away – and I was going to assume for the moment that I could – then I could go back to Lerwick and forget him, forget the plan, forget my ambitions. Or I could trust him, up to a point.

He softened, or seemed to soften. 'Carol, I'm sorry. We're both under hellish pressure.'

'Yeah?'

'Damn.' He pressed his hands against the sides of his neck, giving himself a massage. 'You meet someone who you think could share your soul, and then…'

Then you manipulate her?

I had to manipulate *him*. If I stayed alive, who else could help me frame Eric?

I said, 'I know. I'm sorry too.'

He said, 'How's our plan going? Any developments?'

An abrupt swerve. But I'd decided: I wasn't going to give up on my ambitions.

'Well,' I said. 'Some.'

I told him about Joy's trip to Edinburgh next weekend and the window of opportunity this offered. I told him about Sven starting dinner at exactly eight o'clock every Saturday. And I told him about Charlie Mann and my very sketchy ideas on how we might use his name.

He heard me out, then said, 'Next weekend? Not much time to establish whether Eric would be likely to choose Charlie Mann as a fall guy. Is the good Charlie a family man, for instance, or given to socialising? Either of those would rule him out.'

'I'm going to investigate as soon as I get back to Lerwick.'

'Assuming he *is* plausible, let's think how that part could work.'

We discussed it, and he added a few refinements. I would visit Sven between six and seven, somehow swap the wine, and – if at all possible – wipe his phone clean of fingerprints. The fake message would be sent at five to eight, when Sven was about to unscrew his wine and dish up his dinner; it would say that Charlie had visited because he wanted to make peace. The police investigators would soon find out that Eric couldn't have taken over

his father-in-law's phone remotely because he wasn't computer literate; therefore they would wonder if he or someone acting on his behalf had physically picked up the phone, sent the message and then wiped the fingerprints. (After all, who else could have been involved?) Together with the other evidence, Gregor said, this should make Eric a very firm suspect.

'Other evidence?' I said. 'Apart from the motive and the opportunity?'

Gregor nodded. 'If you could plant the aflatoxin as we agreed, that would help. I'll also arrange for a package to be delivered to Eric. When you get the batrachotoxin, you'll find that each container is inside a book, in a space that has been cut out to accommodate it. Eric will get a similar book with the same space but without any container. We'll hope that he doesn't immediately throw it out and the police discover it, as well as the aflatoxin. Put it all together and it'll be damning.'

It sounded convincing. In fact, we didn't need Eric to be tried and found guilty; we just needed to throw enough doubt into the minds of the voters that they'd turn away from both him and Free Shetland.

'The wine,' I said. 'I don't think I should buy it. Any pupil or member of staff could see me in Tesco and, once the news was out about how Sven was poisoned, go to the police.'

'Okay. I'll buy it, or I'll get one of the men to buy it. We'll do it on Friday afternoon or Saturday morning. Then I'll get it to you. But I'd recommend that you buy some other screwtops and experiment with glue in advance. You don't want to start your trial and error on Saturday'

'True.'

All this plotting and planning implied that he wasn't going to kill me. *Maybe.*

I checked my watch. Ten to nine. 'Look,' I said. 'I think I'd better get Jason home.'

'Of course.' Gregor stood up. 'You know his father's got a problem with drink?'

'Yes.' So the whole of Unst knew.

'Is he – Jason – coming to any harm?'

Was this concern genuine or part of a persona? The worm of suspicion wriggled in my head.

I said, 'Hard to be sure, but I don't think so.'

We walked back the way we'd come. About halfway along, he stopped. 'Carol.'

'What?'

'Are we… will we be… okay?'

Wait a minute. Would a man who intended to throw you off a cliff *really* say this?

'Do you want us to be okay?'

'Of course.' He had an embarrassed air; he wasn't quite the confident Gregor I thought I knew. 'I don't want to let you go.'

I rested my forehead on his shoulder, although it was in part a stage direction from a well-worn script. 'Tell you what. Let's not let each other go.'

His arms went round my shoulders, at first lightly, then pulling me into one of his bear hugs. My cheek was against his stubble, and I couldn't unravel all the tangled threads that ran through me.

I wasn't the one to break the hug. He released his grip, then kissed me on the cheek.

Jason and Joe looked up from a chessboard. Jason said, 'All right?'

It occurred to me that he imagined the two of us had been away having mad passionate sex. 'Sure,' I said.

Joe conceded the game. Goodbyes were said, hands shaken. Gregor said he'd run us to my car.

On the way, we talked about the snow and the mist. The only thing of significance Gregor said came as he dropped us off.

'Catch you both later. I should be back in Lerwick by the middle of the week.'

The middle of the week? I really didn't have long to check out Charlie Mann. And I didn't have long to gear myself up for… yes, for killing Sven.

There was no light on when we reached Jason's house. 'Thank you for everything,' I said. 'You'll be all right?'

'Why shouldn't I be? Dad will either come staggering in after midnight or he won't. Either way, I'll be fine.'

I thought he would. Perhaps, after a certain age, we'd all be better off without parents.

I took a glass of wine to my hotel room and drank it slowly, waiting for fresh hypotheses and interpretations to pop out of my brain. They didn't. You know the technique the CBT people – or maybe it's the mindfulness people, I forget – recommend when worries float around your head? You imagine a big canvas bag, you stuff your concerns into it, zip it up and shove it in a cupboard. The idea is that then you'll forget all about it. I tried this now with my worries about the sonar experiments. *Should* I tell Pamela about them? *Did* I have a duty here? I folded and refolded the questions, trying to tidy

them, and concluded that, since Gregor had let Jason and me go free, the experiments couldn't be absolutely top secret. Even if they were, by the time I had told Pamela and she had mounted an investigation, the Russians would have developed some cover story that couldn't be disproved. Besides, I'd thought a thousand times about my 'duties' to the country in which I'd happened to be born, and I didn't feel these 'duties' existed. I felt a duty to *myself*. If I reported to Pamela, she would sniff around the trail of my relationship with Gregor, with a high probability that she'd thwart my plans to get rid of her.

I didn't have too much difficulty in zipping this bag closed.

There was a second bag, containing my doubts regarding Gregor, which was altogether harder to tidy. He had deceived me, mightily, and the chances were that in some measure he was deceiving me still. On the other hand, did he *want* to deceive me? Wasn't it *possible* that when the moment was right he would be happy to tell me everything? Then – the crucial question – was he deceiving me when he told me how he saw me as a soul mate? That body, those eyes, that touch – it would be easy to *let* them deceive me. My intuition told me that he was telling me the simple truth about how much he wanted me. Yet what seems to be intuition can be an unreliable friend. I gave up trying to close this bag, threw it into a corner, brushed my teeth and went to bed.

Chapter 17
Monday 22ⁿᵈ – Tuesday, 23ʳᵈ

The waitress at breakfast said that the gritters had been out, but there was a forecast of more snow to come. I set out as soon as I could, since the last thing I wanted was to get stuck on Unst. Shetland was at its bleakest: dirty snow by the roadsides, sheep that looked cold and miserable, that eternal mist weighing on the hills and moors. Still, the roads were open, and I made it back to Lerwick by early afternoon.

All those questions about Gregor were still rolling around my mind. But thinking too much can paralyse you. So, as soon as I had had some lunch, I started investigating Charlie Mann. I hit a bull's-eye on Google at once. 'Charlie Mann and Son, Builders, Lerwick.' Not 'Charles', I noticed. Two addresses were given – White Knowes and 3 Masons' Place – and two phone numbers. One was a landline, which Bt.com obligingly told me was the number for 'Charlie Mann, White Knowes by Lerwick', and one was a mobile. I checked Google Maps for Masons' Place and found it was to the north of the main part of the town, not far from Gregor's flat. My next step was a visit.

Someone knocked at my door. It was Betty, holding two parcels, one in the familiar Amazon packaging.

'Hello. Postie here.' Betty was always upbeat when she spoke to me; I think I reminded her what it was like to be young. 'These came for you, both by carrier in fact. The men didn't want to leave them on your step.'

'Thank you.' I took the packages, then wondered if Betty might be as good a source as anyone on the character of Charlie Mann. 'Like a cup of tea?'

'That's very nice of you.'

'I'm a bit short on the home baking,' I ushered her into the living room. She didn't glance at my laptop, which still showed the map of Lerwick, but lowered her ample backside onto the couch.

She patted her stomach. 'All the better for my diet.'

I made tea, fetched digestive biscuits, wondered how I could direct the conversation.

'So,' Betty said, when I sat beside her, 'what have you been up to?'

'I had a trip to Unst, to see Shetland in all its winter glory, and now a friend of mine has roped me into finding a suitable builder to point the outside of her flat. If I said she was fussy, that would be the understatement of the century.'

Betty munched her biscuit. 'No shortage of builders in Lerwick.'

'Somebody's given her the name Charlie Mann. Know anything about him?'

'Charlie Mann? I'm sure he's competent.'

'He's not the kind who would rip off an unsuspecting single girl?'

'I really don't think so. You can't get away with that sort of thing in Lerwick. Word gets round faster than a hungry seagull.'

I was looking for a way to push the subject when she added, 'I heard that Charlie Senior had more or less retired – the steam went out of him when his

wife died – and most of the work is done by his son, who calls himself Charles so that you don't mix him up with his dad.'

'Steam?'

'Oh yes, he used to be very hot-headed. His boiler was always ready to burst. He used to curse his employees so much so that they all left – except, of course, his son.'

I pondered this. Charlie had a temper; that was a good start.

I didn't glean any more detail, because Betty soon changed the topic to maths, of all things. Her grandson, David, was having 'a spot of bother' with his teacher, so she said, and I wasn't entirely surprised when this turned out to be Matthew. She felt, though she was very diffident about saying it, that Matthew tended not to explain and illustrate mathematical points but to issue rules of thumb that his pupils had to memorise.

'Rules of thumb?' I said. 'Like what?'

'Well, suppose you have a number raised to a certain power and it's to be divided by itself raised to a different power – I mean, ten to the power six to be divided by ten to the power three, for example – he gives them a rule like "the index of the answer is found by subtracting the index of the divisor from the index of the dividend."'

'For goodness' sake.'

'Quite. All he has to do is *show* them enough examples so that it's crystal clear inside their heads for the rest of their lives.'

We talked some more. I recommended another Maths teacher, Alexander, whom I'd always found kind and considerate. Perhaps, I suggested, he might give David a little tuition to restore his confidence. Betty was most grateful.

She left me shortly before four o'clock, and I wondered when builders finished for the day. Between four and five? What would be the best moment to visit Charlie?

The boxes that Betty had brought still sat on my table. I hesitated. If I left them unopened, that would be a sign to myself that the plan was a phantasy, that I could return to 'normality'.

Hesitation, thinking, paralysis: I was back to them? No. I'd tried normality and I couldn't stand it.

I tore open the larger package, the one that was supposed to be from Amazon. The contents looked like two books, an omnibus edition of Len Deighton and another of John Steinbeck. I opened Len Deighton and found a little bottle lying snugly in its hiding-place. John Steinbeck offered the same: batrachotoxin – for sure, although it was unlabelled and the quantity unspecified. The bottles were transparent and I could see a dropper inside each, so that you could transfer the liquid without fear of spilling. There was a seal of plastic round the top, such as you see on water bottles in countries where the tap water is unsafe. I put the two bottles to one side on the table, and consigned the packaging, including the books, to the black bag that I transferred every so often to my recycling bin.

The second package was a plain cardboard box. In it lay another bottle, slightly larger than the other two, this time not hidden in a book but wrapped in layers of cardboard. There was no dropper, and, again, no label or specification of dosage. I assumed this was the aflatoxin and if I had to use it, the dosage would be the entire bottle.

I put all this cardboard too into the black bag and took the bag out to empty it. The pick-up time for the bin was Thursday morning, which should mean that the evidence would be destroyed long before anyone could possibly be

poking around. When I came back in, all three bottles were like witnesses waiting to testify against me. I took them through to the bathroom, and stowed them in a medicine cabinet that sat above the toilet cistern. Betty had a key to the flat, but it was inconceivable that she would come in and rummage through the cabinet.

I locked up, went out to the car, and drove towards Masons' Place.

I may have described Lerwick as an overgrown village, but that doesn't really do it justice. It's a funny old place, with layers of history, like the lanes and the New Town, easily discernible. Another layer was added by that herring boom, when thousands of workers descended on the town and all sorts of yards, alleys and tenements were built so that fish merchants and processors could do their business.

Masons' Place, now no more than a small gravelled square surrounded by a near-quadrangle of low buildings, belonged to that era. A date carved on the wall facing the street left no doubt: 1885.

On my first pass, I saw two men unloading a big white van on the back of which, though the doors were open, I was fairly sure I saw the name Mann. I couldn't stop, but managed to park thirty yards or so down the street.

I strolled back and glanced in. The van was shut, and on the rear doors I could now read clearly, 'Charlie Mann and Son, Builders'. At a doorway beside a display window – showing not much more than a bag of cement and a pick – a man whom I judged from his white hair to be at least in his sixties was talking to someone inside. Was this Charlie? I had no idea. I heard him say, in what I would have described as deferential tones, 'Right. No worries.' He was an employee? Betty had been wrong?

I had to get answers to some key questions. Did Charlie drive to the pub on a Saturday night? Did he have cronies out to his house for a booze-up? But I couldn't just walk in and start firing off questions. I heard the words 'See you tomorrow', and saw Mr White Hair cross the yard to a smaller white van that was parked off to the side. It was dirty, but again I could make out the words 'Charlie Mann and Son'. I doubled back quickly to my car.

The little van nosed into the street and turned right, which meant that I had to do a U-turn to follow it. Parked cars made this difficult, and by the time I had driven back down to the T-junction at the end of the street, the van had disappeared.

Left? Right? Had I seen it winking right? Nothing to do but follow my instinct.

But it was useless. After about five minutes, I gave up and circled back to my previous position.

Minutes passed. Was the big van gone? I pulled out my phone so that I could pretend to consult it, decided I would wait another five minutes – and then saw the white shape coming out, turning towards me. I pretended I was typing on the phone, but glanced up to catch a glimpse of a youngish man, shaven-headed. Not Charlie. *Charles*.

I couldn't help feeling that Mr White Hair, if he *was* an employee, was my best hope. I knew when he finished work, I knew the direction he took when he left. Tomorrow, I would be ready to follow him.

But he might go straight home. Then I'd have to investigate *him*, to find the best place and time to make an approach. This was the kind of operation that could take weeks. And the clock was ticking. If the plan was to go ahead, we had to reach a decision on Charlie Mann by Friday. It seemed all but impossible.

When I walked into school on Tuesday, I was so busy thinking about Charlie Mann that I almost didn't notice the altercation in the English corridor.

Joy and Sharon were confronting each other at the door to Sharon's room. As I came up, Joy was saying, 'You're supposed to be neutral. How can you be neutral when you're feeding them your own ideas?'

'I'm not feeding them my ideas.' Sharon's face was tight; I didn't like the signs. 'I'm asking them to deconstruct *their* ideas so that they can be ready to deal with objections from the opposition. It's a standard technique of debate.'

Their voices were shrill. I wasn't surprised when Peter appeared from his cupboard. 'Problem?' he said.

Joy put up her hands in a *Don't shoot* gesture. 'Sorry,' she said, beginning to move away towards her own room. 'A minor tiff. ' She was smiling, because nothing fazed her. She'd switch her mind to her first class within minutes.

Sharon also apologised and went into her room. But she wasn't smiling. She would brood on this encounter for days.

Peter jerked his head towards his cupboard and said to me, 'Got a minute?'

'Sure.'

We stood just inside the cupboard door, not taking the time to sit down. This is how you deal with problems when you're a teacher – hurriedly, in the thirty seconds or so before the bell imposes its iron law.

Peter said, 'Do you know what's up with those two? There's something going on.'

'No, I don't know.' I assumed the argument over pornography was too trivial to be the root cause of anything.

'But you're friends with both of them?'

'Yes. I'd say so.'

'Mm.' His square-framed glasses always gave me the impression that he was looking me straight in the eye. But, then, he always was. 'Feuds,' he said, 'can take on a life of their own. I hate to pass my dirty work onto you, but if you could, perhaps, talk to Joy and see what's behind their animosity, I'd be most grateful.'

The bell rang. 'You want me to report to you?' I said.

'Like a spy?' He shook his head. 'Actually, I'd much prefer it if you could work some magic on your own. I feel in my bones that your magic is likely to be more powerful than mine.'

This pleased me, of course. 'Blessed are the peacemakers?'

'Indeed.'

At morning interval, I didn't see Sharon, but there was a spare seat next to Joy.

I sat down and turned on a full beam.

She said, 'What did Peter want you for? Let me guess.'

'You'll guess right.' I smiled at her. 'You know how he hates quarrels.'

'Sometimes they're inevitable, for example when a person starts being snide about your sexuality.'

I was astonished. 'Sharon's snide about your sexuality? To your face?'

'Even worse. To a pupil, who repeats it to me. Of course, the pupil's trying to wind me up, but that's beside the point.'

214

'That is awful.' Well, it *was* awful if it was true. 'But I didn't think you were arguing about that.'

'No. That was the warm-up. When you came along, we'd got on to the next item: the way she's putting words into her debaters' mouths.'

'Maybe I've misjudged her,' I said. 'I really thought she'd be neutral in mentoring the girls. And as for her being snide, I had no idea she was narrow-minded.'

Joy glanced at me. 'Don't worry about it,' she said. 'Life's too short.'

'Yes.' I caught her drift. 'How's your friend in Edinburgh?'

'Not great. I'm going down on Friday after school. But we can't let death spoil life.'

The bell – that damn bell – would ring any moment. I said, 'Eric's away again this week?'

'He is. Not coming back till Thursday. I'll be all on my own.'

'Want some company?'

'That would be nice. Maybe I could try a bit of drawing again.'

And I could plant some aflatoxin.

'Why not?'

'Tomorrow night?' she said.

'Works for me.'

I didn't see Sharon all day. She wasn't in the staffroom at morning interval and she was nowhere to be seen at lunch. That suggested she was avoiding people.

When she appeared at my door after classes, I waved her in, even though I wanted to get away and get in position at Masons' Place.

215

Her face was flushed. 'Have you *seen* what people are saying about me on Twitter?'

'Sharon, you must not look at Twitter or Facebook. It's a sure route to misery.'

'They are so unbelievably *nasty*. There's a whole thread about my supposed sex life before I came here. They're saying I'm a lesbian, which is a total lie. And even if I was, even if I was a total whore, none of it would affect the case for or against Shetland's independence. It's all... what d'you call it?'

'An *argumentum ad hominem*? You don't need to tell me.'

She walked about the room for a minute or two, looking at the meagre displays on my walls. Then she sat down, hanging her head. 'I don't know how the girls are going to manage on Thursday. Joanna – I'm afraid she's a lightweight. Debbie – she's in a class of her own, but she's unpredictable; she'll either win by a mile or crash and burn.'

'I hear the atrium will be bursting at the seams... Agh!' I'd glanced at my watch and it was later than I'd thought. Twenty past four. I could miss my chance at Charlie Mann's.

'What's wrong?'

'I'm sorry. I forgot I had an appointment in the town. I'll have to go.'

The smaller van was leaving Masons' Place as I drove down the street from the northern end. I braked, to leave a gap between us, but the driver had to stop at the T-junction and I had no choice but to come in behind him. He turned right – it was the older man, the one I thought was an employee – and immediately left.

216

There was no traffic at all. I was able to follow him, though cautiously. It was fortunate that Lerwick wasn't the kind of town where a small-time builder would expect someone to be tailing him. Very shortly, he pulled off the road and stopped.

It was a piece of waste ground, across the road from a pub. He was going for a drink.

I couldn't find another parking space. I had to settle for a spot not far from the van. It wasn't ideal; I'd have to make sure I came out before my target, because I didn't want him taking notice of my car.

The pub was old-fashioned, rather dull, lacking the zany touch of Captain Flint's. Two old men were playing dominoes at a back table, and Charlie Mann's man was sitting at the counter talking to the bartender. Otherwise, the place was empty.

I approached the bar and said, 'Hi.'

The barman was a tall young fellow with a big tattoo on his arm. He seemed amused by my presence.

'Hi. You lost?'

'That's what I call a warm welcome. I thought this might be the kind of place where no one would try to chat me up.'

'You find that a problem?' He was a confident bastard. 'Well, you're in no danger here. Bobby's a married man and I'm gay.'

Bobby spluttered in his beer. 'Aye right.' He had a kindly, avuncular air. 'Oor Wullie is as gay as Don Juan.'

'Where's your bucket?' I said to the barman.

'My bucket?'

'I thought Oor Wullie always had a bucket to sit on.'

'Ah. You wanna stop reading that *Sunday Post*. What'll you have?'

'A half pint of cider.'

We all watched reverentially as Willie poured the Strongbow. I paid, then Bobby said, 'So, what do you do? How come we haven't seen you here before?'

'I teach at the high school.'

'And you've slipped in for a quick one where none of your pupils can see you?'

'Exactly. What do *you* do?'

'I'm a builder. No, I'm a serf.'

'You work for a builder?'

'Yeah.'

So Betty was wrong. I thought he might volunteer the name of his employer, but he didn't. I had to ask, 'Which one?'

Willie, who couldn't keep his nose out of the conversation, supplied the answer. 'Bobby works for the legendary Charlie Mann.'

'I don't, in fact,' said Bobby. He addressed me: 'I work for Charles, his son. Charlie is pretty well out of it.'

'Charlie is, or was, legendary?'

Bobby made a face. 'Willie knows better than me. I've been in Glasgow for twenty years.'

'Aye, he was,' Willie said. 'He was the darling of all the matrons, even though he was a bit volcanic when he had a drink in him.'

'He isn't any more? The volcano went dormant?'

'Aye, when his wife died and he stopped coming in here to drink. Now he's a hermit.'

'Don't tell me he doesn't drink. I've never met a Shetlander who doesn't drink.'

'Oh he drinks all right, but not here. He drinks out at White Knowes – that's his house – all on his own. Right, Bobby?'

Bobby shifted on his stool. 'Well, so they say. He still comes in to work, though, occasionally.'

There it was. The information had fallen into my lap.

Bobby and Willie were silent, perhaps contemplating the good old days of erupting volcanoes. One of the domino players came up for more drinks. 'Two halves and two halves, Willie.'

'Well, Hamish,' Bobby said. 'You winning?'

The man was at least eighty. He had a scrawny neck and forests coming out of his ears and nose. 'If you're talking about dominoes, Bobby, I'm the king. If you're talking of the great game of life, maybe not.'

'Never say die, Hamish.'

'We've all got to say die some time.'

A cheery gathering. It was surely understandable if I finished off my cider and left.

But I couldn't drink the rest in one gulp; it was too gassy.

I got them talking about the pubs in Lerwick. They were dismissive of other establishments and particularly contemptuous about the 'posers' who frequented Captain Flint's. As soon as my stomach could bear it, I poured the cider down my throat and said, 'I gotta go.'

Bobby said, 'Have another drink?'

'Thanks, but I can't get sozzled on a Tuesday.'

'Come back on Friday,' Willie said. 'The joint is jumping on a Friday.'

I drove straight to Tesco. On Wednesday evening, I was going to Joy's. On Thursday after classes I had to attend the debate in the school. I was running out of time to experiment with screwtops.

In the car park, I messaged Gregor: *Double checked C. He is perfect.* I waited for a few minutes, but there was no answer.

Then the phone pinged. It was Helen.

Norseman for a drink? Got something else to show you.

If it was another photo, why couldn't she send it to me?

I typed, *Where are you?*

At home.

I'll need to catch you later. Sorry.

That'll be two drinks.

In the shop, I picked up some fruit and vegetables. At the wine shelves, I found the Isla Negra and saw that it was one of the cheapest bottles available. I also noticed that the shelf was well stocked, giving me every reason to believe that there would be plenty for both Gregor and Eric.

I picked up two screwtops of white.

The family goods section offered every sort of cleaner known to man, as well as wipes, scourers, jewellery polish and glue. I picked up a five-pack of glue sticks, two packets of wipes, one moist, one dry, and moved on to look for latex gloves. Good old Tesco had two kinds, one medium-sized, one large. I bought the medium size, in a packet – more than I needed – of twenty.

The self-service checkout provided suitable anonymity. I paid with cash, and met no one. Back at the flat, I put the wine, the glue and the gloves beside the kitchen sink, and thought about how I would dispose of everything after the deed was done.

Chapter 18

Tuesday, 23rd – Thursday, 25th

I didn't experiment on Tuesday evening; I was edgy. On a rational level, I was wondering if I should have bought more than two bottles, because the amount of trial and error required might be considerable, and on a trivial level – you wouldn't believe this but it's true – I was afraid that I'd do something stupid with the glue and render a whole bottle of wine unopenable. Who'd have imagined that at this point in my life I'd be worried about wasting some Sauvignon?

After I had my meal, I messaged Helen: *I'm at home. Too tired to come out. Have you photos to show me?*

She sent them, with a message: *Phone me.*

There were three photos, all showing the same object. It was like an upside-down microphone with a little cage built round it. Tendrils of green seaweed clung to the cage.

I called her. 'What d'you think?' she said.

'Haven't a clue. What is it? Where did you get the photographs?'

'On a beachcombing website. A Scalloway skipper dragged it up in his nets, a mile or so off the west coast of Unst.'

'That's hardly beachcombing. So what *is* it?'

'That took a lot of searching, I can tell you. It's a sonar device; the cage is to stop it banging against rocks or whatever, and the microphone thing is to pick up sounds coming through the water.'

I didn't know much about sonar. This gadget could originate from Yuri's experiments – though I wasn't going to tell Helen about meeting *him* – but it could equally well come from an oil survey vessel or even a fishing boat.

Helen, by her own account, was equally ignorant of sonar, but that didn't stop her jumping to a conclusion. She whispered down the phone as if Natasha might be listening. 'It's *got* to be connected to that submarine thing that Natasha photographed. If Shetland Isles Council is taking money to close their eyes to some fucking Russian plot, I'm going to make sure the news gets splashed across every fucking newspaper in the country.'

I couldn't have said why, but I was irritated. Helen saw plots everywhere, especially if Shetland Isles Council was involved. 'Plot?' I said. 'What kind of plot?'

'How the fuck would I know?' She was in full flow: 'Don't you know someone in Edinburgh – a journalist, maybe – who could dig into this for us?'

For *us*? 'I don't have any journalists at my beck and call. Anyway, I'm sure you're as likely to get to the bottom of it as anyone.'

'Huh.' She didn't like the brush-off. After a brief sulk, she said, 'Well, a drink later this week?'

'I don't know, I'm sorry. I'm busy tomorrow, Thursday, Friday and Saturday.'

'Fuck me. Must be great to be popular. Okay, text me when there's a gap in your social whirl.'

'You know I'll make it up to you.'

'Huh.'

She didn't need to be so grumpy. I'd have plenty of time for drinking after Saturday.

But first I had to get to Saturday.

My Wednesday started with Jason Young's class. And they were aggrieved.

'Miss, why can't *we* go to the debate?' (George the Second had decreed that there wouldn't be room for everyone; he was restricting the audience to Years Three to Six.)

'Miss, how can this be fair?'

'Miss, what happened to our freedom of speech?

'Miss, can we have a debate in the class?'

My first instinct was to brush their complaints aside, because I had *so* much to think about, but, just in time, I sensed that they were on the very edge of rebellion and agreed that they should have their own debate, as long as *they* agreed to be totally well-behaved and totally respectful of each other's opinion. They said that wouldn't be a problem – they would, wouldn't they? – and they set about dividing themselves into two camps, Remain and Leave, choosing their speakers and electing scribes and a chairperson for each group. We wouldn't let the process drag on: they'd spend just one period – this one – preparing their arguments and we'd have the debate on Thursday. They were totally on my side now, because they thought I was on theirs, and I took the whole process as a warning that even my impending status as a murderer shouldn't induce me to relax my concentration in the classroom.

They were straggling out, still animated, when I thought I should ask Jason how he was. He had seemed comparatively subdued.

'You all right?' I said.

'Yeah, yeah.' But he wasn't rushing to pack up.

'You sure?'

He didn't reply immediately. He let the desks round about him empty, then said, 'My dad's cracking up. His mates brought him back at lunchtime on Monday.'

'Hung over?' I spoke quietly, although no one was left to hear us.

'Half dead. Smelling of booze and sick.'

'God.' I didn't know what to do or say.

He said, 'I'm scared for him. I'm scared he's going to kill himself with the booze. And I'm scared I'm going to get taken into care.'

'Oh Jason.' I'd have liked to give him at least the comfort of a hug, but I couldn't, because Peter was at my door with a clipboard, waiting. 'Is your mother back?'

'Yeah, but he just disgusts her when he's like that.'

'God,' I repeated, still unable to think what to say. 'Would it help if I spoke to your mum?' Now why on earth did I offer *that*? What experience did I have as a marriage counsellor?

His eyes filled with tears. 'Would you, miss?'

'I could try. I could come out on Sunday.' *I'm busy on Saturday. I've got a man to kill.*

He brushed a hand across his cheeks. 'Thank you, miss.' He turned abruptly and rushed out – no young lad wants to break down in front of his teachers.

Peter came in, eyebrows raised. 'Should I ask?'

'Probably not. Parent problems.'

He shook his head. Peter was as humane as any man I'd known, but he was long enough in the tooth to know that you couldn't pursue every

deserving cause; there were just too many of them.' George,' he said, 'has asked heads of department to twist as many arms as possible so that there's a big turnout of staff at the debate tomorrow. At the same time, I'm trying to organise tellers, because I'm assuming that we'll have to count the votes. Can I put you down to help?'

'Of course.'

'I thought I'd give you the back six rows – that's in front of the stairway – to the right of the aisle as you're looking towards the speakers.'

'Is George expecting trouble?'

Peter wasn't an alarmist sort of person. 'George is just being George, preparing for every eventuality. But feelings are running high, and he's under pressure from both the council and the parents to ensure a neutral – and orderly – contest.'

'Well, I'll be there, with my deputy's badge.'

'Good.' He hesitated. 'Any progress on the other peacekeeping front?'

I wasn't going to overstate that. 'I think I may have dug up one of the root causes, but I'm a long way from a resolution.'

He looked relieved. 'Even finding a cause is progress. Let me know if I can help.'

'I will.'

I watched him go. 'Decent' – the word Sharon had used for Colin – would also suit Peter perfectly. Too bad neither of them could add a dash of devilment.

At lunchtime, I finally had a message from Gregor. *Good news about C. All systems go. Get the refreshments to you on Friday?* I assumed he was referring to the wine and I typed back: *Fine.*

Joy had told me to come out around half past six, so that we could have some of her father's lamb for dinner 'before we started'. By the time I was home from school, that left me an hour and a half to test the glue and take a shower.

An hour and a half? How long did it take to apply touches of glue to the neck of a bottle? I made a cup of coffee and took it through to the living room.

I sat on the couch, drank half of my coffee, laid my head back meaning to clear it – and did the opposite. I dislodged an avalanche of images, sensations and memories.

When the debris cleared, one image was stark. My mother, her eyes red and swollen, holding a scrap of a note, all that my father had deigned to leave her. She couldn't believe what it said, and neither, at first, could I. My father, the rat, was sure that my mother and I would 'cope'. Well, my mother 'coped' all right, with massive doses of alcohol and citalopram. And I 'coped' by making up my mind that no person and no circumstance would ever make me a victim again.

I heaved myself off the couch. No more procrastination.

The instructions for the glue said that you should put a 'dab' on both sides of the material to be glued. I opened the first bottle and did that: three 'dabs' on the inside of the screwtop and another three on the neck of the bottle itself. Of course, I couldn't guarantee that the dabs would line up.

And what constituted a 'dab'? I opened the second bottle and put three bigger spots – smears, I suppose – on the screwtop and bottle. Then I screwed both bottles shut. The instructions were that the objects being glued should be left for two hours.

226

To hell with worrying, I thought. I would have more time to experiment, if necessary, on Friday or Saturday.

The only other sliver of indecision concerned the aflatoxin. Should I hide it in my parka or my jeans? The latter, I thought, because they'd come off some time after the parka. I could camouflage the shape with a wad of Kleenex, and in any case the jeans weren't particularly tight.

A pair of latex gloves wasn't a problem: they went into my back pocket without creating any discernible bulge.

I drove out a little early, arriving about a quarter past six. Joy had said, in what might have been a joke but probably wasn't, that this time I should definitely bring my toothbrush. I'd gone one better: I'd packed an overnight bag with a change of clothes, though I intended to leave these in the car in case I got cold feet.

Joy helped me off with the parka. She was wearing one of her white tops and, as usual, no bra. A necklace that ended in a green crescent hung in the scoop where the gentle slopes of her breasts began. I felt like a country girl, in my teeshirt and cardigan. She kissed me on the cheek, letting a trace of that lily-of-the-valley stir some primitive response centre in my brain.

Another smell, much less subtle, came from the kitchen. 'Dad's lamb,' she said, 'will be ready in ten minutes.'

She took my hand and led me through to the living room. 'A drink? Wine?'

If I was driving home, I could have one glass.

I wasn't driving home. Indecision flew away like a bird. I had to find a hiding-place for the aflatoxin and the morning might be easier than the evening. Besides…

'Thank you. Wine.'

She fetched two generous glasses of white wine and sank onto the sofa beside me. The bottle of aflatoxin – I had made sure of this – was in the pocket away from any possible contact.

Her hand brushed my knee, then squeezed a little. I gave her a smile of encouragement.

She put her glass on the floor, took mine and did the same with it, then leaned over and kissed me on the lips.

I kissed her back, quite urgently. Why not?

'Well,' she said. 'I'm glad we're not going to shilly-shally.'

I tried to remember if I'd ever kissed a girl before. Once? In the heady days at university when I was eighteen and drunk and everything was possible?

Joy turned back and picked up the glasses.

When she went through to carve the lamb, I prowled round the living room. There were model ships on the mantelpiece and I couldn't remember if I'd seen them before. Their decks might lift off, but the mantelpiece was so tidy that it was unbelievable Eric would try to store a toxin here; the ocean-going yacht in the dust and clutter of the studio would be a much more plausible hiding place.

I prowled some more. On the dining table was a big hardback – I hadn't noticed it earlier. A Graham Greene omnibus. Some warning bell told me not to touch it.

Joy pushed through the hatch a plate of meat, one tureen of potatoes and another of vegetables. Then she came round from the kitchen, saw what I was looking at, and said, 'That book arrived for Eric. It's very odd.'

Chapter 19

Thursday, 25th

The wine bottles still stood tall and slim on my draining board. I tried the one to which I'd applied a liberal amount of glue.

It was stuck, completely stuck. Someone with a strong grip might manage to open it, but I thought that a man with Parkinson's would not.

The second screwtop resisted too, but only for a second. I judged that this was about right.

So, three 'dabs'.

I put both bottles in the fridge, making a mental note of which was which.

This was the day of the big debate. But first, in the period before the morning interval, my Second Year were going to hold their full, free and frank discussion.

They were so well behaved that I felt a sense of anticlimax. The Leavers, as you might have expected, concentrated almost entirely on the money and what they would do with it, while the Remainers were full of lofty sentiments like fraternity, generosity and open-mindedness. The Remainers won by sixteen votes to thirteen, which pleased me, because it seemed to indicate that they could see beyond their immediate self-interest.

I went to the staffroom for morning coffee. At the interval, the staff – at least, those who didn't hide away in cubbyholes throughout the school –

divided themselves into three distinct groups, each forming a big circle round a table and each with its own mode and tone of conversation. In particular, Matthew's group, which occupied a prime position near the window, passed comments among themselves in such low, muttered voices that you couldn't avoid the conclusion they wanted to exclude everyone else. This morning, I noticed that Matthew noticed *me* as I came in, but I didn't anticipate what was to come.

From where I sat, no more than three or four feet away, I could see his profile. He glanced towards me with his customary supercilious smirk and said something to Vince, a sidekick of his who was invariably on his left-hand side. Matthew – I'd seen this before – didn't throw his own bons mots round the table; he passed them to Vince who was happy to earn the guffaws. Now Vince leaned back, turned towards me and said, 'Your friend's too scared to face the music?'

His open hostility angered me. What happened to good, old-fashioned civility? I tried to be nonchalant, because Matthew and his cronies would love it if I lost my temper. 'Vince, you're implying I've only got one friend in the world?'

He sniggered. 'That's possible, but I'm talking about the one who can't do arithmetic, like eight billion divided by twenty thousand.'

I knew what he was talking about, of course, and the underlying premise annoyed me. 'So what's the answer to that sum? Peace and contentment?'

He ignored that. 'She's not too hot on basic English either, like the meaning of the word "neutral".'

Given my manoeuvring behind the scenes and my own judgement on Sharon's impulsiveness, I was sure that this attack was well aimed. But, of course, I wasn't going to give an inch. 'You have witness depositions to that

effect?' I said. 'Or you're listening to rumours from those who are already biased?'

'It's common knowledge.'

I didn't reply, unwilling to give him the pleasure of an argument, especially one that he might win.

But he was relentless. 'And you're aiding and abetting her. George the Second should discipline both of you.'

Somebody at his table made a guttural comment that I didn't pick up. It might have been a joke, but it might even have been some kind of moronic threat, because a couple of men growled agreement like wolves about to move in for the kill.

I was sitting next to Iris, an art teacher who specialised in multicoloured leggings. She turned in irritation and snapped, 'Vince, will you give it a rest? All we're wanting here is some peace and quiet to finish our coffee.'

Even Vince was reluctant to start a war. He took from Iris the rebuke he wouldn't have taken from me and subsided. I flashed Iris a grateful look and everyone settled, or appeared to settle, into their customary torpor. Nonetheless, I was rattled. Sticks and stones wouldn't break *my* bones, but Sharon's were a different matter.

My concentration was blown. The day passed, but it was one of those days when time seems to stretch to infinity. When classes were finally over, I took a quarter of an hour to prepare for Friday morning, then hurried along to the atrium.

Today, the janitors had set out perhaps four hundred seats, facing what I would call the back of the hall, where five chairs had been spread out in a shallow semicircle round a microphone. The debaters were chatting and the

Voice of God was booming out as Peter tested the sound system. Members of staff had either positioned themselves throughout the audience – one every three or four rows on either side of the aisle – or had congregated on the steps at the far end from the debaters. George the Second was standing in the aisle, scanning for trouble among the jean-clad senior pupils. (This was the only high school I had ever known where the headteacher didn't waste hours trying to enforce some archaic, quasi-militaristic uniform.)

Sharon was by herself on one of the steps, as if she had already been sent to Coventry. I sat beside her. 'What have you done with Robert?' I said. 'Mary babysitting?'

Her smile was thin, but at least it was there. 'They're bosom buddies. Least of my worries at the moment.'

'Nervous?'

She *looked* nervous, her eye bags pronounced. 'I just hope the girls can do themselves justice.'

'I'm sure they will.'

'Everything's resting on Debbie. She's speaking last.'

'If anyone can carry the day single-handed, Debbie can.'

I'd been observing Debbie for a week or so. She was pretty – that was putting it mildly. She had a perfect complexion, long light-brown hair curling round a sweetly oval face, and the whitest teeth I had ever seen. She also had an air of maturity, an indefinable steadiness in her gaze that told me she would see through all pretension. Her co-Remainer, Joanna, was more of a bundle of blonde fun, famous for her infectious laugh; she was bright enough in her own way, but she wasn't in Debbie's league.

'What about the boys?' I said. 'What have you heard?'

'Nothing.'

I knew the boys by sight, and I'd picked up a little information through staffroom gossip. Unlike the girls, they weren't bound for university. Wayne, a big, square-built, crew-cut bruiser, was set to be a fisherman, and Duncan, red-haired and pugnacious, was about to follow his father into the engineering business. Both of them already had a reputation as drinkers and lads about town, and I suspected that neither would be Sharon's cup of tea.

The Voice of God, which needed no amplification, silenced the muttering masses. 'Ladies and gentlemen, mesdames, messieurs, meine damen und herren,' – Peter wasn't showing off; he was poking fun at the supposed seriousness of the event – 'welcome to our debate. You all know the motion – "That Shetland should remain part of Scotland" – and the final vote will be on a simple show of hands, to be counted by your infallible teachers. The debaters have drawn lots and the order of speaking will be: Wayne, against the motion,' – a burst of cheering erupted from a group in the rows I was supposed to be supervising – 'Joanna, who is for the motion, Duncan, who is against,' – another cheer – 'and, finally, Debbie, who is for. I am sure that you will give the speakers your rapt attention. Please keep your questions until the speeches are concluded. So, I call upon Wayne to start the debate.'

Wayne stood up, taking his time, surveying the audience like a Mafia boss who would send his minions out to silence any dissent. 'You know,' he began, his voice gravelly, 'you don't need me to state the case for Shetland. You all know the riches we have: the fish, the lambs, the tourists who flock to see our savage scenery and our wild life – and our oil. Let's be blunt about our oil. Are you aware that, on the basis of present discoveries alone, conservative estimates are that over the next ten years every single person in an independent Shetland would be – I beg your pardon, *will* be – half a million pounds better off. Work it out for yourselves' – he said this with an

air of scorn – 'eight billion divided by twenty-two thousand. You don't need a calculator to realise it's a lot of money.'

I didn't think he had done his long division correctly; also, he had his dollars mixed up with his pounds; and, thirdly, if Eric was going to plough the money into investments, it couldn't also go straight into Shetlanders' pockets. Still, Wayne wasn't doing too badly at all. He wasn't stumbling with maybes; he was hitting his audience hard with 'facts' – all right, perhaps 'alternative facts' – that got at once to the heart of the matter. If his sums were wrong or his 'conservative estimates' were unattributed, that didn't matter; state something confidently enough and a lot of people will believe it.

Wayne rolled on like a Sherman tank. I soon realised that he was restating – with considerable freshness and fluency – the arguments made by Eric eight days ago in this same venue. After the confident claims about Shetland's natural wealth, we heard the same paean of praise about Shetland's way of life: the work ethic, the community spirit, and the 'vibrant scene' in music and crafts. Then he turned on the 'couch potatoes' of the 'sprawling housing estates' of central Scotland; if he was to be believed, the average Scot had no entrepreneurial spirit, no understanding that the world didn't owe him a living, no appetite for risk, no concern for his neighbour or community, and in many cases no desire to get out of bed before midday.

His peroration too could have come straight from Eric's notebook. 'It is in no one's interests that Shetland's wealth should be squandered on handouts to the lazy, in Glasgow and Paisley and Cumbernauld and Motherwell – handouts that enable them to over-eat, over-drink, over-smoke and over-indulge in watching trashy television. No, it's time for us to show the rest of Scotland some tough love, and to use this gift of fortune to

establish a Republic of Shetland that will go down in history as one of the most splendid civilisations of all time.'

Wayne sat down to thunderous applause. He deserved it, I thought; he was eloquent, despite his hard man image.

Joanna started quietly; I sensed she was trying to tone down her natural effervescence, and perhaps that wasn't a good idea. She homed in on the very phrase I'd noticed – 'conservative estimates' – and began to pick apart the assumptions behind the figures. Her approach was very methodical – did these estimates take into account the costs of production in deep and stormy waters, a probable worldwide glut of oil, a fall in demand as manufacturers switched 'inexorably' to electric vehicles and more and more consumers and governments preferred renewable energy? – but the reactions from the audience proved that, while cool reason might win you marks in your discursive essay in Higher English, it didn't necessarily win hearts in a live debate. Legs were crossed and uncrossed, sweet wrappers rustled, and comments, some muttered but some perfectly audible, exchanged. George the Second began to scowl at the disruption and I felt I had to climb down from my perch to let my charges know that they were being watched. Joanna didn't seem to realise that if you 'went negative', you still had to appeal to the emotions of your listeners, and the best way to do that was to ensure that the arguments of the other side were laughed out of court. She might have been labouring towards that end when she fired a few volleys at the notion that Lerwick could become an Athens of the north. Could twee tales of the Mirrie Dancers, she asked, and boozy nights at the fiddle club and multiple conventions of tea-sipping knitters ever compare with the culture that produced Plato and Sophocles, Aeschylus and Aristophanes? But here too she didn't really engage with her listeners, most of whom probably didn't

239

know their Sophocles from their Sappho. When she sat down, she met the fate that public speakers dread: half-hearted, polite clapping.

Duncan stepped up to the microphone. Like the others, he had a clutch of notes that he didn't look at. Though he affected jollity, I detected an underlying nervousness, because he spoke too quickly, not allowing one point to sink in before he went on to the next. 'Roll up, roll up,' he bellowed. 'Are you tired of false news? Then lend me your ears and I'll tell you the real news. The real news, which neither Joanna nor anyone else can undermine, is that the Scottish Government's own figures show that the Republic of Shetland will be one of the richest nations on earth. Joanna can waffle all she likes about declining demand and a shift to renewable energy, but the hard fact is that the world can't wean itself off oil overnight. Overnight? It's doubtful that the world can manage this within twenty years. And within these twenty years Shetland can build up a sovereign wealth fund that, per capita, can rival anyone's.'

If I'd heard the phrase 'sovereign wealth fund' once since I came to Shetland, I'd heard it a dozen times. Still, I was impressed by the fact that Duncan had quotations from Shakespeare and phrases like 'per capita' on the tip of his tongue. I wondered if Brian had given him a lot of tutoring. Anyway, after he'd given us yet more figures on energy, he went on to ridicule Joanna's every argument and even to ridicule her ridicule of Shetland culture. 'Something wrong,' he asked, 'with dancing to the Mirrie Dancers? Something wrong with fiddle music? Something wrong with your mother or your granny or your sister using the best Shetland wool to produce the warmest and most attractive clothing? Better to head to Edinburgh and do your useless degree in media studies or equality issues or the history of posing throughout the ages?'

Large sections of his audience loved this. They stamped, they cheered, they clapped furiously, and Duncan's confidence grew with every burst of applause. Despite his blatant sexism, he sounded convincing, and especially so when he came to a pithy analysis of Scotland's fiscal deficit.

'Let's do some more arithmetic,' he said. 'I know there's nothing you like better. According to the government's figures, Scotland has a deficit of "only" three billion. Now take out the revenue from Shetland's oil; at once you're up to at least eleven billion. Now remove the income from renting out bits of the country to Russians and Chinese and Arabs; the figure's at no less than fourteen billion...' Again, I wondered about the figures, but he went charging on: 'The Scottish Government and the SNP before them have been promising for years that they will eliminate – well, maybe reduce – this deficit by "growing" the economy. They make it sound like growing potatoes, but you only grow your economy by producing more stuff and more services that other people actually want. When Wayne and his dad get up before it's light to catch fish that people want to eat, when my dad and I stay up half the night to repair an engine that some Norwegian skipper *has* to use, that does more for the economy than any number of committees sitting in cosy chambers in Holyrood.'

The cheers were growing ever louder and more frequent. Duncan sensed that he could go out on a high. 'This' – he was back to bellowing – 'is what Shetland's good at – working – and this is why we should – no, *must* – go it alone. Thank you very much.'

He sat down abruptly. The applause rang on for several minutes, and I felt that the debate was lost.

When Debbie came forward, the first thing she did was give everyone a long, slow smile. It was a good ploy, if it was a ploy. She was saying that she

241

wasn't here to fight with anyone; she wasn't here to create bitterness; all she wanted was to tell us what was in her heart.

'Fake news,' she began. 'I don't have much to say about that. The Athens of the north – I don't really have an opinion on that either. Our culture is important, of course, but every culture has its strengths and weaknesses, and we could waste a lot of breath on questions that can't be answered. No, I think Wayne and Duncan are to be congratulated, because they have with great honesty put their finger on the real issues.'

She paused. Some smart Alec shouted, 'Well, get the finger out.' George the Second glared.

Debbie turned a benevolent beam on the heckler. 'Yes. The first real issue is the money. Wayne and Duncan have gone to great lengths to persuade us that *we* will be richer – far richer; we'll be rolling in it; we'll be like King Midas; when we have our sovereign wealth fund, everything we touch will turn to gold. What could possibly be a better outcome?'

'Nothing,' one of the boys in my section shouted.

'Ah,' Debbie said, 'but remember King Midas. Remember how he touched his daughter and she turned to gold. Then he wanted her back. He wanted a warm, living, breathing, loving human being. He learned, too late, that greed doesn't create value; rather, it *destroys* what *is* valuable. It's a lesson that's been repeated again and again throughout the centuries, repeated because people tend to forget it. We can all be seduced…'

'Speak for yourself,' someone suggested loudly, and even George the Second had to be amused.

Debbie suppressed a giggle, or appeared to; perhaps she was just telling the audience that she was one of them. 'Yes,' she said, 'it is so easy to be hypnotised by shining objects of desire – by fancy cars, by bigger and better

televisions, by bigger and faster computers. But ask yourself: at this moment, what would make you happier? Isn't it something to do with relationships? That boy or that girl whose hand you would love to hold? Those parents you would like to stop arguing? That brother or sister who you would like to consider *you*? That best friend forever who has drifted away? And what difference would a lot of money make? None? That's the *best-case* scenario. The probability is that money would make things *worse*, because the more people have, the more they want, the more they compare themselves with the next person and feel aggrieved. That wealth *might* make Shetland happier, but equally it might not. It might tear apart families and communities.'

The audience was quiet now. They knew that Debbie was talking sense. Speaking softly, like a therapist counselling a troubled client, she went on to develop the thesis that money had often proved the root of all evil, and therefore the people of Shetland, who already had a caring, compassionate society, shouldn't risk it all in the hope of finding a bigger pot of gold.

She concluded what turned out to be the first half of her speech with a warning delivered in the gentlest of tones. 'So, when Wayne and Duncan and others tell you – quite rightly – about the virtues of Shetland's way of life, don't let their enthusiasm become a fig leaf for greed.'

A fig leaf? I knew where that phrase had come from.

She began to build the second part of her argument. 'Both Wayne and Duncan – but Wayne especially – gave the game away regarding a second reason – the real reason – why you might want, or might think you want, Shetland to be independent. This reason is subtler than the simple desire for money; subtler and more insidious, and much more destructive. What was Wayne really saying when he talked about Shetland's work ethic and community spirit? He was saying what groups of people often say, all over

243

the world and in every age. He was saying, aren't we great? Here's tae us, wha's like us? Aren't we – let's get the word right – *superior*? The group or the nationality that is cast as *inferior* varies with time and place. In the bad old days of Brexit, it was those who lived on mainland Europe. In the campaign for Indyref2, it was the class-ridden, self-seeking English. And now it's the couch potatoes of the Scottish mainland. It doesn't make a lot of difference.'

She paused, very serious now, willing her audience to think. 'But wait. Remember Hitler? He said that the Germans, or Aryans, were superior and the Jews, gypsies and homosexuals were definitely inferior. No one's suggesting that the Republic of Shetland would start to exterminate any Scots that they found in their midst, but, when our wealthy, attractive Shetland sucks in migrants from Scotland and England and Europe and across the globe, who's to say what conflicts and what perceptions may arise? In short, once you form an in-group and decide that the out-group is threatening or hostile, anything can happen, most of it nasty. The truth is that creating such groups in one's own mind comes from a basic insecurity – not primarily economic or financial, but personal, psychological, existential...'

'Wow! Existential?' someone called out. All right, I thought, 'existential' wasn't in the vocabulary of your average teenager, but they all got the gist.

'And the problem with insecurity,' Debbie went on, unruffled, 'is that it isn't solved at all when you've created your in-group and started to defend it against out-groups. No, the problem is no more than masked. The only way of dealing with the question of who you are and what your existence means is, first, to admit that there is a problem and, second, to think and talk calmly about it. Here's what I want to suggest to you. I asked you already what was really valuable to you and you told me – oh all right, *I* told *you* – that what's

truly valuable is relationships. Well then, your life can have meaning every time you interact with someone – provided, that is, you are hiding nothing, holding no axe to grind, accepting that no man is an island unto himself, believing that it is your duty – and your highest pleasure – to *give*. But a country is exactly the same, because people make the country. So a country is healthy, generous, rich – in the fullest possible sense – if it rejects xenophobia, narrowness, prejudice – the kind of xenophobia, narrowness and prejudice that threatens to sweep across the world – if instead its people want to reduce divisions and inequality, if they see, not different ethnicity or skin colour or religion or sexual orientation, but fellow humans, brothers and sisters, with whom empathy is possible.'

'In-groups'… 'insecurity'… 'meaning'… 'value'… how much of this had come from Gregor to me, from me to Sharon, and from Sharon to Debbie? Still, even if Gregor, Sharon and I provided the spark, the fuel for this fire had been building in Debbie for a long time. She was truly an orator.

She gave us a brief history of those figures throughout the ages who had the best answers, in her view, to the problem of the existential void. She started with Jesus, then dallied with Buddha and his analysis of desire, and finished up with John Lennon. She even sang to us: '*You may say I'm a dreamer…*' I was waiting for her to start some community signing, but quite soon she concluded: 'All right, I *am* a dreamer, but I put it to you that the world *needs* a dream, not in the sense of something unachievable, but as an attitude, a programme, a direction, something we can work towards. I beg you, therefore, to make Shetland memorable, not for its money or its blatant self-congratulation but for its political philosophy of empathy and compassion. Thank you.'

There was none of the cheering and foot-stamping that had been accorded to Wayne, but the applause was warm. The very quietness that in Joanna's case had been a bad sign now suggested that Debbie had forced the audience to reflect on their own emotions. We would soon see if she had actually won them over.

A few questions followed, but they were mostly tentative and about economic details that had already been covered. Debbie didn't have to say much more, but she brought the house down when someone asked her if she truly didn't want to be rich.

She shook her head. 'Honestly. What can I say?' Then she sang, '*I don't care too much for money, money can't buy me love.*'

'Love *me*, Debbie,' someone called.

'No, *me*,' shouted someone else.'

'*Me.*'

'*Me.*'

The Voice of God was required to still the storm. 'I think,' Peter said, while everyone was laughing, 'it is time to put the motion to the vote. Those in favour, those who say that Shetland should remain part of Scotland, please raise your right hand.'

Hands went up, some at once, some more slowly. I couldn't have said if they represented a majority.

Peter said, 'We'll have to have a count. Colleagues, please.

The tellers, me included, counted quickly and reported to George the Second. He entered figures in a notebook.

Peter repeated the process for those who were against the motion. George made his notes and added everything up. We could see him checking his addition again before he tore off the page and handed it to Peter.

The Voice of God was at its most sonorous. 'In favour of the motion, two hundred and eight. Against, one hundred and ninety-six. I declare the motion carried.'

Cheers and boos rose in what seemed like equal measure, but I didn't care how narrow the margin was. Shetland's youth had set an example which perhaps the adult electorate would follow. Perhaps Arnold had, as Pamela declared, been worrying too much. Perhaps, then, all my plotting was unnecessary. And perhaps I didn't need to be a murderer.

It took half an hour for the atrium to clear. I don't know why I waited for Sharon; maybe I had a premonition. When we went out to the car park, there were still groups of pupils hanging around, and someone hissed at us. Wayne and his cronies were standing near the front door of the school; the hiss could have come from them. A rumble – a growl – pursued us to our cars. I let Sharon drive off first, and I hoped she didn't notice as a missile – an empty can – missed her rear bumper.

Chapter 20

Friday, 26th

A text from Colin waited for me in the morning. *Dinner tonight?*

'Dinner' meant 'dinner followed by sex'. I could do without it. I hadn't slept all that well, and I had a big day, after all, on Saturday.

But I was still nervous about Billy. So I texted back, *Sure. 7? How about the Phu Siam?*

Good. I'll come by.

I swept the glue, the gloves and the screwtops into a cupboard before I went to school.

Joy and Peter were at the door of Joy's classroom, looking sombre.

'Something wrong?' I said.

Peter said, 'Sharon.'

'What's happened?'

'You're not a Facebook person?'

'No.'

He shook his head. 'Joanna went on Facebook last night, thanking Sharon for all the help she'd given them. Facebook and Twitter erupted with people accusing Sharon of feeding the girls ideas. She's with George right now. He's had complaints by the ton. I think he'll suspend her until he investigates how neutral she really was.'

I was aghast, because *I* was to blame. So I leapt to minimise Sharon's responsibility. 'But of course she'd *help* the girls. Otherwise, what was her role?'

Joy said, 'Well, there's help and there's help.' She had a miserable air about her, which I couldn't imagine was caused by Sharon's fall from grace.

'In the meantime,' Peter said, 'she has a class first period.' He glanced at Joy. 'I'm afraid you're the only one free.'

She rolled her eyes. 'Damn. I've got a hundred things to do.'

'I'm sure you have. Sorry.'

Peter went off to his own room and Joy shot a glare at me.

I tried to make a joke of it. 'Not *my* fault.'

'You're her friend.'

'Oh Joy, I hardly control her every move.' She looked so downcast that I said, 'Something else wrong?'

Her shoulders sagged. 'It's Eric. He's had word that the sale of the hotel is probably not going through. We're going to have to go begging to my father.'

Really? Well, Eric could always kill him.

At the interval, there was only one topic of discussion in the staffroom; if you could judge by the comments of those who spoke up, lynching would be far too good for Sharon.

Eleanor worked in Home Economics. She seemed a warm person, and she baked a mean fruit scone, as I'd discovered at a coffee morning shortly after I arrived, but today she was icy. 'This,' she said, 'could swing the whole debate across the islands. George had no option but to suspend her.'

'Too right,' said one of Eleanor's departmental colleagues, famed for her stovies.

'Whoever heard' – this was Matthew – 'of a school girl who could trot out words like "existentialism"?' He turned to me, challenging. 'How often have you heard "existentialism" bandied about in *your* classroom?'

I wanted out of this argument before it started. 'Never.'

'There you are. You still going to defend your friend?'

'I'm not on the jury.'

'Yes, you are.'

'Well then, I'd say that one word doesn't put the case beyond reasonable doubt.'

'You would say that.'

I couldn't produce a riposte.

During the last period of the day, I nearly lost it, as they say. I had to take a Third Year class for Sharon, and two of the boys were out to goad me, asking if I agreed that Sharon was a traitor. They knew, of course, that we were friends.

'A traitor to what?' I said.

'To Shetland,' one said. He was an untidy youth; the collar of his shirt was dirty. I didn't like him.

'Don't be ridiculous. Are you saying that all these people who agreed with Debbie were also traitors?'

'So why has the headmaster suspended Miss MacIntosh?'

'Why don't you ask him?' My voice was rising, an engine revving out of control.

'All right, I will.'

'Now get on with your work.' I had set them a passage for interpretation. It wasn't fascinating, but I was so tired that I couldn't think of anything else. I was, of course, making the exact mistake that I had warned myself against just two days ago

They didn't get on with their work. They tried to stare me out and I could feel my body stiffen. I've talked about the tedium of the classroom, and I've talked about the joy you can find there once in a blue moon. But what I haven't talked about is the teacher's nightmare. Do I need to spell it out? It's the end of the day and you're drained, because you're only human; the class is out of control; the adolescents in front of you are more interested in last night's mayhem and next weekend's drinking than anything you have to offer; they're hurling insults and threats at each other; you're praying for the period to end and, having seen your self-esteem shattered, the only other thing you can pray for is that no one gets seriously hurt. After a period like that, you just want to curl into a ball and die.

I'd had quite a few experiences like that in my first job – do you wonder that I'd have given anything to get out? In Shetland, I'd had none – so far.

I was about to bawl at the boys, which they would have loved, or send them to Peter, which would have been an admission of defeat on my part. The shout rose in my throat, then I coughed and stopped myself.

The untidy one smirked. 'Bad cough, miss. Too many cigarettes.'

Humour. That was always a chance to lighten the tone. I made a face, pretending that I was in despair over my own health. 'And I don't even smoke.'

I proceeded to ignore them. They didn't do any work, and the hubbub in the class rose and rose. I pinched my forehead, trying to imply that I wasn't well, to save some face. Apart from that, all I did was let my eyes float in the

direction of any who were becoming too outrageous. Sometimes that calmed them down and sometimes it didn't. Exhaustion – it seemed absolute – swamped me.

The period crawled to a close, the day finished. I sat at Sharon's desk and checked my phone. One message from her – *Can you come over?* – and one from Gregor – *Mareel car park at 4.30?*

I texted back to Gregor – *OK* – and after some thought replied to Sharon – *Sorry. Tied up just now. Be over asap. Before six?* I didn't know what she wanted. Some reassurance? I could give her an hour's worth and still be back in time for Colin.

I pulled into the Mareel car park at twenty-five past four. It was suitably anonymous. People parked there if they were going to the cinema or were meeting someone for afternoon tea at Hay's Dock or had preparations to make for a cultural event at the Mareel itself. There was no sign of Gregor's Landrover.

The momentary optimism of last night had gone. There was no guarantee whatsoever that the voters of Shetland would be influenced by the result of a debate in the high school. It was absurd to think so. The logic was the same as it always had been: I had to discredit Eric to scupper Free Shetland, and the only window of opportunity was this weekend.

The car quickly became cold as I waited. Gregor arrived at twenty to five, slipping into the passenger seat, holding something in a Tesco bag.

'We were in luck,' he said. 'Only one kind of Chilean red at a price anywhere near the price of this.'

'Isla Negra?'

'Isla Negra. And there's plenty left. It's unimaginable that it will have gone by tomorrow. So you won't need your second bottle of toxin. Just dispose of it.'

'Right.'

'You ready?' He put the bag on the floor by his feet and thrust his hands into the pockets of a leather jacket that I'd never seen before.

I didn't feel ready. I felt shaky. 'Don't know. I'm thinking, won't my tyres leave tread marks on Sven's drive?'

Gregor was calm – it was all very well for him. 'With the amount of rain Lerwick gets? Marks won't last long. Besides, the forensic people can't test all the tyres in Shetland. There would have to be a clue pointing to you. And there won't be.'

'And you want me to wipe Sven's phone clean?'

'Carol,' – he was soothing; it must have been obvious how nervous I was – 'it's not *me*, it's *us*. We've been through this. I have arranged for a text message about Charlie Mann to be sent from Sven's phone to Eric's, at five to eight. The sound will be turned off on both phones. When the police investigate, it will be a huge help if Sven's phone has been cleaned, because – as we said – the assumption will be that Eric went out to Sven's, sent this message to himself to establish a red herring, then took a wipe to the phone.'

'But I might not have the chance.'

In fact, I had a ploy ready, a ploy that would also allow me to swap the bottles. Only thing was, my confidence was low.

'Of course,' Gregor said. 'If you can't do it, you can't do it. But it would be the icing on the cake.'

A commotion to my right distracted me. I'd parked beside a big estate car and a bulky woman carrying multiple parcels was fumbling with the handle

on the passenger door, cursing. Another woman – I couldn't see her very well – was loading bags into the boot. The bulky one dropped a parcel and swore ever more loudly, prompting her friend to come round from the back of the car and relieve her of some of her burdens. I never knew that getting into a car could be so difficult.

I turned back to Gregor. He'd removed his hands from his pockets and was blowing on them. 'It's cold in here,' he said.

I didn't think it was *that* cold. 'No gloves?'

'I've misplaced them.'

I'd never had the impression that he was absent-minded. But my thoughts swung back to the task in hand. What had *I* forgotten? What had *I* misplaced?

'Want to come round tonight?' he said.

'I can't.' I told him about Sharon, but not about Colin. Did I really imagine he'd be jealous?

'You're very empathetic. A loyal friend.'

'That's me.'

The bulky woman and her friend, having settled down, backed out of their space and drove off. Gregor watched them go before he opened the door. 'See you next week?' he said. 'When the dust has settled?'

'Sure.'

In fact, I was so edgy that I couldn't imagine relaxing in his arms again.

When I came back from the Mareel, I couldn't eat. I put the Isla Negra on the draining board, took out both containers of batrachotoxin, a pair of the latex gloves, and a new stick of glue. I couldn't believe how I was trembling. Me?

I realised I could already have put fingerprints on the bottle of wine. Putting on the gloves, I wiped it down, first with a wet cloth and then with a piece of kitchen towel. I twisted off the screwtop. How much wine did I have to pour off?

I tipped a little down the sink. Enough? Hell, I didn't know. But the batrachotoxin was so powerful – hadn't Gregor said so? – that even a small amount would work.

I placed the Isla Negra on the bottom of the sink, took a deep breath and opened one of the bottles of batrachotoxin. The dropper was attached to the top, as you would expect, and I could see that if I used it to transfer the toxin, I would take forever. *Damn it.* I put the dropper carefully in the sink and then, decisively – because a liquid dribbles when you pour too cautiously – I topped up the level of the wine.

Almost done. A little of the batrachotoxin remained. I put that beside the Isla Negra, opened the glue and applied it to the neck of the wine bottle and the cap. Then I screwed the top shut, getting the perforations perfectly lined up.

My phone rang. I had left it on the work surface beside the sink and I saw at a glance that the caller was Sharon. She would have to wait.

I moved the wine to the worktop. Then – I didn't stop to think – I poured the rest of the batrachotoxin down the sink, and rinsed both bottle and dropper with immense care – again and again and again and again. Putting the top back on, I placed the bottle, the open stick of glue and the other three sticks in the Tesco bag. Our bins for non-recyclable material would be emptied on Monday. No one was going to search my flat before Monday. Correction: no one was going to search my flat *ever*.

The second container of batrachotoxin sat there, a piece of damning evidence. I realised I was panting – and the phone rang again.

Sharon. There must be a crisis. I pulled off the gloves, deposited them in the bag and pressed the Answer button.

'Carol.' Sharon was whispering. 'They're at the foot of the stairs. Boys, men, I don't know. They're chanting. And they've thrown something at my door.'

I didn't process her words for a second or two. Then I understood: she had a mob of Free Shetlanders outside her flat.

'Sharon, it'll be okay. They're all bluff. They won't hurt you. Have you phoned the police?'

'I tried.' Her voice was still an agonised whisper. 'It's a central number. They asked for my postcode, I couldn't remember it. They asked what the threat was, and I started crying.'

A central number? Police Scotland had a call centre in Stirling or Falkirk or Grangemouth or somewhere. An operator would have a script to follow and would never have heard of the Lerwick lanes.

'Why are you whispering?' I said.

'So that Robert doesn't hear me. I'm in the kitchen. He's in the living room with the door closed. He's watching a very noisy cartoon and he hasn't noticed *anything*. Thank God.'

'Okay. Listen. I'll come round. Don't answer the door until you're sure it's me.'

I phoned Colin. He said he'd meet me at Sharon's in ten minutes. Putting another pair of gloves on, I grabbed the second bottle of batrachotoxin and poured the whole damn lot down the sink. Then I did my rinsing and dumped the bottle in the bag with the first one.

256

When I went out, I told myself I wasn't scared of a mob. What could they do? They'd be all bluster and bravado. Yet, as I climbed the rise opposite the library, I had a moment's unease. Lerwick's lanes were all very atmospheric – they made it easy to imagine Dutch sailors back in the 1890s, clomping up and down in their clogs while they waited for the herring season to begin – but you couldn't exactly cross to the other side of the road if you saw trouble coming.

Going down the hill, before you reach the lanes proper, there's a big car park. I was halfway across this when I heard male voices and almost at once a group of lads appeared, coming up. I thought about retreating, but I was too slow.

One of them accosted me. 'Hey. Going to see your traitor friend?'

I peered. It was Duncan, swathed in a hooded parka. At once my courage came back, because I couldn't see Duncan and his friends being truly dangerous.

'Maybes aye, maybes no, Duncan. What about you? Been busy?'

He hesitated. 'Don't believe her if she blames me. I wouldn't waste the eggs.'

Eggs? What brave warriors. I edged round them, and another one, whom I didn't recognise, said, 'We'll be back with the heavy mob.'

I didn't bandy words any more, merely went on down the lane. When I reached Sharon's flat, Colin was striding up from Commercial Street. We climbed the stairs to the front door, which was sticky with egg white and yolk and bits of shell.

I rang the bell and called through the letter box, 'Sharon, it's me.' No reply. I called again, 'Sharon.' Now I heard footsteps. 'I've got Colin with me, and the boys have gone.'

She pulled open the door, her face tear-streaked, and I stepped in to give her a hug.

She burst out sobbing. 'Carol, it was awful.'

I held her, patting her back. 'It's okay, it's okay. They've gone. They're just kids anyway. All bark and no bite.'

She let me go. I said, 'You know Colin?'

'Of course.' She wiped her eyes. 'Thank you for coming, Colin.'

'No problem.' He looked sheepish.

'Listen,' I said to Colin. 'I don't think they'll be back, but I can phone you if necessary. I'll stay with Sharon. You go for a drink. I'm sorry about dinner.'

He was glad of a way out, but didn't want to show it. 'Well, I'll be at Captain Flint's. I can be back in a couple of minutes.'

I talked with Sharon for half an hour or so – in the kitchen while Robert watched more cartoons. She told me that George the Second had been 'stern' with her, saying he had to conduct a full investigation. When she left the school, she'd sat in her car and cried. Then she phoned to make an appointment at the doctor's because she was 'totally cracking up'.

I asked what the doctor had said.

'She was very kind, perhaps because I was crying my eyes out. She gave me sleeping pills. Strong ones. Nitrazepam. And she said, when I went back to school – she seemed confident I would be going back – I should keep a low profile for a long time.'

'Sounds like sensible advice.'

Sleep was exactly what Sharon needed. Her eyes were hollow, and at the same time puffy from her tears. I wondered what else I could do for her.

'Want a day out on Sunday?' I said.

'That would be nice.' Her look brimmed over with gratitude. God, did she need a friend.

I explained about my visit to Jason's parents. She said, 'You're a saint.'

That was a good joke.

We agreed on a carry-out. I detoured to my flat, fetched one of the bottles of white wine, the one I was sure I could open, then I went down to the Phu Siam. The Thai girl, who now wore a duffel coat with her woolly hat, gave me a wan smile when I told her that spring would be here soon.

Sharon divided the food into three – Robert, apparently, was not averse to chicken and cashew nuts – and she and I settled in the kitchen.

She tried to talk brightly about Debbie, saying how intelligent and mature and attractive she was, but the brightness was only a brittle surface. Beneath it lay – what? Envy? Because she couldn't be where Debbie was – on the threshold of a life full of adventures? If I had been in her shoes, I'd have been envious too.

The wine went down. She asked about Colin. I said I wasn't sure. We danced round the topic of men until we'd finished the wine and most of the food. Another high tide of exhaustion crashed over me and I realised that if I didn't go soon, I'd be in no fit state to deal with tomorrow.

'Can I ask you a favour?' I said.

'Of course.'

'Thing is, I can't sleep either. I don't know what the problem is. Maybe it's all the nastiness that's floating around. Could I scrounge a nitrazepam?'

'Oh.' She hadn't imagined that I could have a weakness. 'Sure. There's twenty-eight in the packet. I don't think I'll need them... all at once.'

'Don't joke about it.'

She fetched her handbag from the living room, popped a pill out of the foil and wrapped it neatly in a Kleenex like a little present.

'Thank you,' I said, and stood up.

'Thank *you*.' She gave me a hug.

I saw no one at all on my way up the hill and across the douce streets of the New Town. I poured a glass of water to wash down Sharon's pill, then I texted Colin and apologised, implying that I was staying with Sharon. When I'd brushed and flossed my teeth, I went to bed.

The nitrazepam didn't work at once; my thoughts were whirling, the pendulum of doubt swinging wildly. How had I got into this madness? Why couldn't I settle for a safe and comfortable existence?

But I could, I could, I could. Of course I could. All I had to do was abort the plan. It would be easy.

Chapter 21

Saturday, 27th

I woke, heard the rain, got up and looked out of the window. The pendulum of resolve had swung again, because the sky was totally overcast and this had to be an omen, a final warning from the Norse gods that either I grasped my fate in my own hands or I would be trapped for the rest of my life in greyness.

After breakfast, I took the car to Tesco, because there were a couple of items that I needed for my visit to Sven's. I also needed food, because your life doesn't stop when you end someone else's. My trolley soon became piled high, everyday groceries obscuring the one purchase that might catch someone's attention.

The checkouts were busy, only two offering human assistance. Helen was at one of these, and I chose her queue. When my turn came, she said by way of a greeting, 'Weren't you going to take me out for drinks?'

'Drinks, plural?' I started to empty my trolley. 'Yes, I was. I will. But – I thought I told you – it won't be tonight. I'm tied up.'

She passed things across her barcode reader with practised speed – until her gaze fell on my single remarkable item. 'Bloody hell,' she said. 'A *twelve*-pack? You havin' a good weekend?'

I did that modest shrug of mine.

'Who is he?'

'Don't think you know him.'

'Well, he's going to be a busy boy, whoever he is. Some of us' – she lowered her voice – 'have fucking forgotten what it's like.'

'Don't believe you.'

'You should. Between you and Natasha, I feel like a fucking nun.'

'How *is* Natasha?'

Helen spluttered. 'Never been better. She and Ivan can't keep their hands off each other. If she hints one more time at how great he is between the sheets, I'm going to strangle her.'

'Seems only reasonable. Got anywhere with that sonar device?'

'Not yet.' She beeped the last of my shopping. 'Clubcard?'

'Forgotten it.'

I paid in cash. At the best of times, I wasn't keen on Tesco knowing what I'd bought.

With another vague promise to take her out for a drink, I left Helen to her beeping.

My intention was to go out to Sven's for six, when it should be fully dark. That gave me, after I'd unpacked my shopping, almost seven hours. Too long.

My brain seethed with good advice. *One thing at a time. Fill your mind. Don't give doubts a chance.*

I prepared my backpack, which I was going to take from the car into Sven's house. He was going to say, 'What have you got in there?' and I was going to say, 'A couple of presents for you, but you're not going to get them until…' Then came my ploy. It had to work.

The 'presents' were the packet of condoms that Helen had made such a fuss about and a Genoa cake that I'd just bought at Tesco. Why a Genoa

cake? It had seemed to me to be the kind of offering you might take to an old widower who had no one to do his home baking. It was also a way of hedging my bets: if swapping the wine turned out to be impossible – if, after all, Sven had someone visiting him – I could produce the cake and pretend that this was no more than a social visit.

I put a jersey at the bottom of the little rucsac and wrapped another round the bottle of Isla Negra. The last thing I wanted was the clunking of glass if I had to put my bundle down on a hard floor.

That left the gloves and the wipes. They went into a zipped front pocket where they would be easily accessible. They would go back in the same place.

I phoned Sharon. Robert was crying in the background. 'Don't want to,' I heard him whine.

'What's happening?' I said.

'Nothing.' Sharon sounded harassed, but I detected nothing out of the ordinary, only the stress you'd expect from a single mother with a difficult child.

'No more trouble in the lane?'

'No. We're meeting my parents for lunch. They think I need support.'

'So all you have to do is reassure them, calm down Robert, avoid indigestion over lunch, do the washing and the shopping and generally have a good day?'

'That's about it.' She laughed. 'You've made me feel better already.'

I laughed too. 'Good. Maybe talk to you later.'

When I put the phone down, I realised that *I* had wanted to talk longer to *her*. Time yawned in front of me.

Nothing for it. I would clean the flat. Kill two birds with one stone.

Housework. Hands up all those who love it. Like anyone else, I normally just wanted to get it done.

But not today. Slowly and methodically, I cleared the surfaces in the kitchen, wiped them all down, and cleared away the salt and the sugar and the miscellaneous utensils that rarely rested in their proper place. I cleaned the hob until it shone, and brushed and mopped the floor. Turning to the bathroom, I scoured every blemish from the toilet bowl, took cleaner to the sink and shower, and tidied the arrays of shampoo and conditioners and shower gel.

About one, I had a break for some soup and an apple. There's an old Buddhist trick someone taught me in university, a simple way of calming a jumpy stomach. The nub of it is that you concentrate totally on your food: you think about where it came from; you think about the rain and the sun that gave it life; you think about the farmers who planted it and nurtured it and harvested it; you think about it sliding down your gullet into your stomach; you think about the microbes that get to work extracting the energy and sending it round your body; you think about the waste that starts its journey down your intestine; whatever you do, you *don't* think about anything that might upset you.

It worked. It even had a knock-on effect, because, as I lay down on my couch after eating, I was able to continue my mind control. I was an ordinary person; I was taking a decisive step to ensure that I had a good life; that was all.

Nitrazepam also has a knock-on effect. It leaves a reservoir of drowsiness in your system, which for many people is a good thing. It was a good thing

for me now, because I slept for twenty minutes and when I awoke I was refreshed.

I took the afternoon more slowly. The living room, by the time I'd finished, had never been so free of dust.

At last, it was 5.30. I spent ten minutes in the toilet, staring at my knees. Then I wrapped up warmly, lifted my backpack and went out to the car.

Nobody saw me. Nobody *would* see me. At that time on a Saturday afternoon, with the light fading, nobody cared about anything except their evening meal and the television programmes they were going to glue their eyes to. I drove up to North Road, past the Toll Clock Centre, round the roundabout, past the ferry terminal, and away up the hill onto the moors.

Sven's track was completely black; I wouldn't have seen it if I hadn't reconnoitred. The rain, which had given way to a light drizzle during the day, was back to a full downpour, making me worry again about tyre marks in the mud.

In fact, the track wasn't particularly muddy. Most of the potholes had been filled with pebbles, on which a tyre wouldn't leave a discernible trace.

There were more pebbles on the space outside Sven's front door. My tyres crunched, as effective as any alarm.

Sven had the door open for me before I knocked. '*Well*,' he said.

There were a lot of nuances in that word, the main one being *Well, I know what you've come for.*

I said, 'Is my Viking warrior fit for receiving visitors?'

His eyes gleamed with anticipation. 'Could be.'

He was wearing an old sweater that had smears across the midriff and tufts of straw sticking to the cuffs. As I came in, I caught a whiff of what might have been sheep dung. Perfect.

The kitchen was untidy, the work surfaces even more cluttered than mine. His Isla Negra was on the table, unopened, and his phone lay besides a heap of junk mail and discarded envelopes. The oven was on, leaking the first hint of roasting lamb.

'Cosy,' I said.

'What's in the bag?'

I didn't take it off my shoulder. 'I have a couple of presents for you, but…' – I flicked my gaze over his sweater – 'I'm not going to give them to you immediately.'

'Why not?'

'Even Viking warriors sometimes have to think about… having a shower.'

He hesitated. Viking warriors didn't like to be bossed about.

I gave him a little encouragement. 'Go on. Cleanse yourself – first.'

He caught the implication – he could hardly fail to. 'Don't go away.'

'No fear of that.'

He went out into a hallway, leaving the door open. I resisted the urge to get my gloves on at once, because he might come marching back through, telling me to pour a glass of wine or make a cup of coffee. It was only when I heard another door close that I swung the backpack to the floor and took off my parka.

Gloves. Wine. Swap the bottles. Wrap his in my jersey and stow it in my backpack. Place Genoa cake and condoms on the table. All done in little over a minute.

I hesitated, but no one could have a shower so quickly. I pulled out a wet tissue and wiped his phone meticulously. Then I dried it with a Kleenex and put gloves and tissues back in the zipped compartment. The little rucsac I put in a corner by the door, so that he couldn't stumble over it. I stood at the window and looked out at the dark.

He didn't take long. Flip-flops slapped along the hall and he stood at the door wrapped only in a towel. The Genoa cake and the condoms caught his eye, as I knew they would.

'What's with the cake?'

'It's to make up for the fact that I'm very inadequate at home baking.'

'Nobody's perfect.'

I stepped forward and smiled. A protuberance appeared in the front of his towel. Having done what I had come for, I had no alternative but to pay the penalty. The best thing to do, as always, was to put on a good performance.

Another step. I whipped his towel away. He was quite big. And getting bigger. I glanced down. 'So, my Viking warrior?'

His left hand grabbed the condoms, and his right grabbed my arm. 'Let's go.'

The bedroom was on a par with the kitchen: clothes on the floor; a curtain rail that had lost two hooks; an unmade double bed; crumpled sheets that were certainly not fresh. I pulled away from him and stripped off my jersey, teeshirt and bra. 'One second,' I said. 'I need to go to the toilet.'

In the bathroom, I removed the rest of my clothes and applied some of my trusty lubricant. I wasn't going to let him hurt me.

He was lying on the bed, his erection reaching for the sky. I sauntered up, swaying my hips, leaned over and brushed my breasts against his lips. He responded as any man would.

I wasn't completely turned on, but I wasn't repulsed either. 'Mm,' I said after a few minutes. I couldn't prolong this, I'd realised, because the stronger that aroma from the oven grew, the harder it would be to refuse an invitation to dinner.

He'd put the condoms on his bedside table. I took one out, released it from its wrapper and rolled it onto him. Then I gave him a shove. 'Get over the bed a bit.'

'The missionary position?' he said.

'I'm an old-fashioned girl.'

To tell you the truth, he wasn't bad. His enthusiasm was obvious and his stamina impressive for an old chap. I gave him an alpha double minus.

But when he rolled off me, I saw problems looming. If I let him use the bathroom first, get dressed and get into the kitchen before me, he could have two glasses of wine poured before I could do anything about it. I had to escape soon, and yet not so suddenly that he'd be suspicious.

I reached the bathroom ahead of him. 'No bidet?' I said.

'Huh.' He was trying to peel off the condom while his hand shook. 'Slap some water on yourself like anyone else.'

I did that, although I would have liked a cleaner towel. Then I swept up the clothes I'd abandoned and carried them into the bedroom. I was half dressed when he reappeared.

I thought it would be better, if I had to pass a little time, to do it where we were. So, when I'd finished dressing, I sat on the bed and glanced towards the condoms.

'What's the betting? How long will those last us? Six weeks at two a week or four weeks at three?'

He frowned, making me wonder if distrust was dawning in him for the first time. He could understand a one-off fuck, but an *affair* was something he'd never imagined.

He said, 'I heard you were seeing Colin Carruthers.'

I rolled my eyes. 'Sometimes you get fed up with *boys*. Anyway, you don't mind sharing, do you?'

'You serious?'

'Who knows? My moods can change with the tides.'

He took a clean shirt. 'You're a strange lady. Thought you said you were old-fashioned.'

'So I did. I might need to reconsider my self-evaluation.'

'You'll stay for dinner?' Not only had he chosen a clean shirt; he'd unearthed a fresh pair of trousers.

'What time you having it?'

'Eight o'clock.'

'Ah.' My grimace of disappointment was worthy of an Oscar. 'I said I'd be at Sharon's at eight.'

'Who's Sharon?'

I told him about Sharon, and the reaction to her girls' triumph in the debate.

'Her?' he said. 'You're friends with *her*?'

'Why shouldn't I be?'

I could see that half of him wanted to argue, but the other half wanted to keep me sweet, because he really wanted me to stay.

'You could ring her,' he said.

I pretended to think about that, before shaking my head. 'One thing I do like to do is keep my promises. I should have thought this out more carefully.'

'So now you're going to bugger off?'

There was hurt in his voice. Aren't men strange? Nine times out of ten, they don't just want to fuck you; they want *you* to want *them*.

'I can come back some other time, now that we've broken the ice.'

He grunted, because his pride wouldn't let him agree all at once.

Hold on, I thought. If I was really going to come back, the obvious next step would be to exchange phone numbers. But I couldn't have him typing mine into his Contacts.

I had to get out *fast*. 'Listen,' I said. 'I'm sorry I forgot about Sharon, but I'm going to go before we fall out. I wouldn't like that.'

I strode out of the room into the hallway and along the hall to the kitchen. He didn't follow me. I put on my parka, picked up my backpack, pulled my cuff over my hand to open the back door, and hurried out to the car. My guess was that he'd fume for half an hour, then pour himself a large glass of wine. After that – goodbye, Sven.

I drove gently up to the road, watching out for other headlights. There were none. Squalls of rain battered against my windscreen, overwhelming the wipers.

Cars passed me, of course, as I approached Lerwick. But I felt invisible, and invincible. No one was going to peer through the dirt on my windscreen to identify me. And Sven wasn't going to tell anyone I had been there, not in the short space of time before he opened his wine. I might have left traces – perhaps a hair or two in the bedroom or a spot of vaginal fluid on that towel in the bathroom – but what Gregor had said about the tyres applied equally

well here: no such trace would be usable unless there were a finger of suspicion already pointing at me.

And where could that suspicion possibly come from?

I had done it.

I parked outside my flat at a quarter to eight. I had barely switched off the engine when my phone rang.

Sharon.

Her voice was panicky. 'They're back, a whole crowd. Robert's screaming.'

I could hear him. 'Have you phoned 999?'

'No. I'm going to go mad.'

'Listen. I'll phone Colin, get him to phone his brother. That'll be faster than going through 999.'

The police station was a short walk away, but would anyone listen to *me*? They'd listen to Billy, one of their own.

'They're chanting something,' Sharon wailed.

I couldn't believe that other inhabitants of the lanes hadn't phoned 999 already. 'Don't do anything. Just hang on.'

'Okay.' She began to sob.

I called Colin. 'Billy's off duty' was his first reaction, but then he added, 'I'll phone him. Don't try to confront the crowd yourself.'

I drove over and parked across from the library. The rain had eased. As soon as I got out of the car, I could hear the chanting, although I had to go down the hill about twenty yards before I could make out the words. 'Traitor, traitor, traitor…' The low growl went on and on.

I went back to the car and waited. No police car with flashing lights. Nothing. Yet from the police station to here you could have thrown a stone.

After a long quarter of an hour, an emblazoned car with two uniformed policemen pulled in near me, while another two figures appeared from Lower Hillhead. Colin and Billy. Colin saw my car and signalled to me to stay put. Then he and Billy joined the policemen and started down the hill. I let them get out of sight before I followed.

The chanting had faded. Voices were audible, some of them raised, but there wasn't the shouting that you'd expect from a full-scale riot. Some sort of stand-off must be in progress.

I risked a peek down the last thirty yards towards Sharon's stairway. The policemen, with Colin and Billy close behind, had advanced into the middle of the mob – I reckoned there were about forty bodies, nearly all of them young and male – and were simply standing there, nodding in sympathy. In the circumstances, it seemed a wise course of action.

Various youths were shouting in anger. 'Who does she think she is?' 'She's an enemy of Shetland.' 'We've got the right to disagree.' The older policeman, who was taking the lead, let the attacks bounce off him. 'Yeah,' he kept saying. 'Yeah, yeah.'

This went on for some time. The policeman was an adept negotiator; it was clear how he expected the confrontation to end. Eventually, he achieved his purpose, for the crowd began to drift off down the hill, perhaps hastened on their way by the downpour that had returned.

When the last complainant had gone, I rounded the corner and made myself known to the police.

'You a friend of the lady's?' said the chief negotiator. 'Come up with me and see if you can reassure her.

We climbed the stairs. When I pushed open the letter box, I could hear that Robert was still screaming. 'Sharon!' I shouted.

She opened the door, red-eyed and haggard. 'They're gone,' I said.

Robert was beyond hysterical. The policeman clearly decided that he didn't want to go inside. He started to question Sharon about whether the crowd had done any damage or threatened her explicitly. She stuttered and said 'I don't know' half a dozen times.

I interrupted. 'Perhaps, if Sharon wants to make a statement, she can come round to the station later.'

He was relieved at that. 'You can stay with her?'

'Of course.'

His radio squawked. He went halfway down the stairs before he answered it. 'Oh?' I heard him say. 'Right.'

He went all the way down to the others and held a brief discussion. I realised that three of them – all but Colin – were leaving. 'Hey,' I shouted. 'What if those yobbos get drunk and come back?'

It was Billy who answered. 'Sorry. We have to go. If that happens, you'll need to phone again.'

Colin waited where he was until I joined him. 'Where are they going?' I said.

He was pale with shock. 'Sven Henderson's been found dead.'

Chapter 22

Saturday, 27th – Sunday, 28th

I knew, as I stood at the foot of Sharon's stairway, that I had to act my socks off.

'What happened?' I said.

Colin shook his head. 'I don't know, but there may have been foul play.'

'*Foul play*? Oh my God. Who found him?'

'Eric.'

'Oh no. Poor Eric. But who on earth would do something to Sven?'

'They don't know.'

I was furiously calculating times. It must now be about twenty to nine, although I didn't like to check my watch. That meant Eric must have found Sven and phoned the police – when? – say a quarter past eight. So he left his house to go to Sven's at perhaps eight o'clock. That would fit; he saw the message even though the sound on his phone was off, and he set out to see what was going on. I breathed a sigh of relief, because by a quarter to eight I was back in Lerwick. In short, Eric couldn't have seen either me or my car.

I said, 'Eric will have to phone Joy.'

'*Phone* her?'

'She's in Edinburgh this weekend, seeing a sick friend.'

'I didn't know that.'

'She'll be devastated.'

'Yes. She will.' He glanced up the stairs. 'You have to stay with Sharon?'

What did he want? That I should help him make it through the night?

I said, 'Yes.'

'I'll just go home.'

It had occurred to me that I might keep abreast of the police enquiries through Colin and Billy. Not that I needed to, but I was going to be bursting with curiosity.

I pulled him in and brushed his cheek with my lips. 'Colin, promise me you won't brood?'

'I won't brood.'

But he would.

Sharon, who didn't know Sven, was much more concerned with Robert's screaming. 'He won't let me near him,' she said.

Robert was sitting on the couch bawling his lungs out. The noise went through my head like a shard of glass.

I switched on the television and found a cartoon channel. At first, I turned the volume up high, but then, having second thoughts, I turned it down until it was virtually inaudible. This worked. Robert stopped his screeching and said, 'Turn it up. I can't hear him.'

Poker-faced, I put the volume up to a reasonable level. Sharon and I exchanged glances and withdrew to the kitchen. She sat down heavily, dropping her head into her hands. 'I'm done,' she said. 'This is a nightmare.'

I went round and put my hand on her shoulder. 'Sharon, you've had a dreadful couple of days. The storm will pass.'

She twisted her head towards me. She looked awful. 'Oh God,' she said, 'Robert's had nothing to eat. No wonder he's crying. What kind of mother am I?'

It was just past nine. Robert should be in his pyjamas with his teeth brushed.

'What does he like to eat?'

'Fish fingers and chips.'

'You have some?'

'I always keep some in the fridge.'

'Let's go for it. Better than another carry-out.'

She came alive, a little bit, when she had something to do.

Robert's eyes were drooping as he stuffed in the last of his chips. Sharon almost had to carry him to the bathroom.

I did the clearing up. When Sharon had tucked Robert into bed, she was at the end of her tether, both tense and exhausted. She flopped on the couch, squeezing her eyes shut. 'I'll never sleep,' she said.

'Sharon, you'll take a nitrazepam, or even two.'

'What if the yobbos come back? I'll not be able to deal with it.'

'Listen. I'll stay the night. If they do come back, *I*'ll deal with it. Get me a blanket or two, give me one of your pills, then get yourself to bed. Follow this doctor's orders.'

There was only one bedroom in the flat – did I mention that? – and Sharon, a selfless mother, had given it to Robert. Now, too beaten to argue, she pulled out her rollaway bed in a corner of the living room and retrieved from a recess her downie, two pillows, two blankets and a pair of pyjamas that were styled to look like camouflage gear. I refrained from making any jokes about the pyjamas, accepted one of the pillows and both blankets, and assured her I would be fine on the couch. Before we said goodnight, we downed a nitrazepam each.

276

We slept for more than eight hours, which seemed to me a miracle, and agreed that a visit to Unst would do us both good. I scrounged another nitrazepam because I thought I would need one more night to re-establish my sleeping pattern, then I went back to my own flat to have a shower and a change of clothes before we started on the road to Toft.

I also phoned Colin. He sounded very downbeat.

'Colin, have you slept?'

'I did sleep, but I spoke to Eric this morning. He found Sven with his limbs all bent and stuck out at awkward angles. One of the policemen said he thought some kind of poison had paralysed him.'

'*Poison*? For God's sake.'

'Eric says he went to Sven's because he got a very odd message from him.'

'What d'you mean, odd?'

Colin sighed. 'In the first place, Sven and Eric *never* exchanged messages. In the second, this one said that Sven had had a visit from his neighbour, Charlie Mann. But Sven and Charlie were at daggers drawn because of some boundary dispute a while back. Sven won and Charlie never forgave him. It's inconceivable that Charlie would pay a visit.'

I thought. Did this mean the police would find it inconceivable that Eric would choose Charlie as a fall guy? No. 'Inconceivable' was only Colin's judgement, which the police wouldn't necessarily accept.

'There has to be an investigation?' I said. 'A post-mortem and that sort of thing?'

'Yes.'

'Billy will be involved?'

'Well.' Colin sighed again. 'That's not how it works. The local boys don't do much. They just rope the scene off and leave everything to a major enquiry team from Glasgow.'

'I see.' I'd asked enough questions.

But I could still enquire after Joy.

Colin said, 'Eric spoke to her last night.'

'Poor Joy.'

She'd get over it. I'd saved her a lot of trouble. She wouldn't have to watch her father going downhill with Parkinson's. She wouldn't have to bring him to stay with her or put him in a nursing home. She should be grateful to me for getting rid of the carnaptious old bastard.

'Colin,' I said, 'thank you for your help with Sharon. You're very kind.'

'I'm kind, am I?'

Oops. No suitor wants to hear that he is *kind*.

Yet the word was right, for it summed up exactly what I felt about him. When the time came to break up, I could replay this conversation, to point out that I always thought he was a really nice person, I always really liked him, but...

'Of course you are, among other things.'

He didn't reply.

I said, 'I'm going to Unst today, with Sharon and her son.' I gave him a summary of the Jason story.

His only comment was: 'That's surely beyond the call of duty.'

He was right. In fact, I was probably acting inappropriately – I had cleared this with no one in the school – but I'd made a promise. Besides, a trip to Unst would keep my mind off other matters.

'Listen,' I said, 'it's going to be a hellish week, with Eric and Joy in shock, and Sharon in goodness knows what kind of state. I'll ring you?'

'Sure.' He was desperate to believe in me.

I picked up Sharon and Robert, and we were passing the Toll Clock Centre at 9.02. Forty-three minutes to get to Toft. We could do it.

We did. The old Honda touched sixty miles an hour at some points as we romped across the moors. While Robert fell fast asleep in the back seat, Sharon and I talked about last night's visit from the mob. She was much calmer about it, accepting that the high tide of emotion would pass.

Toft looked empty but lovely: blue sky, calm sea, gentle wavelets lapping on the stony beach. I found it relatively easy, in this tranquil, beautiful scene, to compartmentalise my mind. If thoughts of Sven threatened to intrude, I simply shut them out.

But, if you close down one page, another pops open. As we waited for the ferry, Joy's allegation about Sharon came back to me, and I saw that a friend wouldn't fudge this; a friend would talk from the heart.

'Sharon,' I said, ' there's something I need to talk to you about.'

'What?'

'It's about Joy.' I ploughed on, telling her straight what Joy had told me.

'Oh no,' she said, and I could see she was embarrassed. 'No. I remember talking to the pupil, I remember saying to her – this was after the class had gone – something to the effect that same-sex relationships weren't part of God's plan, but I swear I never mentioned Joy's name.'

The pupil had twisted the story for her own ends, whatever those ends might be.

'I'd never have thought you believed in God.'

'I don't. It was a flippant way of expressing my... my...'

'Disapproval?'

'Yes.'

'There's the point, Sharon.'

'Oh.' She massaged her forehead and looked out at the ferry, which was opening its jaws. 'You know, I've rarely thought about this. I've just always been... what word would you use?'

'Prejudiced?'

'Intolerant?' She was quick to find her own faults. 'Oh dear. So that's why Joy doesn't like me?'

'Yes.'

'Do *you* like me? *Will* you like me if I grow up and put prejudice behind me?'

I felt for Sharon. While the rest of the world, or most of it, had accepted same-sex marriage, she'd been stuck in a time warp. She'd had so many other conflicts to resolve that she'd never got round to this one.

'Of course I like you,' I said. 'And never mind God. If a person is truly penitent, I think he or she should be forgiven.'

'Carol,' – she was relieved, as if confession had cleansed her soul – 'if I did believe in God, I'd say he sent you as his angel to save me.'

We boarded the ferry. Robert woke up and we had to pay him some attention. On the boat, across Yell all the way to Gutcher, we sang songs: nursery rhymes, pop songs, anything with a catchy chorus. Sven was a blur at the back of my mind, a blur that I had no intention of bringing into focus.

I don't know how I managed it, but I missed the Unst ferry *again*. It was pulling out as we pulled in. I hadn't been concentrating. If I'd saved just a couple of minutes by speeding up on Yell's good roads, we'd have saved – how long? Two hours and twenty minutes.

But it was still a beautiful morning. We played on the beach, throwing stones into the sea, trying to skim them, looking for crabs and shells, watching the water gurgling out of a narrow channel from what I think is called the Loch of Gutcher. I suggested going to look for the otters, and we found two where I'd seen them before, stretched out on their rocks, working on their tans again. Robert was fascinated; he watched them from a good distance at first, then stepped closer and closer. We went with him, holding a hand each, Sharon putting a finger to her lips, until one of them opened an eye and they slipped into the sea. 'Wow,' Robert said.

We were on Unst at one o'clock. I took Sharon and Robert up to the hotel, where I hoped that lunch would be on offer, before going on to the Youngs'.

Jason was at the window of the car almost as soon as I had parked. 'I told my mum you were coming,' he said, 'and then she got out of me why. I heard them talking about it last night and for once they weren't arguing.'

'Is she annoyed at me?'

'Don't think so. She's broken up with her boyfriend. And dad's sober.' It was easy to see that Jason was excited. He hoped that I could wave a magic wand and reset his parents' relationship.

His mother, who had a wiry frame and hair like straw, met us in the porch. 'Call me Tina,' she said.

'I'm Carol.'

She took me through to the living room, which had been tidied beyond recognition, and introduced me to her husband, Tom. He was older than her, his hair thin and greying. He'd scrubbed up, had a shave and possibly a shower, but he couldn't hide the drinker's veins. Husband and wife were very different: where she moved with a certain sensual grace, he shuffled, slouching under his pullover; where she spoke easily, asking about my experience of Lerwick, he was taciturn and uncertain, perhaps mistrustful.

'You'll have some lunch,' Tina said.

'That's very kind of you. Thank you.'

The table was set for three. It had been cleared – and polished! If I could judge by the speed with which Tina served the broth, lunch had been ready for a while.

We pretended this was a social visit. Tina set the tone, talking about Unst – its lack of shops, its remoteness, its insufficient public transport. (I hadn't noticed any car outside.) Jason, deliberately or not, counterbalanced his mother, praising the 'amenities', by which he seemed to mean the swimming pool, the football pitches and, especially, the fishing. Tom uttered hardly a word, beyond a few grunts of agreement about the abundance of cod and mackerel.

Then, when we'd finished our broth and were halfway through our rabbit stew, Tom said abruptly, 'Hear Sven Henderson was murdered last night.'

'*Murdered?*' I was completely taken aback. He knew Sven? More important, how could he know, and know so quickly, about his death and the suspicion of murder?

Tina said, 'He's dead. That's all you can be sure of.'

Her husband was defiant. 'I'm sure. Everybody's sure.' He addressed me: 'Eric Sorenson found him. You get what that means?'

'No.'

'It means they'll try to pin the murder on Eric.'

'Who will?'

'Police Scotland. The Scottish parliament. Take your pick.'

'Why would they do that?'

But, before he even replied, I could see that this drunk on the island of Unst had guessed the truth.

'So that they can derail Free Shetland, and keep the money from our oil.'

Tina was scornful. 'You love your conspiracy theories.'

I said to Tom, 'You want Shetland to be independent?'

'Too right. With a share of that money, we could buy a car. Tina could go to Lerwick for shopping every week.'

Tina didn't argue with that. 'Tell you something else,' Tom said. 'The Scottish government will have sent someone to plant evidence on Eric. If the police try to use that to frame him, there's going to be trouble, big trouble. We're not the only family who needs Shetland to be independent.'

There was nothing to be gained from pushing Tom.

'I see what you mean,' I said.

We returned to safe topics – the weather, the ferries, the buses. When we finished our stew and Tina offered me coffee, I suggested that I help her tidy up first.

Everyone knew what that meant. Tom sat where he was. Jason carried plates to the kitchen, before making himself scarce. Tina rested her backside against the sink, waited for a couple of moments until she was sure Jason had gone, then blurted out, 'So, who the fuck do you think you are?'

At least she got to the heart of the matter.

I hung my head in full contrition mode. 'Tina, I'm sorry. I absolutely shouldn't stick my nose in your business. It's just that Jason…' – I spread my hands in that gesture of honesty that Gregor made – 'was so upset.'

She crumbled at once, biting her thumb, letting the tears glisten in her eyes. 'Shit.' She held her head. 'All right. It's a mess. I can see that. Every time I put Tom down, it makes him worse, he's ever more likely to reach for the bottle. But I can't help myself.'

I decided that if I was to be a counsellor, I might as well go for broke.

'Tina, did you ever do amateur dramatics?'

'No. Why?'

'Because, if you want to save your marriage, you have to make yourself act a part. You have to make Tom believe that you care about him. You also have to act like someone who's really upset. Very few men will turn away from a woman who's weeping.'

She contorted her face. 'Do I *want* to save my marriage? *Can* I save it?'

'I don't know. But the answers will become clear.'

I wasn't going to tell her my doubts, which centred on Tom. Self-destruction is a terrible thing. People can pursue it long after they've recognised that they are being held prisoner by some chemical reaction in the brain. And I didn't think that Tom had even got that far.

I was here to do my best; that was all I could do. We talked about Tom's self-esteem, and the things she might do to nurture it. We talked about Jason, and how he would feel if his parents broke up. Though we didn't talk about sex – which was perhaps a mistake, because it could be a deal breaker – when we went back to the living room, I hoped I'd achieved something.

We had coffee, I said goodbye to Tom, and Tina and Jason walked me out to the car.

284

I gave Tina a hug, whispering, 'Good luck.'

I gave Jason a hug too. *That* broke all the rules about never touching pupils.

'Thank you, miss,' he said.

Sharon and Robert were at the hotel. They'd had lunch, walked down to the harbour, scoured the rocks on either side for any sign of otters, and come back for scones and afternoon tea – or, in Robert's case, afternoon lemonade. We had plenty of time to catch the next ferry, at 4.45.

I managed to give Sharon a summary of events at the Youngs' before Robert started babbling about otters. He wanted to know where they slept, how they stayed warm, how many babies they had; he wanted to come back to see them every weekend; he wanted to keep one as a pet – we had to smile at that. He kept up his near-monologue until we rolled off the second ferry onto the mainland. Then he fell asleep.

Sharon said, 'Phew. I'm exhausted too. D'you mind if I have a doze?'

'Not at all.'

Now I could try to assess Tom's guesses and predictions. How important were they? Not very, I concluded, because, as Tina said, they sounded far too much like a conspiracy theory. The police would take no notice of *that*; they would act on the basis of *evidence*. As for the 'trouble' that might lie ahead, that could actually be advantageous, since rioting or civil dissent by the independence fanatics would make the ordinary, sensible, law-abiding Shetlanders *less* likely to vote yes in a referendum.

I had nothing to worry about.

We reached Lerwick about twenty to seven. I checked that there was no mob in Sharon's lane, then said goodbye and drove over towards my flat. As I parked, I saw Kirstie coming down the side of her house with her children. Her son, who was called Simon, was running ahead, pointing a stick at something in the gutter.

I locked my car. 'What have you got there?'

Simon looked up, waving his stick. 'It's a rat.'

So it was. A very dead rat. There was a gap round a drain cover where rain and frost had caused the road surface to subside, allowing the creature to crawl through. Its legs were splayed in a strange, contorted position. I knew at once what had killed it.

Kirstie glared at me, for some reason. 'Don't touch it,' she said to Simon. 'Rats can carry fleas.'

'I'm not touching it.' Simon was belligerent.

'You poked it with your stick. Any organisms from it will now be on your stick.'

Simon sulked. 'Your mother's right,' I said.

Kirstie said, 'It's disgusting. I'll phone environmental health tomorrow.'

I didn't want Shetland Isles Council to run tests on the rat. They probably wouldn't bother – a lowly employee would just throw it in an incinerator – but you never knew.

'How long will *they* take?' I said. 'The body may decay quite fast. The fleas, or other things, might escape.'

Kirstie frowned. 'You're right. I'll tell Gordon to take it down and dump it in the sea.'

Gordon, her husband, would do what he was told – anything to stop Kirstie whining.

'That would probably be a good idea.'

She spoke to her son. 'Go and tell your father to bring a spade and something to tip the body onto it.'

Simon hesitated – he didn't want to miss any fun – but, as his mother drew breath to scold him, he capitulated and went into the house. A few minutes later, he came out with his father.

Gordon, a big, bald man in a blue anorak, was carrying a spade and a small weeding fork. 'All right,' he said. 'Stand back.'

We all stood back, though I doubted that the rat was going to explode. He manoeuvred the carcass out of the hole in the road and onto his spade. His wife said, 'Now there could be bugs on the fork and the spade.'

He snapped, 'I'll wash them in the sea.'

'Can I come, Dad?' Simon had a proprietorial interest in this rat.

'Yes, you can. Bring that stick and don't touch the end of it.'

Father and son went off towards the lanes and Bressay Sound. 'Glad that's over,' I said to Kirstie.

And I *was* glad. When the rat was in the sea, that would be the end of the matter. Once again, I had nothing to worry about.

Still, I felt relieved when I remembered that I had one more nitrazepam.

Chapter 23

Monday 1st March

On Monday, the English department had two absentees – Sharon and Joy – and the one free period I should have had was consumed by a please-take. I'd have gone to the staffroom either at morning interval or at lunchtime, even if it meant another fight with Vince, but I just didn't have time. The result was that I didn't pick up any news until a quarter past five, when I was heading to the front door.

Eleanor and Matthew had paused to zip up their coats. 'It's postponed indefinitely,' Eleanor was saying.

I butted in. 'What's postponed?'

They both gave me a look that said, *Piss off*. But Eleanor replied, 'The indicative referendum. The council decided this afternoon.'

Matthew said, 'They're a bunch of pussyfooters. But you'll be pleased, you being a unionist. It probably means they're never going to hold it at all.'

Good news, if Matthew was right.

'Why have they postponed it?' I said.

This time, Matthew's look said, *Stupid woman*. His actual words were: 'You been living in a cave over the weekend? You haven't heard of Sven Henderson's murder?'

I was annoyed. 'Of course I have. But why would that lead them to postpone the referendum?'

Eleanor was scornful. 'This isn't Edinburgh. We honour our dead in Shetland.'

That wasn't the whole story. They weren't going to tell me what rumours about Eric had reached the councillors' ears. But I could guess.

I drove out to Joy's. There was hardly a space to park. Apart from Joy's Toyota and Eric's BMW, there was a marked police car, a police van, and three vehicles from Bolt's Car Hire. Had the attack dogs from Police Scotland already sunk their teeth into Eric?

A uniformed police officer opened the back door like a butler. 'Who are you?' he said.

'I'm a friend of Joy and Eric's.'

'Wait a second.'

He went away but quickly returned. 'You can come in.'

Joy and Eric were sitting on the couch in the living room. They both looked drained and white. Another uniformed policeman stood to the side.

Joy came over and I gave her a hug. 'Joy, I'm so sorry about Sven.'

Her eyes were red. 'This is hell,' she said.

'What are the police doing *here*?'

'Good bloody question.' This was Eric, spluttering with anger.

When Joy didn't answer, I said, 'Colin told me there was a suspicion that somebody called Charlie Mann was involved.'

'Charlie?' Joy shook her head. 'He's been on the phone giving me all sorts of abuse. The police searched his house yesterday – "ransacked" was his word – and took him in for questioning. They kept him overnight, and he's blaming us.'

Eric spluttered some more. 'They let him go pretty damn fast, though everybody knows that he hated Sven'

'But they did let him go,' Joy said.

Eric erupted. 'So they've got the right guy now? Is that what you're saying?'

Joy sighed. 'No, Eric, I'm not saying that.'

'All because of some stupid book that I know nothing about.'

I said, 'What stupid book?'

Joy was trying to be calm. She said, 'You remember that book I showed you, with the space cut out in the middle? The Graham Greene omnibus? I hadn't thrown it out. They found it when they searched this room – not that it was exactly hidden – and seemed to think it was a big deal.'

'Oh yeah,' Eric said. 'Everybody knows that reading Graham Greene is a crime.'

I was tempted to say that reading Graham Greene wasn't the crime, it was the punishment, but it wasn't the moment for jokes.

Eric's fury dissipated. He stared into space. Joy, who was still standing in the middle of the room beside me, opened her mouth to say something – probably to invite me to sit down – when the door from the hall opened and yet another uniformed policeman came through with a big cardboard box. It held labelled plastic containers which I assumed were evidence bags.

Eric challenged him. 'Where are you going with that?'

'I'm sorry, sir. I've been told to take it out to the van. I'm just the porter.'

Another man appeared, in a sharp grey suit. A woman followed, younger but equally smart in jacket and trousers.

The man said to Eric, 'I'll have to ask you to come to the station with us, sir.'

Eric clenched his fists. 'I'm under arrest?'

'No, sir, but we'd like your cooperation.'

'Christ.' Eric stood up and half staggered across the floor. He didn't reach out to Joy, and neither did she to him.

The woman stayed. She was in her forties, I'd have said, her face a little lined, her short hair blonde with dark roots. A detective, certainly, but her rank I couldn't guess. She said, 'Our people will be finished very soon, Mrs Sorenson. We will need to take a detailed statement from you too at the station, but may I ask you one question now?'

Joy was punch-drunk. 'Yes?'

'Would you say that your studio was a room that collected dust easily?'

'Not particularly. Why should it?'

Our detective didn't answer. She said, 'So, if an item was covered in dust, that would imply that it had been there for some time?'

An item? The model of a ship?

Joy looked blank. 'I suppose so.'

The woman looked at me. 'I'm D.I. Haddow,' she said. 'May I ask your name?'

I told her. She wrote it down, took my address, noted that I was a friend of Joy and Eric's, and instructed me to come to the police station 'after work tomorrow'.

I was comfortable. She hadn't the slightest reason to suspect me.

Then she slipped one in: 'Did you see Mr Henderson during the weekend just past?' I realised she was alert, like a cat ready to jump at a bird.

'No.'

'Have you ever been to his croft?'

'No.'

I felt the merest bite of unease, but she was only being thorough.

She turned back to Joy. 'Thank you for your help, Mrs Sorenson. I know this is a very difficult time for you.'

She went out. A few minutes later, the rest of her troops – three men and two women, all wearing latex gloves and plastic hairnets – passed through with a cardboard box each. I noticed that one box held books and another rolls of drawing paper.

By now, Joy and I were sitting on the couch. We'd said very little, but as soon as we were alone, she grabbed my hand.

'Carol, what am I going to *do*?'

In undercover work, you play many parts, but The Loyal Friend is about the easiest of them all. This is because it rarely matters what you say, as long as your body language and the expression in your eyes convey unending sympathy.

So I squeezed her hand and said, 'What d'you mean? You're not saying the police *really* suspect Eric of killing Sven?'

She wailed, 'Carol, *I* suspect Eric.'

'Why on earth?'

'Eric himself told me dad's body was twisted with every muscle spasmed; he thought at once of poison. And there was an empty wineglass on the table. The police have already established that I was away and Eric bought dad's shopping, including the wine. If the poison was in the wine, who could have put it there except Eric?'

'What about this Charlie Mann?'

'They must be satisfied he's in the clear.'

'But, Joy, you can't believe your husband would kill his own father-in-law?'

292

Her voice was still a wail. 'I don't *know*, Carol. You never really know anyone. Eric and dad didn't get on. Eric was pretty bitter that dad wouldn't help us out financially. And... and...'

'And what?'

'The bank is about to foreclose. The sale of the hotel has completely fallen through. Eric's going to be declared bankrupt.'

Bankruptcy? This was a bonus.

But I groaned like someone who'd been hit in the solar plexus. 'You're saying Eric had a motive?'

'A very strong motive.'

'You've told the police this?'

'Not yet. But I'll have to. Won't I?'

She was in agony. I held my head, to tell her I shared her torment, and couldn't see a way out. Then I pretended to recover.

'Joy, wait a minute. If Eric knew – as he must have known – that his financial difficulties were going to be discovered, then he'd also know that he'd be a suspect. He wouldn't be so stupid.'

Joy's face lightened for a fraction of a second. Then it darkened again. 'So what if... what if he tried to frame Charlie Mann?'

I was silent. She'd think I was shocked beyond words. In fact, I took the moment to congratulate myself. Hadn't Gregor and I done a first-rate job?

I said, 'Where's the evidence that Eric tried to frame Charlie?'

'This message that he says he got from dad. It's unbelievable. He and dad weren't exactly WhatsApp buddies.'

'But Sven must have sent it. Surely.'

'Maybe not. That detective asked me if dad was obsessive about cleanliness, if he was the kind of man who would wipe his phone clean of prints. I laughed at the very idea. Then she gave me a look.'

'Oh, Joy, a look. That could mean anything.'

'But what if Eric went out to dad's on Saturday evening, somehow added the poison to the wine, sent the message to himself and then cleaned the phone?'

Exactly.

'Joy,' I said, 'you're overwrought because your dad's died. I don't believe any of this stuff.'

My phone buzzed. I apologised and looked at the screen. Sharon had sent me a text. *Coming back to school tomorrow. Got an official reprimand.*

I typed back*: See you tomorrow. Xxx*

I put the sound off and decided not to pass the news to Joy. She was too lost in her own misery to care.

We went over the question of Eric's guilt about three times, Joy prosecuting, me defending. Round about eight o'clock, she said, 'We should eat. You hungry?'

I'd thought she would never ask. 'Got something in the freezer?'

'Smoked haddock?'

'I'll do it.'

'No, we'll do it together. My life is damn well going to go on.'

I peeled the potatoes, she defrosted the fish, then opened a bottle of Chardonnay. As soon as I had my first sip, I knew I wasn't driving home.

We'd finished our meal, and the bottle, when the phone rang.

Joy snatched it up. 'Eric?'

But it wasn't Eric. 'Paul?' I heard her say, and I listened to her side of the conversation. 'Yes. How did you...? God Almighty... No, I haven't heard. They might be keeping him overnight... You want to *what*? Say that again... Well, *of course* I want to help Eric. Listen, what it comes to, Paul, is that you can do what you like. I'll speak to you later.'

She put the phone down and said, 'I don't like Paul.'

'What did he want?'

'First of all, he wants to tell me that Eric's arrest is all over social media. Why tell me that? To cheer me up? Then he wants me to endorse his brainwave that we can turn the arrest to "our" advantage, "us" being all the people who think that Shetland's independence is the most important thing on earth.'

'What's his brainwave?'

'He wants – he's got all the bloody jargon – to "make another attempt to take over the narrative". He wants to flood social media all over again with hundreds more posts about the devious Scottish government.'

'But, Joy, maybe he's right.'

'You think?' She was agitated beyond measure, flicking imaginary specks off her jeans, shooting me agonised glances, then getting up, walking about and sitting back down. 'So somebody in the government buys my dad's groceries for him, poisons his wine, sends Eric a message and wipes my dad's phone? What other fairy tales can we think up?'

I let my gloomy face say that she'd convinced me.

She jumped up. 'I'm going to open another bottle.'

'Joy, you don't want to be sick.'

'You're right.' She threw herself back down. 'Hold me. I want to live.'

295

I put my arm round her shoulders and hugged her close. She was in her usual bra-less state, and I thought again that she really did have a nice body.

After a while, she wriggled from under my arm and pulled her top off. I was excited; this was *so* inappropriate.

'Kiss my tits,' she commanded.

'Joy, are you sure?'

'Sure I'm sure. Why shouldn't I be sure? Just kiss them.'

I was happy to oblige. No suckling infant had pulled these breasts out of shape. I kissed and licked and sucked and marvelled.

She groaned. 'What's wrong with me?'

I paused. 'Nothing.'

She didn't seem to hear me. 'My husband's being questioned by the police on suspicion of murdering my father, and I'm encouraging you to suck my tits.'

'Joy, you said it yourself. You want to live.'

'You'll stay the night? You'll have to, after all that wine.'

'I'll stay.'

'Oh God.' She groaned again. 'What if the police let Eric go, after all? What if he came home and caught us naked in bed? Then he'd really go mad.'

The lust seemed to drain from her. She picked her top off the floor and put it back on.

'I'll sleep in the spare room,' I said. 'There will be other times.'

There might be other times. If you shed your inhibitions, sex with another woman can be quite pleasant.

But it's not the same – now this is really stating the obvious – as with a man. I would never hunger for Joy as I hungered for Gregor.

We got ready for bed. I used Eric's toothbrush again and she brought me my pink pyjamas. She took me by the hand to the door of the guestroom.

'To other times,' she said, and brushed her lips against mine.

As I lay in bed, I hugged my blanket of satisfaction.

Chapter 24

Tuesday, 2nd

I left Joy straight after breakfast – there was no sign of Eric – and was back in Lerwick by eight. I had a flurry of panic as I approached my flat, because a Scottish Water van was parked where my car should have been and a man with 'Scottish Water' stencilled on a high-visibility jacket was sitting, apparently fishing, at the drain where the rat had expired. He had in his hands an instrument from which a line, or cable, fed down the open drain.

I parked behind the van and walked down. 'What you doing?'

The instrument was a computer of some sort. I guessed he might be operating a remote camera.

His appearance reassured me. He had a weatherbeaten, ruddy face which suggested he spent a lot of his days outdoors – in other words, he looked like a genuine Scottish Water employee. And his reply also calmed my fears.

'Ever heard of a fatberg?'

'Yes. Have we got one?'

'I'd say so. Not quite blocking the whole sewer, but not far off it. You live here?'

'Yes.' I pointed to Betty's house.

'Toilet blocked?'

'Not on the last occasion I used it.'

'Lucky you. You can get nasty pongs coming up from a fatberg, not to mention toxins.' He was very cheery about it.

'There was a dead rat lying at that drain on Sunday. My neighbour's husband dumped it.'

'I know. She phoned it in.'

'What have you found? More dead rats?'

'Not so far. Just the fatberg.'

'How do you go about getting rid of it?'

He pressed a button on the screen of his computer. 'My ROT will slice it up.'

'Your ROT?'

'Remote Operated Tool. Ten years ago, we'd have had to send a man down. This is much more civilised.'

'Well, good luck.' I had decided that, once again, there was nothing to worry about. Even if there were a few more dead rats, Scottish Water wouldn't care; their priority was to get the sewer flowing again.

He grinned. 'And good luck to you when you flush the toilet.'

I had a wash, put on fresh clothes, and set out for school. Sharon arrived in the car park just after me.

'You all right?' I said.

'Nervous.'

'Don't be.' We walked towards the door. 'You're bound to get abuse, from both pupils and staff, but you'll handle it.'

'I'll ignore it?'

'Even better,' I said. 'Smile at the attacker. Pretend you're ready to be best friends. Maybe they'll believe it and maybe they won't. Even if they don't, they'll see you're not going to be riled, which will annoy them. So either way you win.'

'I like it,' she said.

'If you need any more advice from your agony aunt, drop into my room.'

She did drop in, at lunchtime. We ate a sandwich together and she told me she would carry on smiling. 'It's working so far,' she said.

'Good.'

I resisted the urge to keep checking my phone, which I'd put on silent. If Gregor didn't contact me soon, I wouldn't be able to resist texting *him*. I was bursting for him to join me in celebration. Besides, I was more and more convinced that we didn't need to wait any longer; I wanted to tell him to release the film of Pamela's adventures as soon as possible.

Sharon prattled on. With about ten minutes left until the bell, I said, 'Listen, I'm sorry, but I must do a little preparation.' I wanted, of course, to check my phone again, but also I thought that *she* should do her preparation; she should calm down; she should try to get her moods on an even keel rather than bobbing up and down like a dinghy on a choppy sea.

'Oh gosh. Sorry. Right. I'll catch you later.'

She went off. I looked at my phone. Nothing.

At the end of the school day, I had one message, but not from Gregor. Joy had texted half an hour ago.

Can I come to your flat?

I typed back: *Sure.* I had to go to the police station at some point, but Haddow could wait.

Joy was outside my flat in her Toyota. There was no sign of the man from Scottish Water. We had a hug and I could see that she was still upset.

I took her in, sat her down and, before I could even make her a cup of coffee, she said, 'It just gets worse.'

I stopped in the doorway to the kitchen. 'What's happened?'

Her face was taut. 'Eric's still being held. They pulled me in this morning and showed me something. It was a phial they found in the studio. It looked like medicine, but I knew it wasn't medicine. So did they.'

'What was it, then?'

'Poison. I'm sure of it. They asked me if I'd seen it before and of course I hadn't.'

'It was in your studio?'

'Inside one of Eric's models, the model of a schooner. They asked me again about the dust. I think *they* think Eric put it there ages ago and forgot about it. Or perhaps thought it would never be found.'

I came across and sat beside her, holding her hand. 'But, Joy, that doesn't make sense. If Eric was going to poison your father – which I don't believe – he would never keep some of the poison in the house. All the police would have to do would be to match it to whatever's in Sven's body.'

She held my hand so tightly that it hurt. 'I know, but they also asked if I'd noticed any dead wildlife about. So what else are they thinking? That Eric was experimenting with a range of toxins? That he rejected this stuff as unsuitable and then forgot all about it?'

They might conclude exactly that in due course – and Gregor's little finesse would have paid off.

'God knows what they're thinking,' I said. But what about Eric? Have you had a chance to talk to him?'

'No.' She removed her hand and pressed both palms hard against her temples. 'And I told them about his finances.'

301

'Oh.' I wanted to imply a lot with that word: *Well, that's it, then. Any idiot would find him guilty.*

She sobbed. 'I grassed on my own husband.'

'Joy, stop it. You had to tell the truth.'

I put my arm round her, smelling her sweat, and gave her a long hug. She cried on my shoulder. A lot of guilt lurked in her soul, I felt. How often had she wished she could be free of Eric?

Still weeping, she said, 'You know what else they asked me? Had I read *The Human Factor*?'

'*The Human Factor*? Graham Greene?'

'Yes. Eric had a copy. He must have read it.'

'Have *you*?'

'Not that I remember. What could that be about?'

'No idea.'

I couldn't hurry Joy. It was half past five when I reached the police station.

Haddow and a youngish man took me to a narrow little interview room with high, barred windows. She waved me towards a plastic chair.

There were four other chairs: two along the side, under the windows, and two, facing me, beside a cabinet from which poked the snout of a video camera.

Haddow said, 'This is D.C. Cameron.'

'Hello,' I said.

He didn't reply.

'You're not a suspect,' Haddow said, 'but if I tape the interview it saves me making notes.'

She switched on the recording device, took a disc from a drawer in the cabinet and slid it into place. In a routine that must have been second nature to her, she identified herself and Cameron, stated the place, date and time, the subject of the enquiry – 'the unexplained death of Sven Henderson' – and asked me to give my name, age, address and profession.

Then she coughed. Cameron seemed to take this as a signal, because he produced from a cardboard box a plastic evidence bag which he handed to Haddow. She showed it to me. It was the phial of aflatoxin.

'Recognise this?' she said.

'No.' I felt the faintest flush on my cheek. But the room was hot; they couldn't deduce anything from a flush.

'You're sure? Have you seen it before?'

I frowned. 'No. I haven't seen it before.'

'Do you know what it is?'

'No.'

She waited, the bag against her knee. I waited too, deadpan.

Eventually, she gave the aflatoxin back to Cameron and he said to me, 'What's your relationship with Mrs Sorenson?'

I didn't see this as dangerous. 'I told you, I think. We're friends. We work in the same department in the school.'

'Anything more than friends?'

'I'm not sure I understand you.'

'Are you or have you been in any kind of sexual relationship with Mrs Sorenson?'

Ah. Joy hadn't mentioned any questions like this, but to Joy it wouldn't have seemed important. Well, it *wasn't* important.

I didn't care what they thought about my sexuality. 'Very mildly so. Some kissing, some hugging. Hardly a full-blown *relationship.*'

Haddow inclined her head towards Cameron, giving him some barely perceptible instruction. He brought out a roll of drawing paper that I should have noticed. It was, of course, the drawing of me in the nude, complete except for my feet.

'You recognise *this*?' Haddow had taken back control of the questions.

'Yes.'

'Did you ever spend the night with Mrs Sorenson?'

If she thought the nude drawing might put me on edge, she had another think coming.

'Yes.'

Haddow leaned forward and raised a finger. 'Let me make the question clearer: when we say "spend the night", does that mean you simply stayed at the Sorensons' house or did you sleep with Mrs Sorenson?'

'The latter, not that it's any of your business.'

'And you describe this as a very mildly sexual relationship?'

'Yes.'

Cameron broke in again. 'Have you ever been to Mr Henderson's house?'

That did catch me off guard; it seemed such an abrupt change of subject.

I frowned. 'You asked me this before, and I told you no.'

'*I* didn't ask you. So you're sure you've never been to Mr Henderson's house?'

I had to calm down, get back to deadpan. 'I'm sure.'

They couldn't have found the tyre tracks, not after all that rain. And they certainly couldn't have matched them to my car. Haddow had told me I wasn't a suspect. They were only probing.

Haddow said, 'Why did you frown?'

'I'm sorry. When did I frown?'

'When my colleague asked if you'd ever been to Mr Henderson's house.'

'Oh. I just don't understand why you're asking me these questions.'

I thought I'd said that with enough spontaneity to make it convincing. Haddow tightened her lips, which I imagined was a gesture of frustration.

'Mm,' she said. 'You know that no one can profit from their crime?'

Now I was lost, but I said, 'Yes.'

'So if Mr Sorenson were found guilty of murdering his father-in-law, he couldn't benefit from the inheritance.'

'I don't get this.'

'But Mrs Sorenson could.'

'I'm still not understanding you.'

Haddow was in no hurry, perhaps calculating how she could throw me off balance. Then Cameron spoke.

'Did you and Mrs Sorenson ever talk about being together permanently?'

I looked at him in disbelief as I finally saw the scenario they had in mind.

'Are you *kidding* me? Are you suggesting that Joy killed her own father and tried to frame her own husband so that she and I could take her father's money and run away to some sapphic paradise?'

The words had just poured out of me. I stared at Haddow and she blinked. I guessed that was her way of showing embarrassment.

She said, 'It is our duty to consider every possibility.'

'Bloody hell.'

That was the interview as good as over, I knew it. The fact that Haddow had said I wasn't a suspect meant that they'd never seriously considered the

lesbian angle, they'd just been making sure they could rule it out. And my reaction, I was certain, had caused them to do precisely that.

They asked me a few more questions about the relationship between Joy and Eric and I was able to say truthfully that, although Joy's tendencies were obvious, I felt that she and Eric had a bond of companionship, that they were actually quite happy together.

Then they moved on to Eric's financial difficulties. I replied briefly that Joy had mentioned these, but I hadn't known the full extent until yesterday. That seemed to satisfy them. In fact, their manner had become, if not deferential, at least polite, so much so that I wasn't on the back foot any more. When Haddow finished up by thanking me for my help, it was all I could do to keep a smirk off my face.

Eight o'clock. I'm finishing my evening meal when my phone rings. It's Colin.

He says at once, 'Have you heard?'

'Heard what?'

'Eric's been charged.'

'Oh no. How can they do that?'

I was a little surprised that the police had reached a decision so quickly. What had tipped the balance? That phone which somebody had wiped clean?

Colin had a theory, which he offered in gloomy tones. 'Billy overheard something to the effect that there might be a South American connection.'

'South America?'

'They haven't confirmed it yet, but there's a possibility that the poison came from a frog species in the Amazon. And Eric went to and from South America when he was in the merchant navy.'

Poor Eric. He had no luck at all.

There was a silence, before he said, 'I guess we're all in shock.'

'Say that again.'

'Will we meet up this weekend?'

That was said with diffidence. He *knew* I wanted out.

'Colin, I'm not sure. I think Joy might need a friend. How about we meet for something to eat on Thursday?'

'Thursday?'

Well, with any luck, I'd spend the weekend in Gregor's bed.

'Just a quiet drink, so that we can talk.'

'Oh? Right.'

'How about eight o'clock at the Norseman?'

'Okay. Okay. Right.'

He sounded like a man who'd been told the day of his execution.

I'd hardly put the phone down when I picked it up again. It was definitely time, while my star was high, to make a move on Operation Pamela.

And it was more than time to stop being so cautious about seeing Gregor.

Despite WhatsApp's encryption, I was cagey about what I typed.

Hear about e? Time to move on p?

The reply came back within two minutes: *OK. I'll get going with p. Celebrations on friday night? My place?*

I was wet in an instant. *Around 8?*

Perfect. Just like you.

Oh boy. I'd earned a reward, and on Friday night I was going to get it.

Chapter 25

Wednesday, 3rd – Thursday, 4th

At school, I was marking time. (Yeah, yeah, it made a change from marking jotters.) Indecision began to plague me. If I assumed that I had done everything I could in Lerwick, should I hand in my notice to George the Second? And if I also assumed that Pamela was about to be forced out, should I take the weekend in Edinburgh to have coffee with Arnold? But which did I want more, to go to Edinburgh or to cuddle up with Gregor?

Two things pleased me. One, Jason gave me a thumbs-up as he left the classroom. (I'd missed him on Tuesday because the Second Year had to go to a talk on subject and career choices.) I knew it would be stupid to assume that his parents' problems were over, but I felt hope for him, and some satisfaction that my trip to Unst might not have been in vain

And there was Sharon, in sheltered waters. It helped that people were so preoccupied with the news about Eric. At lunchtime on Wednesday, when word filtered through to the staffroom that he'd been in court and been remanded in custody, even Matthew could only mutter about 'a bloody conspiracy'; nothing he or anyone said was directed at Sharon.

There was a message on my phone when I switched on the sound in the late afternoon. It was Helen, 'inviting' me to her house in the evening. It was hardly a formal invitation: *Bring a fish supper and some booze if you like. Got something interesting to show you.*

Again? Eating with Helen wasn't a fine dining experience. But I wasn't doing anything, and I was restless. So I typed back: *OK*.

I did my detour to the Coop for the wine before I went home. Then I called Joy.

She was very subdued. 'He's been remanded to Grampian Prison,' she said. 'He'll be leaving as soon as they can arrange an escort.'

Grampian Prison was on the mainland somewhere. Near Peterhead, I thought. That would make it all but impossible for Joy to visit.

But she wouldn't want to visit when she'd already found him guilty.

'Joy, I'm so sorry.' Well, I was, a bit.

'I had to go into the police station again. They asked me if dad was in the habit of sending Eric text messages and I had to say no, never. It's pretty clear they think Eric sent the message himself. And they asked whether Eric still had connections in South America. At first I said no, but then I remembered there was a family in Manaus he was friendly with, whose photographs he sometimes viewed on Instagram.'

'Where's Manaus?'

'In Brazil. On the Amazon.'

'Colin told me about this crazy Amazon frog theory.'

'I don't know if it's crazy.'

Who was I to argue with Joy? I let her pour out her heart for a good twenty minutes. The police had told her it was unlikely Sven's body would be released before next week 'at the earliest', and she thought this was 'heartless'. What kind of state would the body be in? And how could she face arranging a funeral? I soothed her as best I could, reassuring her that I would help with the arrangements. It was all I could do.

At a quarter to seven, I was outside Helen's door with room service.

When she let me in, I noticed that her hair was sticking out, in need of a wash, and the side of her face had acquired some new blotches that would surely benefit from a soothing cream. I shouldn't be feeding her fish and chips and encouraging her to wash it all down with wine. But Helen was Helen; she lived for the moment because she had nothing much else to live for..

'I didn't bring anything for Natasha,' I said. 'Is she in?'

'No.'

'Out with Ivan?'

'No. Just out. But – you're not going to believe this – she's talking about getting married and going to live in Russia.'

'She's mad.'

Helen shoved aside a new bundle of washing, then she fetched two tumblers – no glasses today – and filled up one for herself. On my instructions, she poured only half a tumbler for me.

I wasn't very hungry, but it was clear that she was. 'What have you found?' I said when she'd cleared half her chips.

She chomped another mouthful before replying. 'Remember that sonar device the man from Scalloway caught in his net?'

'Yes.'

'Another four turned up: one on Greenland, two on Iceland and one on the Faroes. I found out by lurking in chat rooms and groups on the Internet.'

'You're sure these are the same devices?'

'You can judge for yourself in a minute. But let me tell you about my big breakthrough.'

'Okay. Go.'

'There's this group on Yahoo,' she said. 'They interpret patterns of data to work out the military movements of the major powers. You give them the facts as you've observed them and they come back with explanations. I gave them what I had: Russians on Unst, the micro-submarine that Natasha photographed, and the locations of all the sonar devices that have been found.'

I imagined the group would be called *Conspiracy theories for utter nutters.*

'And what did you get back?'

She took a pull at her wine, and said, 'Well, I only got one reply, but the guy knew what he was talking about. He was an expert on naval warfare. According to him, some outfit called the British American Security Information Council produced a report years ago saying that swarms of drones could be used to keep watch on the North Atlantic – the Greenland-Iceland-UK gap, he calls it. These would make nuclear submarines more or less obsolete, because they couldn't pop up unforeseen to flatten Moscow with a missile or two. Now, he thinks, the Russians may be trying this in earnest. Didn't I tell you it was all a fucking Russian plot?'

'You did. But how does he know the devices are Russian? Why not American or British?'

'Something to do with the design. I didn't follow that bit, but he seemed confident.'

Though I was sceptical, I didn't want to show it too much. Helen could be prickly if you disagreed with her.

I did say, 'It would need a hell of a swarm to cover the North Atlantic. And where would the micro-sub come in?'

Helen had yet another slug of wine; she was drinking Pinot Grigio like lemonade. 'He suggests there is a hierarchy of data collection and transmission, with the micro-subs somewhere in the middle.'

I remembered my intuitive certainty that the black, shark-like craft had some military purpose. Even so…

Helen cleared away the remnants of our meal – though the aroma would cling to her laundry for days – washed her hands and began to load up images on her computer. In one window she had the device caught by the man from Scalloway, and in another she positioned the four from Greenland, Iceland and the Faroes. Some of the devices were more battered than others, but I had to admit they were all very similar.

Yet Helen's 'expert on naval warfare', no doubt self declared, could be wrong. Did the design of sonar devices really differ all that much from country to country? Besides, these things, as Gregor had said, were used for a whole variety of purposes. None of Helen's evidence was conclusive.

I began to get bored. She polished off her changing-the-balance-of-naval-power presentation, and took me on a tour of the social media posts about Eric. This was altogether more interesting. McIntyre had clearly been at work, because there were lots of accusations from people in Shetland who'd come to the same conclusions as Jason's father – that the Scottish government wanted to 'castrate' (a favoured term) the Free Shetland movement by framing its leader. This, many argued, was merely an extension of the Scottish government's 'well-proven' technique of using dirty tricks to silence dissent.

They were right, of course, except for that phrase 'well-proven'. I knew that nothing would be 'well-proven' – unless someone stumbled across a treasure trove of evidence like the data stored on my cloud account.

'Where are the posters going with all this?' Helen asked.

'I'll tell you where they're going.' I was confident. 'Nowhere.'

I went home, I slept, I went to school. On Thursday evening, I watched two news channels. And there was the Pamela story.

Although no news editor – this was hardly surprising – saw fit to run the film, the reports on her indiscretions in the Ross Hotel were quite detailed, and included the name and rank of her short-term boyfriend. Analysts gave their opinion that the evidence was 'incontrovertible'; various politicians declared that, since Pamela's companion had been shown to be Russian, the breach of security was 'unacceptable'; and Arnold, very statesmanlike, agreed that Mrs Grey had 'done the right thing' in resigning. I whooped.

Pamela couldn't blame me. Could she? Even if she did, she couldn't get her own back by ratting on me about Sven, because that would be an admission that she knew he was about to be murdered. She was a foul-tempered, jealous bitch, but she wasn't suicidal.

I plunged into Twitter, looking for the film.

That didn't take me long. Various helpful tweeters had posted links to websites where the antics of Pamela and Mikhail were shown in commendably high resolution. I clicked backwards and forwards, checking that Gregor's original recording hadn't been altered in any way. As I did this, I noticed that there were hundreds of tweets, even more than Helen had shown me, about the deceitfulness of the Scottish government. But I didn't pay much attention.

Ah, I wasn't the first, and I wouldn't be the last, to underestimate the rabble-rousing powers of social media.

I went out about ten to eight, meaning to meet Colin in the Norseman on the hour, and at once I realised that something was going on. Groups of people were going along King Erik Street and when I glanced right I could see more groups walking up Market Street. At teatime in Lerwick, this was unheard of.

I tagged along. When I turned into Market Street, I heard a rumbling of voices that seemed to come from the police station.

It did. A sizeable crowd had gathered, swelling with new arrivals every minute. They were growling, 'Free Eric *now*. Free Eric *now*. Free Eric *now*.'

'What's going on?' I asked a girl whose boyfriend was filming with his phone.

'Don't you read Twitter?'

'Yes, but...'

'That woman who resigned at Holyrood – she was up here in Lerwick.'

'The woman in the Intelligence Services?'

'Yes, her. She was staying at the Ross Hotel. She was up here to plan the murder of Sven Henderson and to frame Eric.'

'How do you know?'

'Come *on*. What *else* was she up here for? It's all over Twitter and Facebook.'

That made it a 'fact'.

The mood of the crowd was ugly. As yet, no one was throwing anything, but some hotheads, perhaps assuming that it was too dark for the cctv to capture their faces, were screaming obscenities at the door of the station and all who sheltered behind it. The black gates, which could have been pulled across to protect the yard, were yawning open, allowing bodies to pour in

and swirl round the parked vehicles. I heard a scrunching and then a defiant cheer as a windscreen caved in.

Headlights swept up from behind, and I turned and squinted towards them. From the passenger door of a marked police car, a bulky man in full regalia – I guessed he might be a chief inspector – stepped out with a megaphone. He addressed the crowd at once.

'Could you please listen to me?'

Some of them jeered, some didn't even hear him. He repeated his request and the hubbub subsided, though not completely. A group of young men moved towards him clenching their fists.

Give him his due, he was resolute. He bellowed into his megaphone, 'I have to tell you that Eric Sorenson was transferred to Grampian Prison this morning. There is nothing that I or you can do about it.'

This produced a howl and a torrent of catcalls. Gradually, the insults coalesced into one: 'Traitor! Traitor! Traitor!' The Chief Inspector – if that's what he was – waited with admirable patience.

A long five minutes elapsed, giving lots of people the chance to film the chaos. Then, in a slight lull, the Chief Inspector let loose again into his megaphone. 'All I want is that justice be done. Believe me: if Eric Sorenson is innocent, he will be found to be innocent. You can put your trust in our system of justice.'

'Rubbish!'

'Whose system of justice?'

'Traitor! Traitor! Traitor!'

The impasse seemed solid. But abruptly, out of the dark, another police car came screeching up behind me, its headlights helping to illuminate everyone at the gates. At the same time, arc lights came on in the yard.

'Bloody cctv,' someone shouted, and at once bodies began to edge away into the shadows.

When a few sheep move, the whole flock follows. As those in the light tried to push into the darkness, those who were already there had no place to go except out into Market Street. Within a very short time, the yard was all but empty; a trained collie couldn't have done a better job.

I went on to the Norseman, trying to assess what effect this near riot might have. I'd argued to myself on the way back from Unst that civil dissent would *deter* people from voting for independence, but now I had to convince Arnold of this. In other words, I had to convince him that I had done a good job in Lerwick and therefore deserved promotion. The truth was another matter – it was dawning on me that once you set a ball rolling in the bumpy field of politics, it could bounce anywhere – but who cared about the truth? I had to strike while the iron was hot, meeting Arnold face to face and letting him pick up the hints that I was, and would be, ruthless in protecting the Party's interests. In short, I definitely had to be in Edinburgh.

I was supposed to give a month's notice to George the Second, but there was a way round that – my mother. I could catch a plane south on Saturday morning, then phone George from Edinburgh to give my mother's deteriorating health as an excuse for not serving the month.

I found Colin nursing a half pint. For some reason, the fact that he was already there irritated me.

I slid onto the banquette beside him. 'Sorry I'm late.'

'It's all right.'

'Weren't you at the police station?'

'I was, but I left. It was going nowhere.'

No. He'd left because he didn't want to be late, he was worried about annoying me. He was so *needy*. I had to steel myself to tell him, in words that allowed no misunderstanding, that we were through. He deserved a clean break. Besides, there was no risk to me now: once I was back in Edinburgh, Billy would surely not bother to investigate me.

He said, 'What would you like to drink?'

'I'll get it.'

'No, I'll get it. What would you like?'

'I'll have a half of cider.'

As he went to the bar, I looked around. On the other side of the room, with an older man who had to be her father, was Sharon. That was a surprise.

She caught sight of me and I waved. The man beside her said something. She replied, put down her knife and fork, and stood up. She was coming over.

She almost bumped into Colin. At the last minute, he raised his eyes from the cider he didn't want to spill, and I saw them exchange smiles.

They reached the table simultaneously. Sharon sat down opposite me and said, 'Hi.'

Then she turned to Colin. 'Colin, I want to thank you for helping me the other night. I was in a bad place.'

Colin glanced round the pub. 'Well, you're in a good place now.'

She looked more relaxed than I'd ever known. With a mischievous tone that was something else I hadn't witnessed before, she said, 'Do you come her often?'

She wasn't... she couldn't be... *flirting* with him?

Colin said, 'This is my brother's favourite watering hole. But I haven't seen you here before.'

'No.' Sharon smiled again. They'd be making eyes at each other shortly.

317

Not that I minded.

Sharon went on: 'My parents thought I needed a break. My mum's busy; so my friend Mary's babysitting while dad takes me out for a booze-up.'

'Yes, you'll need a chaperone here.'

'I know.' She stood up. 'I'll push off. See you both later.'

'See you,' we said in unison.

Colin said, 'She seems to have recovered well.'

'Yes.' Was he really sizing Sharon up as my replacement? Because he knew what I was about to say?

I was going to say it anyway. 'Colin, I've been thinking.'

His face set. He did know what was coming.

'I like you. I think you're a really nice person. But I don't want to continue in our relationship.'

There. I couldn't be blunter.

'Why?'

There was a light in his eye. I couldn't work out what was going on in his head. Anyway, I'd let him have it.

'It's mainly the sex, Colin. It hasn't been good.'

'Too rushed?'

'Too rushed.'

'And I'm not confident enough?'

'That's right.'

'But you could see that as soon as you met me. So why did you take up with me in the first place?'

'I don't know. I liked you. And I guess I was lonely. I'm sorry. You deserve much better than to be mucked about.'

'I think you're a bitch.'

'Right.'

We sat in silence. Not much else to say, really. But finally, to make some peace, I said, 'Shall we have another drink? Can we be friends?'

'No!' He jumped to his feet. 'I don't want friends like you.'

And with that he walked out.

I couldn't blame him. In fact, his reaction made me respect him a little more. I waited for a few minutes and then, realising that Sharon must have seen the manner of Colin's departure and could come over to ask what had happened, I got up to leave. Tomorrow I'd give her an edited version of events.

I waved. Her frown was questioning, but I didn't go across.

On the way back to my flat, I asked myself how I felt. Relieved? Oh yes. Oh yes, oh yes, oh yes. Now I could be with Gregor tomorrow without worrying about being caught. Still, something else was hiding. Sadness? Guilt? Oh all right, I felt a touch of guilt. But it would pass.

Chapter 26

Friday, 5th

The weekend beckoned. I'd booked my flight for late Saturday morning and I'd texted Arnold. His reply was warm, suggesting we meet on George Street for afternoon tea. Before I made my pitch, I'd just listen and let him know that he was the most thoughtful person in the world. I was good at that.

I'd only have Friday night with Gregor, but I was looking forward to it.

I was in school early and got my first surprise when I saw Joy at her desk. She was surveying the chaos – the scattered jotters, the stray pieces of paper, the jumble of books – from a week's please-takes.

I went in and put on my best air of concern. 'How are you?'

She didn't get up, merely swept a hand at the wreckage on her desk. 'Awful, but I couldn't stay off forever. It wasn't doing anyone any good, least of all me.'

I said, 'How can the police be so sure that Eric's guilty?'

Her shrug was one of miserable acceptance. 'Too many clues that they couldn't miss.'

I shook my head, which was meant to convey the message, *Yes, it's awful, but you're right.*

'But what do I do?' she said. 'Life goes on.'

It was then I got my second surprise. There was a knock at the door and Sharon came in, walking right across to where we were. That took a fair bit

of courage, because a rejection from Joy would have made her feel very small.

'Joy,' she said. 'I'm so sorry about Eric. And I'm sorry about us falling out. Carol told me why you were annoyed with me. The story got twisted quite a bit, but I still owe you an apology.'

'Thank you.' The Joy I used to know might not have been so forgiving. 'I appreciate it.'

Don't forget, dear reader, if you're on that panel assessing my application for sainthood, it was I who brought about this reconciliation.

'You're very brave,' Sharon said, 'coming back to pick up the pieces.'

'Not really. I was going mad in the house.'

Sharon glanced at Joy's desk. 'Your please-takers have left a mess.'

'Tidying up will be something mindless to do.'

Now Sharon glanced at me. 'I guess we'd better let you get on.'

In other words, *Carol, I want to talk to you.*

Joy said, 'See you both later.'

In the corridor, Sharon hesitated, but only briefly. 'What happened with you and Colin?'

It's best to stick close to the truth. 'I had to break it off. I've met someone else.'

'Oh?' Did I detect excitement? 'Who?'

'A scientist. He's got a hatchery on Unst, for researching sex determination in halibut.'

'Sex determination?' She said it as if the subject were truly distasteful. 'But you like him?'

'Yes.'

'Oh… well…'

321

A twitch came to my lips. *Yes, Colin's free. Go for him, sis.*

The school day was uneventful, though at lunchtime I did hear an amusing exchange in the staffroom.

The initiator was Maggie, a spinster lady who'd taught chemistry as long as anyone could remember. 'Dreadful scenes last night,' she squeaked – I'd been told that she had 'nodules' on her throat. 'Just goes to show that those who shout the loudest should be paid the least attention.'

Matthew heard her, and for once he didn't have Vince to be his mouthpiece. He turned and snapped, 'You mean, those who don't meekly accept the status quo should shut up and go home.'

'No.' Maggie, who I'd never heard speak out before, was firm. 'I mean they should engage in tolerant, civilised debate.'

'If the Bolsheviks had engaged in civilised debate, we'd still have serfs in Russia.'

'And if Hitler had engaged in civilised debate, we wouldn't have had the Holocaust and the Second World War.'

Matthew had no answer to that, and round the table where Maggie and I sat most people smiled, supporting the underdog. I smiled too. If someone had asked me ten minutes ago for my honest opinion, I'd have said that civilised debate was on the verge of extinction. Now I wondered if there was hope.

My mood was up as I walked to Gregor's. There's a song somewhere that says, *We've got tonight, babe.* I suppose that's pretty well how I felt.

I had with me only my toothbrush and a spare pair of panties, because I planned to go back to my flat in the morning and pick up an overnight bag

before I took the Honda down to the airport. I wasn't dressed up for a date – just jeans and a top – but clothes didn't matter with Gregor.

He opened the door with a welcome in his eyes and pulled me against his chest. If I'd been a cat, I'd have purred.

'Well, fellow plotter,' he said, 'we did it.'

Yes, we'd done it. Whatever the outcome, we'd proved that, for us, anything was possible.

He pushed the door shut with one foot and squeezed my shoulders. My Russian bear. Why would I doubt him?

Then he led me up to the living room, where one of those basso profundo choirs growled from his speakers. Just as we came in, a man whose voice plumbed the very depths of sound sang a few solo phrases.

'Who's that?' I said. 'It's not you?'

'No. I'm in the choir, but it's not me. It's our oktavist.'

'How low can you go? What song are you singing?'

'It's famous in Russia. It's called Krestu Tvoyemu, which means, "Thy Cross We Worship".'

'But you don't believe in Christianity.'

'Of course not.' He walked over and switched off the music. 'We're merely role-playing, as you often do when you sing. To the writer of the song, belief in God was all-important. So we who sing his words have to enter into his psyche. Don't you agree?'

'I suppose so,' I said. Then, teasing, never expecting what came next, I asked him, 'What *do* you believe in, Gregor?'

He stood beside one of his speakers and looked me in the eye with total calm. 'I believe in you.'

Unease gripped me. 'What do you mean?'

I didn't like his look; the seriousness that had attracted me that first night in the Norseman wasn't what I wanted now. '"Believe in",' he said, 'is ambiguous, yes? It can mean you believe in something's existence, like believing in God or ghosts, or you believe in the value of something, like democracy or your country. Yes?'

I agreed, though I was a little impatient with his semantic analysis

'So, if I believe in you, I believe you have value for me. That sounds very calculating and egocentric, but if I say you're an inestimable treasure for me, or you make my life infinitely richer or, even, you bring my life meaning, that sounds much better. Yes?'

I couldn't fault his logic, but that was the third time he'd used 'Yes?' like that. It grated.

'Of course.'

He said, 'Enough. A drink?'

'Yes. Please.'

'Wine? Slivovitz?'

'Wine to start with.'

'Georgian white?'

'Good.'

'Dry? Mtsvani?'

'Fine.' *Any bloody wine, as long as it's alcoholic.*

I was a lot mellower after two glasses. Probably, I'd been more on edge than I'd realised. The Mtsvani had a delicate, fresh flavour, the product, Gregor said, of eight thousand years of tradition. It did complement the hake that he'd baked in a nutty paste.

We talked about the Free Shetland movement, agreeing that it was dead if Eric was convicted. Then I moved the conversation on to my application for Pamela's job.

I was beginning to worry that I was counting too much on Arnold's influence. After all, I had no idea about who would serve on the selection committee. On the first burning issue of the day – Shetland's independence – opinion would be unanimous, but on the second – Scotland's neutrality – there would be a whole range of attitudes, varying from fierce anti-Russian (and pro-NATO) sentiment to support for a neutral position like Switzerland's. Strictly speaking, it wasn't the function of SIS to *make* policy for the Party, merely to deal with those who opposed policies already decided on, but if I were asked a direct question about my own position, that could be awkward. Other interviewees, especially those who worked in Edinburgh, might have a better finger than I had on the collective pulse of the committee. That could put me at a huge disadvantage.

I put all this to Gregor and reminded him that he'd said the Russian government could help me with information. If I found out from Arnold the names of the committee members, could his friends in Moscow establish where these individuals stood on the neutrality issue?

'Probably,' he replied.

That surprised me, because it had to be an understatement. His 'friends in Moscow' would have gigabytes of files on all the main players.

Gregor did point out, quite reasonably, that I'd have to provide the relevant names before the SVR could produce the information, yet something in his voice told me he didn't see the matter as urgent. Maybe that upset me. Or maybe Helen's theory about swarms of Russian drones was buzzing like

a bee in my brain. I don't know. What I do know is that when I spoke again I spoke impetuously.

'It would definitely help in my interview if I brought some knowledge that the panel didn't have.'

'Like what?'

'Like the possibility that your government is seeding the North Atlantic with sonar devices that can detect NATO submarines.'

I watched his face as I said this. At first I thought he was pulling down a curtain, but his expression quickly eased. 'If I knew about a strategy like that, you must realise that I couldn't tell you.'

'Why not?'

Another shift in his face. Into thoughtfulness, or concern. Real concern?

'I have to assume that even I am under surveillance. If it was suspected that I had leaked anything to you, I would be interrogated, perhaps forcibly. But so would you.'

It was my expression that changed now, because these few sentences reminded me that Gregor played in a league well above mine. My mood somersaulted, because suddenly he was once again a man of mystery. And power.

And physical power. He'd poured me a third glass of Mtsvani. As I sipped it, my body remembered the muscles beneath that loose shirt, I remembered his hardness, his staying power, his ability to satisfy me completely. To hell with everything. Why was I here?

We'd finished the fish. He produced a dessert – Greek-style yoghurt and defrosted Scottish raspberries – that was as delicious as it was unexpected. I drained my wine.

'Slivovitz?'

I shook my head. 'Sex.'

He nodded, like a philosopher agreeing to some important ethical issue, then suddenly he came round and whipped me off my seat. I yelped in his arms and started to giggle.

'Now, Mr Muscle.'

He carried me through to the bedroom, dumped me on the bed and contrived to take off my clothes. My pelvis was contracting in anticipation.

Well, we were frenzied, outside of our selves, like people who had starved for a long, long time and didn't know when they would eat again. It was only a pity that he spoiled it as we lay in post-coital exhaustion.

'We get on well,' he murmured. 'Wouldn't you say?'

'I would.'

'You know, it's once in a lifetime, or it can be, that you meet someone who can be your soulmate.'

'Yes.'

I said 'Yes,' but the unease was nibbling at me again.

'When you go back to Edinburgh, I'd like to keep on seeing you.'

'I'd like to keep on seeing *you*.'

That was true enough. I could see us meeting, when I was installed on Pamela's throne, to dance round each other and trade a few secrets. A tango now and then would be very pleasant, especially if it ended in bed.

'Suppose for the sake of argument,' he said, 'you did not get Pamela's job – though I'm sure you will – would you consider a change in direction, even a change in location?'

An amber light started to flash. 'A change in location? Where to?'

But I knew what was coming.

'Well, Moscow.'

And I had had just long enough to compose my response.

'*Moscow*? Gregor, what are you proposing? *Are* you proposing?'

He laughed. 'Put it this way: you wouldn't rule it out?'

I damn well would rule it out. That light had changed to a solid red. Gregor was intelligent and desirable – highly desirable – but I didn't want to *marry* him. I didn't want to be installed in some dacha or Moscow apartment and become a little Russian housewife or – God forbid – a housewife and mother.

But I wouldn't spell it out to him immediately. Caution, caution was my watchword. Never prick the bubble of a man's vanity until you're sure you can do without him.

'Gregor,' – I nuzzled his shoulder, hoping the action would speak for me – 'how could I turn down a suggestion like that?'

A man hears what he wants to hear. He turned and kissed my forehead.

I lay and imagined what *he* might be imagining: the wedding; a bride from the west, a trophy; his family, admiring their successful son; his basso profundo chums, grunting out a Tsarist love song; the distinguished guests, quaffing champagne. It wasn't going to happen.

So now I wanted Pamela's job more than ever. I lay and fretted. What questions could the selection committee put to me that I had no answer to, that I hadn't even thought about? Suppose they accepted that the main role of the intelligence services was to shut up dissenting voices and then said, 'But how would you do that? How would you *anticipate* dissent?'

I decided. I'd trot out the adage that Google and Facebook know you better than your own spouse. So, to get inside a person's head, you have to get inside his computer. I prepared a few modest sentences, adding a

judicious sprinkling from Helen's keywords: 'I won't pretend that I am an expert in meterpreter shells or rootkits or keyloggers, but there's the nub: I should be. In short, Mrs Grey's policy of centralising computer skills should be reversed. These skills, and the concomitant responsibilities, should be diffused throughout the services.' Arnold, for one, would approve; he'd see that such 'diffusion' implied that every attempt to hack or to snoop would be, for him and the head of the service, much more deniable. Pamela should have seen this too; it would have been a far better solution than farming out sensitive cases to lone hackers like Helen.

Yes, Arnold would see the point, and make sure it wasn't lost on the rest of the committee.

I was just about to drop off when another thought hit me, one that was rather more disquieting. Gregor had said, 'Suppose you did not get Pamela's job' and then he'd more or less proposed that *in that case* we should get married. But Gregor played chess; he worked out every move, leaving nothing to chance. So he *knew* I would not get Pamela's job.

So – somehow – he was double-crossing me.

I didn't sleep well after that. On the other hand, if I'd known what was waiting for me in the morning, I wouldn't have slept a wink.

Chapter 27

Saturday 6th

After breakfast, Gregor gave me a kiss and wished me good luck. I stepped out into a southeasterly gale, checking in my head as I went that nothing I had done or said could have leaked a clue about my changed perceptions.

I was almost at my flat, head down against the wind, when I realised that there were far more vehicles parked outside than usual. Then I saw that one was marked 'Police Scotland'. And a uniformed officer was standing at Betty's gate. I never dreamed that this had anything to do with me.

'What's happening?' I said to the policeman. 'Hold on,' – I'd just noticed – 'my car's not there. Someone's stolen my car.'

'You live here?' he said.

'Yes.'

'Are you Carol Rutherford?'

'Yes. What's happened?'

He didn't answer, but spoke into a radio or walkie-talkie. I didn't pay attention, because I was worried about Betty. Had someone broken in and attacked her, and then made his getaway in my car?

D.I. Haddow came out of *my* door, not Betty's, and marched down the garden path, trailed by Cameron. 'Where have you been?' she said.

'Mind your own business.'

She fired an order at Cameron: 'Cuff her.'

I was stunned. He produced a pair of handcuffs, snapped one on my wrist and one on his.

Now I screeched, 'What are you doing?'

'Carol Rutherford,' she said with no inflection and no expression, delivering lines in a pattern that must have been burnt into her brain, 'I am arresting you on suspicion of involvement in the murder of Sven Henderson. You do not have to say anything, but anything you do say may be taken down and used as evidence against you. Do you understand?'

'No, I bloody well don't understand. What the hell do you think you're doing?'

'Don't get smart with me. Do you understand the warning I'm giving you? I'm arresting you...'

'Yeah, yeah. I understand that. It's you who's the idiot, not me.'

She pressed her lips hard together, then said to Cameron, 'Take her to the station. Get her processed.'

I saw my life disappearing down a plughole. But what evidence did they have against me, all of a sudden?

A car took us to the station. How often had I walked past this grey but pleasing building? Apart from the barred windows on one passageway, it could have been a manse or a well-kept council office.

I was hustled in. A duty sergeant asked if I consented to my DNA and fingerprints being taken.

I said no.

He'd heard this a thousand times. 'It's your call, but I should tell you we'll get a court order. Mind you, that'll take till Monday. So you'll be kicking your heels till then.

Bugger it. There was nothing to be gained by postponing the inevitable.

'Oh all right.'

As he poked his scraper inside my mouth, I felt dehumanised. The police operated a giant sausage machine; once you were inside, no detail about you was left out of the mix.

There was worse to come. When he'd taken my prints, I was marched along a corridor, still handcuffed to Cameron, but accompanied by two uniformed women, one of them clutching a plastic bag that seemed to hold a bundle of rags. We stopped, a cell was unlocked and the handcuffs sprung. The women took me inside and closed the door.

'Your clothes,' said the one with the rags. She had a lined face and bright orange hair. No spring chicken.

'My clothes?'

'We need them as evidence. Please take them off.'

If I refused, she'd tell me they'd get a court order. Slowly, I undressed.

They looked at me like a slab of meat. The younger one, who was pretty, if chubby, produced an empty plastic bag, put my clothes in it, folded over a label and asked me to sign it. Then Ms Orange Hair took out the rags.

'Put these on.'

'What?'

'Hold on, Jennifer,' said the chubby one. 'I need the clippings.' She brought out a small pair of tweezers and said to me, 'I need clippings from your head hair and your pubic hair. Please stand still.'

My pubic hair? I had a visual replay of Sven grinding away on top of me. *Every contact leaves a trace.*

The clippings went into small plastic bags, of which Police Scotland had an inexhaustible supply. The small bags went into a larger bag, and again I had to sign the label.

I'd have almost preferred to be naked rather than put on the rags, but they didn't give me a choice. The underpants, an indeterminate shade of grey, were too big, sagging round my crotch. This was what it meant to be a criminal.

They left me alone for a long time, although the younger woman did bring me a cup of tea and a digestive biscuit. When she left, clunking the old-fashioned key in the lock, I was filled with a sense of doom.

Then I remembered that DNA could be derived only from a hair root, not from an unattached fragment. So, without the root, any hair I'd left on Sven would not, I was sure, be conclusive. Or was I sure? Something I knew, something I'd read was floating round my mind and wouldn't come back.

The big question was: what had led them to me? Here, I hadn't a clue. I puzzled over it obsessively, because I couldn't see what I'd done wrong.

They gave me a meal – chicken, potatoes and cabbage – before they hauled me along to the same interview room as before. Haddow and the older, sharp-suited man I'd seen at Joy's were waiting for me.

Haddow started the recording apparatus and did her introduction, identifying herself and her colleague – DCI Webster – and repeating what she'd said to me outside my flat. Then she told me I could have a solicitor present if I wanted.

I didn't know a solicitor and I didn't want to confide in whoever Police Scotland might provide. So I said I didn't need one.

'Fine,' she said. She was clearly going to ask the questions while Webster, a solid fellow with a big, well-shaven face, watched me and looked for a chance to pounce. 'Right. You told us before that you had never been to Sven Henderson's house. Do you want to change that reply?'

'No comment.' I was working on a story, just in case, but it was going to stay inside my head in the meantime.

'Right.' She was very calm. 'I'm going to give you some information that may persuade you to answer the question. What do you know about hair proteins?'

'Not much.' What *was* it that I couldn't remember?

'Uh-huh. Well, even if you don't have a root, you can still identify the hair of a particular person. You see, our DNA codes for proteins, and that includes the proteins in our hair. So the proteins in each person's hair are unique and can be linked backwards, if we can put it that way, to the DNA.'

'Fascinating.'

So it was. The article I'd read came back to me now. It was in some magazine like the *New Scientist*, and the emphasis was not so much on the straight translation of DNA to RNA to proteins as on the way drugs could affect the translation and so leave traces in your hair. I didn't have any drug use to hide, but the long and short of it was that Haddow wasn't bluffing; she knew, and I knew, that they were going to prove I had sex with Sven.

So I had to produce that story now, whether it was ready or not.

'All right,' I said, framing an expression that was full of penitence. 'I'm sorry. I did mislead you. It's embarrassing. I did have sex with Sven on the afternoon of the Saturday he was murdered. I was in a relationship that was very unsatisfactory in a sexual sense, and Sven had hinted, when I met him at Joy's, that he was interested. I was sort of fascinated by him. Joy had told me he had Parkinson's, but to me he seemed brimming with life and vigour and… well, naughtiness. But I didn't want to tell you or anyone because Shetland is such a small place and I'm a schoolteacher and I could see parents

complaining on moral grounds that I shouldn't be overseeing their children. That sort of thing. I'm sorry.'

Haddow had been listening without showing any reaction. 'So,' she said, 'you lied.'

I sighed. 'If you must use that word, yes.'

'So tell me, at what time did you go to Mr Henderson's croft on Saturday?'

'I don't know. About two o'clock.'

'And when did you leave?'

'I think it would be around four.'

'Did you take anything with you?'

'Yes. A packet of condoms and a Genoa cake.'

'So you intended to have sex?'

'Yes.'

'Why the cake?'

'I thought we might have a cup of tea before… or after.'

'And did you?'

'No. He'd been having a shower and he came to the door wearing only a towel. It fell off and we more or less went straight to bed.'

'Ah.' I wasn't sure what that meant. 'Did Mr Henderson use any of the condoms?'

'Yes. One.'

'Did he force you?'

'Not at all.'

'Did he force you on any other occasion?'

'No.'

She was scrabbling to find a motive. She'd wondered if I'd plotted to murder Sven because he'd raped me brutally at some earlier time. I realised with a flush of optimism that here was one huge hole in their case. And there was another: how could a schoolteacher get hold of a potent toxin?

Haddow glanced at Webster. For help? If that was what she was looking for, she didn't get it, because all he gave her back was a blank stare.

'All right,' she said. 'Now tell me how you account for the dead rats found not far from your sewage outlet?'

'Rats?' I said, but I was thinking, *This is how they found me?*

She compressed her thin lips. 'Poisoned with the same toxin as killed Mr Henderson.'

Shit. 'I've no idea, but a man from Scottish Water told me that there were lots of toxins in a fatberg that was almost blocking the sewer.'

'A man from Scottish Water?' The tiniest glimmer of satisfaction came to her eye. 'Yes, they're very thorough. We're grateful to them.'

Damn Scottish Water.

'Tell me about the toxin?' Haddow said. 'Where did you get it from?'

She didn't know where to start. I said, 'How would I be an expert in toxins?'

'Answer your own question.'

Aye, right. The dead rats might not be as damning as I'd feared. You could raise a hundred doubts about the movement of fluids through sewers, and she really was stuck about the source of the batrachotoxin.

I shook my head in the manner of someone who would love to help. 'I'm sorry. I'm lost.'

Haddow paused for breath, or inspiration. As she glanced at Webster again, there was a knock at the door and in came Cameron with something –

a slip of paper – in one of those little bags. He gave it to Webster. 'This was found in Rutherford's car, sir. Among other debris in the passenger door.'

'Thank you.' Webster dismissed him, examined the piece of paper, raised his eyebrows, and passed the bag to Haddow. She blinked, registered whatever it was, and visibly brightened.

Holding the clear plastic so that I could read the paper, she said, 'As you heard, this was found in your car. What comment do you have to make?'

It was a receipt from Tesco, showing only two items: a four-pack of lager and a bottle of... Isla Negra.

'I don't understand,' I said. And I didn't. I had never bought Isla Negra.

Haddow said, 'Look at the date and time.'

The date was a week past on Friday, and the time was 16.05. When I *could* have gone to Tesco.

As Haddow pointed out. She added helpfully, 'This was the day before Mr Henderson was murdered.'

But *Gregor* bought the wine.

Gregor? My mind jumped to the Mareel car park. He'd been doing something with his hands while I looked out the driver's window at the two women who were huffing and puffing.

He'd left the receipt deliberately? *Why*? Why *would* he? *Why* had he double-crossed me? I felt sick, and couldn't stop the blood draining from my face.

Haddow noticed. 'Something wrong?'

I had to rally. 'Yes. I heard that Mr Henderson was poisoned through a bottle of wine. Now I think you're trying to frame me. Or someone is.'

'Who would do that?'

'I've no idea.'

337

Haddow said, 'You keep your car locked, I presume.'

A small opportunity. 'No. Not always. This is Shetland. No one steals cars in Shetland.'

She didn't like that; it was a complication. 'You're saying you leave your car outside your flat unlocked?'

'Quite often. Yes.'

'Did you go to Tesco on the Friday afternoon?'

I thought for a second. 'No, I didn't. I went on Saturday morning. Wait. They have cctv. You can check their footage. You won't find me on Friday afternoon.'

She scowled, but said, 'Not conclusive. You could have asked someone to get it for you.'

'Find that person and I'll give you a reward myself.'

She scowled again, because she could hear the spontaneity in my sarcasm. 'We will.'

'Good luck with that.'

Webster intervened. 'Tell us about your knowledge of computers.'

'That won't take long. My knowledge is minimal.'

'All right. Tell us about those of your friends who have knowledge of computers. Of hacking, perhaps.'

I frowned at him. This frowning business killed two birds with one stone: it declared your innocence and gave you time to think. What was he getting at?

Then I had it. If I had murdered Sven and tried to frame Eric, then I had arranged for that message to be sent to Eric's phone from Sven's. He was nearly right.

'I don't think I have any such friends. I teach English literature, for God's sake.'

Webster stroked his sturdy jaw, and I wondered if I was winning. They had things against me, certainly: the hair, the rats, the receipt. But they also had huge areas of doubt.

Another knock came to the door, and Cameron stuck his head round. He said to Webster, 'Could I have a word, sir?'

'Pause the recording,' Webster ordered Haddow. He stood up and went out.

Haddow and I were silent, both of us trying to listen to the voices in the corridor.

There were several of them, all male. And there was a degree of argument. I heard a trace of incredulity in someone's tone – Webster's? More argument.

Webster opened the door and said to whoever was behind him, 'You do it with us present or not at all. Your authority is dubious, to say the least.'

Two men came in with him, both in suits and ties, both tall and shaven-headed, in the manner of faux thugs who hope to intimidate you. Webster gave one of them – he was darker-skinned, perhaps of Pakistani origin – his seat, while he and the other sat under the window. My nausea grew.

'Do I record this?' Haddow asked.

'No,' said the dark-skinned one. I christened him Omar, because I like to give my adversaries names.

'Go ahead.' Webster said, though his feathers were clearly ruffled.

Omar stared at me. He imagined he was scaring me. In truth, I felt sicker and sicker, because I knew who had sent him before he opened his mouth.

'Carol Rutherford, I know who you are and I know who you work for, really.'

Webster said, 'Wait a minute. Spell this out. You told me she worked for people in Holyrood. But for whom, precisely?'

Omar didn't look at him. 'She's supposed to work for the same employer as us. The Scottish Intelligence Services. But when I say "supposed to", there's a story that you need to know.'

'No,' I said, desperate. 'I *used to* work for the Scottish Intelligence Services. Now I'm a schoolteacher.'

Omar shook his head. 'Thought you might try that.' He had a little black attaché case with him. From it, he produced a single sheet of paper which he handed to Webster. 'A printout of her bank statement. Note the two salaries: one from Shetland Isles Council and one from the Scottish government.

Webster read it. He was struggling to process everything Omar had said, but he'd get there. In the blink of an eye, he was going to have my motive.

Chapter 28

Saturday, 6th

Webster could only listen as Omar, who had done a lot of homework, started his attack. 'On Friday, the 19th February,' he said to me, 'Mrs Pamela Grey visited Lerwick for a weekend break. Mrs Grey's personal life is not our concern, but it is a matter of public knowledge that she was illegally filmed in the Ross Hotel. We have cctv footage of you meeting her in the lobby of that hotel; so it is clear that you knew she was staying there. We also have cctv footage of you, her and a woman we have identified as Helen Flett in the Norseman Bar. We have interviewed Flett and established that she has a history of hacking and unethical use of electronics. She also provided us with some other useful information.'

He paused, and Webster said, 'What other information?'

'Get to that in a minute.' Omar was intent on staring me down. I think he fancied that his piercing Pakistani eyes could burn through me like a laser. He addressed me: 'I take it that you – or Flett, acting on your instructions – set up the equipment to film Mrs Grey.'

I'd have liked to spit in his face. 'You take it wrong. And don't try to tell me that Helen has confessed, because she wouldn't confess to a lie.'

'Flett will cooperate in due course.'

'In other words, she's told you that you're talking rubbish.'

Omar didn't blink; he had great faith in those lasers of his. 'So you're claiming that you set up the equipment by yourself.'

'I'm *stating* I had nothing at all to do with it. You're barking up the wrong tree.'

Being accused of filming Pamela was the least of my worries. Webster had been watching me intently. I'd hazard a bet that he'd already closed in on the fact that I was a servant of the Scottish government, who had a lot to gain from framing Eric.

Yet something was strange, because Omar and whoever sent him would hardly want to implicate the government.

This point too had not been lost on Webster. He interrupted Omar with some impatience. 'Hold on. Let's leave Pamela Grey out of it for a moment. We have a certain amount of evidence that Rutherford was involved in the killing of Sven Henderson. You said that she works for the Scottish Intelligence Services. Are you therefore saying that the government *commissioned* her to kill Henderson?'

'Absolutely not.' Omar switched his lasers onto Webster. 'You'll remember that I said Rutherford was *supposed to be* working for the Scottish Intelligence Services. In fact, she has a history of being a loose cannon, with no respect for any rules. Our hypothesis is that she plotted to frame Sorenson for the murder so that she could sabotage the Free Shetland movement and claim credit for *that*, and she also plotted to get rid of Mrs Grey so that she could then use this credit for her own advancement. There is no indication that anyone but Rutherford, and possibly Flett, was involved in this plot.'

Of course. Pamela knew nothing about killing Sven – that would be the cry – and neither did Arnold. Webster would put me in jail for a long, long time and everyone in Holyrood would be happy. Despair gripped me and, beyond that, a feeling of utter hollowness that Gregor had betrayed me.

There might be one tiny flaw in Omar's narrative. If I was going to claim credit for killing off Free Shetland by framing Eric, then I would also be claiming credit, more or less, for Sven's murder. So the person from whom I was claiming the credit – Arnold – would have to be complicit.

But I wasn't quite convinced by my own logic. It was tortuous and probably inconclusive. And Arnold was as slippery as the next politician.

Another knock. Another sight of Cameron poking his nose round the door. 'Very sorry, sir,' he said to Webster, 'but there's yet another development I need to inform you of.'

'God!' Webster wasn't hiding his irritation. 'Deal with that, will you?' he said to Haddow.

Haddow bridled – she didn't like being snapped at – but followed Cameron into the corridor. Webster scratched his chin and seemed to be unsure what to say. I could see his dilemma. As a policeman, he wasn't inclined just to accept Omar's story – perhaps he saw the same flaw as I did or perhaps it wasn't in his nature to leave stones unturned – but at the same time he'd hesitate to open an investigation into the very government who paid his salary. After a good scratch, he said to Omar, 'To go back a step, to the filming in the Ross Hotel, what proof do you have, or what proof do you expect to get, that Rutherford set it up?'

'We can prove she was scheming for promotion.'

'That's circumstantial,' Webster said.

'Yeah, of course.' Omar was the kind of guy who had the answer for everything. 'But Rutherford will confirm it eventually. Or Flett will.'

There was cursing in the corridor – I heard Helen's voice say, 'Fucker' or perhaps 'Fuck her' – and Haddow pushed the door open. She said to someone behind her, 'Bring her in, but keep a good hold on her.'

Cameron came in, with a firm grip on Helen's upper arm. She was wild-eyed and red in the face. I thought at first she was drunk.

Webster exploded at Haddow. 'What the hell is this?'

Haddow was no meek little mouse. 'You told me to deal with it,' she said, 'and that's what I'm doing. I think it's in everyone's interests that we hear what these two have to say to each other.'

Helen struggled to break free from Cameron. She started shouting at me, 'You're a fucker. You're a fucking lying bitch. You fucking *used* me.'

Cameron held her tight, which was just as well, while Haddow said, 'How did she use you?'

Helen ignored her, losing all control. 'You fucking pretended to be my friend,' she screamed at me, 'when all the time you were working for the fucking Scottish government.'

'No, Helen.' I had to shut her up. 'Don't believe a word he says.' I pointed at Omar.

Her screams got louder. 'He showed me your fucking bank statement. Two fucking salaries, one from the fucking Scottish government. Don't fucking lie to me any more. I thought you were about my only friend. You didn't want to discredit Eric Sorenson because it was a good joke. You were fucking working.'

Haddow said to her, '*You* hacked into Eric Sorenson's computer?'

Helen glared at her, while jerking her head at me. '*She* said, "Let's have a laugh. I've got the name and password of a guy who's forever sending Sorenson spreadsheets." Some guy she was fucking. Her and her fucking fucking.' She turned her glare on me. 'Did you ever fuck anyone for the fun of it? Did you hell. Every fuck was part of your game. And every "friend" was someone to be used.'

She was incriminating herself, but she was past caring. In any case, her time in jail would be negligible compared to mine.

Webster was perking up. 'Your story,' he said to Helen, 'is that Carol Rutherford was behind the attempt to discredit Eric Sorenson by hacking into his computer?'

'My *story*?' Helen sneered. 'Isn't it bloody obvious?'

'It's obvious now.' He addressed no one in particular. 'And it's also obvious that when that failed she had to look for something else.'

The room was unbearably hot. Seven bodies were sweating in a cubbyhole designed for three. I began to think I'd faint. The venom that Helen spat out was leaching into my blood.

Helen twisted with a force I didn't know she was capable of. She was out of Cameron's grip and halfway across to me, nails ready like the claws of a cat, when Omar's colleague grabbed her by the left wrist and swung her round as her right hand flailed at me.

'Right,' Webster said. 'That's enough. Get her out of here.'

Somehow, Omar, his colleague and Cameron hustled Helen out. Haddow called for reinforcements and in no time Omar and his friend were back. Webster said to them, 'May I suggest you have a window of opportunity with Flett? She's agitated, to put it mildly, and much more likely to spill the truth about the Ross Hotel. Anyway, Rutherford's not going anywhere.'

Omar rubbed his nose. 'Maybe you're right.'

The two of them left. Webster said to Haddow, 'I'm going to charge her. Record this and then we'll pause the interview.'

Haddow clicked the recorder and stated the time. Webster addressed me: 'Carol Rutherford, I am charging you with the murder of Sven Henderson. You do not have to say anything…'

Shit, I thought. There had been two holes in his case: a small one and a big one. The big one was my motive. Now that he'd filled that in, the small one – where I got the toxin– was a minor crack.

They dumped me back in the cell. I fully expected to be hauled out again – when Webster had had a cup of coffee and a think – and subjected to a rigorous interrogation about my relationship with the Scottish government. But it didn't happen. Webster was no fool. He had me; I was the immediate perpetrator; he could take days or weeks to consider his conscience and his career.

I was given a meal of potatoes and mince – I think it was around six o'clock, though keeping track of time was difficult – and left to my own devices. Not that I had any devices: no phone, no radio, no books. All I had was my imagination and that wasn't serving up anything very cheerful.

Then, some time in the evening, the key turned and in came Billy and Colin, closing but not locking the door. I stared at them, my mind dull.

'How's it going?' Billy said.

'What do you want?'

They stood between me and the door, Billy with his arms folded, Colin with the look of someone who was inspecting a foul-smelling lizard. Billy said, 'You know Webster's got you over a barrel?'

I didn't reply. Why give them the time of day?

'And you'll go to Grampian Prison with a life sentence?'

'Stuff you.'

'Unless you cut a deal.'

A *deal*? What deal could I cut? I could try to implicate Pamela, but I'd no evidence. I could tell them about Gregor, but then I'd face the additional

346

charge of conspiring with a foreign power. Besides, I still couldn't get my head round Gregor's betrayal.

'A deal with us,' Billy said. 'That's to say, with me and Colin.'

'*What?*'

'Yes.' In his posture, he was about as flexible as a granite statue. 'Here's our reading of the political situation. Despite the attempt by the Intelligence Services to push all the blame for Sven's murder onto you, we think that the people of Shetland are not stupid. They will blame the Scottish government, whether the justice system tries to hold its own government to account or not. Then Shetland will swing massively towards independence. There will be an indicative referendum; it will become impossible for the Scottish government to resist the call for a full, legally binding vote; Shetland will become an independent state.'

'Get to the point,' I said.

Billy wasn't deflected from his monologue. 'For a decade or more, we'll have a big fiscal surplus, which we'll invest in our sovereign wealth fund. But in the long run we'll be dependent on what we're dependent on today – fish, lamb, tourism, etc. And we'll need trading partners. The obvious candidate is the European Union.'

I remembered the glances I saw between them during the discussion in the town hall. 'You and Colin think this,' I said, 'but not everyone agrees with you.'

'Of course. We have to make our case.'

I was weary. 'Why are you telling me this?'

He nodded, which was probably the first movement he'd made. 'Our exact relationship with the EU will be a matter for discussion. But the EU as a whole is very opposed to the splintering of countries. You can't blame them.

No one in Brussels wants to negotiate with a multitude of tiny states. So we have to expect a degree of coolness towards us.'

'All right, all right. So?'

'Be patient. I'm nearly there. What we have to establish beyond a shadow of a doubt is that we were escaping from a tyrannical government, one which spat at multi-party democracy, which rubbed out criticism and opposition by underhand means, especially intimidation and blackmail. There have been lots of mutterings that this is what the Scottish government does, but there is damn little proof. That's where you come in. We suspect, given your behaviour in Lerwick, that you've been involved in this intimidation for some time and – like any prudent agent who thinks about insurance for the future – you have evidence of the means the government uses.'

I thought of the films, the audiotapes of Pamela giving me instructions, the notes of dates and times and places – all the material that I'd transferred to my cloud storage – and had to admire the accuracy of Billy's deductions.

'What if I have? Why should I give the evidence to you?'

He managed another nod. 'Understand that we don't care about you. You're scum. Your guilt is clear and it's going to be exposed whether you turn up in court or not.'

Hope jumped in my heart. I might not turn up in court?

'What we care about,' he said, 'is Shetland. We don't *want* you to have your freedom, but we'll trade it to safeguard Shetland's future.'

'Who's "we"? You and Colin?'

'I'm not answering that, but it's a measure of Colin's loyalty to his native land that he's willing, after you've behaved like a pig, to consider letting you have your freedom if it will benefit Shetland.'

I didn't look at Colin, only Billy. 'How would I get this freedom? You're going to sneak me out of jail in the middle of the night?'

'First thing that will happen is that you'll give us the evidence we need. I presume you've got it in some electronic form.'

'Suppose I do. You didn't answer my question.'

'*We*'re not going to sneak you out.'

'Who is?'

Billy unfolded his arms. Then he folded them again and sighed. 'I had my suspicions about you from the start. When Colin told me, on Thursday, that you'd dumped him, I was worried about him, because he's always been a romantic. I was worried that he'd pine for you, and I was absolutely sure that you weren't worth it. So on Friday night I tailed you, to a flat off North Street. This lunchtime, I went back and I met your Russian boyfriend. I'm assuming he was your source of the toxin.'

'Assume whatever you want.'

'Yes.' Billy's demeanour suggested that he didn't really care, that Webster's investigation was none of his business. 'He said he was shocked that you'd been arrested.'

'Oh?'

Billy did his folding and unfolding; he seemed embarrassed by what he had to say next. 'Then *I* got a shock, because you know what he told me?'

'No, I don't.'

'He told me that he loved you and he'd do anything to set you free.'

I goggled at him. That didn't make a bit of sense.

Billy waited. I said, 'Really?'

'Yes, really. I wanted to tell him not to be stupid, but I didn't. Instead, I struck a deal: you give us our evidence and I give him the information he

needs to get you out. The two of you scarper to Moscow, where you can rot for the rest of your days.'

I couldn't understand this. Why would Gregor shop me and then rescue me? He'd be playing some fiendish game of chess in which it was a basic rule never to throw away a pawn.

'Well?' Billy said.

I stalled. 'If I got out of here, there would be a massive enquiry. This visit of yours would put you high on the list of suspects.'

He shook his head. 'We've thought this out. Everyone knows that you hacked into Eric's computer through Colin's. Naturally, Colin wanted to find out how you did this. That, in a nutshell, will be the story of why we came to see you. How *did* you do it anyway?'

'I watched him typing in his email password.'

'Simple as that, eh? But listen: you don't need to worry about me.' I took it that he was being ironic, though no smile crossed his lips. 'You deceived my brother. I should hate you as much as he does. No one is going to dream that I would connive at your escape.'

I could imagine that.

'So?' he said.

I still wasn't sure. 'Suppose I gave you this evidence, what guarantee would I have that you'd keep your end of the bargain?'

'None, except my word.'

'And what's that worth?'

He dripped with scorn. 'That's a bit rich, coming from you. Decide for yourself. But remember this: if you go to jail, carrying a lot of secrets that the Scottish government want *kept* secret, they could reach inside and cut

your throat or push you down a stairwell at any moment. You'd be looking over your shoulder forever.'

That had a ring of truth.

'I'll trust your word.'

'So where's the evidence?'

I gave him the username and password for my cloud account. He wrote them down.

They were about to leave when Colin spoke for the first time. 'What turns someone into a bitch like you?'

I surveyed his beaten face: the worry lines and the sad eyes. I could have asked what created a loser like him.

Instead, I said, 'Everyone uses everyone, Colin, in one way or another.'

'Maybe in Edinburgh, but not in Lerwick.'

'Dream on. Next you'll be telling me about Lerwick's community spirit.'

'I would, but you wouldn't understand.'

'Come on.' I don't know why I bothered arguing with him, but I was exasperated. 'How many people through the ages have had Utopian phantasies?'

'I'm not talking about Utopia. I'm talking about a warm and honest heart.'

Billy intervened. 'Leave it, Colin. She's not worth it.'

They went out and locked the door. I stared at the wall. What did I care about Colin's bitterness? What did I care if Gregor was using me in some big game of chess?

As long as I got out of here.

Chapter 29

Sunday, 7th

The night passed. For a long time, I dozed or lay awake.

Then I fell into a deep sleep and at once, or so it seemed, I was dreaming. I saw a skull, which somehow I knew was Sven. He had his teeth open in a hideous guffaw. I tried to speak to him but couldn't. I woke up, shaking.

What in hell was he laughing at?

Breakfast came: porridge, toast, coffee. At first, the food didn't tempt me; I was too spooked by Sven's visitation. But, gradually, I talked sense into myself: feelings of 'guilt' (if that was the right word) were to be expected after a lifetime of conditioning. These feelings would fade – *should fade*, because in reality I'd saved Sven from years of suffering. Still, why was he amused? I couldn't work *that* out.

I ate. After breakfast, there were more empty hours, lots of them. Colin and Billy would be checking my data, deciding if it was enough to buy their cooperation. But even if Billy intended to keep his word, what information could he give Gregor that would ensure my freedom?

None. Police Scotland didn't design their holding cells to give you a sporting chance of escape.

Lunchtime. More hours. Evening meal, served by a burly sergeant who told me cheerily that I would be 'up with the birds', to be taken to court and remanded in custody.

'Where?' I said.

'Grampian Prison.'

'I'll be taken there at once?'

'I'd say so.'

So Gregor had one night.

That night began to slip away. I lay on the bunk and didn't want to sleep.

Something happened. At first, I didn't realise what it was because I had my eyes closed. When I opened them, there was total darkness where before there had been a glimmer of light. I heard low voices, and feet on the corridor outside. One voice was anguished.

Then, the tiny sound of a woman on the phone, a woman who was sobbing and croaking in fear. The sergeant speaking, no longer cheery.

'Okay, okay. Hold on. He says he'll let you go.'

The key turning in the lock. Gregor's deep tones: 'Thank you.' A short scuffle. The sound of a body slumping to the floor. Gregor – on the phone? – saying calmly, 'Let me speak to my colleague.' Then: 'In half an hour let her go. Tell her not to phone the police for another hour if she wants to see her husband alive and well. See you later.'

He came in. 'Let's go.'

'What on earth?'

'*Now!*'

He had a pencil torch, but I almost stumbled over the policeman's body. I smelled unfamiliar chemicals.

'You killed him?'

'No. He'll be fine in an hour or so. As will his wife and children. Now come on.'

Except for the thin beam of his torch, the station was in total darkness. He led me by the hand to the door, and out.

Market Street was black too. I glanced at the cctv cameras. 'They're out,' he said, 'along with everything else.'

'No backup power?'

'Oh yes. That's out too.'

The street was deserted. He still held my hand; it might have been in case I stumbled in the dark. But it didn't feel like that; it felt like a gesture of affection. I was about to shake him loose in anger, but I thought better of it.

Play along.

His Landrover was parked across from the library, a little way back from the road. He put me in the back seat and covered me with a rug, telling me to be ready to get on the floor if he thought we were going to be stopped.

'It'll hardly pass a close look,' he said, 'but it's better than nothing.'

We turned left, probably because he didn't want to go past the police station. He had his headlights on, which would make us conspicuous, but we'd be even more conspicuous without them.

I could see just enough to recognise Scalloway Road when we reached it. He turned right. My bet was that we'd go round the roundabout at Tesco and head north past the school.

I was right. It was strange to think that I would never go up South Lochside Road again.

The whole town was dark and we were the only people on the road. When I heard the sound of sirens, my pulses raced, but after a minute I worked out that they weren't coming towards us. We were on Holmsgarth Road now; not much longer till we turned up the hill out of town.

The streetlights came on just as Gregor changed gear for the incline. I would have liked to bombard him with furious questions, but I was too tired and disoriented to think straight. Besides, I was cold, because I had only the clothes that the police had given me, and the shoes from which they'd taken the laces. I curled up under the rug and shivered.

What was Gregor going to do with me? Take me to Unst and put me on a submarine? No. To get to Unst he'd have to take two ferries, and in the light of dawn – which couldn't be far away – some ferryman could easily cast a glance into the back of the Landrover.

We couldn't have been travelling for more than fifteen or twenty minutes when there was a brief crunching of gravel and the car slowed right down. We were off the main road.

We slewed to the right and stopped as I sat up. Gregor killed the lights.

'How are you?' he said.

'Cold, and angry.' That 'angry' was out before I could stop it.

'Sorry. I forgot. I have clothes for you.' He swung a plastic bag over to the back seat. 'As for you being angry, I understand, of course I do. But I can explain everything.'

'And you think I'll believe you?'

'I very much hope so.'

I had to control myself. What could I do, when all was said and done, but go wherever he took me.

'Where are we?' I said.

'Tingwall Airport.'

Tingwall Airport had a few desolate lights shining on its emptiness. I imagined that it operated a few flights a week to the outer islands. We were in its small parking area, and a white van was beside us.

355

Gregor said, 'I'll be back in a second.'

I delved into the bag and found a thick sweater, long socks, gloves and a woollen hat. They were all needed.

When I stepped out onto the tarmac, there was a smudge of grey in the sky towards what must be the east. I made out a barbed wire fence cordoning off a grassy sward. A sharp but not unpleasant smell hit me. Sheep dung.

From my left came the sound of low male voices. Three dark shapes stood on the far side of the van. One came round to me. 'Ready?' Gregor said.

'For what?'

'An early morning flight.'

The other shapes were bulky – I thought they might belong to the two heavies who'd plucked Jason and me off our feet at Woodwick beach. Neither spoke, but one led us to a white waist-high fence and indicated that we should climb over. Tingwall Airport was hardly well protected.

A tiny plane stood at the edge of the runway. It was two-toned, one broad band being white and the other a shade of green or blue that I couldn't distinguish. Gregor installed me in the passenger seat, went round to the other side, fastened his own seat belt, then mine, and showed me how to use a headphone-and-microphone contraption that would enable us to communicate easily during the flight. I could see the need for it as soon as he switched on the engine.

He examined his gauges and instruments, but didn't talk to anyone. Registering a flight plan was for wimps.

We taxied the short distance to the end of the runway – and the starkness of my situation came home to me. I had nothing: no passport, no proof of identity, no certificate of my birth or my educational qualifications, no

money and no bank card, no book or photograph or other memento of my life.

The light was stronger now; we could see thirty or forty yards down the runway. That was enough, apparently, for we took off without trouble, swinging right almost at once towards that ever-brightening glimmer.

In minutes, we were over the sea, flying so low that I could have waved to a fisherman or watched dolphins at play. Gregor glanced at me and spoke into his microphone: 'All right?'

'No. That policeman – you intimidated him and his wife?'

'Yes. I didn't like doing it, but I had to be sure of getting you out.'

'Billy knew you were going to intimidate him?'

'No. He only gave me the man's name.'

And Gregor had used his own resources to do the rest. Billy would have that detail covered too; he would let the enquiry conclude that someone had tailed the sergeant to his home.

'Why did you want to get me out at all?'

He glanced my way again and said, in that serious way of his, 'Because I love you.'

Why would he say that if it was a lie? He didn't need to manipulate me any longer.

Yet he'd shopped me.

I smiled, because that was what he wanted. I would keep my questions.

He didn't say any more, just gave me another look, then concentrated on his flying.

We flew for hours. I dozed or tried to bring some order to my thoughts. After a long time – two, three hours, I didn't know – we were over land, mountainous and snow-capped. It had to be Norway.

More hours. I dozed again, waking with a start as we bumped down on a rough landing strip. I couldn't see a single building.

In fact, there was one, a hut with a brick base, wooden walls and a roof of corrugated iron. This place made Tingwall Airport look like Heathrow. A young man came out, strolled across to our plane and exchanged a few words with Gregor – in Russian, I was sure. A wad of banknotes came out of Gregor's back pocket.

'Food,' Gregor said, and took me into the hut. On a concrete floor sat a white plastic table with two orange chairs on either side. In a corner, a stove that was fed by a gas cylinder had three rings; one was empty, one held a kettle, and on the third a big pot contained something that was steaming gently.

He found plates and mugs, doled out a stew with vegetables and chunks of meat, and made coffee. Then he sat down opposite me. If he hadn't – if he'd sat beside me – I'd have wanted to move so that I could read his face.

'Where are we now?' I said.

'Sweden.'

'The boy spoke Russian?'

'Yes. He's half Russian, half Swedish. His mother used to be a masseuse in Moscow. When he was about ten, I think, she brought him back here.'

There would be a tale there, a narrative of sex, manipulation and unrequited love. But I had my own narrative to think about. I ate most of my stew, because I was famished, then I said, 'Well, Gregor, why did you put that receipt in my car?'

358

His gaze was steady, which might have been simply the mark of an accomplished actor. 'Because I was told to. My superiors wanted the blame for Sven's murder to fall on you, and therefore on the Scottish government.'

I processed that. 'They wanted to boost the case for Shetland's independence? But you told me the Russian government was neutral.'

He hung his head. 'I lied. I know it doesn't sound like a valid excuse, but, again, I did it because I was ordered to.'

Even if I believed him now, that wouldn't make up for the fact that he'd lied so comprehensively. I wasn't going to tell him that. So I said, evading the issue, 'Gregor, that throws up a dozen other questions. Tell me why your government wants an independent Shetland.'

'That bit is easy.' He seemed almost relieved to answer. 'Why do think they wanted the UK to leave the EU, and Scotland to leave the UK? Divide and conquer – hardly a new principle. Each fragment is weaker and more open to manipulation than the whole.'

'So you toyed with me from the start?' Maybe I shouldn't have put that quite so bluntly. On the other hand, he would expect me to.

He grimaced. 'Actually, I argued hard that you would be a good replacement for Pamela, because you would be much more pragmatic, but the men above me became adamant as events unfolded that it was more important to use you to discredit the Scottish government.'

'Are you aware that the Scottish government now claim I was acting on my own accord, that it had nothing to do with them?'

'They won't get away with that. Maybe in a court of law, but not in the court of Shetland opinion.'

Billy's verdict exactly. I finished my stew, gathering strength. The Russian-Swedish boy came in, said something, and went back out. 'What was that?' I said.

'Just that the plane has been refuelled.'

'Are we in a hurry?'

'We have all the time in the world.'

'Just as well. Now you have to tell me how you even knew that the police were going to investigate me. You heard about the rats?'

'Yes.'

'You couldn't have anticipated that. So how did you know...?'

'They would arrest you? My instructions were brutally clear. If it seemed likely that you would *not* be arrested, I had to make an anonymous phone call, informing the police that you worked for the Scottish Intelligence Services. They would then deduce your motive and search your car and flat.'

I wanted to say, *You bastard*, but I couldn't spill out my hatred. The warning voice was strong: *let him think you hate him and he'll dump you in a Swedish bog.* My was spinning.

'Carol,' he said, 'one thing I have never lied about: the moment I saw you in that bar, the moment we spoke, I knew in my gut that I wanted to spend the rest of my life with you.'

'And that was why you put me in jail?' I just managed to avoid the hint of bitterness; the tone I picked belonged to someone who wanted to forgive but couldn't quite understand.

'I let you go to jail because I knew that I would get you out. Somehow.'

'Wait, wait, wait. It never occurred to you – when you were so madly in love with me – to tell your bosses you weren't going to do this, you were

going to quit?' I had tried for a bantering note, but I heard the distinct clang of anger. It wasn't inappropriate, but, *damn*, I had to be careful.

'There's something you don't understand.'

I gave him a fake smile. 'Go on. Amaze me.'

He rubbed his chin – he needed to shave that black stubble – and looked at me with eyes I'd have sworn were pleading. 'The thing is, a Russian can't quit. A Russian who quits is a traitor. He will be hunted down wherever he goes – and, believe me, I thought of running away with you to New Zealand or Canada or Paraguay – and then it is very, very likely that he will be killed. Toxins, funnily enough, are a favourite method. Anyone with him will be killed too.'

I believed *that*. I could see he'd faced an impossible dilemma. All right, I would admit that some of his actions might have appeared to him unavoidable. But some definitely weren't, for example when he implied that I could take over from Pamela even though he knew for sure I wouldn't. He'd said that just to secure my cooperation.

In short, he'd run rings around me.

And no one ran rings round Carol Rutherford.

'Okay,' I said. 'I get it.'

'We *are* okay, you and I?' He'd said that before. On Unst. A man could protest too much.

He held out his hand, and I put mine in his. It was an instinctive movement, but don't get me wrong: it was instinctive only because a good actor has an instinct for the movement that fits the part.

'I think so,' I said. 'What now?'

'We'll go to Moscow. I hope you will live with me, though I don't know exactly what you will do.'

'I'll find something.'

'I'm sure you will.'

'Shall we go?'

'You need the toilet?' He pointed to a door I hadn't noticed.

I was happy to go to the toilet. It gave me a chance to think. He might want me, at some level; I'd concede that. But... I sat, but couldn't work out all the buts.

On the way back to the plane, I said, 'Anything else you haven't told me?'

He took my arm. 'Full disclosure? Remember that news conference when Popov Systems claimed they had traced the hack into Eric Sorenson's computer to the Scottish Intelligence Services?'

'Yes. Paul McIntyre – you know him? – claimed to have set that one up.'

'Well,' he said, 'he didn't. It was me. The hope was that this by itself might be enough to discredit Pamela.'

'Whereas it didn't. She seemed to ride it out.'

I was thinking, *McIntyre?* It wouldn't be surprising if he'd claimed the credit for something he didn't do, but was there more to the McIntyre story? Colin had wondered how he had the money to use Facebook's repertoire of advertising tricks. Did he and Gregor have an arrangement?

I said, 'Tell me about McIntyre.'

'What about him?'

'You knew him?'

'No.'

I couldn't see into Gregor's eyes, but there was something too firm about his voice. McIntyre spent money he didn't have. McIntyre, by his own admission, had trained in St Petersburg. It was too much of a coincidence.

362

But I'd slipped. I'd come perilously close to hinting that I didn't trust Gregor any more.

We reached the plane; he let go of my arm and opened the passenger door. 'More disclosure,' he said. 'I knew the hack was down to you and Helen.'

I had thought I was beyond surprises. 'How did you know?'

'Did you notice, that time in the Norseman bar, that I was wearing what seemed to be Bluetooth headphones?'

'I did notice. You were listening to us?'

'I have to confess that I was.'

But he didn't have to confess. This was a detail he could have kept quiet about. So why was he admitting it now if not because he wanted to be entirely honest?

Wait. He wanted me to *think* he was being entirely honest.

Why? What was he *not* being honest about?

McIntyre. It had to be. I didn't care that McIntyre was a Russian agent, but I cared that Gregor still thought he could deceive me.

Now an old saying echoed round my head: *revenge is a dish best served cold.*

Chapter 30

Here I am, two years and two months since my flight from Lerwick. It's spring in Moscow, and the trees are budding in the manicured gardens round our apartment. Gregor's off to his 'tutoring job' at the SVR, where he's training recruits – so he says – to speak and listen to English, and in particular to pick out nuances in British tones, gestures, phraseology and sentence structure. I do wonder if this job is a demotion, a slap on the wrist because he blew his cover when he helped me escape, but he seems to be paid well. Either that or his family are supporting us; as I understand it, they are 'comfortable'.

I won't hide from you the fact that my first few weeks in Moscow were very difficult. It was freezing cold, and I was cooped up in the apartment; I didn't speak a word of Russian; and no one – not even the SVR or the FSB – seemed interested in me. Worst thing of all was dealing with Gregor, who expected us to be 'okay', especially in our lovemaking. I pleaded stress for about a fortnight. Then I made him use condoms – he'd always been adept at rolling one on without losing momentum – and I insisted that I wasn't ready for children. Even so, there was a problem: Gregor, being not quite so confident, had lost some of his touch, and I, being not nearly so randy, had lost a lot of that wonderful wetness. I had to look up the Russian for 'lubricating jelly', write the words down laboriously – I was learning the alphabet – go to a pharmacy and suffer the condescending smirks of the shop assistant. And still I wasn't sure whether Gregor, super-sensitive as he is, would notice the change in my responses.

Eventually, however, our sex life did settle down. I polished my act, never rejected him, even put on a little show now and then to tell him how keen I was. And he seemed content.

By the way, did I write the words '*our* apartment'? It's Gregor's, you'll gather, but I know full well I could become his lawful wedded wife if I just said the word. He's *so* eager to start a family. I've watched him smiling as he drops hints about the ticking of biological clocks – and the more he smiles, the readier I am to change the subject. I've lost count of the number of times I've diverted the conversation to our social circle in Moscow or my increasingly fluent Russian.

For a long time, he was delighted with my Russian. I really threw myself into it: the alphabet, the vocabulary, the grammar – oh the grammar! – the sounds, the slang I heard on the Metro, all the differences you'd expect between the social classes. Gregor saw my dedication as a sign that I intended to put down roots in Moscow, and therefore I would some day be all his. More fool him. I had only two ambitions: one, to get even with him and, two, to get back into the great game.

A full six months after my arrival, I was debriefed by the FSB – not the SVR. Freely admitting to a complete lack of concern that my attempt to sabotage Free Shetland had rebounded, I declared that I was never motivated by patriotism, but by the intellectual challenge of a complex puzzle. 'If I fail in one puzzle,' I said, 'I just like to find another.' Then I was very scathing about those figures in Edinburgh – I may have mentioned Pamela! – who thought that Scotland could stand apart from the great power blocs of the world. They homed in on this, asking me which power blocs I considered most important, and I named Russia, China and the USA – 'natural political entities', which would always be more stable than 'cobbled together'

alliances like the EU or ASEAN. Then they asked if I saw these 'natural entities' as competing or cooperating.

It was obvious what they wanted: *not* namby-pamby musings about the moral high ground of international cooperation, but a blunt statement about nature red in tooth and claw, with the Russian bear having the sharpest claws.

So that was what I gave them. One of the debriefing team, a handsome, charming chap called Alexander, wondered if I could see myself contributing, at some point in the future, to the economic power or political influence of the Russian Federation. I said that I certainly could, though I'd have to polish my Russian first. They all nodded sagely.

Alexander was very quick. When the debriefing was over, he took me for a drink and dropped into the conversation an enquiry about whether I was 'comfortable' in Gregor's apartment. He said this with faintest of stresses on 'comfortable', making me think he wasn't talking about the central heating or the softness of the mattress. I looked straight at his eyes, which were sharper than Gregor's, and I *knew* that he knew what I'd bought in that pharmacy. (Well, he would, wouldn't he? The Russians wrote the book on surveillance.) There and then, I decided to make him an ally, and confided in him that there was a looming conflict between my desire for active service and Gregor's hopes that I would become a mother.

He was sympathetic. 'Domesticity doesn't appeal to everyone. And it would be a huge pity if Mother Russia didn't benefit from your talents.'

We left it at that, but agreed to keep in touch. Over the next year or so, we met a few times. Since I had no idea about factional loyalties within the intelligence services, and therefore no idea whether anyone might carry tales, I told Gregor that Alexander wanted to get my input while Shetland was in transit to independence. (In fact, that was one of the topics Alexander and I

did discuss. He'd taken out a subscription to *The Shetland Times* – it was posted to him every week from Lerwick – and quite often he'd give me half an hour to catch up on the fishing news or the police news or the independence news before we had our talk.) I did *not* mention to Gregor, however, either the range of our conversations – the entire gamut of international relations – or the way Alexander would on occasion quietly check whether my ambitions had changed.

Then came my breakthrough. Alexander decided my Russian was fluent enough; if I was keen, he would get me enrolled in the Moscow Centre for Strategic Studies, so that I could bring myself up to date on current thinking – before, perhaps, I went 'into the field'. *Was* I keen?

Well, of course I was, I thought; it was *exactly* what I wanted. But it was something of a shock to Gregor, even though I stressed that my aim was simply to sharpen my wits and get my brain back into gear; in other words, I wasn't leaving him.

Not yet, I said to myself. But I was imagining the moment when he'd come home to find me gone and Alexander would explain to him that the needs of Mother Russia had to take precedence over his plans for marital bliss. He'd learn, too late, that if deception was sauce for the gander it was also sauce for the goose. The cold dish would be perfect.

I enjoyed the process of studying and writing essays again, despite a few difficulties with the language. I thought my supervisors would want me to suggest ways in which Scotland's now inevitable fiscal catastrophe could be exploited, but they didn't. They asked me to concentrate on how Russia might outmanoeuvre – that's to say, weaken – their major rivals, China and the USA. They had big problems, I realised, with China. I'll give you an

outline, in case you're not familiar with it, of the major stumbling block, the Chinese social credit scheme. The authorities have two lines of attack: first, they force the population to do almost all of their transactions online, usually by smartphone, so that these can be recorded; and, second, they have cameras everywhere that feed into facial recognition algorithms. The result is that you can't buy a bottle of wine, visit the wrong barber, talk to or message the wrong person, read – never mind write – the wrong blog, and so on and so on, without a computer somewhere registering this and feeding it into your social credit score. When your score is too low, you can't get a decent job, your chances of a decent flat are minimal, and you can't even buy a train or air ticket. The overall outcome is that the slightest dissent is snuffed out before it can get properly started – and so the Party keeps an iron grip on power.

How do you weaken a power structure like this – when even Covid-19 couldn't shake it? I suggested that China's Achilles' heel was the economy: their dependence on external trade, their mountains of housing and other debts, and the way everyone and their granny indulged their passion for gambling by speculating on the stock market. Suppose, I said, discreet intervention, through Chinese intermediaries, could drive stock prices to unsustainable heights and then to a catastrophic collapse, could the Party become so entangled in controlling dissent among its own people that it ceased to bother Russia?

'Interesting,' said my supervisors. 'But what could your role be?'

The question floored me. What *could* I do in China when I was quite ignorant of Mandarin?

'All right,' they said. 'What about the USA?'

Now my morale surged – in retrospect, I think the Russians may have choreographed my moods – because the implication was that if I could map out a role for myself in the destabilisation of the USA, I could indeed go back into the field.

They already had a strategy of sorts: to chop bits off the USA, literally. They planned to start with Texas and California because both these states have secessionist movements and also huge economies. The good people in St Petersburg's Internet Research Agency had been hard at work setting up multiple networks to micro-target alienated voters who might be turned into secessionists – using all the old tricks and probably a whole stack of new ones. So far, so hopeful. But they'd run into a brick wall when they found the 1869 ruling of the Supreme Court that said bluntly no state could secede from the union. Their question to me was: how do we get round *that*?

I attacked the problem with enthusiasm. I found a sentence in the Declaration of Independence which says that a government derives 'its just powers from the "consent" of the governed'. Well then, I argued – and I laid this out in a paper that I submitted last week – what was needed was a new amendment to the constitution, one which allowed a state to secede if there was clear evidence that its citizens no longer gave their 'consent' to the federal government. A new amendment needs a two-thirds majority in both houses of Congress as well as ratification by three-quarters of the individual states, but, I wrote – getting carried away on the flood of my own argument – nothing was impossible. Suppose an indicative referendum in Texas showed a majority for independence; suppose the Texans made such a nuisance of themselves that the other states were eager to get rid of them; suppose lawyers hammered away at the issue of consent... at very least a coordinator on the ground could light huge bonfires of resentment. That

coordinator would have to be an English speaker, I said, someone highly skilled in manipulation. I was implying, of course, that it would have to be me.

Now they've summoned me to a meeting – this morning. I should be pleased. But when I woke up, I found that I wasn't. Sven, who hadn't visited me for a while, was in my head again, laughing with that awful bony rictus. As I tried to work out what *would* amuse him in my present situation, I hit on a possibility: the FSB must know all about the US constitution; they must have picked apart the logic already and seen that to get an amendment such as I've described would be a long and difficult task; in short, if they *were* going to send me to America, they would be playing some deeper game.

What might it be?

Nothing that was in my interests. They could set me up as a British spy. Then, a few years down the line, when it suited them, they could expose me to the CIA, causing an almighty bust-up between the US and what remains of the UK, and in the process they could consign me to a federal prison for the rest of my life.

Or am I being paranoid?

So, on this fine spring day, as the birds chirp and the solid matrons take their dogs for a walk, I'm nervous. The meeting's at eleven, in the Savoy Hotel of all places. (Is this because they want to impress me?) Before I go, I have a skim, because I have time to kill and I can't settle, through some of the news on the Internet. One item catches my eye: 'Americans panic over North Atlantic' – that's my rough translation of the Russian. The website editor has helpfully provided a link to the original article in English, and at

first glance this seems to be presenting a scenario about the Greenland-
Iceland-UK gap that's very similar to the one put forward by Helen's
conspiracy theorist. But there are two developments: the photographs in the
article show sonar detectors that have a sleeker design and, as far as I can
judge, are smaller than those Helen showed me; also, the writer – an
American intellectual – refers to the finding of 'scores' of such devices. I
conclude that either the Russians have really seeded the North Atlantic or
they're seriously trying to bluff NATO strategists into thinking that they
have. It's plausible, even likely, that they were working on a trial, or proof
of concept, while I was on Shetland, and that what I'm seeing in the
photographs in front of me now are second-generation devices.

Did Gregor know about it?

Of course he did.

I take a look at the Scottish papers, wondering if they've picked up on the
story. None of them have, but a paragraph in *The Scotsman* catches my
attention. Susan Ferguson, *Deputy Director of the Scottish Intelligence
Services*, said…

What did she say? Something about it being 'inconceivable' that the
Scottish government would eavesdrop on phone calls or text messages or
emails of innocent people. But that's not what I notice. 'Susan Ferguson' was
the name Gregor squeezed out of me when he was talking about who I would
recommend *if* I didn't get Pamela's job. Susan Ferguson, I told him, is
distinctly pro-Russia. And now – with, surely, a little help from her friends
– she's Deputy Director.

I feel both nauseous and furiously angry, because this reminds me how
Gregor was pulling my strings at every step.

But the FSB, or the SVR, were pulling his.

Suddenly, the game that I sought to re-enter seems utterly hollow. For there is no honour among spies. It's beyond doubt that the FSB would use me and then discard me.

I take the Metro to Lubyanka and walk round to the Savoy. Alexander is in the ornate lounge, reading *The Shetland Times*. He stands up as I come in and kisses me on the cheek. He's all smiles, and I think that maybe this *is* the meeting at which I'll get offered a job.

That would be truly ironic.

Alexander says, 'I have to go to the toilet and make a call before the others arrive. Have a read at the paper.'

The Shetland Times. A call from another life. I see from the front page that some of Harry Watt's predictions about squabbling in an independent Shetland have come true, because, at the latest session of the alting (as they've called their parliament) there was a heated debate on whether a proper runway on Foula (population about forty when I was there) should be postponed to leave sufficient cash for the upgrading of Baltasound Junior High School to a six-year academy. (Both daft ideas, if you ask me.)

Then I turn over a couple of pages and I can't believe what I'm looking at. It's a photo of a wedding in the Shetland Hotel and there, cutting the cake, are Sharon and Colin, the light in their eyes telling a tale of bliss that neither expected.

Sharon and Colin. *My God*. But I'm happy for them. I'm *so* happy for them. I wish I was there to give them both a hug.

Now I'm not at the Savoy. I'm not in Moscow. I'm in Shetland. I'm at the Skipidock with Sharon and Robert and Mary. I'm in the Norseman with Helen or Colin or even Billy. I'm drinking Sauvignon Blanc at Joy and

Eric's. I'm walking along Commercial Street with Betty. I'm in Anderson High School with Peter and George the Second. I'm at the Phu Siam talking to that shivering girl from Thailand. I'm in Baltasound with Jason and the Browns, Malcolm and Annette and their child.

But I can't go back. *That's* why Sven was laughing.

60453226R00213